THE SWORD
OF GABRIEL

Ten Days on Earth

Tom Holloway

ISBN: 0692813683
ISBN 13: 9780692813683
Library of Congress Control Number: 2016919745
Sword of Gabriel, Louisville, KY

For my true partner, my loving wife; and, for my mother who always believed in me; and, for my fantastic family plus all my friends who encouraged me----with love and gratitude always.

CHAPTER 1

ARRIVAL

The *Cyclone* is coming in fast, much faster than I want, as this limitless light-speed starship is not used to putting on the brakes in such a short distance. We're heading into this solar system at exactly 10,828 million miles per hour, a lot faster than the speed of light, braking hard, and it's not easy to slow down at this speed. Glad to be here finally. It's been a long trip. After traveling trillions of miles across a universe of mostly cold black emptiness, blasting through several galaxies, I'm finally closing in on Earth, my destination target. Earth isn't easy to get to, and it's been ten years since I was here last. I'm thrilled to be here again; it's hard to contain my anticipation. I have ten precious days to be a human again.

I definitely need to slow my speed more, or this visit might end before it starts. We're still too hot, way too fast to try to penetrate the atmosphere of Earth. Yes, it's now urgent! I have no time to be stupid; I need to reduce speed quickly. I have to slow to 450,000 miles per hour *right now.*

At this speed it normally takes several million miles to come to a stop, and I need to pull it off in less than a million, trying to hit Earth with some degree of accuracy. It's also a moving target as it is traveling at orbit speed. I'll hit the atmosphere hard and level, with a thunderous explosion, then skip off like a flat rock hitting a pond, trying to slingshot around its only moon using its gravity to slow me down. Coming in the second time will be better, slower, a reasonable seventy thousand miles an hour. I'll use the top layers of Earth's air coming in at a six-degree plane to slow down more—any steeper would cause a huge inferno—then orbit once, probably twice, slowing more each time. The air friction will result in lots of superheated air, maybe more like a blazing firestorm. It'll be enough to light up an entire continent for several minutes. Then I'm not sure of the next step. Probably best to take the *Saber* down to do some reconnaissance on Earth's surface. The *Saber* is an attack star-jet much smaller than an intergalactic starship like the *Cyclone*. It's housed in Bay 5.

I have many things to do and not much time to do them, thus the foolish haste. Unfortunately, coming in so fast with the massive air friction on the hull will alert the whole planet. It's stupid to light up a dark sky. I have no illusions; surely all this will be noticed. Best to be cautious after this error, to park the *Cyclone* in a high orbit, let things calm down, stay hidden. Maybe use the *Saber* in stealth mode, check the planet out, and look around. I need to plan this, think about my visit, as every minute is valuable.

I'm coming in solo, one starship and no backup. A confrontation with some military force wouldn't be good for anyone, and that's not my purpose. This is recreation only, time off, a chance to see my home planet after many years of being gone. It's a wish granted because of my rank and a reward for my deeds. However, it comes with limitations, and the first is a big one: I have only ten days, and then I'm gone for another ten years. It's never enough time and too long gone.

I work for a Consortium of Civilizations with 14,651 members and one pending application. Unfortunately, Earth is not considered part of its membership nor a possible applicant, as it's too far away and too small, really too primitive. Earth's star, or sun, is one of three hundred billion stars in this galaxy, and there are maybe a hundred billion galaxies in the universe, more than I can count. Actually, hardly anyone knows about Earth except for me. This solar system is just a tiny part of an immense area I roam, which spans more than forty-five billion light-years across space in all directions. This is more than a quadrillion miles— and sometimes many times more, depending on what direction you go. I've covered more miles than a googol, the highest number known on Earth. I've seen thousands of solar systems. I keep busy.

A light-year is the distance light travels in one year. It's an actual distance of about six trillion miles; if calculated, the speed of light is about seven hundred million miles per hour. This is fast yet not fast enough to cover the distances I travel. You need the fastest starship in the universe. You need speed many times the speed of light, and with the starship *Cyclone*, I have the tremendous power to get the job done.

I call it the *Cyclone* as I was allowed to rename it, after asking permission. The previous name was impossible for me to pronounce—too alien and way too weird. *Cyclone* was much more fitting, as it's like riding a cyclone when you generate that much power and speed. Yet even more essential, after further discussion, it was determined it was critical that the starship agreed to the new name, as this ship was opinionated. At the time this was curious to me as it was explained the starship was a being of its own and actually much smarter than me. This process wasn't easy, and we, meaning the starship and me, argued about it at first, but reason prevailed. The deciding factor was that it wasn't practical to use the real name, for my sake a nickname was necessary. It will always be too long for me to say and will not help our working relationship. That was many years ago, and we now laugh about it after it accuses me of being really primitive in those early years. I have come a long way since then, and our relationship is close now.

The *Cyclone* is an incredible starship, capable of amazing feats. For example, breaking through the speed-of-light barrier is not easy; it can be messy if not done right. The *Cyclone* must bend space and time, which requires huge amounts of energy, exact timing, and the manipulation of gravity, including negative gravity, or the physics of dark matter. Everything in the universe moves with the colossal power of the flow of gravity. If you can handle and control gravity, the universe is yours to take, as it's God's engine. And if you can't, stay home, as starship travel is dangerous on many levels.

No matter—Earth is home for me, my first home, where I was born. It's impossible to express how good I feel, other than saying I'm more than overjoyed to be here. It's night over North America, and you can see the millions of lights coming from the cities spread over the globe. Dawn's not far off, and I'm looking forward to seeing the sunrise. I'm excited about my first day here—ready to go, eager to see everything.

Probably smart to look around some, see what's going on, and check to see if there are any military conflicts in the works. Earthlings have their issues sometimes. Something is always going on. Maybe there's a war or hurricanes, maybe a typhoon. Bad weather is always possible; bad stuff is always possible. Need to be careful.

Yes, it will be good to take a spin around the world. Maybe a quick surveillance will be interesting. No question, I'll use the *Saber*, as the *Cyclone* is too massive for an unseen reconnaissance on Earth. Better to let it orbit in stealth mode, unseen by prying eyes. It's also suitable to use the *Saber* for another reason. It's one of my greatest joys. It has tremendous power and incredible acceleration; then there is the pleasure of the adrenaline rush. On

Earth it could be compared to driving the ultimate sports car. It's a light attack military starship capable of great speed, yet it has the flexibility of a smaller starship, thus it's used for reconnaissance and simply a lot of fun to fly. Actually, I love flying it!

The *Saber*'s look is stunning, too, the surface a polished, dazzling black silver, like a black mirror, blinding to the eye when shimmering in the sun's reflection. It's long and aerodynamically slender, curved with knife-edge wings off the stern, with a slanted tail fin on a tapered cylinder with an elongated extensive forward hull, finishing with a long frontal knifelike spear, the blade side down. On the whole it has a wicked and dangerous look to it.

The *Saber*'s engineering makes it good for this mission. For one, it has a complete visual operations package, including video cameras with extreme magnification, and drones that are invisible for close-in surveillance, including sensitive sound collection. We can see and hear conversations of beings on the ground, even though we might be in orbit.

The design of this sleek military starship includes an extended flat underside, which helps give it extra lift when there's atmosphere. Overall its appearance is like a big sleek eagle with a long pointed beak. It has a hull length of 478 feet, with a hull width of 130 feet plus 86 feet of razor-sharp wings sweeping back at the rear, off both sides, for a width total of 302 feet. The total hull height is 70 feet, yet it reaches 138 feet with the tail fin centered on top, sweeping back severely, off the rear at 68 feet high, razor sharp. The wings are severely slanted off the port and starboard sides, going farther back, next to the aft thrusters.

Generally, for a military starship, the craft is heavy, weighing 996,000 tons in Earth's gravity. With a weapons package the weight increases dramatically, as it adds 950 tons. In comparison to most reconnaissance military starships in this class, it's much heavier. Most of the extra weight is because it's well armored.

It can be used to ram other ships, as it's almost impossible to penetrate its armored skin. Any craft the *Saber* hits will fragment on impact. The entire *Saber* is made of a metal alloy that's almost supernatural; nothing damages it, including mega hot temperatures. The wings are also like titanium knives and will slice through anything, even asteroid rock. A starship may hit many things at high speed and must survive the impact.

As good as it was when built, it's even better now. I've improved many features of the *Saber*. For one, it now has six fusion rocket burners aft, powering it. I'm proud to say I rebuilt four of them and then added two more, which also made the starship heavier. I wanted the extra backup thrust. Plus I could use the backwash as a weapon. The fiery blast creates a hot tail for miles, burning up anything in its path. Just by swinging away from a target, the *Saber*'s fiery tail will do damage. The massive thrust will destroy anything in its way and achieve terrific speeds quickly. The forward air shockwave, at mega sonic speeds, is an issue to any structure in front of the concussion wave. I have to be really careful when at lower Earth altitudes to avoid damaging buildings with the massive wind hit.

The far rear of the ship is mostly an elongated circle of massive dull-black rocket engines, then the fusion blast funnels, real serious looking, and each impressively protruding another 82 feet back from the hull.

I've changed the front of the ship, too. It's extraordinary. I enhanced the ultra sleek design with an additional length added to the slender nose spear, and making it more knifelike, a deeper cut downward, as it is now a twenty-foot blade protruding 102 feet out forward, proportionally sweeping gradually to a sharp point, starting from the front cabin nose. Like a razor-thin knife, it will slice through anything it hits, including enemy starships. It is a saber made from metal compounds that are forged at a heat equal to the sun, with metals harder than anything existing in the universe. With this forward razorblade spear and the aft rocket extensions, the ship's hull stretches out to a total length of 662 feet. The starship itself is formidable, extremely fast, and deadly, even without firing a weapon.

Because of the knife-blade nose tip, I call the ship the *Saber*, a fitting name for a warrior starship.

As the captain, I sit at the base of the frontal spear structure, in the pilot's cockpit or front cabin, which is raised up over the front fuselage. It's thirty-six feet wide, shielded by a black diamond crystal "see-through" windshield, sitting on the top of the total hull width of 130 feet, thus the width without the wings. Plenty of room for two pilots high up front, with a lot of equipment panels, and behind them there is room for four crew members, part of the team needed for long-range operations. There are living quarters farther back and also space to carry ordnance, troops, or millions of drones. The dark-black windshield is also thirty-eight feet long, sweeping from the pilot's cabin and slanting forward, narrowing onto the nose spear, aerodynamically perfect. It is stronger than metal.

The *Saber* looks powerful standing still, ready to burst free, fierce, tightened to spring; dangerous, just like a crouching jaguar. They both are spectacular engineering miracles.

This light starship's six nuclear-fusion reactors at full heat will create a total horsepower of 968 million units at thirty thousand degrees Fahrenheit. At full power it will leave a blast tail behind it for hundreds of miles that will simply vaporize anything that tumbles into its firestorm.

I have never powered up to full capacity or even taken it close to its top speed. However, I know I can take it up to 250,000 miles per hour real quick. This is very easy to do, depending on gravity and atmosphere. It's helpful to be in thin air or no air, as in off-planet space. Also, the g-forces on a human body on Earth, or any similar heavy-gravity planet can kill you if you're not careful.

The human body is too fragile for much pressure. I have to control gravity, or adapt to it both ways; when it's too much or too little. Both can be critical, leaving my survival in question. The ship will offset the g-force pressure on me as much as possible, with some counter-internal-gravity absorbers.

No matter. I have arrived, made my Earth destination as planned, with no incident. The slowdown worked. The *Cyclone* has automatically piloted into a safe orbit and is now on course about two hundred miles above Earth. I figure I need to let it run at about eighteen thousand miles per hour to maintain this orbit, keeping the *Cyclone* from falling into Earth's gravity. Currently the *Saber* is embedded in the *Cyclone*'s lowest cargo hold, with an escape door for fast getaways. Within a few minutes, I am belted in. The starship is ready. I open the outside bay doors, hear the locks disengage, and then I silently drop out, down toward Earth, waiting to completely clear the *Cyclone*'s airspace. The long free fall is pleasing, serene, and quiet, as in the calm before the storm. I drop down to about a hundred miles above Earth, looking out at the planet from outer space, seeing the horizon of Earth, a line separating the blackness of the universe. Not much atmosphere at this altitude and little air for wing lift pressure, nor much gravity.

I fire the ignition, readying myself for the massive surge forward. I feel the initial thrust blasting, accelerating, the thunderous roar, then the impact of the enormous speed, my body pinned back, the *Saber* streaking up over Earth's atmosphere, still in black outer space, the rockets smoking hot, the unlimited power. I love this part.

The part I don't like is being in Earth's gravity field, as I am pressed back to the seat from the colossal surge forward. My entire body feels the terrific pressure. It takes my breath away, and I am gasping for air until I reduce power. I wonder if it could turn me into a pancake if I didn't let up. Sure feels like it. I do imagine at times it's pulling my toes backward, then it feels like my ears are stretching, and maybe my eyelids are being pasted to my forehead. Yet I always come away with no side effects. Apparently my body adapts. There is not much I can do about it.

Quickly I'm hitting tremendous speed, running at fifty-five thousand miles per hour, gaining altitude fast, maybe 160 miles up from Earth's surface. I'm in Earth's exosphere, using the very thin air in the upper layer of the atmosphere, as it has less friction and little gravity. I'm looking out at the Earth, the beautiful blue world a stunning sight from this outer-space loft, and the ride is exhilarating. Moving this fast, this high, is thrilling and much smoother in comparison to when I plunge down into heavier air. Then it is thunderous, the air-shock waves exploding like a tsunami blasting forward, the concussion jerking me about. The sensation of the massive ground speed is dramatic; Earth's surface flashing by below me is exhilarating. Then the heavier air is forcing me to let off the gas as I descend. The heated fireworks from the friction on the hull also slow me down, as I am dropping altitude.

CHAPTER 2

SABER RECONNAISSANCE FLIGHT

I am always awed by the sparkling colors of Earth's bright sun; although ninety-three million miles away, it provides a bounty of sunrays hitting the top of the atmosphere: golden, magical, and breathtaking. The sun's rays sparkle with a full spectrum of incredible colors outlined by the background of outer space's total blackness, with the sparkling pin lights of millions of stars in the unlimited vastness. The sunrise is spectacular; my view from this starship is amazing, a miracle that I have missed deeply.

Still moving supersonic, I am looking down again as I nosedive toward the many clouds below, seeing brilliant flashes of the Atlantic Ocean's blue water underneath. The billowing white clouds of moisture are awesome. At this loft, seeing Earth from above, observing the golden reflections of the sun's light shimmering off the many cloud surfaces, sometimes almost a blinding brightness, you can see the flowing currents visible when watching the clouds, like seeing rivers of ocean air. It's so dramatic to grasp both the power and the velocity of these massive movements of air as the atmosphere and clouds flow across Earth's surface. Some of these vast jet streams of air are powerful, approaching three hundred miles an hour.

I drop fast, pull up, and then level out about fifty miles above the surface. The air is thin and cold, yet there's more of it, and I've dropped my velocity to twenty-five thousand miles per hour to keep within a moderate turbulence level. I'm at a good place, where the heavy-air atmosphere starts to end and the lighter air of outer space begins, which is about sixty two miles up, the point where the speed of the ship hitting the air creates no lift, not that much friction, and less turbulence from the air pressure. Currents of air moving fast crosswise also increase the turmoil of atmosphere below this point. To reduce the concussion and the rough ride as I accelerate, I climb back to an elevation of sixty-eight miles, and then increase my speed to fifty thousand miles per hour, more than what I need to orbit. No question, the atmosphere below is perfect for the *Saber*'s flights, sailing through an ocean of air, so like the sea, with currents and temperature variations similar to any large body of water.

I circle the planet, covering the twenty-five thousand miles in about thirty minutes, then drop speed severely to fly lower, under any military detection, at about five hundred feet off the surface of the Atlantic Ocean in the Southern Hemisphere. Dropping speed fast, I'm moving at six thousand miles per hour, close to Mach ten at ground speed, traveling northwest. Still at this speed, and with the heavier air due to the low altitude, I'm feeling much wind velocity and even more turbulence. I'm kicking up a lot of ocean behind me. Looking back, I figure my exhaust tail is at least a couple hundred miles long, maybe five to six miles wide. The speed and the tail blast of the fusion mega-heated air, temperatures close to thirty thousand degrees, is vaporizing billions of tons of water behind me, the blast trail looking like hurricane-powered clouds. This air is thrusting up, maybe a three thousand feet high, caused by hot steam, moving fast, like billowing white clouds from a volcano blast. This is surprising to see, even for me. Other eyes see it, too, I am sure.

There is always some military satellite surveillance, eyes from above. Not surprising, as there are so many satellites spinning around Earth I have to be careful not to hit them. Many different countries and private companies put them up there for many different purposes: communications, GPS navigation, military, surveillance, entertainment. They clutter up the higher atmosphere. They detect me on every trip back here. I can process the pings when they see me, as they try to zoom in for better focus; it's impossible to avoid them. Not all of them are surveillance. Some are much more dangerous to me. They aren't just harmless satellites. They're armed. Actually they're missile platforms, really scary, not good things for all those below. Doubtful if too many on Earth know about these weapons, probably just the leaders of the larger countries. The satellites are probably ultra top secret; it's awful to think they might be used against human populations.

I'm sure the surveillance satellites detected me when I first came into orbit. I'm sure more than a few nations or their governments know I'm already back, an alien unidentified flying object. They're maybe wondering if this is the one that's been here before. It is always hard to hide my being here. In the past I was always gone before they could figure out how to find me. I know it excites the hell out of them, yet it is my time to be here, and maybe it's for the overall good. I figure it gives them the opportunity to think about the big picture. A few scientists should be starting to figure out there is much more than Earth's population in this massive universe. This civilization is just one of many thousands.

I'm now running slowly at a critically low altitude of only two hundred feet, and then drop the speed to a drift mode, about seven hundred miles an hour, still over Mach one, yet my lowest speed before a stall. I am still over the Atlantic Ocean heading southwest toward South America. Then, before I can change course, I'm suddenly up close next to a huge ocean liner. I knew it was there and had wanted to see it, slowing down for it, just not this close. It's a vacation passenger ship heading due west. It's not much past dawn; unfortunately there are still a few passengers on deck, spotting me as I veer portside, rocking the big ship even with my slower speed, as I'm still pushing a lot of air, creating booming supersonic shock waves. The resulting air mass hits the ocean liner. It is much louder than any military jet on Earth. I'm just too close to them. I can see the passengers, even barely make out their faces and big eyes, shocked to see something they've never seen and never will see again—a brief glimpse at a real alien starship moving very fast and close. They can feel the heat off the fusion rockets plus see the blistering exhaust trail stretching for miles behind me. This is foolish on my part; any closer and my exhaust tail could hurt them. I'm lucky to veer away just in time. I immediately bank and accelerate straight up to an altitude of forty-five thousand feet and then slowly drop down, leveling off at fifteen thousand feet.

This ride is sheer joy for me as the *Saber* blasts over the Earth. On these trips I always play all kinds of Earth music, maybe rock or classical depending on the need or my mood. It calms me and enhances my senses. It also clarifies this event in my mind, something to remember in the long years ahead. When I'm listening to the Rolling Stones, their blasting away matches the excitement of the moment. The *Saber* is shooting through Earth's upper air at twenty-five times the speed of a bullet, invisible to the naked human eye, except for the fire tail. The thrill of exploding through the top of Earth's atmosphere accelerating at mega hypersonic speeds fits the momentum of a first-class rock band, my ride a true partner of rock and roll. The Boston Symphony Orchestra is also good, as the power of an orchestra is remarkable. Without question, music is the lifeblood of the drama of life.

In these Earth visits, I reclaim my soul. Every time I restore my ability to stay human. The planet and people are extraordinary, beyond any other world in the universe; no place feels this good to me. This is my home, always feels right, and a wonderful gift from God. As I fly over this magnificence, observing from this height, I can see the colors everywhere, and all are extraordinary, the splendor coming from everything: the golden horizon, the bright-blue skies, white clouds, the deep blue-green ocean, rich tan sandy beaches, undulating hills with light-green grassy fields, emerald-green forests, towering majestic mountains with white snow tips, dark-green valleys and winding blue-white rivers, dark-green lakes, massive brown plains. Even better, there is the colorful patchwork of thousands of square or rectangular fenced fields, snug farmhouses, easy to see during the day. Then impressive cities spring up with high-rise skyscrapers and miles of roads.

Then at night, a total changed appearance, still amazing to see, looking down at the busy high-rise cities with millions of bright lights coming from thousands of glittering structures. As you expand your view, you can see more lights coming from millions of homes spread out for miles around the cities, interrupted by the lighted crisscross roads, connected to the interstate highways with lights flowing like hot lava from a volcano, caused by the headlights from thousands of moving cars.

Then, best of all, the cause of all of it, at every sunrise, the supreme gift from God, the radiant light coming from Earth's sun, with the nurturing warmth of a sun giving life. The abundance of energy, delivered just perfectly, not too much nor too little. Just wonderful. To feel it once more is a luxury, and I have been looking forward to this moment for ten years.

All of it is pleasing! The ten years between visits is tough, a long time gone, hard to keep my sanity. Finally I am home.

As the *Saber* covers the surface quickly, I again drop to a lower altitude and also try to avoid damaging the surface buildings with hypersonic air shock. I am at five thousand feet off the surface, moving slowly for the *Saber* at three thousand miles an hour, as high as feasible to avoid damaging Earth's structures. I want to see everything, especially any changes or, maybe more critical, possible issues for me. I see random passenger airplanes and a few military jets, ocean ships, and more. Maybe some spot me, and they may even be wondering about me. However, there's no real issue, as I am moving too fast for them to get a photo of me or even to see the *Saber* clearly. It probably adds to the excitement of the day for these Earth men (and Earth women) to see a possible alien ship.

I miss Earth men and women, the beings on this planet. I especially miss my father and mother. If only I could see them again. It's impossible not to think of my family and friends when I make these return visits. Most are dead.

Maybe this trip will be even better than visits in the past. Just the idea of this one excites me. Even the scent of everything on Earth is awesome. My sense of smell is more acute now, much better with my recent rebirth. Yes, I love the Earth smells: sizzling steak, baking bread, pizza, hot dogs, wildflowers, newly mowed grass, fertile soil after a light rain, apple trees, pine trees, honeysuckle, mountain air, the ocean breeze, leather, horses, dogs, hot coffee...even the scent of humans.

Just having natural air with the right mix of oxygen and moisture is good, so satisfying, rewarding to my lungs and energy levels. To inhale the air here is a pleasure. Earth air is just right—refreshing and sweet, like a cool drink on a real hot day. Then the feel of all of it, always the right air pressure against your skin and the delight of a cool breeze on a hot day. Yes, to be a human again on Earth! Just the expectation of seeing it all again and remembering it when it's gone. In all the past years, it has kept me going, knowing I'm coming back. It's too bad there's never enough time when I'm here. As usual, I must quickly see and do as much as possible. I'm wasting time. I need to get back to the *Cyclone* and begin the real visit.

━┼ ┼━

The Atlantic Ocean is a big sea with plenty of room for many ships, including one large liner traveling at wake speed, coming from London with a heading of due west, now close to the Caribbean island of Antigua. It's unfortunately in the same parallel path as the *Saber*'s, the air concussion of the backwash causing the ship to shift, moving it off course and leaning it over about ten degrees, its tail wash veiling the ship with hot cloudlike water vapor, this thick spray misting all passengers on the deck. Henry's flyby makes quite an impression.

John and Molly are two of those passengers on the upper deck of the magnificent *Queen Mary*, a massive ship that's like a traveling city. This is their first vacation cruise, and they're up early to catch every minute. Now both of them are astonished. It's impossible to imagine the impact to the huge ship; John and Molly hear and see it before they feel it. They hear the rumbling, almost a roaring sound like massive rolling thunder, powerful, coming from a long way off, and they know something is coming fast up close to them. Then there are massive sonic booms, causing their eardrums to vibrate painfully. John catches a glance of something in the distance, something black and massive; he's not sure what it was. He thinks it looks like some kind of extreme experimental military jet as it blasts by the ship, causing a horrific supersonic windblast, rocking the huge ship sideways, so loud it hurts their ears, and then the fiery heat from the jet engines, the hot vapor, hitting the liner with a massive air shock concussion.

John holds on to Molly as she almost falls. He grabs the handrail but keeps his eyes on the aircraft. It's totally weird-looking. It's big, long, and mirror black, with a bladed spear nose not like anything he's ever seen. It's traveling fast, like supersonic fast. He has just a brief glimpse as it passes. He has never seen anything like it; it's extraordinary, huge, and definitely military. Another odd thing, it also looks alien, not of this Earth, real scary. John feels the hair rise on the back of his neck and then fear, real cutting fear, his stomach starting to react, getting sick. He wonders if Molly or anyone else sees it. Others have to see it, too. This is shocking, once in a lifetime…It couldn't be just him seeing it.

The captain and crew see it for a brief moment and catch vague radar shadows of it. They are alarmed, yet it happens so fast they cannot react, then it is gone, whatever it is, probably some experimental military jet. They will report it. They wonder about it, and then they conclude it's one of the mysteries of being out at sea.

⚔

Later, at the end of the day, *Chicago Tribune* editor Bill Simkins is at his desk trying to decide how to run a story about a huge meteorite almost hitting Earth or maybe a possible UFO. There have been sightings reported all over the world, the massive bright light in the night sky moving really fast, barely missing Earth. Hundreds of phone calls to the police and military. Then there are the hundreds of videos all showing this bright stream of light scorching across the heavens, actually lighting up the Earth for thousands of miles, just like the sun.

Then there is a report from a cruise-ship captain of a definite sighting of a UFO; passengers say they saw an alien spaceship that came close to hitting them. Not inconceivable, as it about knocked the ship over from the air concussion alone and lots of heated vapor. Could this have been some military jet? Not as it's described.

The question is, is all this worth including on the front page of today's edition? Maybe. It was real weird; never happened before. For about three minutes, it was bright daylight, the night just evaporating over most of the United States and a good part of the Atlantic Ocean. The official statement by the US spokesman, John Jacobs, head of Section 58, is that it was not one of ours or any aircraft we know about. He suggests it was a meteorite, bigger than most, and it burned up with no Earth hit.

However, there were some guys with amateur telescopes, and more than one is saying no way it was a natural phenomenon. It was not a meteorite or anything like it. It was a UFO.

They all agree. It is impossible to explain the velocity and trajectory of this object, as whatever it was hit us twice, first time moving at an incredible speed, too fast to calculate. Then, about forty minutes later it hit again, traveling not as fast, running parallel with Earth's surface. Then it continued orbiting at about sixty miles above the surface. It was big, large enough to create enough friction to light up the sky for hundreds of miles, finally slowing down to about twenty thousand miles an hour. Then it disappeared, just vanished. Millions of people saw the light. No meteorite does this. We have no idea what it was, maybe just another ghost spaceship checking Earth out.

Maybe run a small headline on the front page then again as a science feature on the fifth page, just in case another news group runs it, too. *It's probably nothing*, Simkins thinks.

⤛⤜

The *Saber* feels good and sounds good, humming the right tone, the thrust stream perfect. I'm now over South America heading northwest, running about five thousand miles per hour at fifteen thousand feet, looking around some, seeing more mountains, valleys, and vast prairies. Hard to think there might be military craft here, as I'm going too fast for them to catch me. They're trying to see me, too, but it's not easy although I am leaving a sizable heat signature, as the *Saber*'s fusion burners are always real hot. As I come up to the Pacific coast, I decide to follow the shoreline.

Then, out of nowhere, I pick up the signals of three F-16s that have come off of a US aircraft carrier about four hundred miles west of my heading, and they're coming my way, which is an issue. The aircraft are flying toward an interception point on my flight path to the United States. I decide to bank east bearing forty-five degrees crossing over Mexico, then the US border—drop to a much lower altitude of about three thousand feet, running slow at about two thousand miles an hour, ground speed, mostly over desert, partially in stealth mode. There's good chance they can see my hot fire tail behind me. I hear radio frequencies as my communications tracker picks up the pilots' conversations with an overhead AWACS surveillance aircraft about thirty-five thousand feet up, a hundred miles portside, due northwest. It's the one that was tracking me.

The F-16s are coming up behind me with all they have to burn, fast as they can, desperately trying to catch me. No plane on Earth is much faster than three to four thousand miles per hour. The F-16s' top speed is about 1,200 miles per hour, and they cannot catch me unless I let them. I decide to do just that, as it gives me a chance to look them over, satisfy my curiosity. After our meeting I'll head out, rocket straight up into outer space. It will be impossible for them to follow me. Plus, I'll be moving faster than they can see, going mega hypersonic. Escaping Earth's gravity requires a velocity of 25,800 miles an hour, impossible for any military jet on Earth.

The three fighters catch up to about four hundred feet behind me. We're all at the same elevation. I hear them clearly on their radio frequency as they start to panic. They're not sure what to do, requesting direction from their command center. They keep coming closer, only two hundred feet away.

The lead fighter pilot is excited and blurts out, "Come in, this is Charlie Nine...Holy hell! I can't believe it. What is this thing? It's huge...just massive...never seen anything like it! Covered with some kind of weird metal; totally black yet it glows in the sun. Wow!...Look at the aft frontal spear...hard to believe...it's a long pointed sword blade like an old-time cavalry saber. This is definitely a military ship! Over...and stand by."

Captain Gawlik, the command officer, reacts from the aircraft carrier: "Copy that; this is T-bone, request ID...Start video of the craft with starboard cameras...Report back...Say again? And over."

"Wilco," responds the pilot. Then, after a few seconds, "Come back T-bone, this is Charlie Nine...Video in progress...It has enormous outer-space rocket burners off the rear; looks like it's used for off-planet thrust, probably nuclear, and really strange-looking. Copy?...Come back...You should be getting a visual off my nose camera...Stand by."

"Roger that; this is T-bone! And stand by," the captain responds.

"Charlie Nine here...What do you think? Over...Come in... Should we try to make contact?"

The aircraft carrier captain responds, "T-bone here; I copy, we see it...The starboard camera video is transmitting...Be careful. It's massive...Don't do anything hostile...Zoom the camera in on it if you can. Scan to the starboard, then port, back again... We can see it clearly and are searching our database...Nothing like I've ever seen...No one here can recognize it, and our systems analysis report says it's not known. It could be experimental from somewhere. You're now in Mexican airspace. We will notify the Mexican authorities...Copy?"

"This is Charlie Nine, copy that..."

"Roger, T-bone here, we will stand by...Try to make radio contact. Ask for identification...Over."

The pilot replies, "Charlie Nine...copy...will do...I'm tuning in all wavelengths and frequencies...Stand by...Could it be Mexican experimental? It's freaky strange or a major weird-looking rocket ship...My guess, it's not Mexican...No country could build this. It has massive fusion burners...A real chance this is not from this planet. No one today could build those nuclear thrusters off the stern. They must weigh tons. We have a real UFO. Maybe it really is an alien ship. Certainly not a Chevy, guys. Definitely built for outer-space travel, lots of thrust; looks like it's powered for massive speed. Just really look at those red-hot nuclear burners pushing it...amazing! I am transmitting now on all frequencies...I will try to make contact. Stand by."

The pilot then says through his intercom, "Attention...Come in...Come in...Attention, starboard aircraft...Please identify your craft and origin...Need for you to respond...Do you copy? Affirm...Come in, black ship! Do you copy me?...Please confirm your identity."

No response.

The other pilot, the second F-16, shouts, "George Two here... Roger that...we have no reply...T-Bone, none of this is good; it knows we're here...It has to be military and real lethal, built to kill, really scary, one bad-looking dude! I don't like this. Come back...Over...Affirm."

Captain Gawlik shouts over the radio, "Roger that, George Two...T-bone here...You're right! We do not engage! It's looking like extraterrestrial time, guys, Time to call Section 58. The big boys need to know about this one. I'm relaying your visual to the Pentagon. Over and out."

My turn to look them over; it's time to change the game. I hit the brakes using *Saber*'s antigravity traction force field. They zoom on by me. I hit the gas, and I'm up behind them. I smile as I hear their chatter saying I've vanished.

Of course then the AWACS controller sees me behind them. He panics, yells that I'm about a hundred feet behind them, maybe twenty feet higher, right on top of them. I'm now following them really close, so close I might be able to read their name tags. I'm for sure in position for looking them over, good to see them up close. The ships are slow, with primitive technology and simple weapons. All three pilots panic, each peeling off in a different direction, scattering fast.

I think it's a good time for me to go, too. I hit my burners, blasting forward, feeling that tremendous surge, vanishing again as I head up into the skies. The fiery blast is trailing behind me for miles, and I'm moving fast enough to feel the pain of gravity, making it hard to breathe with the massive chest pressure. Climbing at seven miles a second, I'm up fifty miles from Earth in seconds, beyond reach, and heading cross-country to have a delicious lunch at my favorite restaurant in Manhattan. I need to make it there by eleven thirty. The reservation was made ten years ago. It would sure be disappointing to miss it and wait another ten years for the next one. I know my law firm has called them to remind them I'm coming and to confirm my reservation.

CHAPTER 3

DAY ONE—VISIT TO NEW YORK CITY

I n Manhattan, in a paneled van, pulled off into a vacant lot, two
men are making the life of one teenage girl really miserable.

Heidi is sobbing, afraid, fighting for her life, trying to break
free; as they bind her with duct tape, she cries out, "Why are you
doing this? Please don't hurt me. I'm supposed to be home; my
mother expects me. Please let me go. I'll tell no one. I can't see
you. My eyes are taped shut. Please, please, please don't hurt me."

The blows are coming fast and hard, hitting her face with
loud smacks, her cries now muffled by the tape over her mouth.

Heidi feels overwhelming terror, knowing she is doomed; she
tries to struggle against the tape on her wrists and ankles. She
wails, "Someone please help me! Please, God, I pray to you in my
time of need—please save me," yet the cries are muffled by the
tape. Again she feels a painful blow against the side of her head,
then more against her face, to her chest, and a hard blow to her
stomach. She passes out.

Her name is Heidi Nealfertie. She is fourteen and a freshman
at Saint Patrick's High School, a good student and well liked. She
helps out at the school's food bank one evening a week, coming

home later, when the streets are not so busy. She walks many times to save money and because she loves to walk.

She wasn't paying attention, as she was on her cell phone with her best friend, Kati, who has many problems—being sick and in a poor family are just two. Heidi helps Kati with everything. As she has no sisters, Kati is her sister, and they share everything, including cell phones—Heidi pays for Kati's. Heidi works cleaning her grandmother's apartment every Saturday. She loves her grandmother dearly, and her grandmother adores her and is delighted by the weekly visits. Heidi then helps Kati with the money her grandmother pays her. Kati would go hungry except Heidi pays for her lunches without her knowing it.

The men caught Heidi by surprise on her way home from the food bank, grabbed her, and put her in the van. She never had a chance. They kidnapped her roughly off a side street, at an alley entrance, making a quick getaway. She happens to be the only daughter of a New York City Department of Health worker. He inspects restaurants and has the power to evaluate them or even shut them down.

Heidi comes to, still dazed, dried blood on her nose and mouth, now in a filthy old abandoned warehouse. The duct tape is gone; her wrists are shackled with metal chains, a collar around her neck, chained to a beam, and she is naked. She immediately feels sick, vomits. Then, looking at herself, shocked, then looking around, terrified of what she sees, and she knows her nightmare is coming, her papa had warned her so many times. The men see her, knowing she is looking at them, and they have taken off their masks; she sees their faces. Heidi now knows she will not survive this. She braces herself as they come for her. The next couple of hours are as bad as she imagined: she is beaten, then she is strung up by her wrists, hung from a beam, her feet barely able to touch the floor.

Normally Heidi is a bright, happy girl, is fun to be around, and loves her parents and her friends. They appreciate her for her kindness; she is always there for them. She's pretty with long dark hair. She's always been sheltered, surrounded by kind people, never had much in material things, yet she is loved dearly by her family and friends.

Now she is naked, petrified, severely bruised, in a lot of pain, humiliated, and sobbing, desperately pleading for her life, looking small and fragile. One of the men is taking a video as another one is whipping her hard with a belt. She is suffering, each hit painful; her screams are loud and woeful. She is frantic, begging them to stop, trying to evade the blows, hysterical from the belting. Red welts are covering her body, her face bruised, bloody, and more pain added with the loud smack of each hit.

One of these two men is in charge, yells at her: "Look at the cell phone camera, you little bitch!" Then he tells her to ask her father to save her, to start talking and look directly at the cell phone camera's eye. She wails with clenched teeth, tears rolling down her cheeks, and then begs for her life as she looks directly at the phone camera. She cries out, "Papa, Papa, please help me." Then, sobbing: "I love you, Papa. Tell Mama I love her."

The boss scans her naked body with the cell phone camera, the lens showing the ugly marks on her. He laughs! He is a cruel man enjoying her pain; he has done this before with other young girls. He knows it works.

He e-mails the video to her father, and then Marco, the one they call the boss, calls him. The call is answered on the second ring.

In a heavy Italian accent he says, "George, my name is Marco; do you hear me? Did you see the video? You know who she is, right? Do you love your daughter?"

Heidi's father shrieks, "You son of a bitch! My daughter, why? Who are you? You have her? You've hurt her! Why? Why are you doing this? I am not a rich man. I am just a city worker. I can't pay you much. Have I done something to you? What do you want? Why would you hurt a child? Do I know you?"

Marco laughs, responds, "No, you don't know me. You have the video? Good! Yeah, I have your daughter. Stop talkin'! Be careful what you say. Now listen carefully! Yes, your daughter, Heidi, is still alive, and yes, I sent you the video. If you want this to stop, and if you want to save Heidi's life, you need to do exactly what I tell you. If not, believe me, she will suffer badly because of you. First of all she will be whipped again many times. She will be raped. She will suffer. We will then drug her with our best heroin; she will become addicted. I personally promise you she will end up in a brothel in Thailand, as she will be sold. She will bring a good price, and you will never see her again. You understand, right?"

George, with much fear in his voice, says, "Yes, yes. Why did you do this? Please, I will do whatever you want. Please, she is our only daughter! I beg you, please don't hurt her! What do you want from me?"

Marco tells him, fortunately for him, he does not need money to save his daughter, just to follow his instructions exactly. He continues, "George, listen carefully! It's easy. There are three restaurants you will inspect for me. Make the arrangements as soon as possible. I will e-mail their names and contact information. You will give them bad marks after your inspections. You will call and threaten each restaurant with shutting it down due to health violations. You will tell them if they cooperate their problems will go away. You will call and tell them they will be contacted by me, then hang up. That's it. George, it's easy, your daughter comes back to you when this is done. For her sake hurry, and no police. No police! You understand, right?"

The father is crying on the phone, begging Marco not to hurt his daughter. He moans in misery, frantic to save his daughter, then blubbers out that he will take care of it exactly as requested, and no police.

Marco smiles and says, "Call when you make first contact with the restaurants and then when it is done. Call me at this phone number. I will make arrangements to give your daughter back then. Her life depends on you."

After the phone conversation, the men take Heidi down from the rafters, clean her up, and put her in a steel cage the size of a big closet, over in a corner of the warehouse. There is a filthy mattress and a thin dirty blanket on the floor and a bucket to perform toilet needs. A small worn-out table with a lamp with a bare bulb is in one corner. A pitcher of water and a cheap plastic glass sit next to the lamp. There is a sack of candy bars and some packages of chips on the table. Heidi's backpack and books are on the concrete floor. She sits on the mattress, naked under the blanket, shivering, sobbing hysterically, and then she slowly lies back on the mattress, wrapping her arms around her legs, pulling the blanket around her, exhausted.

Marco closes up the warehouse, locking all doors. The warehouse is his, in a deserted bad neighborhood. No one will ever hear Heidi, and she will be sold off soon, at one of the foreign storeroom auctions, and probably for a nice price, just like the other girls. She will clean up well and probably be a quick sale; virgins sell better. He smiles and thinks how easy this was; young girls are his specialty. The father will have to be taken care of, too, and the mother, no loose ends. Dead people can't talk.

It is good to enjoy one's work; rewarding, too. His plan is working well so far. All three of these restaurants will be paying him, and the current management will be gone in time. Eventually he will put in his guys to run the operations. He laughs in anticipation, thinking money is a good thing. He smiles at the thought of one more small chore. He needs to revisit one restaurant today, a little Italian place on West Ninety-Fifth Street in Manhattan. The real owner does not live in New York yet will be there today. He will be surprised by this visit. Smiling, Marco is thinking it will not be a good surprise for the owner. He laughs. These rich guys are all the same when cornered. Sometimes they even cry and beg. It's something to look forward to. He laughs.

⊷ ⊶

The *Saber* is hovering above Manhattan, about two thousand feet up, in stealth mode, maneuvering for my visit, now over my destination on West Ninety-Fifth Street.

I say to myself, "Good to be in New York City."

I've barely arrived on time. I plan for one hour to eat lunch at my little Italian restaurant in Manhattan. The food is fantastic. I love the spaghetti! The place is not far from Central Park, and I plan to walk in the park, too; I will enjoy seeing it again. I've already called my law firm to let them know I'm here and will be having lunch at the restaurant.

It's surprising to me even now, sixty years later, that I still own this restaurant. On my first trip back to Earth in 1954, I stopped to eat at this little family Italian eatery in New York. My law firm recommended it and gave me directions. It was late in the evening. Wanting some really good spaghetti and not having had any for ten years, I finally found the restaurant on Ninety-Fifth Street in Manhattan. I sat at a well-worn table and ordered spaghetti, and the meal was terrific. I loved the place.

The restaurant was mostly empty in the late evening when I finished. Sitting there waiting for the bill, the dining room quiet, I could not help noticing there was much crying in the kitchen. So I left my table and found a young couple, both in tears—Alfonzo and Rosa, the owners of the establishment. Both were dressed in worn-out, weathered clothing; both with faded, stained aprons; standing among all the pots and pans; both in great despair. They were an attractive couple yet aged more than their youth, lines on their faces from worry, yet still fine-looking people.

Neither could speak English well, and they were alarmed at my presence. Before they could say much, I asked what was wrong, and with a lot of coaxing they told me their story. They had emigrated from Italy four years previously, looking for work in the United States. Italy had been a mess, as it had been not long after the war, so they had come to Manhattan. They had struggled to start their restaurant and had two more children, adding to the three they had brought from Italy. Unfortunately one child had become very ill and required extensive hospital care. The huge medical cost was bankrupting them. After all their efforts, they said, they were going to have to sell the restaurant to pay the medical bills and might lose their children, as they were unable to feed them.

There was lots of discussion between us. I met the whole family, and there were more tears, many tears. The end result was that I bought the restaurant. I gave them twice their asking price. I also leased it back to them for a dollar a year on a ninety-nine-year lease. I gave them complete control, and they would receive all the revenue. It was a very good deal for them.

I made only two requests. I asked for free spaghetti dinners on my visits there, as every ten years I would be back. The second condition was secrecy. They needed to close the restaurant for the hour I would be there. It would be critical to always keep me a secret and confidential partner, to never ask questions, and to tell no one when I would be there for a visit. Alfonzo and Rosa were stunned by my offer, even suspicious, not sure about me, questioning why I was so generous, why I was helping them. Yet after a while, they took the deal. Later, through the years, they were happy and grateful for the partnership. I became part of the family, and they gave me credit for saving them—for being sort of their guardian angel. They forgave me for the ten-year absences and were delighted to see me on every visit back.

At the time I had my law firm follow up after the deal. The next day the firm gave the couple the money, drew up the contract, and worked out the details. The law firm also took care of all their legal issues as the years went by, for no charge—rather, I paid for it. The law firm was there to advise them.

Now it's time once again for an excellent lunch! I am looking forward to the wine, too. I hope Alfonzo and Rosa are well.

The *Saber*, in camouflaged mode, drops altitude, down to two hundred feet, to allow me to use a power beam. When no one is around, I quickly take a single-person power beam down. It's invisible. I drop off in the alley behind the restaurant, close to the back door, look around. I see no one in the alley and hear people talking, voices coming from the door. It's open, maybe waiting for me. I immediately smell the wonderful aromas of the Italian kitchen: the tomato sauce, the different cheeses, garlic, coffee, baking bread. I know Alfonzo and Rosa are expecting me, as my law firm arranged the time and notified them of my arrival. I smile, walk in the door.

Alfonzo and Rosa are both sitting in the kitchen, sitting at a little side table, drinking coffee. The place is busy, staff in well-used aprons, cooking, washing pots; the working space is bigger now, remodeled since my last visit. They are delighted to see me and stand up to hug me, both smiling big smiles, laughing, excited, and saying hello in Italian. I am delighted, too, smiling back at them although I am shocked by their appearance. The extra weight and the hair that is now grayer I can understand. However, they are both showing ugly dark bruises on their faces and arms. Not good, bruises? They are looking their age, the last ten years may have been hard, and they're in their late eighties. Both seem weary.

I can see they are truly pleased to see me although I know they are uneasy about my continued youthful appearance. I have always looked young on these visits, and they have speculated about it but never asked me. This year I can tell they are really wondering about me, even more so than usual. They are closely examining me, maybe a little stunned by my youth. To their amazement, they tell me, I look just like I looked when I first met them fifty years ago, when they were young like me. I smile and give another big hug to each of them.

To my amusement their children, their grandchildren, and several great grandchildren are there, too, all in the dining room. There must be ten little ones, all happy and full of energy, running around, into everything. Two of their grown children have taken over the operations of the restaurant, and they and their families, including all the children, are introduced to me. It's great fun to meet them; they're all impressive people. Also the business has become very successful and quite famous, now a New York favorite. Per our agreement the restaurant is now closed, and one table is set for me in the main dining room. I am delighted to be part of the family, to sit, eat, and listen.

There is a plate of hot spaghetti waiting for me on the table and a bottle of my favorite red wine. One of the sons lights candles, and another places my meal in front of me. I have been thinking about this moment for a long time, anticipating how good the sauce would be, how tasty the meatballs. I am not disappointed; the meal is superb. I can smell the tomato sauce. The aroma is splendid, and it tastes like I remembered. I drink the wine, and I feel human again. Happiness surges through me.

Then a surprise: suddenly everyone leaves except for Alfonzo and Rosa. They sit down across from me, and while I eat they talk, more serious than usual, telling me about the last ten years—the kids, their health, the neighborhood, and the restaurant. Sadly, for the first time in all these years, they are nervous about being with me. When they talk about the restaurant, they act strange, anxious, and fearful. Definitely something is wrong.

I have finished the meal. I look intently at them, with some concern. After a long pause, I ask, "What's wrong? Where did the bruises come from?" They do not reply. I continue, "Alfonzo! Rosa! You can talk to me. We've known one another a long time. What's wrong? You're acting strange. How did you both get the bruises? Tell me, please."

Rosa starts to cry. Alfonzo has a serious sad look, afraid to talk, fear on his face, as if preparing to tell bad news he does not want to share. He starts to cry then attempts to gather his composure, takes a breath, makes eye contact, and starts to talk.

"Mr. Johnson, please forgive me! I am so sorry. I have not been able to bring myself to tell you." Alfonso catches his breath and continues, "I've put you in a terrible dangerous spot you do not know about, and I have no excuse. I'll tell you everything. I have to confess, I have betrayed you. You have always been our friend, yet I've failed you. I've broken our promise to you not to tell anyone about your visit. We have a visitor coming in a few minutes. He is coming to see you, as he knows you are here. I told him you own the restaurant, and you would be the one he would have to talk to about his so-called proposal."

He pauses, asserts: "By the Virgin Mary, I had little choice, and I claim no excuse. It is bad, really bad; he is really a tough local Mafia thug, dangerous and threatening us for money, and now you. The Mafia is into many terrible things, crimes that are cruel and brutal. They enslave young girls into prostitution, extort money from small-business people, murder people, and then are never caught by the police. This one, Marco, is vicious and clever. He says he will have the health department close us down if we don't do what he wants. The city inspector has already called to say he will visit us tomorrow. Marco, this thug, is also demanding we give him part ownership of the restaurant, allowing him to become our new partner. The bruises are because he roughed both of us up last week, wanting to know about the restaurant's ownership. He slapped Rosa, knocked her down, and then hit me when I tried to protect her. We held out as long as we could, not agreeing to anything. When it looked like he might kill Rosa, I finally told him about you. Rosa could not walk for a week because of him. I told him about today's visit, and we are so sorry. I was afraid for Rosa! I hate to tell you all this. And even worse, there is little time. He is coming to see you today."

Alfonso continues. "I apologize. I could not prevent his coming to see you today. Mr. Johnson, please, we have nowhere to turn. We do not know what to do. We cannot go to the police. Marco has done terrible things to other local businessmen who have refused him or gone to the police. He has even put women we know in the hospital after severe beatings, has cut off fingers and killed people. He's never been arrested, so I think he's paid off the police, or they are afraid of him. He will come with his thugs today and may do awful things to you and to us. I am so sorry. We will do whatever you want."

They're so serious, I can't help but laugh. They're confused by my reaction and look hurt, maybe offended by my lack of sensitivity. I realize I need to make it up to them and explain my response.

Now serious, I say, "Alfonzo, Rosa, I'm sorry for what you went through, yet no worries are needed now. I'm not laughing at you, just amused that you think I would be angry with you. You need not be afraid of this thug, especially for me. In this kind of situation, it's always better to tell me. This is a very small problem. Do not be concerned about his visit here today. I'm happy to talk to this fellow. After hearing your story, I'm in the mood to meet him. I'll try to reason with him. Either way, he'll never bother anyone again; let me assure you. There will be no health-department issues, no reprisals, and no beatings from him. There will be no payments to him either. I want you both to leave right now, before he gets here. When you leave please keep the 'closed' sign up, leave the front door unlocked, and turn the lights down. Do not come back for two hours. Tell no one about his visit or our meeting. If asked, you know nothing. We never had this conversation. I will lock up when I leave."

"Also, I will see you again ten years from now. Please stay well. You're both getting older, so please take care of yourselves. If you have any more problems like this, contact my law firm. Thank you for the spaghetti and your wonderful friendship. Don't worry. You have done nothing wrong. This issue will be taken care of today."

They both look at me in amazement, concern on their faces. Alfonzo starts to cry, gets up from the chair, and comes over to me. I stand. We hug each other, Alfonzo blessing me in the name of the Virgin Mary. He smiles at me, tears running down his face, then turns and helps Rosa up from her chair. Then they are both looking at me intently, maybe a little awe on their faces or maybe real affection, or maybe it's gratitude. Not sure exactly, and I would never do a mind probe to find out. It doesn't matter. I can feel their love for me, and it makes me feel good, really good.

Alfonzo's eyes are still tearful. He finally speaks: "Mr. Johnson, thank you, thank you for helping us again. I thought or hoped you might be able to handle this horrible man. I know you are much more than what you appear, much more! Maybe you are a real guardian angel. We have always kept your secret until now, told no one and will tell no one about today. You have been so kind to us; we owe you so much. We do not understand about you but do not need to know more. We know you are a good man. Please be careful, as Marco is a ruthless, brutal man who kills without conscience. We look forward to your return visit. If we can do anything for you, just ask. Thank you and bless you!"

After they have left, I finish the meal with an apple, the first one in ten years. An apple is priceless, the perfect Earth food. I think life is good. Yes, and I can be of help to them once more. Even now, with these issues, I am in a very good mood. What a wonderful meal. What wonderful people, splendid grandchildren. What a wonderful family. Earth is such a treat!

I am glad to be here for them. It's easy for me, always has been. I know basically I am a predator by profession; it's part of who I am naturally; and, I was rebuilt, and then trained to be the predator of predators. It's my role in this life, and I have become really good at it. Yet I think I work for the betterment of those who cannot defend themselves. It makes me wonder about myself, though, as I look forward to meeting this Earth predator, glad for the challenge, pleased about him. He is a cruel one. His treatment of Alfonzo and Rosa left a bitter taste. I know I can kill him without any remorse or complications. It makes the universe a better place to cancel a wicked being, especially right here and now. Cut out the cancer. Then again, some may say he will do me in. I am sure he thinks so. Maybe he plans a cruel death for me as outnumbered by his thugs, treating me like his other victims? He might end my existence. Many have thought they could do so, and many have tried in many different worlds. I smile then I laugh!

Right on cue he comes in the front door with his two large thug bodyguards, as if he owns the place. He looks around, as it is a little dark in the room with no lights on. He sees no one at first. Alfonzo was accurate: Marco looks like a bad man. He is big and muscled with cold beady eyes, dark bushy eyebrows, a big chin, and black hair to his shoulders. Yet he is dressed well, with a tailored black suit, a blue silk shirt, and a red silk tie. He smiles when he sees me, actually an ugly smile, and then lets out a really wicked laugh as he crosses the room toward me. He turns angrier as he moves, staring at me, swearing under his breath.

No one could ever forget his laugh. I am impressed. He must practice the laugh. It's really wicked.

I'm sitting at the table drinking the last of the wine, waiting for him. The wine is excellent, and I pour another glass. I hear him getting closer.

He pulls out the chair facing me, intensely staring at me, frowning. He slowly sits and then, very slowly, pronouncing each word in a thick Italian New York accent, says, "My name is Marco, and I knows your name: a Mr. Henry Johnson, and you are the owner of this here restaurant. You look real comfy sittin' there drinkin' your wine. I know you know who I am, right?"

Intently looking at him, making eye contact, exclaiming: "Marco, why don't you tell me what I can do for you?"

"Mr. Johnson…I am not like you. I have earned my way in this world. You're probably some kind of smart-ass Wall Street banker with a lot of money. Youse guys like taking advantage of poor little men like Alfonzo. You might be rich because of takin' money from restaurants like this, or maybe your family gave you lots of money. It don't matter. I think you're smart enough to understand me. You look like you know what insurance is all about—like protection from unforeseen events, critical to your continued good health. I am a businessman sellin' you some really good insurance. I need fifty thousand dollars from you right now for past-due coverage. The restaurant will be payin' me directly in the future. By the way, I'm goin' to be takin' this business. You'll sell it to me for ten dollars. We can do this the easy way or the hard way. Your choice, dipshit."

I laugh, saying, "Marco, I think it would be much better for you if you were not a predator. You're not that good at it. You're too predictable. The easy way for you to survive this is not what you think. Pay me everything you have, walk away, never come back to New York, and thank me for sparing you."

Marco's face turns red in rage, and he blurts out, "Go screw yourself! You think you're going to walk away from this? I guess you're not as smart as I thought. This could be very painful for you!" He leans across the table, menacing, his eyes cold. Then his two mean-looking thugs start to come in behind me, one on each side, ready to close in and grab me.

Marco spits out, "Do you know why I'm here, asshole?"

I don't reply. Ignoring him, slowly I take another drink of the wine, finishing it off.

He shouts, "Do you have the money?"

I respond in a quiet severe voice, staring into his eyes. "Marco, stop. Slow down while you're still alive. It will be a bad death for you. Try to save yourself. Maybe tell me about this situation, think about saying you're sorry, and make amends. Ask for salvation. You must have some regrets. Did you not have a mother who cared about you? Can we work this out? It doesn't have to be this way. You have one opportunity to save yourself. It's a procedural process for me that benefits you now, a guideline for me. It means even though you don't deserve it, I will give you one chance at redemption. I'm warning you not to pursue this; instead, ask for salvation. Do you believe in God?"

Marco has lost all control. Wild-eyed, in a guttural New York accent, he spits out his words. "Listen, you stupid asshole, you are the one needin' redemption. I'm going to start cuttin' off your fingers, then I'm gonna burn this place down with you in it. Maybe you think you're a tough guy! You'll be beggin' me to stop before I'm done with you. Are you goin to be payin' or not?"

Shaking my head no, with a hard stare, penetrating his eyes with my anger, I say, "Marco, it's going to be a bad day for you. You should have taken my offer."

Marco is not fazed. Now he's completely in control, his eyes cold, heartless. He smiles an ugly smile, pulls a big closed knife from his side pocket, and opens it, a brutal, lethal-looking tool, razor sharp, something you might use to skin an animal, effective for his intent. Marco's thugs are also big tough-looking guys, probably ex-military. Both move in closer, their eyes vicious, starting to reach for me.

They are caught off guard, as I abruptly rise up, knocking my chair backward, grabbing the nearest thug by his hair and jerking his head hard, ramming it down on the table with a crashing thump. His face is smashed and bloody. I then punch him through the ribs, the force of my fist crushing and shattering bone as it penetrates, one rib splintered, stabbing into his heart. He screams in pain. He tries to pull away, with his back to me, and then he feels my second punch to his kidney as it explodes inside his body, creating an internal bloody mess. He shrieks, pisses and then passes out from the pain, almost dead before he hits the floor.

The second one momentarily freezes, fright in his eyes, yet fares better as I grab his throat, easily lifting him off the floor, snapping his neck loudly, like a branch of a tree. He gasps, his eyes roll back, and then he dies. I gather him up as he falls forward, jerking him into the air, throwing him back about fifteen feet like a limp rag doll, and he hits solidly, with a loud crashing detonation, ending the future use of a good table. All this happens in just a few seconds.

Now focused on Marco, loathing him, I can't help letting out a low, deep growl. My eyes are meeting his, penetrating his brain, my thoughts searing his consciousness as I feel my own rage. Marco is astonished, all his confidence gone. He is trying to stand and back up as fast as possible, to make a run for it. I can see the shock, then bewilderment, and then terror across his face as he panics. His feet tangle, and he falls backward with the chair, dropping the knife and grabbing hard at the table, knocking it over.

On the floor, spread-eagle on his back, and with his right hand, he is desperately trying to pull his gun out from a shoulder holster then finally jerks it out and fires at me. The first two rounds miss, but the next three are dead-on, striking my chest. I feel the pain penetrations but not for long; it's gone quickly as my body repairs the damage immediately, no effect as I close in on him. He is screaming in absolute terror as I grab his right shoulder with my left hand, gripping and lifting him like a child, my left hand gripping hard on his shoulder, compressing it like a steel vise, fracturing bone, causing him to shriek in pain; the gun drops from his hand.

Still holding on to his right shoulder with my left grip, I slap him hard and fast several times across the face with my right hand, back and forth, each time a sharp whacking sound, a skin-to-skin pop; he is dazed, disoriented, his mouth bleeding now. At the same time I squeeze more, my left grip crushing his right upper arm more, still holding him tight and up in the air, just a little off the floor. He squeals in pain. I grab his mouth and chin with my right hand, fracturing his jawbones, smashed with a crushing squeeze. His eyes bulge in pain and terror, and he makes babbling sounds, breathing not easy, not able to use his mouth. I grab his left shoulder with my right hand, crushing it with my grip, hearing it rupture, then moving down to his left elbow, crushing it, too. I work my way down to his left knee, which I crush with the same right-hand grip. He tries to escape, trying to squeal in pain through his mangled, broken jaws. I drop him to his knees while at the same time hitting his right shoulder with my right fist, breaking his rotator cuff into splintered fragments. He can hardly move, both shoulders useless, and he falls on the floor, helpless, writhing in pain like a wounded animal hit by a car, sobbing, then let's out short shrieks of agony.

He desperately tries to crawl away, and I grab his right leg, the only limb not damaged, twisting it, lifting him up like a rag doll, and his leg bones snap like peanut brittle. I drop him, and he lands hard. He almost passes out, squealing at the top of his lungs. I roughly grab the hair on his head, pulling his face toward me, forcing his gaze to meet mine then hitting him in the nose. His eyes are wild and crazy as blood spurts out his nostrils.

Staring into his eyes, I project my thoughts into his brain. "Marco, focus! I am reading your thoughts. You know it. I know you feel it. I know you also understand my thoughts. You have a lot more pain to go through before you die."

He knows I'm in his brain as our eyes lock as I probe, causing more pain. His eyes reflect his pain and horror. The pain is now beyond his brink, and he is approaching insanity, and now his mind is totally vulnerable to me. I'm alarmed by his memories as I force his mind open. Marco is truly a bad man, more than I expected. He also has been busy. I can see into his memories and can see many of his previous ugly activities, what he has done. I see the terrible damage he inflicted on many young girls, and one real recently, today, a young girl, Heidi. She should be alive still, although suffering in some warehouse. It is a fresh memory. I understand now. I know how he was going to get the health department to shut down the restaurant. I ask him where she is and her father's name and number. Marco wants his own death; I feel it. He is pleading, begging for an end to his agony. I reassure him mentally that I will kill him quickly after he tells me about the girl. I will put him out of his misery and pain.

He tries to scream again, as adding to his terror, he finally comprehends he is hearing my thoughts mentally. This bewilders him. He can barely talk, barely able to breathe, mostly because of the broken nose and crushed jaws; his speech is now a garbled, blubbering blood. His eyes wild from the extreme pain, he blurts, "Who are you? Are you a demon?"

I ask him again, this time out loud in a snarl. He cannot speak; it's impossible with his jaws swelling and his face a bloody mess. No matter. I can hear his thoughts. I know where Heidi is, the warehouse's location, and her father's name—George—and his cell number.

I don't need Marco anymore.

I immediately finish him off. It ends fast. He never knows what hits him, my right fist exploding into the middle of his chest, crushing his sternum and exploding his heart. The pain is intense only for a moment as he dies of a massive heart attack. I stare into his horrified eyes, penetrating his last thoughts as his life drains from him. He is a dismal, violent, cruel man who is afraid to die, his soul beyond redemption. He receives the bad death he deserves.

I then call George, Heidi's father, using Marco's cell phone and tell him I know about the kidnapping of his daughter. I know where she is located, and I give him the address. I tell him to tell no one and not to do what was asked of him for her return, saying, "It's all over. Your daughter may need some medical attention. She is in bad shape. Hurry! Go get to her now!" I tell him. "Her kidnapper will never bother her or you again—ever." He's weeping as he thanks me. He asks who I am. I do not respond. I hang up.

The *Saber* sends down a cleanup crew, specialized debris-eater drones. They take care of the blood, the gun, the knife, and the bodies. They look like swarming termites humming away. Then nothing remains: the bodies vanished, blood all gone, no sign they ever existed. They all become recycled waste. I straighten up the room as much as possible and lock the door as I leave.

I need to head back to the *Saber* quickly, no time for Central Park. I also have to change clothes, as mine are covered with blood and smell awful. The spaghetti dinner took more time than I wanted. I have things to do. It was good, though. Poor Alfonzo and Rosa. I hope I helped them.

CHAPTER 4

RUSSIAN OVERFLIGHT

I need to figure the velocity at the current latitude and longitude of the *Cyclone* to navigate my trip back to it, as it is moving fast over Earth's atmosphere. The *Saber* immediately gives me the starship's location. The interception point will be plotted automatically.

The *Cyclone* is currently orbiting the Earth about 170 miles up, not far from Russia, moving in line toward Moscow, with a heading due southwest at a speed of thirty-eight thousand miles per hour including Earth's rotation speed. The *Saber* calculates the intersection point, changing course, tracking a new destination plot, then notifies the *Cyclone* of the intersection point.

Our direction takes us up over Siberia, not far from Alaska. We are accelerating to make a quicker hookup yet keeping an altitude of thirty thousand feet. I want to see Alaska and Siberia. The vast pristine wilderness there is amazing, worth the time. Siberia alone is three times larger than Alaska or half the size of the United States. Last time I was here the cloud layer was too thick to see much. It was a carpet of clouds for miles, earth not visible from above.

Today is much better, blue skies. I drop to ten thousand feet, enjoying the scenery using the *Saber*'s video magnification lenses, seeing the magnificent forests, the coastline of Alaska, then the miles and miles of heavy forest in Eastern Siberia. Suddenly I am surprised to see a massive area of forest that is not all forest. My infrared scanners are picking up much higher temperatures under the tree canopy, what may be lots of people and moving vehicles spread for miles. This is mostly uninhabited Russian territory, no towns, no cities—nothing is supposed to be here other than wilderness. I see nothing at first, and then there it is. I'm barely able to see them, camouflage and forest hiding a lot of tents and tanks and thousands of troops. They are truly hidden. Even with the magnification lens, which gives me a view at a thousand times normal, really a close-up, it's not easy to see them from above. Still, I know they're there.

What is all this? *Not possible,* I think. This is a real anomaly. Very odd, and hidden by someone who went to a lot of effort. I see something, maybe a tank moving along the edge of the forest. Whatever this is, none of it is good. Maybe it's thousands of military tanks and millions of troops. Unfortunately for me I can't ignore it; it is certainly worth checking out.

The *Saber* changes course instantly, reading my thoughts and knowing exactly what to do. We swing back and reduce altitude severely, still maintaining supersonic speed, letting the air friction slow us down. Much to my surprise, several missiles are fired at us from multiple ground locations, none of them sophisticated. They are primitive and not a real threat. The *Saber*'s defense systems destroy all of them instantly. More missiles are fired and destroyed. Why all this? They are serious about killing me. Something important is down there, with so much effort to protect it. I suspect it's a large troop encampment, maybe millions of soldiers. This could not be possible. The infrared signature is massive. Does Russia have that many troops?

Now that they know I'm there, there's no reason to be coy. I am definitely an enemy target, as they have fired at me, though without success. I need to take a closer look, and I can show some teeth. They deserve it. I drop down to two hundred feet above the ground, extremely low since I am moving at fifteen thousand miles per hour. The supersonic air concussion from this velocity will come close to blowing out most of the eardrums of any troops below or burn them with the mega heated air from the hull's friction burn; even worse, this causes a lack of air that will suffocate many of them. And more terrible, the ship's mega hot fusion tail-stream blast will literally blow a channel four miles wide behind it, burning and erasing ground brush, roasting the trees, burning troops, tumbling buildings, overturning trucks, destroying camouflage covers, and starting many fires. It will scare the hell out of the other troops, and as I'm moving so fast they won't see me, just hear the thunderous booms and feel the massive blast of mega hot air. There will be casualties.

Actually the sweep caused much worse destruction than I expected; because of troop density it caused a lot of instantaneous death and obliteration, no escape possible from the massive megahot tail-blast thrust. Too bad, this was predicable.

Then it seems I was premature in my confidence that I escaped other military threats. There they are. Many fighter jets are now descending upon me firing missiles, yet they have little chance of keeping up with me. They can see only my exhaust trail. It's still irritating, though. Maybe time to show them a real military ship. Circling high, I come roaring back, accelerating, and blasting out a massive fiery tail thrust for miles. I'm white hot, the blast resulting in sweeping the air clean of their fighter jets behind me. Between the massive air concussion and the air-friction firestorm coming from the hull with the twenty-five-thousand-mile-per-hour acceleration and the thirty-thousand-degree fusion heat coming off the two-hundred-mile thrust tail, most of the planes are simply destroyed or evaporated. The rest try to escape. I accidentally run over several as they attempt to leave. They are so thin-skinned, the result is obliteration. They are also disintegrating from flying debris or just losing control from the whipping air whirlpools and then crashing.

The *Saber* is armored. Nothing can penetrate it. The collisions and debris have no effect on it, and my flight continues. I accelerate up and away, heading for the *Cyclone.*

The troops' commanding officers will be shocked at the sudden catastrophic loss. They will realize it was caused by some kind of supersonic military jet, massive in size in their perception and many times faster than anything they know about. They will feel instinctive fear, much anxiety and apprehension, or maybe even dread as they eventually realize someone has discovered them. They will also be terrified by the knowledge that there was a military confrontation and they were so vulnerable as well as by the realization that they have a powerful unknown and certainly strange new enemy. Who did this to them? Who has discovered them? They will ask themselves, "Who has this kind of technology? Maybe the United States?"

Of course I realize it is my first military engagement on Earth, which is truly unfortunate. Gabriel will not like it.

The only possible good result to hope for is that maybe it will scare them enough to rethink their plan, whatever their intent.

Still, it puts me in an awkward situation. What do I do? No question this massive army being there is not a good sign, so close to the United States, so many troops. Does anybody know about them in the States? Need to find out what this is as might be critical, will go ahead and implement a reconnaissance survey. Really strange, and bad timing for me. What is happening on Earth? Why are they there? I have no time for this. I circle back to make the drop.

I release several hundred reconnaissance drone slips with a host oversight drone, before leaving the area. They will give a detailed report of what is down there. It sure looks like a lot of troops, shocking enough and hard to believe, just bad news. Crazily enough it looks like a lot of Chinese army divisions sharing the same site, with just a couple of Russian divisions. Are they allies? They'll be wondering about me.

No time to mess with it now. I'm approaching the *Cyclone* and need to load the *Saber* back on board. The bay doors open and I lock in, on track, the starship happy to see us. Time to start my real visit.

CHAPTER 5

EMPLOYMENT BY CONSORTIUM

I am back on the *Cyclone*, the *Saber* loaded up and now heading for Louisville, Kentucky, in the United States, the location of my hometown, or what was my home many years ago. For
many decades I have roamed the universe and thus know it well.
Because of this I now know the Earth to be an unusual planet,
really a precious jewel. It has a very small population as far as
inhabited worlds go. Plus it's a long way off the starship trajec-
tories, the well-traveled trade routes, which are the hyper speed
corridors. Earth unluckily—or maybe luckily—is much too far
away in an immense universe, even for starships, to get much
attention. Worst of all, unfortunately there is almost nothing on
Earth anyone wants.

I know not to meddle too much in human affairs. Actually it's
forbidden. I have been warned many times not to make contact,
as too many issues would come out of it. Earthlings are too primitive to be trading partners, not like the other civilizations. No
one is interested in Earth except for me. I am also told the people of Earth are not ready for trading—too many complications
would result, maybe even serious harm. Even with our good intentions, it could be disastrous for Earth. The massive difference

in technology plus an alien culture would be shocking for Earth humans; there could be worldwide panic.

I have tried many times to advocate the admission of Earth into the Consortium—and been turned down enough times to quit trying. Since no one knew of Earth, the Consortium felt it did not need protection for now. Earth's best defense is to be unknown.

Maybe they are right. Contact with an advanced civilization from some other world in the universe would be problematic. Many issues would be created with real contact or continued interactions, such as when Europe's population met the North American Indians; a lot of Indians died, and there was much suffering, too. Even if someone could give the human race starship technology for effective space travel, the cost would be prohibitive for Earth. The price tag is about $300 trillion for one no-frills starship. The other challenge is the nuclear-fusion energy a starship requires. It has huge fuel needs. To fill the gas tank for just four months of starship travel is equal to three years of Earth's total energy production. Think about creating enough starship fuel for several years, the resources required. It's just not possible on Earth at this time.

Still, Earth is my home planet. I was born there on April 17, 1920, in Louisville, Kentucky. It was a great place to live and grow up: friends, school, family, and lots of boyhood adventures. My biggest wish was to return there and raise a family. However, this was not meant to be. After four years at Indiana University, I graduated, and then I joined the US Army in 1942, not long after Pearl Harbor, and became a pilot. Then I died, or maybe almost died, on June 6, 1944, at Normandy Beach, part of the invasion force on D-Day, flying a P-51 Mustang fighter plane for the US Army. I was, unfortunately, shot down; there was no escape for me. My Mustang hit the water hard, and I was badly injured, couldn't get out of the sinking plane. My last memory is that I was in a lot of pain. It was dark and cold, and I would miss my friends and family, especially my mother. My last thoughts were about her. She would be sad, and she would miss me. I wished I could have seen her one more time.

Then I woke up, and, to my astonishment, I was still alive. However, life had changed for me in a big way. The first thing was I was a long way from Earth, trillions of miles. I would learn later that an interstellar reconnaissance robot starship picked me up. It was assigned to find someone like me, the right military DNA, beyond hope, dead to my world, ready for a new life to be granted on new terms.

I was rebuilt, as a damaged car is fixed, put back together with new parts and good as new, actually better, an improved version when they were done. It was pleasant—no pain, no fear. My new comrades were kind, certainly strange, not human yet very human, as empathetic, compassionate, and concerned about me.

I had a purpose, which was explained to me, and I understood. This new world to which I was introduced was really beyond my comprehension, yet, I learned fast. The learning was mostly telepathic. Words were rarely spoken. Really hard to explain, just that I had a constant stream of information coming in, like a software download, and amazingly enough I retained it permanently. I learned later a small microcomputer processor (part synthetic, partially organic, as it was nurtured by my body) was implanted in my brain when they were rebuilding me, which has turned out to be quite handy. For one, I am now telepathic. It has also increased my brainpower by giving me access to massive computer data links. It can be used anywhere and everywhere. My brain has a language communications link, too, given to me by the use of telepathy. I needed to communicate with my benefactors in their way—cerebral: a mental exchange of facts, emotions, and thoughts. Being able to talk with them directly, with my mind opened up to everything, is a much better way to give and receive information.

Remarkably enough, I can even link to any computer software program. For example, I can access Earth's phone communication system anywhere or any communications system on any world, even check into anyone's e-mail on Earth. It also gives me the language capability of all the populations of the civilized worlds known by my benefactors, which is a lot.

And yes, there are trillions of beings throughout the universe, spread over the immense trillions of miles of empty space in many different galaxies. Unfortunately for all of us, the universe is mostly empty space, with vast distances with no mass, nothing, just long, lonely voyages between planets. Most of the worlds we know about, that are inhabited, are in the Consortium. Those that are not members are too young and primitive or just too far away. Most of the member civilizations are very old, existing for millions of years, in a universe that is about fourteen billion years old, older than Earth by three times. Earth is about four and a half billion years old. The Consortium leaders are the most ancient of all the civilizations. Most are more ancient than I can comprehend, maybe counted as in billions of years. They are not sure either. I feel privileged to be part of it all, maybe even a key player, a small one anyway. Who could ever imagine this for my destiny?

Always the real gift to me, bringing me up to maximum effectiveness, is this imbedded little microcomputer synthesizer/processor in my frontal lobes and all the downloaded software it contains. It gives me the technical knowledge and the telepathic ability to command or communicate with the *Cyclone*, my command starship. As I am always linked to the *Cyclone*, anything is possible, with access to its unlimited data and unlimited power. I can also ask it to do anything I need, no matter where I am. It has the capability to do everything, absolutely no limits to its power. No entity in the universe can withstand this power and intelligence. I don't think we can be compromised in any way.

The *Cyclone* will also link me to everything. For example, I can contact all my fleet commanders no matter where in the universe, although many times it's delayed because of distance. They all report to me by way of *Cyclone*'s communications center. This is a huge amount of communication flow. The crew of the *Cyclone* knows how to handle much of this activity, especially now, during my visit home.

My only real issue with all of this is that I am accountable for results. My benefactors know mostly everything that happens to me, including what I do. If they decide to check on me, I am always available. Luckily for me they like me, and I do not hear from them often. Their thought processes are beyond my comprehension, and many times they know outcomes before they happen. Yes, they can predict the future to some degree. I know they respect me; at least they know exactly what I am required to do and know it is difficult. In a universe of free choice and free will, my attempts to achieve good results do not always bring about great endings. There are so many variables and judgment calls, all giving me decent chances at total failure, which is misery for many others and me. My benefactors understand, yet the accountability is rough sometimes. Not that they are angry, just disappointed, sad, and unhappy. I feel the same, too.

I do hear sympathy from them when things go bad, but they also acknowledge or praise good results. When we need one another, or if they have something specific needing to be done, I just know it, as I hear their thoughts. Sometimes I feel something like love from them, similar to the affection I had for my dog as a boy. Most of the time, I am sure I've satisfied their expectations, and I have been able to do great things for them at times. There have been some truly great military victories over the years, and I have earned their admiration.

My purpose for them was surprising to me because of why they picked me. Mankind on Earth is still young or primitive, an evolution in process. Humans' genetic programming is still enabled with the ability or capacity to kill. For example, a very kind woman still has the capability to harm others for the right reason: to protect her young, to protect her family, to protect her country, and maybe to sacrifice herself if needed. Those genes or DNA codes are no longer part of advanced cultures. No, my new home is a much kinder place. There is no war and no death, as humans know it. It is a wonderful civilization, hundreds of thousands of years advanced, or maybe much more than that. For sure they are far beyond my comprehension or my body's evolutionary status. They have achieved technology beyond belief, maybe even reaching a status of supernatural, maybe spiritual. You might imagine heaven would be like this, with the angels as ancient scientists, all-knowing and wise.

Thus my purpose does make sense. This is why they saved me, why I exist. They told me this.

In the universe there were threats that had to be contained, dangerous issues that needed to be resolved, and laws to enforce. Simply put, they needed my genetic coding. They needed guard dogs. They needed to use my genes, my virgin DNA code. Although primitive in comparison to theirs, my chromosomes are untainted, with pure traits they wanted and needed for breeding warriors or guardians. I am their warrior-guardian.

They were clear. They said to me, "Henry, we need a warrior's temperament yet one who is civilized as well as smart, honest, and loyal. You have all the character qualities of a good soldier— the best traits, the ones most admired: a sense of duty, protection, courage, endurance, strength, loyalty, selflessness, and, the most critical, a good heart. You have this nobility and all that comes with it and more. You will do fine."

Thus I was cloned, or cyber-cloned, many times…hundreds of times…then millions of times. I was the original, and then, though it was hard for me to believe, I was put in charge of this army of my clones. They are not exactly like me, as they are a mix of both organic and synthetic, more like robots, or you could maybe call them humanoids. I think they're more human than not, much like me. You can easily see the similarity, although they're better than I am, as far as what a soldier should be. They're stronger, hardier, and never ill; they need little food or water and can breathe in almost any atmosphere and function in all weather extremes. They are perfect soldiers. The best part is they still have my character traits: my values, my sense of duty, my honor. They are unselfish, sincere, honest, and without greed. They are as loyal to me as a son is to his father. Actually they are all my sons. My genetic DNA codes are in them, programmed to honor me. They do act like me in a weird way; their mannerisms are just like mine. The astonishing part is there are millions of them spread over the universe.

My job could be described in very simple terms. I was assigned the task of being the policeman of the universe, given command of the largest military police force in the universe (that I know about). I have been given technology beyond human comprehension. Unlimited resources back me. Well, almost unlimited. The long distances with trillions of miles create issues in supplies and sometimes communications.

I have a boss. As I work for a Consortium of Civilizations; their leader is my employer. He is from one of the very old, really advanced civilizations, leading the rest, or at least I think so. Their culture is very functional and kind, plus: unselfish, and filled with respect and love for one another. They are beings that have mostly grown past the need of our type of outlook; humans, at times, can be very self serving.

They have given me this guardian responsibility and the tools to carry it out. They said to me, "Keep the peace, enforce our commandments, cut out the infections when needed"—that's never easy—"and do the right thing. Always make a bad situation better, and then start the healing process."

At times justice is easy and comes only when needed, involving little politics, a simplified due process. It is just a simple set of commandments. I was given some basic laws to enforce, told to use kindness whenever possible. I always have a range of options with resulting outcomes, yet I have never been asked to justify my decisions. Sometimes I think they give me too much power and responsibility. I have never lusted after power. It is a curse with a heavy price demanded and constant payments due regularly. I accept it as a duty to endure.

Of course the main challenge is the massive expanse of my jurisdiction, as it is immense, sometimes impossible, just as the universe is almost infinite in size. Plus, I think I am not the only one to command an army for the Consortium now and in the past. There are other parts of the universe I have not seen. Maybe there are others like me across the vastness of space. I have been told there are other military groups, built similarly to this one, beyond my vision, many quadrillions of miles away.

As for my boss, I call him Gabriel; he is considered one of the smartest guys in the Consortium. I don't know his real name. I think Gabriel might be his real name or should be his real name, not sure. He says it fits. He is part of a group of beings who are very old. I mean really old, many thousands of years old. They are intimidating, and they are constantly teaching me, coaching me, and, mostly, forgiving me. I have become humbler as I've grown older. I now realize the immensity and variety of the universe in its construction: the energy, time, movement, dimensions, the vastness of space, and the other beings of intelligence living in it. I have faced many challenges, many problems to resolve; some I've handled well, some not. I am sorry for those situations in which I could have done better. I have some real regrets and remorse.

I am now ninety-four in Earth years and have seen a life that is beyond belief. I would not change anything. I have many stories to tell, many adventures, although I'm not sure who would believe them, and I'm not permitted to tell. No book deal for me. I miss being a human on Earth. Never having a family or having a special girlfriend has been tough.

All this sounds silly, like some old guy whining. I have ten days to enjoy being here. What to do first?

As severely as I have missed everything on Earth, the most valuable objects for me are its books and music. I take some back with me, trying out new authors and artists. I always need to re-stock. Thus I think a bookstore will be my first stop. Plenty of newspapers and magazines are there, too.

I have also discovered music is distinctive to each world, as are books, or what we call books. Each civilization does it differently. I love the music from this planet. I can't get enough of it. All of it is brilliant: symphonies, rock bands, soloists, choirs, country music, and jazz. On this visit I would be thrilled to go to a concert, see a live performance, maybe at a nightclub. I always make time for a bookstore, just to feel and buy new books, then I review them; how pleasing to review the work of creative new authors. I am old-fashioned. I like real books and real newspapers, as they feel personal, not like electronic downloads. I especially love the charm of a real book, as in the sensation of it, the look and shape of it, even the texture and the smell of it. It's just like when I was a little boy. Having a good book is like holding a little treasure. It is real. The magazines and their photos make me feel good, a quick fix.

There is nothing better than being home.

CHAPTER 6

JUNE 6, 2014 HENRY BENJAMIN JOHNSON

This visit will be the best. I feel it. This time back will be different, in the Earth year 2014, and today's date is June 6, a great time to be here. Although I am ninety-four years old, age has never been too much of a problem. I have not aged like a normal human because of being rebuilt in 1944; my benefactors dramatically slowed the aging process in me by improving my cell regeneration and by using DNA adjustments, changing codes, enhancing them, reengineering me.

Because they are pleased with me, as a reward I was recently given another overhaul. The Consortium's original rebuilding of me worked well, yet they felt an enhancement was necessary. They have given me a new lease on life, making me grateful for their kindness and affection. I smile when I think about their warmth toward me. You could call it a birthday gift from them. They gave me youth and enhanced my immortality.

I am physically young again. Yes, I think it's quite miraculous. I am rid of my ninety-four-year-old body and, thanks to my benefactors, back to around age thirty. At least the physical body I am now using is thirty or even younger, cloned from my previous ninety-four-year-old body. I still feel the same, though. The same DNA and genes were used, just like when I was in my twenties.

All this was done with a perfect clone built with my DNA coming from my body, created two years ago. It was grown in an artificial environment, advanced by enhanced growth hormones plus some synthetic organic material, creating a young physical body, the muscles conditioned by liquid electricity. It is my exact duplicate but better, more enhanced, all within a required two-Earth-year period, so as to meet this deadline for my current visit. My previous body was quite young-looking, even for such an older age, feeling younger and looking maybe more like the midforties. Yet I was starting to feel my age. Now all that is gone.

My personal data was downloaded into my improved body using thousands of microscopic drones copying stored data from my mind, all that I am: every experience, all my human values, memories, military experience, relationships, and spiritual values, all in preparation for the last download, which took place before this trip. These molecule-size magnetic-electron drones magnetized and copied every single neuron in my old brain, then sorted them out, billions of them, loaded them into something like a massive mainframe computer, and prepared the download for the new me.

I nervously made the final transition and know it was successful, as I am now in the new body and feel the same cerebrally. My thinking is the same, no differences. Of course I now feel much better physically than before; I feel young. I am rid of the ninety-four-year-old body with the aches and all the other age-related health issues. All problems are gone. Intense workouts are easy again. The chemical difference physically is remarkable; all my glands are at full output. One big change is I have a sex drive again; it's been a long time since I felt the strength of those hormones. Now I realize what I lost with aging, as I feel completely restored with this update. I am delighted. I stare at my hands, and they are a young man's hands.

Although as far as I can tell, I am the same Henry Johnson. The old memories seem unchanged. I remember the same experiences and feel the same emotions. I am just young again. I have more energy, more strength, and more optimism. I am renewed with purpose—I'm once again excited about the future. I had lost some of that enthusiasm in my old body. I now feel inspired again. I feel the youth surging in my veins. Sometimes being part of a highly advanced civilization is a good thing. And, smiling, I say aloud to myself, "I think a youthful sense of humor sure helps, too."

Also because of some new genetic enhancements, I am better than before. The muscles are better; this body is much stronger physically. Plus they added titanium cement in the bones, which are now more difficult to break. The muscles are much tighter, laced with polysynthetic compounds causing quicker reflexes and overall built for high-sustained performance with great strength. The only drawback is the weight. The new body, because of the increased muscle density and the metallic bones, is heavier. I am still six foot two and have my same slender frame, yet my Earth weight surprisingly comes in at 290 pounds—much heavier than my original 195. To have the increased strength, I must deal with the extra gravity.

The other new rebuild improvement is my intelligence, which has again been enhanced by my benefactors, who thought I was very primitive. Although I still feel primitive, I am smart enough to know I am not smart enough. They laugh at this. They say I am still very young and to stop complaining; I should be thankful.

In this upgrade, the microcomputer processor and its database, that they had implanted in my brain in my first rebuild, in my original body, were replaced. The new ones are similar but much better. They are now 90 percent organic, part of my body, nourished by my blood, part of my DNA. Thus I have cell re-generation. The processor can now develop, evolve, adapt, grow, and become much stronger with time and use. They also give me even more extensive communications capability. My outgoing telepathy is much more powerful; the incoming more receptive. It feels natural, not strange. In the past I was never able to completely use telepathy well. It was always unnatural, certainly never strong enough to overwhelm another mind, and never able to communicate to more than one being at a time.

However, now, because of this new processor, telepathy is a real strength, a terrific tool for me. I have much more powerful access to others' thoughts, including many beings at the same time. I can even use my thought waves effectively to broadcast my emotions and then to pull out or guide the emotions of others, as in a mind meld, to create understanding of the real feelings among a group of beings. Opposite of this, it is an awful instrument; it can be a weapon to overwhelm others and forcefully extract information using painful probing when needed. I can transmit back and forth to the starship over long distances just by thinking of it and by using the energy from the *Cyclone*. The military advantage is useful, too, as by using the *Cyclone* as an energy source I can amplify my telepathy, focusing on beings within five hundred yards or more, sometimes even through a ship's hull. This gives me the terrible option of killing all the beings in this range by overwhelming their brain activity, causing it to cease functioning. Too harsh even for me. I probably will not use the processor for this, as it's hard to tell whom I might hurt, what kind of possible collateral damage there might be, and the flash-backs might damage me. Besides, I find it distasteful to use it to kill. Maybe changing an attitude or controlling a victim's mind might be useful, or it might help listening to extracted memories or communicating my anger. But more than this does not work for me. I live with a lot of remorse now. I don't want more.

Anyway, I am now back in the *Cyclone*, hovering about two hundred feet above Frankfort Avenue in Louisville, Kentucky, close to where I was born many years ago. Thankfully, it is overcast, thus no massive shadow is being cast from the ship to the ground. This huge starship is really near to the surface, maybe too close. It may cause vibrations people can feel, and the massive energy shields cause static electricity, which also can be felt. It causes the hair on the back of your neck to rise, too. I have to keep moving. The *Cyclone* has just caused two electric company transformers on the tops of phone poles to explode. Shorted out by static electricity strikes from the hull. Not good, both strikes were visible.

I need to be close to the surface to allow me to drop down from the *Cyclone* using a one-person power beam, which is fast and efficient, mostly invisible. I want see the house I grew up in. The visual images are terrific as I walk along on the sidewalk, trying to act normal. I see people walking or talking on cell phones on their porches, and I say hi; some of them smile back. I see the old neighborhood, not changed that much, and I have many good memories: my paper route, the tree-house tree, Mrs. Slafkes's oatmeal cookies, and my friends. The people I see can't see the *Cyclone* above us, as it is in camouflage mode, yet they can feel it; they peer upward, with funny looks on their faces. I feel it, too; the static electricity is there; the starship is only a few hundred feet up. I know better, but I just like seeing the old neighborhood.

When I was born I was given the name Henry Benjamin Johnson, born to a good Catholic family, several brothers and sisters, a loving father and mother, just working class people. Life was simple then, and I remember it fondly, as we were a close family. My death was tragic for my mother, especially since I was the oldest, the only child to die in World War II. My friends and family have never forgotten me; they truly mourned me. I think my mother came to my grave every year on Memorial Day until she finally died. My sister Jane was there, too, helping Mom and missing me greatly, sad about me the rest of her life. I was given a military grave with a white cross, even though I was classified as missing in action. My family members are all dead now.

My girlfriend then, Pamela, whom I loved, I lost. She eventually married my best friend, Kevin Norris. They had children, the children who should have been mine. I miss her. I miss them both. I miss the children I never had, and even now after all these years I feel the pain. In my previous short visits here, I checked on my family, always checked on my mother. I could never let her know of my existence, only helped them if I could without them knowing. Their children are still alive and having children, their memories of me mostly lost now, the hero uncle who died in World War II. I always come back to our house, hover over it, look at it, and remember those days. I stay hidden, as it would cause way too much commotion if any family now knew about me—and it would be a serious breach of the Consortium's rules.

The *Cyclone* is a huge military starship, thirty-four billion tons in Earth's gravity. It's easy to see from a long way off. On Earth it's normally in camouflage mode, using technology similar to very sophisticated chameleon stealth craft. No one can see it by sight or radar, nor by heat signature. It's invisible, or almost. If we are in blue skies, it's a sky-blue color. However, I still have to be careful at low altitudes, as it is now. With the sun above the ship, it will cast a large shadow on the surface, similar to a large cloud. It helps if it's a cloudy day. I also have to be careful because the ground will sometimes rumble like a small earthquake. Sometimes concrete roads will crack, or many small splinters develop in concrete. It happens mostly when the *Cyclone* is below a five-hundred-foot elevation, due to the air displacement and the massive pressure from the weight of the ship; even though the antigravity buoyancy compensators float the ship, some massive pressure points are created.

If people on the ground could see the *Cyclone*, they would see a long, sleek spaceship, mostly a slender silver cylinder, with brilliant reflections in the sunlight, with a flat underside, a ship that is aerodynamically perfect with a long, slender nose. It is massive at 26,628 feet long, which is over five miles. The main hull is 10,766 feet wide, or a little over two miles, without the side wingspans. The sternly slanted wings spread out another 1,466 feet at the rear adding almost a half a mile to the width, 733 feet each side, port and starboard. The sleek back tailfin is 520 feet tall, on top the hull height of 4,460 feet, thus a total height of 4,980 feet, close to a mile. It has a wide flatness on the underside, with an additional 480-foot lip as a flat platform extending out from the body of the ship and circling around the entire bottom of the hull.

It has the overall look of a silver killer whale with a long, slender nose, although it would be a gigantic one. The exterior color of the ship is a bright-silver sheen, with a blinding polished brightness, enough to look like a mirror. However, sunlight rays cause massive sparkling in dazzling colors. It is always changing as it has no single color, more like a rainbow of colors with blues, yellows, greens, and reds, all depending on the angle of the sunlight's reflection, and it blinds the viewer at moments, like a star in the galaxy.

As starships go, the *Cyclone* is extremely sleek, even more so with the wide, sharp, thin spade-spear at the front end, which is pointing forward and extends a long way out, a graduated 1,944-foot extension, adding to the overall length. This wide front nose is what makes it look long and sleek. The nose is just 3,266 feet wide, much more narrow than the ship's main body as it is an additional 7,500 feet wider equaling a total width of 10,766 feet; it also has an extra 60-foot lip extension on each side.

The ship is shapely, as it is also much thinner in height in its front because of the long, pointed, slender nose. It adds additional sleekness because it is graduated forward, like a wide, thick nose. Like the *Saber* it will disintegrate anything it hits, even big things. Nothing will bend it. It is harder than any diamond, unbreakable. It is designed to shatter anything it hits. The total length is over five miles without the engine rocket thrusters. The very back of the ship, the stern, is more squared off, with twenty massive black funnel rockets protruding out another 2,592 feet, about half a mile. It is impossible to overlook, impressive to see, truly awesome when powered up, creating fire as hot as a star. The nuclear hydrogen fusion blasts out fire streams thousands of miles long.

The *Cyclone* is extraordinary, more than awe inspiring in comparison to anything in the known universe. It looks like it was built yesterday, yet it is very old, actually ancient; I'm not sure how old, maybe millions of years. When you're immortal, time is not so critical. The ship has evolved over centuries, becoming better: stronger, smarter, and wiser. What more can be said about it? In simple terms it can do everything. It is the ultimate technology. It took many thousands of years to develop, made from materials from a hundred worlds. Its real name is an alien name, long and impossible for me to pronounce. I've renamed it *Cyclone*. It is a wonderful name, although Gabriel laughs when he hears me say it.

The *Cyclone*'s propulsion comes from three main energy sources. Using a combination of these driving forces, the starship propels itself forward in stages, creating an aggregate speed, building up to millions of miles per hour. The first thrust comes from a hot nuclear hydrogen fusion similar to the nuclear chemistry in the Earth's sun, and then, adding to the acceleration, the second stage hits. The plasma burners kick on, thrusting forward with millions more horsepower, resulting in light speed. Finally, as the dark-matter or negative-gravity drives take over, the ship breaks through the speed-of-light barrier.

The starship then can travel many times faster than light, and at these top speeds it is bending space and time with dark or negative energy. This energy is plentiful in the universe although invisible, as no light escapes; it pulls in light, the gravity is so powerful, and thus it is black. The intensity is colossal. We use this, or we use the magnetic repulsive power force or the polar reverse of the massive forces of this gravity, changing the equilibrium, thus creating the massive power to distort or to bend the fabric of space. The strength of this black undulation forces a ripple, which opens a corridor for the starship to plunge through at unbelievable speed.

The negative energy comes from the fusion of antimatter particles. The atoms are so explosive; they actually create an infinite energy source, unlimited power. The same energy is used for both propulsion and weapons execution. A military ship using it can unleash a fury of punishment to offenders; even erase planets, all because of the effective use of this unlimited energy. In addition to using the universe's gravity fields then combining with the repulsive nature of our negative magnetic polarization, we have extreme antigravity power capability.

For one use it gives the starship the flotation to counter gravity, for floating weightless above Earth or another planet. Also, when it is needed, the ship's power beams will neutralize the force of gravity on other objects. Using it against enemy ground troops and equipment leaves them without gravity, making them helpless. They are weightless and eventually float off the planet. We can tow objects with it, too, easily pulling them to us. It also works to use this same drive energy for extreme weapons, as it can be a planet killer, causing a planet to implode into itself. At this point the extreme power of it is difficult to handle. Once it's created you have to do something with it. If you let the tiger out of the cage, you have to be careful it doesn't eat you. We use it carefully.

In addition, the most critical use is using the drive as an energy source; we have enough power to supply the *Cyclone* for centuries or maybe give a world a thousand times the population of Earth an energy supply without interruption, as in forever. I am always impressed when I give out these numbers. It amazes me!

In addition to propulsion and extreme weapons, we need a power source for all general weapons execution plus communication strength. The operation modules and the intelligence processors need large amounts of energy. This ship is the command fleet starship. It uses massive amounts of energy to send and receive many assortments of communications from all over the universe.

I am the captain of this ship, and I am also the supreme admiral in command of all the starship fleets. All are led by admirals I have picked. Most of them are my synthetic clones and are loyal to me—a natural-bred bonding, part of their DNA. Part of this command staff is on *Titan I*, our official military base of operations, where Gabriel keeps an office, as I do.

It is our operations command base. I am there only when I have to be, way too many meetings, and always issues and problems.

The fleets are composed of many kinds of starships. At the top of the list are the massive World Starship *Titans*. At least that's what I call them. They are huge spheres several hundred miles in diameter. They have cities inside, everything you would need, yet are set up for military missions. They are the manufacturers and service industries used to supply the army and starships; many workers produce everything needed by the fleets. They are also troop ships, with millions of soldiers, mostly my synthetic clones, and more weapons.

These ships are supported by starship cruisers I call *Eagles,* and there are many thousands of them spread throughout the universe. They are *Cyclone* size or bigger and equipped about the same. They are protected by *Tiger Threes*, which I also named; *Three* means it's a third-generation fighter rocket. These *Tiger Threes* are like the *Saber* although not quite as fast or as heavily armed and smaller. Each *Eagle* cruiser carries three *Tiger Threes* in its hold.

I am proud of my ship, the *Cyclone,* as it does it all. One special feature of this ship is that it is alive in every sense of the word. It is a being; although it's a nonorganic life form, it is a being with an identity. The *Cyclone* is really my life partner, as it thinks in parallel with me. It knows what I know, feels my emotions, processes information for me, lives a life with it's own emotions, and has centuries of fond memories. It is more like an ancient beast with an old soul. I hear its many stories and have had many long philosophical conversations with it during long voyages. And, luckily for me, the *Cyclone* has intelligence way beyond me, actually thousands of times beyond me and beyond most of the beings we deal with in this universe. The *Cyclone* considers me an extension of itself, and I think the opposite: the *Cyclone* is an extension of me. We have a good laugh at our unique relationship.

To my surprise, according to the *Cyclone,* starship technology has been around for a long time, millions of years. The *Cyclone* is a military starship, thus it has no issues with funding; nothing was left out when it was created and rebuilt many times over the centuries, evolving over the years. It is priceless in Earth dollars. Maybe it could be built now for a million trillion US dollars. Talk about sticker shock!

Monetary values are used throughout the universe. The Consortium pays a stipend to be used off ship or as personal savings. My crew and I are paid salaries. The Consortium, however, unlike Earth, does not use currency or money. Units of value are used, established by the aggregate worth of all the wealth of the members of the Consortium. The use of this money is done with a cyber scorecard. Values change constantly, kind of like a stock exchange. There is no paper currency anywhere in the Consortium's jurisdiction. Your bank account balance floats up and down, updated when the values are looked up at the time of the transaction. It is all done through a financial system tied to your unique brain-wave frequency. It is totally accurate, and fraud is impossible. Extractions of funds are immediate, as is investment tracking. When you make a purchase, it is charged to your individual brain frequency, like an account number. No two frequencies are alike. The Consortium's financial centers process the transactions. Revenue is done the same way, just reversed. It works over most of the universe. I am blessed. I have as much as I need, more than I deserve.

The *Cyclone*, unfortunately, has all the issues of a living being that are caused by intellect and emotion: opinions, prejudices, principles, biases, philosophical thought processes, character strength, anger, personality, charm, love, jealousy, fear, loyalty, and a sense of purpose. It also has been my dear friend for many years. We are more than kindred spirits. We are linked mentally and psychologically, the ultimate team. We know each other more than well. The *Cyclone* has done much for me by teaching me, by guiding me, by advising me, and by helping me complete my missions. The *Cyclone* has saved my life many times during military ventures that went wrong. Unfortunately our lives have been lonely ones, yet the *Cyclone* has helped make it bearable. Our missions and purpose are one, and we have shared the losses and the victories.

Many more ships under my command are much larger and more advanced, yet the *Cyclone* is the most versatile vehicle, the ultimate law-enforcement tool, the killer of killers.

In this business it is difficult to take prisoners, difficult to house them, as space is limited on board. Death is kinder. Only when the offense is truly forgivable, and if it is reparable and we have means to do it, do we take prisoners. Once the law (called commandments) we enforce has been broken within our jurisdiction, after the proper identification and culpability of all parties are finalized, then there is a somewhat quick resolution. Sometimes the penalties require financial payments by a government. Other times individuals face rehab time. We also back up and help local world police units, as no civilization in the Consortium has a military army or military fleet. We provide those services and resolutions. Sometimes we punish the police groups that are in violation of Consortium laws.

Unfortunately there are penalties and some court sentences that end with tragic results. We cannot foresee all outcomes that might eventually take place. We try to be quick, efficient, and relentless to fix any issues. Many depend on us. Regrettably we sometimes do screw up, and I'm not sure I want to think about it, much less talk about our mistakes. The remorse causes too much pain. It is all for the price of free will, a common philosophy throughout the universe. Part of having intelligence is the desire to make your own fate on your life's road. All beings feel it is their right to make their own choices, thus we have free will. We all need help, may God protect us, or "*Calabra*," which means: "May the divine light embrace and guide you!"

CHAPTER 7

DRONES

The best weapons are not the huge ones or large armies of troops or even the lethal *Tiger* fighter starships. It is the little ones you can't see—they are tiny and the most dangerous. You never see them coming. They are the drones. These are the most effective tactical weapons in the universe, the most deadly weapons I carry. They are intelligent, very sophisticated, small or even tiny self-contained satellite robots. I have many millions of them, all kinds, designed to fit various missions. Our drone technology is much more advanced than Earth's current technology or nanotechnology. The current use on Earth is minimal. Drones are part of everything in my world; they do everything. Some are very small, like molecules, and then there are bigger ones. Some are like basketballs, some may be as big as cars or the size of buildings. Many are shaped like little satellites or could be any shape that works for a specific purpose. Some are the size of human cells and can do surgery inside your body with no guidance or repair organic body parts, even change out parts, limbs, or destroy any disease, or maybe inject chemicals that heal or enhance performance.

Drones also do most of the physical repairs on the *Cyclone*, even equipment or wiring or internal parts of anything organic or nonorganic. The massive *Titan* starships are all built by thousands of huge skilled drones in outer space with no gravity. These ships being built are hundreds of miles long. They are the created by builder drones, belonging to a specific guild, owned by the drones.

Many drones can think independently, with a specific mission; or, as partners following specific directions from a host, sometimes on critical assigned missions. They can also become permanent microcomputer data processors hosted in the brains of beings, nurtured by the host. Or they can be just temporary ones, as for example, to help in teaching and translating languages. Some of these little drones are part synthetic and part organic, thus able to repair themselves with regeneration of cells like a living organism, using DNA codes. Others have limited lives, just one job, as do the military drones, used like missiles programmed for specific targets, a dead shot every time. These are the killer-type drones, similar to the ones I use, although mine are more advanced.

Yet, the drones I use most of the time I call my reconnaissance slips. They are very small satellites and can look like silver marbles used by kids. Each looks harmless. At smaller size, when camouflaged, they are almost invisible. They can shrink to be much smaller than the head of a pin. If needed, they can shrink down to the size of a big molecule, or the opposite—they can expand to the size of a football. Yet most of the time, they stay about the size of small diamonds or little round marbles. The permanent cell size drones are different, as created by other cell-sized drones, as in mostly cloning themselves. They are so small only similar drones can build them. All drones belong to the Consortium Drone Manufactures Union; follow specific guidelines and rules, strictly enforced by the Consortium.

When in normal mode, a slip shines like a bright sparkling light, sort of like a flying ember from a campfire. It is quick, darting back and forth, always moving with intent and purpose. It is impossible to see when it shrinks to the size of a molecule, and then it is used as needed, depending on the mission. It can travel much faster than sound and goes anywhere it's directed, even through concrete walls. It is very versatile. And the good news for me is that I have millions of them. The best part is I can carry and store millions of them in a very small space, not like troops that take huge resources to transport and maintain.

As these drones have small computers or artificial brains, as they have intelligence, of various capacities, depending on the level of independent thinking needed, and are skilled in reporting back to an operator, giving visual surveillance activity. They can repair their own wounds, as they regenerate like organic cells, working off their own genetic code. They can also be used as the ultimate computer virus, molecule-size robots going directly into a hard drive, without an outsource software download. They can infiltrate any software system anywhere and plant programs or viruses and are impossible to detect. They are almost physically indestructible.

The other slips I have are military, as they have weapon capability and can be used like missile drones when fitted for target destruction. They can also enter organic brains of any species like parasites and collect data (memories, experiences, deeds) or enter the bloodstream. They can mentally influence the host by probing or releasing chemicals into the brain in specific spots, allowing for some mind control on a limited basis. I also insert them into other beings for communication when language is a problem, as they will provide telepathic brain-to-brain thought transfer.

They can inflict great pain if needed or numb pain and then go completely unnoticed, only detectable with a very sophisticated head scan. Or for a kinder use, they will repair wounds if instructed; they are used for all soldier surgeries. They have saved many a soldier by pulling out bullets or repairing large wounds on the battlefield.

They all can be used as a source of energy, as they can transfer energy, working off of and transferring energy from the mother ship. Because of this it becomes a Taser weapon if needed, automatically thrusting high-voltage strikes when threatened by an enemy. They can kill quickly if they are triggered or become unstable. They explode inside the host, thus causing a quick, messy death. A better kill is when the slip operates just like a blood clot going through the heart. The host dies from a heart attack fast. Plus, there's no evidence of our having been there.

The little weapons are the most effective, the little things you never see coming. I have used them many times in different worlds, and they work better than all the other serious weapons known to the universe.

Unfortunately most of my little slips have one weakness. They depend on energy and activation from the mother ship plus mission support. They can operate only a short time on their own stored power. Then they go into hibernation, waiting for their activation and the energy generated by the operations of the mother ship or an energy host. They need to be supplied mission directives and orders, too. The mother ship must be in range to supply the energy needed, although the range can be a long way depending on the operating conditions.

Anyway, I am now impatient, ready to start my visit, no time to waste and a world to see again!

CHAPTER 8

BOOKSTORE VISIT

S ounds crazy, but as I said, my first stop is going to a bookstore, specifically the Barnes & Noble located up the road on Hurstbourne Avenue. I want to see people, read newspapers, and buy books and music, lots of music; maybe have a cup of real coffee and read everything that happened in the last ten years. It is all critical to me. This is my lifeline to my humanity, my escape from becoming more alien. I need enough humanity to last me ten more years, until the next visit.

I was born at a time when a real book was a big deal. I have loved books since I was a little boy. They were my gateway to the life and opened my mind to possibilities. Books are also healing. Look at me now—I still need them. Books are so human, showing the thought patterns, the emotions, the passion, and the love for life. This helps in opening my mind to opportunities to stay human. It also refuels my humanity by subduing the alien side of me, to once again feel the joy of being human, through the eyes of the many human authors.

I am also delighted by the voice of a woman singing a soothing song; it always touches my heart! I love to feel the depths of her emotion, the passion and the ache. I have learned that being human is living as part of the human tribe, so it's necessary to feel their emotions, as the interaction is critical. Being away so long also creates a deep loneliness, then shyness, then fear of connecting, and then you become a recluse. In danger of becoming this, I desperately need real human contact during these visits.

A home-cooked dinner is a dream, and sitting around a kitchen table with humans making small talk is good, too—laughing, joking, conversation, and drinking coffee...wonderful!

I also like to shop, though I rarely buy. I walk through stores just to see the changes and to people watch. The changes in clothing styles are astonishing, especially the variety between young and old. The tattooed heads are a trip, too. Shopping also gives me an excuse to talk to real people, and so I spend as much time as I can in stores when I am here.

Just looking at people and talking and listening to them are great. Even better is being part of their activities. To see families together and supporting one another, maybe at picnics, laughing, seeing their friends, praying, going to church. A high school baseball game is a delight. Three trips ago, or about thirty years in the past, I attended a game in upper New York State, in a small town. It was a warm summer night, and it was so pleasant to watch families together. The love between them was obvious and it reminded me of my own family many years ago.

I plan to take the *Ship Tender* down from the *Cyclone*, which is now about eight hundred feet up above the shopping center. The ship's tender is our small landing craft stored in a rear lower hold, built for small missions. It is used for landing troops and picking up cargo. It also has a surrounding force field for security—not as good as the *Cyclone*'s but good enough when activated. The little ship is easy to defend, as it is armored. Plus it has offensive weapons and is incredibly fast when needed. However, it is short range, no more than twenty thousand miles of cruise range. I use it in camouflaged mode as much as possible, as I need it to stay hidden when landing in strange places.

The ship is snub-nosed, with a black windshield up front and ugly lines going back, like rectangular blocks fastened together, definitely not sleek, more like an army tank. It is only forty-two feet long and twenty-four feet wide. It has no real wings, just slanted extensions eighteen feet out on each side, ending in extended lips, with two massive rocket-engine thrusters attached by arms underneath the main body. The front of the ship has a ten-foot slant on the front nose. It is about sixteen feet tall from its bottom floor, then maybe another twelve feet off the ground to allow space for the thruster funnels, when landed with landing pods down, for unloading from the back doors. There are hatches that open from below also. It has an ugly dull, flat black finish. The ship is sinister-looking, with a threatening appearance; it scares the hell out of anyone who sees it come in, which is the right emotion. It is lethal. I let it bring me down to the ground. I get off in the deserted back parking lot and send the tender back up about eight hundred feet, reloaded in the *Cyclone*, hovering above.

This Barnes & Noble will be my first stop and my home until it closes tonight. Maybe it will be crowded, and like a man who has been in a desert without water, I will not be able to get enough of it. I will savor the time there. I am out on the pavement quickly, not spotted. I look like I always do when here, dressed to not draw attention, wearing faded blue jeans with a brown leather belt and a blue oxford cloth shirt with a button-down collar, an old brown tweed sport coat, old loafers, and no socks. I purchased all of it by mail order, from L.L. Bean, and had it sent to my New York address. I have been a customer for a long time.

Now I need to find the front door of the bookstore.

In a human assessment of myself, I like to think of myself as good-looking. I am slender and tall, a little over six feet, light-brown or almost-blond hair. Most of the time my hair is a little long yet still military style, as in World War II, and easy to comb. I have big brown eyes and handsome facial features, or I think handsome. My body's best attributes are big shoulders and a narrow waist, as I am always in excellent physical shape. I am military muscled, required to be strong, yet not too bulky. I guess my body looks similar to the one I had in 1944—nothing fancy.

Unfortunately I am awkward with people, especially human females. One real issue is I am behind the times—old-fashioned. I am aware I have not kept up with the culture, and I have to be careful not to give myself away. I'm normally shy with all people, find it hard to open a dialogue, yet once I meet them, I have always found it easy to talk, and thankfully, girls like to talk to me. I think they find me attractive, although nothing has happened since my World War II girlfriend; no relationships with women have been possible. The end result is that my experience on earth is limited. I am not good with human relationships, really never had much chance for meaningful interaction—meaning I have had no real relationships since World War II.

I am also mentally old in comparison to this generation, a man from another era, which is not helpful in mixing with the new generations of people. The other unfortunate part of my looks: I look like who I am, a soldier from another era. Still, I'm proud of my generation. We felt responsible for the weak and the downtrodden and defended freedom from tyrants, the evil men who sucked the life from anyone too weak to defend themselves. I saw firsthand what the Nazis had done, and I think I am still fighting that war.

Of course I know we won World War II, and overall I am delighted and proud of the wonderful things done by mankind in the last seventy years. The rebuilding of Europe, discovering nuclear power, inventing computers, landing on the moon, creating the Internet, developing cell phones, inventing TV and video games, writing great books, creating art and terrific movies, even Monday night football. Then there is the Olympics, plus all the water and snow sports, and the production of amazing music, super spectator sports, golf for everyone, new churches, more parks, and new skyscrapers. I think of mankind as a mostly smart, very kind, and generous people, now almost seven billion strong worldwide. From what I can observe and report back to Gabriel, I think most humans have meaning in their lives, try to help one another, raise their children, and try to earn honest livings. There are lots of challenges in living on Earth. It is not easy. I wish I could help mankind, as there are all these amazing gifts I could bring to them, unbelievable technology; plus I could give them much longer lives and help them be free of poverty. No one would ever be hungry or sick.

Yet Earth is still a dangerous place, not safe for many people, as the weak are brutalized; evil still prevails. I could certainly quickly help with this issue. I always come here prepared for defending against an attack. I am armed, with my troops, in an extremely lethal military ship that can kill any world in ten minutes or destroy all the armies in any world in two hours. Unfortunately I am strictly forbidden from interfering with the events here. Gabriel says Earth is not ready for me. I have to be careful when I do help, pick my best opportunities. As in many worlds, there are some really difficult people here, some probably evil, others just misguided. There are also some bad political situations on Earth, or, I should say, unhealthy cultural issues. The top of the list includes genocide, starvation, crime, corruption, injustice, and oppression.

Another worry about this planet, resulting from natural weather cycles and the nearly seven billion people living here, are the changes in the landmass, the atmosphere, and the oceans. All are under stress. Every time I've come here over the past years, we've measured the chemistry of the Earth, both air and water, which is more polluted on every visit. There are too many toxins, coming from several sources. This, combined with a hotter sun, presents a bad forecast for human survival in the future.

Absurdly enough, and hard for me to understand, the rubbish from human consumption is everywhere. The planet is being covered with trash by every country, some more than others. Also, the methane and carbon dioxide seem to be a real issue, as too much is lethal in the atmosphere. It is coming from lots of places both natural and manmade. Burning carbon-based compounds in land vehicles and forest fires create some problems. Plus the exploding volcanoes cause many of the carbon dioxide issues. Human and animal waste, marshes, bogs, natural gas wells, extensive rice cultivation all contribute to dangerous methane levels. Not sure of the immediate resolution to the problem; it's somewhat complicated to solve yet certainly solvable. Not much I can do to help in ten days. I think it will be solved here, as many smart people know about it, and they are making suggestions.

And, as always, I think it is difficult that Earth is outside my jurisdiction, as I am here only every ten years. If I were here more often, maybe I could have fixed a few things over the years. On the other hand, who am I to talk? I never married, no girlfriend, no children, no family, a lonely military life, and work for an alien civilization. My only real pleasure is my visits to Earth, and they total only seven times, ten days each, or a total of seventy days—hardly enough to make me an expert on mankind. Even my friendly benefactors warn me not to meddle. They say I could make it worse, much worse.

As I had hoped, the Barnes & Noble is crowded, offering more people for me to see. After coming around to the front doors of the store, I am now inside, looking at everything. I am delighted, although I look stupid, foolishly smiling at people everywhere and saying "Hi" like this is a country boy's first visit to the city. I try to take it all in visually and mentally. Looking at everything is wonderful, and even the smelling is good. All kinds of odors—everything has its own fragrance. Then the books. I'm looking in the new-fiction and nonfiction shelves, then in the newspaper section, where I read six different magazines and two newspapers. What a treat! I do reconnaissance of the store; walk around several times to make sure I see everything. There are books everywhere, and my last stop is my favorite, the music section. I decide to go to the help desk first. A lovely girl smiles and asks me if I need anything. I say I need a cart, as I plan to buy quite a bit. She leaves and then comes back with a cart the employees use in the store.

I feel compelled to talk to her. I smile. "Are you in school, or do you work full time here?"

She smiles back and quickly answers: "I'm part time. I go to the University of Louisville. I'm in the nursing program there. I love books, and this is a great place to work. My name is Susan, and I have some time, if I can help you find a book."

I look more closely at her. She is pretty and very young, has big brown eyes, almost soulful, dark-brown hair worn long with bangs. She is small in stature, slender, looks like a book lover. She has the fragrance of a sweet soap. For some reason I feel protective, like a father.

I smile again and say, "Susan, my name is Henry, and I am certainly glad to meet you. Yes, please, maybe you can help me. I need to know about some music groups, maybe singers or bands you like, or recent albums that are popular among people your age."

She says, "Follow me," and off she goes. We are soon in the music section of the store. She points to several rows, saying they are all good; she likes all of them and tells me to look through them. She smiles at me and says, "You will like this music as you don't look that much older than me."

I respond, smile at her warmly and say, "Thank you," and then ask, "Do you have family here in Louisville?"

"I'm from Richmond, Virginia. My parents and sisters are there. I'm the youngest. I just turned twenty-one. Fortunately I do have a grandmother here, and we're close. She is special. Although I stay in the dorm on campus, I see her every week. I also have a roommate who's wonderful, like a sister."

I ask what her favorite books are. She mentions several, recommending three I should buy if I like historical fiction and World War II stories.

She declares, "My grandfather fought in World War II, and I've heard his stories. We're all proud of him."

"You should be proud of your grandfather. Do you know what division he served in, where he was stationed?"

She says, "I'm not sure. Are you familiar with Normandy? I think he was there on D-Day."

I light up and say, "Yes, I know it well. I've studied that part of the war, and it was a real critical battle! Maybe I could meet your grandfather."

She looks sad. "He died three years ago."

"I am so sorry," I say with obvious sadness.

"Do you live here?" she asks.

"No, not now. I used to live here. I still like the area—wish I lived here again." I decide to give her my cover story. "I'm finishing up on a PhD from Indiana University in Bloomington, down here just to look around. I want to teach history and political science someday at the university level. I'm working on my dissertation and going to Washington, DC, tomorrow to do some research."

She asks, "What's your dissertation about?"

"I'm writing about our culture's reaction to other off-world civilizations. Yes, aliens. What thoughts does this culture have about our place in the universe, as if we actually know we're not alone? What if a visit occurred? Just how would we behave differently than we do now if we thought there were others out there who might judge us? What if there was an alien civilization talking to us that was far more advanced, many years ahead of us and much more powerful? Of course they might be much different from us, look strange, maybe better, a kinder species, like angels maybe or wise beings, and able to read our minds. Is that scary? What would our elected leaders do, and how would other countries behave? Or just plain people, how would they react? Would they be friendly or not friendly? Would there be fear, panic? What would the media do, knowing this as a new reality? Real aliens are out there. The universe is more than ten billion years old, plenty of time for many civilizations to develop, and each of them could be millions of years old. That's a lot of time to develop the expertise, philosophies, and technology for starship travel."

A surprised look crosses her face. "That is remarkable. I think it's a wonderful idea for a dissertation, to think others in the universe might judge us. We might scare them, too, just as they scare us. Probably everyone would be terrified. Maybe they'd scare us into doing better. Maybe honesty with one another is a good start, no hidden agendas. Actually, I think real contact with aliens would be a shocker. I'm not sure the world could take it! Just wondering about it happening is a fright."

"You're thinking the right thoughts. I think it would change everything, and I'm not sure the world could handle it either."

After pausing I continue: "Enough of that. You probably have better things to do than listen to me. I need to go find my music and books before the store closes. Would you ring me up when I'm done? I'll have a lot. It might be at the end of the day. By the way, what time does the store close?"

She smiles. "We close at eight o'clock tonight. Don't worry; I'll wait until you're finished."

I smile back. "Thanks! See you in a bit."

The next few hours are pure enjoyment. Drinking lots of coffee, which is so good I buy some canisters of it. I also end up with thirty-eight books and sixty-four CDs of all kinds of music. I go looking for Susan, easy to find, back at the help desk. It is eight o'clock, and they are starting to close. I look at her as I get near, walking quickly, pushing the cart, and she hears me and she looks up.

Susan smiles, saying, "You've bought the store out! Let me help you check out. I can do it from here if you have a check or credit card."

I nod my head. "I can give you a check drawn from a New York bank; will that work?"

She says, "No problem." I'm thinking that helps, as I have no cash and no credit card. I need to get some cash.

I had long ago set up a checking account in New York City. It was on my first trip back to Earth, in 1954. I had raw gold as currency, and banks are not comfortable with raw gold. However, I retained the services of a small, distinguished New York law firm, Lindemann, Noakes & Beagle. I asked them to manage the transfer of the gold to US dollars. Then, over a period of time, they converted it to US currency, about $900 million. It was a lot of money at the time. It wasn't easy making the exchange and avoiding the curious eyes of banks and the government. The law firm was successful, however, and created an investment trust fund for me. Now, many years later, it is worth many times more.

I keep $50 million of it in an interest-bearing checking account, usable immediately. The total value of my trust or investment fund is about $9 billion. The firm invests much of it in equities and about 20 percent in short-term conservative bonds and bank notes that are easy to convert to cash. I give the law firm all the investment returns to reinvest. As their main fee, to their delight, they get 10 percent of the annual investment profit, which is massive, averaging $60 million a year. They receive an additional 0.001 percent of the total investment as their fee, which is another $10 million. They seem more than pleased with the arrangement, as it is very generous. In return I require their absolute loyalty. I do not care about my personal investment revenue, as it stays in the trust, reinvested, and I do not want a large 1099 going to the US government to draw attention to my name.

The law firm goes to great effort to cover my tracks, shielding me from the government and others, keeping me invisible. They use their talents well and are paid well. In addition to their investment fee, the law firm automatically takes out any expenses I use for services as needed. They are making a lot of money for doing a small amount of work, yet it is vital to me. Over all these years, they have prospered, and I am by far their oldest, largest, and best client. They need me, and I need them.

Besides keeping my name hidden and confidential, they also do various odd jobs for me. They supply a limousine and chauffeur when needed and keep a large rooftop luxury penthouse for me in New York City, mostly so I have an address and a normal residence to stay when there. Actually, I own the building. The law firm bought it years ago for me, as it was then two massive parking garages, both able to hold a lot of weight. It was converted to one huge building, with lots of storage space and several apartments; the top floors are mine as I have my living quarters in two full stories. They take up thirty thousand square feet. It has a wonderful panoramic view of the city yet in a secluded area that is mostly warehouse buildings. It has several more stories for storage and then there is staff, housing them and their families. No one else lives there.

In secret, my drones built many parts of the building, partially to keep it top secret, as some of it was off-world technology, difficult to build and highly sophisticated, not Earth stuff. The weird stuff like infrared security systems, grid defense shields, laser communications, cyber lattice, grid matrix armament, fusion direct target weapons, were all installed using drones. The place is an armed virtual fortress, independently supplied with water and electricity. The atmosphere is also controlled in the building, mostly independent of offsite air. Drones secretly maintain the systems, presently staffed there.

It is also fully people staffed, and the employees are still not sure about me, as I am gone for such long periods. The staff is always shocked when they see me after each ten-year period, as I change little in my appearance. They are sometimes even terrified of me, and I spend a lot of time calming them down. I hardly age, and it freaks them out. I think they think I am a vampire, which makes me laugh. They keep the drapes drawn when I'm there, which is really funny.

Most of the staff members have been here thirty or more years, and there are large living quarters for them, too. They live nice lives. The staff consists of a butler, an excellent cook, two housekeepers, and a handyman/maintenance guy. They were sworn to secrecy when they were hired, and they have taken this seriously. They are compensated well to do what they do. Their children, who once lived there, are now grown and gone. They come back, though, visiting, bringing grandkids, as this is the home where they were raised. Interestingly enough, they never come when I am there.

The best part of the place is the roof. I can land the *Ship Tender* or the *Saber* on it, although a tight fit for the latter, yet it has a massive helicopter-landing pad suitable for landing and can be covered with a movable roof. I can land and then use the roof to hide the *Saber*, coming in at night only. The huge building was reinforced to handle the weight. Being a car parking garage helped. Unfortunately, the staff knows about the *Saber*; I use the slips to help them keep it a secret. The slips are mentally inserted and guide them away from awkward situations when issues are presented, thus protecting them, nothing more. I always enjoy being with the staff when I am here; they are like family. All have been faithful to me. I have sent all their children to college as my thanks for my privacy and their loyalty. They are paid well, and they have a nice pension plan. Unfortunately, even with me trying to be extra friendly, trying to be thoughtful, they still fear me. I attempt to reassure them on every trip back.

At times the law firm will provide military mercenaries for me to do odd jobs and provide security for my building or, if needed, for specific issues. They supply me with cash when I am here, pay people off when needed, and donate to several charities and organizations I wish to support. They deal with any government officials when needed. They balance the bank accounts monthly and give the bank an address and a persona, an agent of record, someone to be me when I could never be me. Over the years I have done a few things they needed to cover up for me—nothing terrible, just awkward. They also prepare overview updates for me on the last ten years of Earth activity, which they download to me when I arrive each time. This includes election results, world leaders, any ongoing political crises, a world monetary report, important world events, and scientific innovations.

The law firm has never questioned me, not once. They do not want to know too much about me. They always do as I ask, never question why or ask who I really am or where I am from. I have given them no real identification, no federal ID numbers, and no address outside of New York. I receive little written correspondence. They have seen me only a few times, and I am a complete mystery to them. I have been this way for almost sixty years. When I go to the firm's office, they are totally freaked out, almost enough for me to laugh about. I think they think I'm some kind of old Mafia guy who looks young after many operations or maybe a CIA assassin. Maybe some do think I am an alien, and they are laughed at.

I know the law firm would never cheat me or report me to anyone. I am very sure of that, as I think they are truly frightened of me—go figure. I pay them well, I'm always friendly to them, and I appreciate them.

Unfortunately I can never use Henry Johnson's official identification, not my original social security number, as I am dead, lost at Normandy Beach in World War II. The law firm helped a lot, as it created an identity for me, doing what they could while staying within the law. I am sure this lack of identity concerns the law firm and is of some humor to me. For example, when I call even for little things, they jump, act scared, stop doing whatever they were doing to help me. I know everyone in the law firm knows the name Henry Johnson, and they speak it as if they wonder about me, probably frightened by the possibilities.

As I am essentially a very old client, most of the original attorneys are gone; only two original partners are left who have known me the entire time. The new generation of attorneys now working there hardly knows me. They may wonder why I am still alive and why I look so young. They are nice at all times; they do act as if I am really important and are very polite to me. When I visit they close the law firm to any other visitors, for confidentiality and for my protection. I tell them the fewer people who see me, the better; although, I don't blame them for their anxiety. After all these years, they have no clue who I am or whom I really represent. If they only knew. Not good for them to really know; guessing is fine.

Meanwhile, back at Barnes & Noble, Susan helps me check out my purchases, working quickly, a hard worker and smart. I write a check and give it to her. She looks at me with kind eyes. I think, *What a sweet girl.* I hope she has a good life, although intuitively I know there is a problem. She appears worried, maybe even a little fearful.

I have to ask, "Susan, are you OK? You seem worried."

She looks up, startled, and hesitates. Finally, after a few breaths, she sadly says, "I am fine, just a long day."

I don't believe her, as I am now reading her thoughts, yet I feel uncomfortable about prying. I change the subject. "Do you have a boyfriend?"

She looks at me strangely and says, "Not really."

I say, "It sounds like you did have one. Boyfriend problems?"

She looks at me angrily and says, "Why are you asking me this?"

I am surprised by the outburst and say quickly, "I'm sorry, Susan. You look like a very nice person, and I feel concerned for you for the same reason. Maybe because you look really worried, maybe afraid. I hope I haven't offended you. It is certainly not my intent. You do have an issue, don't you?"

She says, "I really am losing it. I didn't think it showed. I have to go out in the parking lot tonight after we close to get my car, and I'm worried about it."

I am surprised. "Why?" I look intently at her.

She is in tears now and she blurts out, "He may be out there, a crazy guy. I went on one date, and he beat me up, and now, of all the things that can go wrong, he stalks me. Although I have a restraining order from the court against him, he still has threatened to kill me, and he is really scary. What can I say? I don't know what to do. He was out there last night and the night before, and maybe he will be tonight. I'm parked a long way from the store, and it's dark where I'm parked."

"Do your parents know about him?"

She tears up again. "There is nothing they can do, and they think the police should be helping me. The police are nice; however, they can't guard me every minute. I didn't tell them everything. He really beat me up badly. He did more, but I don't want to talk about it, and he said it would be worse if I told the police. He also threatened to burn my grandmother's house down with her in it. He could do it. He scares the hell out of me, and he is bad news, a total psychopath! He actually wants me to date him, says he's sorry. Last night he wanted to give me a gift. I didn't look at him; he really scared me. I just got in my car and left. He started swearing at me and threw the gift at the back of my car."

I smile, and then laugh, which surprises her. "Susan, it's your lucky day. I can be there for you. Actually I'm quite good at this, the right man at the right time. You could say I'm an expert with this kind of person. Truly it will be my pleasure to help you tonight!"

I am thinking, *Lucky for me, too. What a great day, twice today, a second predator.*

Susan looks at me with a questioning, doubtful expression. She looks me over, trying to figure out if I look up to it.

I add, "This is what we will do. We both go out the door. Now that the store is closed, we may be the only ones out there. I'll wait with my packages. You go ahead, get your car, come back, and get me with the car. I'll watch for him from here, so we don't scare him away. If he doesn't show, we can maybe hang out some this evening. Maybe I can treat you to a good meal, stay until you feel safe."

She doesn't look happy, more like confused and disbelieving. She fidgets with her ink pen, not sure what to say, doubting me.

I continue reassuringly, "What have you got to lose? My being here can't hurt. Here's the plan. We wait for him to seek you out. And if he's out there tonight, maybe he'll start to approach you when you get to your car. I can reach him before he gets to you, and it will not be good for him. Let's say it will be a life-changing event for him. I guarantee he will never bother you again. What do you say?"

She looks at me intently, nods her head, with a hopeful look. Then she smiles, actually laughs, and says, "Are you sure?"

I reply, "Without a doubt."

Out the door we go. There are people still in the parking lot. I know it would be better to find him now, know where he is, if he is out there. I have a response about this from the *Cyclone* immediately. I now know where he is. Amazingly enough, yes, he is actually here. He is armed with a knife, which is unfortunate for him.

The *Cyclone* wants to take him out immediately—one shot from the starship and he is gone. I tell the *Cyclone* to send down some reconnaissance slips and have one insert itself into his brain and to do it carefully, so he will not know it happened. I do have plans for him, could use the initial report from the slip to check his DNA, identify him, find out everything about him, and maybe let the slip probe his brain for some memories. He probably has done this before. I know this behavior is habitual, and he probably enjoys it, needs the criminal scores, like trophies. Maybe he has done something really bad in the past, enough to have him arrested.

I just need one crime the police could use so they can put him away. It would be better to let the locals handle this; it's really not part of my jurisdiction or my business. We are hacked into all kinds of Earth databases: hospitals, banks, police, CIA, FBI, IRS, NSA, Secret Service, KGB, Scotland Yard, and Interpol, everything there is in this world. I ask the *Cyclone* for everything on him as fast as possible. I'm starting to get excited. Hand-to-hand combat does not come that often, now the second time in twenty-four hours. I am delighted. I can't help it. I can feel my muscles tense. The anticipation and adrenaline are a rush!

Susan, you and I are both blessed tonight, or at least I think so.

She walks away, looks back, now frightened again. In a scared, quivering voice she says to me, "You'll be there if he comes for me? I am a long way out, at the end of the parking lot."

I smile and say, "If he does something, I will be there. I'm faster than I look."

I am starting to receive data downloads, even some memories from the man's brain, coming from the *Cyclone* communications system, received from the slip embedded in his brain. Yes, he really is one sick guy. He has hurt several human females, and yes, he treasures those memories. No question of what needs to happen to him.

The slip is probing more, and it reports an alarming specific memory from him about a fourteen-year-old girl named Natalie Alder. Several months ago he abducted her from a party as she was outside talking on her cell phone. He took her, beat her, raped her, and buried her alive although unconscious. Her dead body is only eight miles from here in a shallow grave in a forest at a state park. Her parents don't know about her death, just think she is missing. She was very young, and it was a cruel death. It is hard not to feel a great rage toward him. Yes, I think eventually I will let the slip do its final work, to eat his brain. He has earned it; he has done some bad stuff. When triggered the slip works just like a little mind worm, causing havoc in his brain, unbelievable pain coming in waves. It is effective in behavior control also. He will be confessing all his crimes tonight. I just have to keep from killing him myself.

I drop my packages on a bench by the door, standing ready. Susan is still walking toward her car, slower now, looking in all directions. It is hard to see, as the parking lot is not well lit. She makes it to the end, maybe forty yards out, then turns to open her car's door. I see him, a big fellow, not far away, maybe twenty yards. He is going for her!

Startled, I move quick, yelling, "I'll be dammed. Run, Susan! He's going for you!"

The man is making a mad run at her. I am now moving fast, too. She turns and screams! I'm there quickly, and he is there, too, focused on her only, screaming at her, "You bitch!" And his hand is up high, clutching a knife.

He never sees me until I snatch the upraised hand, getting a really good grip. My momentum carries me forward, and he comes with me. Then I stop moving, causing his body to swing out fast. I grab his shoulder with my other hand, gaining speed to lift him off the ground high, then pulling him all the way around me again, gathering more speed. He looks like a golf club being swung by a golfer. At the peak of the swing, I let him go, and his body goes into flight. He has this totally disbelieving, terrified look on his face. He sails seventy feet, maybe twenty feet high, in a perfect arc, screaming the whole way, and then hitting a car hard. It sounds like an explosion of bending metal and breaking glass, then he bounces off and hits the pavement several feet away.

He is now silent, lying there on the blacktop. A concussion has knocked him out, his head bloody. Unfortunately I crushed his hand when I grabbed him, mangled the knife and hand together, bloody, one big gob. It will be difficult to pry apart, most painful. Hitting the car was not good for him either.

Susan is astounded, wide-eyed, as if she saw the end of the world. Actually I'm surprised, too, and it's hard not to laugh. It was definitely a home run. I'm having the slip that is still in the man's brain keep probing for more memories. With him being unconscious, it will be able to move in his brain without concern for his reaction from the pain.

The slip overwhelms his unconscious mind, pulling not only his memories and thoughts but also energy, which could kill him. I do not need him dead yet. He needs to tell the police about

Jennifer's body and any others. It's important for her parents to know what happened to their daughter. The slip will stay in his brain until he has told the police everything and will leave him only after justice prevails. He will be confessing everything he has ever done, in overwhelming pain and in terror only I understand. It will be awful for him, but he gets no sympathy from me. He has earned the reckoning.

Of course with all the commotion, someone did call 911. There are some people here now, asking Susan if she is OK. And then the police come, then an ambulance, all flashing red and blue lights. I'm really not interested in talking to any of them. In total four squad cars are here, several police officers, and then a second ambulance. The police carefully look me over, not friendly, tell me not to move, and ask Susan what happened. She goes into a hyper speed explanation, pulls out the restraining order from her purse, and praises me to no end, crying the whole time.

The *Cyclone* is in full security-operations mode now, wanting to pull me out immediately, send down troops, neutralize everyone on the surface; I say absolutely not. I want the complete data report on the idiot who attacked Susan. I have it coming in and some more of his downloaded memories. He also killed another girl last year. She was really young, too.

Well, he will be confessing now. The slip is probing his brain, painfully now. The EMT guys have him conscious again, and looking at him I can tell he is totally petrified by the slip in his brain. He can feel its presence. It overrides all the other pain in his body. He can't figure out what is wrong with his head, the pain, and this thing in his brain. He thinks maybe a demon has possessed him. He starts talking nonstop, crying, moaning, short screams, bursts of pain, holding his head, pleading for them to help him. The police are all ears now. He tells them he wants to confess, talks about the last girl he killed, gives them names of others, those also raped and those who escaped death. He can't stop talking. The police have to turn on their recorders and hustle the crowd away, hold off the EMT guys. They are all excited, actually forgetting about us for the moment in all the commotion.

I start to slowly move away. Susan sees me. She ducks behind her car, gets in, and waves at me, wants me to get in her car. I open the door and jump in. We drive off slowly, stopping to pick up my packages still lying on the bench. We are gone before anyone realizes it. I look at her and say, "Susan, let's go to your grandmother's house." She nods her head, has a faraway look on her face.

I am now looking at her closely, and Susan is shaking all over. She can hardly drive and looks like she could use a good dose of Grandma. I ask if I can drive, and she pulls over and stops the car. I walk around the car as she slides over. I have never had a driver's license and have not driven a car in at least fifty years, yet under the circumstances it seems the prudent thing to do.

Once I start driving, she starts talking nonstop, tells me where to drive, and keeps talking a mile a minute. I hear her life story from the beginning, and for some reason it makes me feel good, her confiding in me, trusting me, sharing her heartfelt emotions, helping both of us, allowing me to be human again. To be human feels good. And thankfully she stops shaking.

She then looks at me intently. "Henry, how did you do that? It's impossible. You threw him a long way. You must have military experience. I don't care how you did it. I'm more grateful to you than you will ever know. You not only saved my life; you ended this nightmare I've been living." She is crying now. "Thank you, Henry; bless you!"

Smiling and with a fatherly look, I say, "Susan, I'm glad to be here for you. It was meant to be; I think divine providence helped us both. I am convinced it's more than luck that I'm here at this location on Earth at this exact time. Do you believe in destiny and divine providence? For some reason many times in my life, I am at the right place at the right time. Can't be just coincidence, as it happens more than it should. In fact it's mathematically impossible for it to happen so many times. It has to be more than being fortunate." I smile fondly at Susan and laugh. "I think your guardian angel helped me to look after you today!"

The *Cyclone* is close, reassuring, right now about eight hundred feet above us, all thirty-four billion tons of metal and compounds. I can feel it moving along with us, watching over us, following us. Thankfully no one can see it. I know those on board are wondering about me: the *Cyclone*, the crew, and my security-guard troops. They are all thinking this human thing is crazy, my ten-day visit. It is hard not to respect their opinions. They have been with me all these years, through thick and thin. Hardships have mostly been our fate. The years have gone by quickly. We have traveled trillions of miles together, had many experiences together. They do not complain about my migration home, as they understand it is part of my DNA, can't be helped. The Alaskan salmon and Canadian wild geese go home, too.

We end up at Susan's grandmother's house, a nice four-bedroom home in the east end of Louisville, in a middle-class neighborhood. Susan asks me to come in, anxious for me to meet her grandmother. The house is nice, cozy, with a kitchen used by a real cook, as I smell the wonderful aroma of baked cookies and freshly brewed coffee, just like in my mother's home. There are family photos everywhere, showing lots of cute kids. Her grandmother looks nice, too, kind eyes, maybe a little overweight. The weight looks natural, as she is an older woman, and it fits her. I think she is in her late seventies, and then I remember at that age she is a lot younger than me.

Susan introduces us. Her grandmother says Susan's roommate, Nikki, has called her. The police called Susan's dorm looking for her, wanting her official statement. Her grandmother is worried and also wants to know all about it, and about me, which I try to explain as best as possible.

Then Susan takes over, explaining the situation to her grandmother, who is grateful and asks me if there is anything I need. Can she offer me something, a drink, dinner? I tell them there is nothing either needs to do for me; I am happy to have helped Susan. She is on the house phone now and saying her roommate, Nikki, is coming over. Nikki's sister is also coming, an Anna Summers, who is visiting her. The fact that Anna is coming is quite exciting for Susan and her grandmother as Anna is a famous young actress with several major movies and leading roles to her credit. She is supposed to be quite stunning and very charming. Susan and her grandmother forget about me and hustle around the house cleaning up, preparing for the big visit. This is amusing to me, as they are totally ignoring me. I sit down on the couch, take off my shoes, put my feet up on a bench seat, and watch the TV. The news is on, and it is interesting. It has been ten years since I have watched the evening news.

Susan yells at me, "Henry, don't get too comfortable. They also want to meet you, the hero of the day."

I'm starting to think this might not be too good for me, for a guy who wants to stay under the radar, yet it's a good finish to an already strange day. This is almost the end of my first day; nine more days to go. I remind myself that I am on Earth, and it's just splendid to be here. Anything could happen.

CHAPTER 9

DAY TWO

Meanwhile over at Susan's dorm, Anna is there. She is putting the dishes away from a late dinner and is wondering about the wisdom of visiting Susan's grandmother, as it is late, after ten, well into the evening. "Maybe there's no time for this." Anna is also thinking, *I need to get an early start tomorrow, back on the road. I'm still a long way from Richmond.*

She says, "Nikki, you know if we go I cannot stay long at Susan's grandmother's house. It's really late."

Nikki says, "I know, I know, you're leaving early for Richmond. We'll stay only a few minutes. You remember Susan. I've talked about her. She's been my roommate for a long time, and she's a sweet girl. We're best friends, almost as close as you and I are with each other. And she's had a tough few months. She went on one date with a guy; it was a bad evening, and now he's been stalking her for weeks. This guy is really creepy. He petrifies me, too. Apparently he attacked Susan tonight, according to the police who called here looking for her, and this guy she just met at the store today saved her life, and he's also there at the house. Susan wants to meet you, and I thought I should see her, too.

She's been really depressed lately. This stalker thing did her in, and I want to help her."

Nikki laughs. "And seeing you will be a big deal, you being a big movie star, the famous actress and everything. Susan's grandmother will be more than pleased to meet you, too. Plus, I'm curious about this guy. Susan said he's really remarkable, really different, and she became excited when she talked about him, said he is actually extraordinary. She said it's hard to explain. He's someone you just like spending time with. Maybe you can get a date with him for the Academy Awards."

Anna laughs and says, "First I have to be nominated. All right, I'm coming. We can't stay long. But who knows what this might lead to? Some big adventure, right?"

Nikki laughs, too, saying, "Don't get carried away!"

They're getting into Anna's rental car, Nikki saying they need to hurry.

Anna is thinking again about her plans. She's glad Nikki is doing the driving, glad to be on their way, needing to get this over with. Nikki knows Louisville better and is a better driver. Plus Anna always dislikes driving rental cars. She has a chauffeur at home most of the time and is not used to using a strange car. She flew in three days ago and was forced to rent a car for the trip to Richmond, Virginia, after visiting Nikki. She has not been home for several months, home being her parents' farm outside Richmond. It is a beautiful place in the country, with horses, rolling pastures, woods, and a house that should be in the movies.

Her mother divorced her biological father when Anna was six years old. She met Anna's stepfather, married him, and then left Chicago with him, although they keep a house in Chicago, too. Anna was born in Chicago yet calls Richmond her hometown, even though this is the second residence of her mother and stepfather, who is a politician and an attorney. His name is

Sam Jordan. He is wealthy and lucky, as he backed the right senator and then stepped in as his campaign manager. After that the newly elected senator, representing Illinois, asked Sam to be his chief of staff. Unfortunately, the senator died of a heart attack three years later, and Anna's stepdad ended up taking his place. He ran on his own and was elected.

He still has his main residence in Illinois, as required by election laws, yet keeps a small condo in Washington, DC, for when he could not make it back to Richmond, his favorite home, the farm he loves.

Anna's whole family prospered. Nikki was born a year after they moved to Richmond and lived at the farm. Nikki is a great half sister, and she and Anna are close because much of the time Anna cared for her, especially back in those early days. Senator and Mrs. Jordan had many functions and many events. Plus, being the senator from Illinois was not easy.

Anna ended up going to Duke University because she is smart and maybe because her stepfather is a senator. Duke is hard to get into, but Sam made some calls to help her, and she had four great years there. She studied political science and drama. No one thought she could make a living in theater; however, she was a good actress and then a lucky actress. After graduating she was able to get a small role in a soap opera. It did not hurt to have Senator Jordan as her stepfather. She didn't care how she got the role, because she excelled at it. The TV audience loved her. Then there were bigger roles, movie parts, and now starring roles. She is one of the lucky few making millions and is recognized everywhere.

Anna's last movie was about a young family that had been through the Revolutionary War in 1776. The wife, her role, was struggling to feed her children and then overcame losing her husband and moved forward, prevailing against all odds. It has just been released and started out well at the box office, and she hopes she might be looking at an Academy Award. Many say she's worthy, even if she is young. She's just twenty-eight.

Finally she has some time for visits, as she is now between roles. She will also attend a premiere opening in London in a few days. The previous few months with this movie production were grinding, no let-up. And since there were no breaks, she is exhausted. She needs a little R and R and wanted to see her sister, then go on to Richmond. So she left her home in Hollywood and flew to Louisville, and here she is. Nikki just graduated from the University of Louisville and is now starting at their school of medicine. Anna's little sister will someday be a great doctor, and Anna is very proud of her.

They arrive at Susan's grandmother's house and she is waiting at the door to greet them. Meeting her is great.

Anna is impressed, thinking, *So nice, waiting for me at the front door. She is terrific, and Susan is charming. Then there is meeting Henry—wow! Another real surprise; who would think? He is just amazing: intelligent and so easy to talk to, maybe even old-fashioned. He's fun, not like anyone I have ever met. His eyes are unbelievable, sensitive, and sort of sad, like an old soul's, yet penetrating, as if he can see what you're thinking. He also seems all-knowing in a nice way, yet humble, and just very charming. I think he has seen a lot of life. He appears really kind in a compassionate way, like an older man, although he looks only about thirty years old. Actually he does not look much older than me and has outstanding looks! I feel drawn to him, irrational, yet I can feel it clearly.*

She wonders, *Is it possible to fall for somebody on the first meeting? Does Henry feel it, too?*

She knows it's impossible, yet she thinks, *I feel like I know Henry, like maybe he's a kindred spirit. He just feels right; the attraction is strong and difficult to ignore. It's hard not to be impressed by Henry; he's not your average guy. The most striking thing is his bearing. His self-assured dignity is magnificent. He is like a Greek god or a Shakespearian actor: proud yet nice. There is something really special about him. With his light-brown, almost-blond hair and a tanned, a weathered look, combined with his strong shoulders, he would make a great leading man, a navy captain perhaps. He has the look of a really important man, one you would never forget.*

Anna is acknowledging her predicament, thinking fast: *This is worse than any fantasy movie script where I am in romance trouble. This is real trouble! It's crazy. I'm smitten. I just cannot take my mind off of him! I feel warmth deep in my body I have never felt before, like I am hot to touch. The chemistry he creates is intoxicating. I have never felt like this with anyone. I know I need to see him again. I really do not have time for this! How could it happen? I have always scoffed at girls who are this way, thinking,* They're just silly females.

He makes it easy to fall for him—his strong, handsome face; his facial features are almost aristocratic, like an ancient Roman soldier's. He has a slender physique, yet it's really well muscled, strong, looking like a professional athlete or maybe military, like SEAL team military. That's it; he has a certain hardness that is definitely military. Still, he moves so gracefully; he should be in ballet, and he is a definitely a gentleman: polite, even respectful and also smart, in a delightful way. Yes, there is some mystery about him, too, almost enigmatic. Amazingly to me, I can hardly wait to see him again.

She speculates, *He can't be that perfect. There must be flaws I don't see. Maybe he is a con man, or maybe he was in prison. No one is this good. His life story is a little strange. It is the one thing that does not make sense. His work life does not match him. Henry certainly does not look like a PhD student at Indiana University, as he says he is. It's hard to believe; he just does not fit in as an academic type, definitely more of an action guy. Could he be a liar?*

The other unexpected part, making me angry, surprising me, I was so foolish when I was with him. I'm like a schoolgirl with him: flirty, nervous, and silly. I also have a hard time taking my eyes off of him. It's embarrassing how I keep talking to him, excited; my nonstop talking is mindless. I cannot help myself. No question I feel emotions about him in a way I have never felt before. I have lost self-control and all pride.

She thinks, *I guess, maybe luckily for me, I will see him tomorrow. I've volunteered to let him go with me on my drive to Richmond, as it works for him too. He has plans to go to Washington, DC, as he wants to interview politicians as part of his PhD studies, which also seems hard to believe. He just does not look like the type who interviews politicians. He looks like the type who knows most everything a politician says is BS. I guess I will learn more about him tomorrow. I'll pick him up here, as he is staying with Susan's grandmother tonight, sleeping in an extra bedroom. Susan is staying, too. Since she's not coming back to the dorm, I'll sleep in her bed tonight, back with Nikki, giving us a chance to talk. I wonder what Nikki thinks about Henry.*

Later that night, Nikki and Anna have a lot of catching up to do. As they sit in bed across from each other, Anna tells her about Hollywood and how she has missed Nikki. Life there is lonely. Anna explains that most of the men in Hollywood, the handsome actors especially, are extremely self-centered. Most are selfish and act like predators. She dated a Hollywood director she thought was nice, James Algeir. He is famous, powerful, and rich. Turns out he is a very controlling guy, a type-A person, domineering, aggressive, abusive, and it was hard to escape him. He is very possessive and treated Anna like his property. Even now he calls her, still telling her what to do. He expects her to obey him in all things. Too bad. She thought they had connected at one time. He was way too much for her, really intense. She's now trying hard to be rid of him.

They talk about Henry, and Nikki was impressed, too. It's hard not to want to know more about him. He is completely different from anyone they have ever met. He is extraordinary. Of course Nikki gives Anna a hard time about her flirting with him and says he was clearly watching Anna the whole time. Could he be interested in her?

Anna sadly tells Nikki, "I have no one right now, do not date, see no one in sight that might be special, and yes, I still want a family. Thank goodness I have you, as life is really lonely."

Nikki responds, "Anna, you will find someone. You're kind, smart, a wonderful person, and certainly gorgeous!"

Thankfully Nikki talks more. She talks about her classes, homework, and how hard it is to become a medical doctor. It takes all her energy and time just to keep up. She laughs and says she does not have time to date—no guy around for her either. She and Anna will be old sister spinsters living together when they are old and gray, and they both laugh.

Finally they both fall off to sleep.

⟞⟊ ⟋⟝

I am half-asleep, then wide awake; knowing the morning is coming fast, I am up quickly, showering and dressing, thinking: *I do not look great, unfortunately, in the same clothing as yesterday. It will have to do. The* Cyclone *is leaving me alone, taking care of business without me; good to keep it that way, yet I need clothing for tomorrow and a small travel bag with my overnight things for sure, maybe some running stuff; I like to run over Earth terrain, seeing things up close. Running every day is of great value to me. I am thinking today will be an excellent day, and now day two of my trip back to Earth."*

Also, this morning, early, before light, the dark *Ship Tender* drops down to the Earth's surface, meeting me around the corner, in an empty parking lot, to pick up my Barnes & Noble purchases, dropping off my travel bag and clothing. Then I am back to the house, drinking coffee, saying good-bye to Susan and her grandmother. Both end up with tears as we declare friendship, and they thank me many times. I tell them I will visit them again, check on them. Their tears are heartwarming, as such a wonderful human expression of emotion, genuine and meaningful. Then I am at the curb waiting on Anna.

Mentally congratulating myself, I think, *It doesn't get any better than this. Here I am, it's almost seven thirty, and I'm waiting for Anna to pick me up. Her taking me to Richmond is a lucky break. The PhD dissertation is a good cover story, no issues or problems for her and maybe an excuse for me to spend some time with her and maybe meet her family. I hope she doesn't figure out I know little about what's going on here, never seen her films, although I acted as if I have. She is impressive: gorgeous eyes, stunning face, a totally beautiful figure, quick witted, smart, charming, fun, every bit a superstar. Someday some guy will be a very lucky man. She must be in her midtwenties, although she's smart beyond her years. To have some time with her is a lucky break.*

She pulls up in a car that looks like a tall station wagon. They call it an SUV. It is well designed, even if primitive, and does what it needs to do. I jump in, and off we go.

I smell her perfume immediately, and I detect her personal odor, too. Both are pleasing to me. I look at Anna, very attractive in a cream-colored silk blouse over a gray light-cotton T-shirt, the blouse not buttoned until a third of the way down, not tucked in either, and tight blue jeans and sandals. Her blond hair is cut very short, boyish. She is small, a little taller than five feet. Slender, or *petite* is the word, with a classically beautiful face with high cheekbones. She has a nice figure, although small-breasted and not wearing a bra. She actually is just perfect. Her legs and bottom are firm, like those of a runner. It is hard not to stare at her. It has been seventy years since I have felt these kinds of emotions, and warning bells are going off. I realize I am not sure how I am going to deal with this. She is simply a smart, beautiful human woman, and no question, I am very much attracted to her. This is not unusual for a human; it's normal to feel a pull, even a powerful one.

Once in the car, I am surprised I am shy with her. I catch my breath and finally manage to say to her, "Good morning! Thanks again for the ride. Please let me pay you for the gas, and I will pick up any meals."

As she puts the SUV in gear, moving forward onto the street, she laughs and says, "All right, you're on. It's the least you can do." She looks at me, beams. "Henry, I actually appreciate your coming. It makes a long ride not so long. By the way, did the police ever get ahold of you and Susan about yesterday?"

I reply, "Yes, both Susan and I spoke to them. They seemed satisfied. They wanted to know how to reach us if we are needed for a trial. I think they have plenty of evidence, as the man was pleading guilty to everything—other crimes, too, coming clean, as he should. I feel bad for Susan, going through all of it. Maybe she'll be better going forward."

Anna says, "Thank God you were there. He could have killed her. What a terrible man. It is good to know there are good and brave men in the world. I am grateful for men like you, Henry."

I actually blush; I never thought it possible. I have to laugh, and then I say, "Anna, how could anyone do less? You would have helped her, too, and you are sure making me feel good about it. Yes, there will be extra ice cream for you at lunch!"

Anna laughs. "Tell me about yourself. Where were you born; how old are you; where do you live? Do you have family, are you married now or were you ever, in the service, and why did you go to Indiana University? Do you have a job? What do you like to do? What are your plans?"

I am startled, maybe a little astonished. I now know she is actually interested in me, and this is amazing. I feel a powerful surge of excitement I have never felt before—something wild, crazy, and fantastic. My heart is pounding. This is not in the plan. I can't help myself. It is nonsensical. I want to answer her truthfully. I feel I want to impress her. Unfortunately it is impossible.

First of all, there is no way she will believe me; the truth is way too weird. Second, just knowing me, the real me, could put her life in danger. It would be of great interest to the US military. Governments are usually unpredictable when dealing with me, might do whatever they have to do to make her tell all, as politicians are usually afraid of me. I cannot protect her. I am leaving in eight days.

This is silly. I'm like a teenager, acting all emotional. I need to get ahold of myself. I remind myself I am the commander of a huge army. I defeat worlds, a captain of a starship. I have massive power. I have huge responsibilities. I am old and wise, beyond these kinds of things. She is just a young Earth girl. It doesn't have to be complicated. I will just her give her my total cover story.

She then asks more questions, good questions. She is very perceptive as I answer her. Although I am honest about my personal life—my parents, religion, raised middle class, no wife, never married, no girlfriend—I also give her my fake background story.

Looking away, trying to make it sound sincere, I say, "I live frugally on a part-time job for now. I am a political science major, live in Bloomington, a grad student at Indiana University located there, and I want to teach at the college level someday. I have always wanted to teach."

She looks at me and asks, "Do you believe in God?"

I smile. "Yes, no doubts for me; you can count on it. Really, I am serious. My belief is right for a lot of reasons. I have seen many awesome things, been given gifts in my life you would never dream of, beyond my comprehension. I have wondered at the sheer immensity of the universe, of life itself in all shapes and sizes. I have seen beauty that is beyond belief. It does not make it less wonderful or not true. I never doubt these blessings, as they are gifts, and I am grateful. Never worry; you will know what I say

is true either now or later. Inexplicably enough, I think these extraordinary blessings have already happened to you, and I think
these momentous events will continue for you. Miraculous events
take place in everyone's life; just know them for what they really
are; don't deny them. There is a divine light. It will embrace you
and guide your way in the dark."

Anna keeps driving, saying nothing. She then looks at me
and says, "I never have felt your confidence until now, and I am
surprised. You give me hope. You are right. I know it in my heart.
It sounds crazy, yet I think I can actually feel your faith."

She pauses, hesitates, turns her head to me, looks at me intently, straight into my eyes, and asks, "Are you gay? "

I laugh and say quickly, "You better watch the road, and no, I
am not gay. I'm not sure how I should take the question."

She laughs, too. "You passed."

We talk about everything. I love it. She is fun, endearing, and
very honest. She also gives me the benefit of the doubt on some
of my evasive answers. I have almost forgotten about the *Cyclone*
and that life. I am actually happy. We stop, have lunch, chat about
everything. We enjoy the time together and then get back on the
road. We are still in West Virginia, then on to Virginia, going
east through the Appalachian Mountains.

She is driving. It is raining hard. She has not said much for a
couple of hours, and I sense she does not want to talk. I know she
is getting tired; I can see it. I ask if I can drive. She says no, as I
am not insured under the rental agreement, although she does
not like driving, and she is tired.

She then suddenly looks at me and has an angry expression.
She says, "You're lying to me about yourself. Your answers do not
add up. You are not at Indiana University; I am sure of that, and
I do not know who you are. You have been conning me. I don't
know why, as I've been honest with you. I like you. I thought we
had a connection, too. Now I want you to get out of my car."

To my surprise, she slows the car down and pulls over to the shoulder of the interstate highway. We are still in the mountains and in heavy rain, and big trucks are ramming by us, spraying a lot of water on our stopped car. I look out the passenger window over the side of the shoulder. Even in the rain I can see it goes straight down, very deep, maybe thousands of feet. We are over a mountainous cliff, surprisingly with no guardrail. I think how it all went wrong so fast. I feel lost and disappointed, and worse, I have disappointed Anna. I know she will not believe whatever I say. I've lost all credibility. She still cannot know the truth about me. It would change her life and not for the better. It might ruin it. I just can't risk it. Too bad. I already know I will miss her.

Looking at her, seeing those angry eyes, I say, "Anna, I understand, and I am truly sorry I have upset you. I certainly care. Please forgive me. You're right; I have not been entirely honest. I cannot tell you anything more about myself than what I have already said. You would not believe me even if I told you. It's like looking up into the blue sky and seeing very little other than blue sky, then on a clear, dark night looking up again at the same sky and unbelievably seeing the millions of stars and the vastness of the universe. You have to see it to believe it or to understand it. If it makes you feel better, I have no choice. I'm sorry. Please go on to the next exit, and drop me off there."

She looks at me with a pained, disappointed expression and says, "All right!"

Anna puts the SUV into forward gear, gives it too much gas, sharply pulls out onto the highway, and, maybe too upset to look or because of the rain, does not see a big semi tractor-trailer come barreling up behind us. She pulls out in front of him; he swerves to miss us, scary close. He misses us, his water spray covers us, and he goes on with horns blasting.

Anna then swerves back onto the shoulder of the road too fast, hitting the concrete roadside bump hard. The steering wheel jerks out of her hands, causing her to lose control. We are both totally shocked as the SUV lunges forward past the pavement, off the road shoulder, teetering at the edge of a huge drop-off, hanging over the cliff of the mountainside. Then, in a long second, it falls forward. It slides downward, then plunges over the side of the mountain, airborne, straight down. We plummet, tumbling into the black empty space below, no bottom in sight. I am sure it is a long way down, guaranteeing certain death.

I shout, "Holy hell!"

Anna is screaming at the top of her lungs.

Down we go, and even worse, the SUV cartwheels end over end, still airborne, falling faster into the black, bottomless abyss. Anna is in sheer terror, still screaming, holding on to the steering wheel for dear life. We are both thrown around like rag dolls; it's not pleasant. Yet I know we will not die. I wish I could yell out, tell her, and reassure her. I know what she cannot know: the *Cyclone* will use a power beam to catch us and create a vacuum around the car with negative polarization. With no gravity, the SUV will stop falling, and we will be fine or almost fine.

CHAPTER 10

MEETING A STARSHIP

The *Cyclone*'s massive blazing power beam lashes out from the sky, like a six-foot-wide torchlight, blazing down out of the heavens, grasping the truck hard. The rain sizzles on the hot beam. The SUV comes to a jolting, bumpy halt, tumbling one more time, and we are now floating upright in midair. I can't see much other than the power beam because of the heavy rain and approaching dusk. It is really hard to see anything except the blinding light.

I know the *Cyclone* has sent the *Ship Tender* down to come and get us. It will pull the SUV along behind it like a water-skier behind a boat. And there it is. I barely see its shape a couple hundred feet out ahead of us, not camouflaged, barely visible, black and ugly as usual, and now a really beautiful sight. Unfortunately the *Ship Tender* can be seen by radar during this rescue; the camouflage is not able to function during this kind of maneuver. It hooks on to us using another power beam shooting out toward us in a bright bolt about three feet in width. It is very visible now, easily seen by Earth eyes other than ours. It looks like a huge bright shaft of light shining on us, making the whole area around us like daylight.

Off we go, jolting forward, then trailing behind it as we speed up quickly and climbing very fast, maybe reaching ninety miles an hour—a fast flight for an SUV. We are riding a little rough because of the side winds, and the speed causes heavy wind commotion. It is now sunset, and we are moving up through a thick cloud layer. The sun is becoming visible over the clouds.

Anna is speechless, freaked out. She is just staring at the *Ship Tender* with eyes big and wide, more in shock than not. She can't take her eyes off of the tender, gripping the SUV's steering wheel as if her life depends on it. I can actually smell her fear. Her face is as white as a sheet. She then asks in a weird, quivering voice, "What is that? Why are we alive? What is happening? I don't understand…We're moving up, we're flying and gaining height, moving faster now. We're moving really fast; we really are climbing up high! Henry, what's going on? This is impossible! Can you figure this out? What's happening? What the hell is that thing pulling us? Are we going to be OK? Are you all right?"

I say, "Anna, I am fine. You are fine, too, or will be, and we are being towed by a ship's tender; it's like a tugboat and a passenger landing craft for large starships."

Anna is looking at me, not comprehending what I am saying, just staring at me, at a loss for words.

"Anna, I know this is hard to believe. Just know it is real. You are not crazy. You will be fine, and no one will hurt you. You have nothing to fear and a lot to learn. First of all, to answer you about who I really am, I guess I will have to tell you now. This probably feels like a movie scene, irrationally enough, certainly an eerie experience for you. I am telling you what I should not be telling you, could not tell you before. It is hard to believe. You will doubt your sanity or mine. I could not say this before, as you would think I was an idiot with a delusion. You will probably still think I am insane or on drugs when I say this, yet here it goes; you need to be prepared for what is coming up, the reality of my life will soon be your reality. We are now heading up to an altitude of about 10,000 feet to board a starship."

I pause, waiting for her to clear her head, giving her a chance to think, digest my words, to try to sort this out.

I continue, "Astonishing and as strange as it sounds, I am actually a captain of a starship, the starship *Cyclone*, the spacecraft we will be joining soon, as we come up over the clouds. What you see just ahead, pulling us, is the ship's tender that belongs to the *Cyclone*. You will soon be my guest on the *Cyclone*, as we are coming aboard it. Your life just became a lot more interesting."

Anna stares at me then back again at the ship's tender, blinking her eyes as if trying to wake up from a bad dream. She can't figure it out. I can tell this is not going to be easy.

"Anna, listen to me. We are partially visible to radar now, and someone may pick up on us, discover we're here in this airspace. We may attract visitors we don't want, thus we make haste. We will enter and land in the *Cyclone*'s cargo bay in about two minutes, and then off we will go, out of here."

Anna is now staring at me as if I am some kind of lunatic. She looks more freaked out, not less. She is speechless. Her are eyes huge, her face still pale; she is breathing rapidly and looking like she is going to be sick.

In a worried voice, yet more firm, I say, "Anna, *please* just do as I say, and I will explain everything to you once we are a safe distance from Earth. I will answer all your questions, no lies. We will leave Earth for just a short time, then I will take you home. Nothing bad will happen to you; I promise. You will be fine, not harmed, no big deal. Just try to relax."

We then break over the cloud layer at about ten thousand feet up, our eyes overwhelmed by the vivid brightness of the massive blue sky and bright light everywhere. The sun is reflecting off the top of the billowing clouds in a blazing orange mixed with yellow and overall just glorious!

Then, there it is. We see the *Cyclone* in all its glory, waiting for us, lightly floating above the clouds, maybe about ten miles away. It is shimmering in the sunlight like a huge bright-silver mirror, a massive starship. It dazzles from the sun's reflection with all the colors of a rainbow, awesome beyond words. I am always impressed when I see it. I can feel it welcoming me back. I respond in kind.

I look at Anna to see if she sees the *Cyclone*. She is all eyes, a look on her face of total amazement. Thankfully she seems much better, not so pale. It might be the sunshine. She is staring fixedly ahead at the *Cyclone*, the fear gone, replaced by the thrill of seeing a real starship for the first time.

She is excited and yells over the wind hitting the car, "Henry, do you see that? It's some kind of spaceship. It really is a spaceship. It's incredible! It's huge. Do you see it? It's just floating above the clouds. It looks like a bright star hovering, ready to escape back to the heavens. Can you believe this? Are you seeing what I'm seeing, or am I dreaming this? This is wild! Is that where we're going?" Eyeing me, she exclaims, "Henry, am I hearing you right? You really are its captain? How is that possible? Do you work for NASA?" Looking at me with a more bewildered expression—no, maybe it is more of an electrified look, certainly not calm—she cries, "It was you who saved our lives!"

I look back at her attentively, needing to reassure her. "Anna, the starship saved our lives, not me. It will be all right, and you have nothing to fear. You are not crazy, and you are not dreaming. And I think you probably need to prepare yourself. You might be a little bit overwhelmed. You need to trust me. I can explain everything. Please don't worry; this will be a new life experience. Think of it as an adventure."

The *Cyclone* opens her cargo bay doors. We quickly slide in, the *Ship Tender* going in first then drawing us in, the SUV landing with a jolt, tires squealing. This all is happening fast.

Unfortunately, when the bay doors opened, we created more of a radar signature. Radar, although primitive, still works well. We have to move out quickly, need to leave Earth fast. Maybe we were spotted; the US Air Force might be coming. Yes, the *Cyclone* is telling me fighter jets, F-16s, are coming fast out of Andrews and will be there soon. A confrontation with them would be bad, though we have nothing to fear other than them knowing we exist. The *Cyclone* has a security field they cannot penetrate, and I do not think they can clearly see us now. However, invisibility shields have vulnerabilities. If we leave this planet, life will be easier for us.

We are moving out. I can feel the ship starting to accelerate, the pressure of the gravity, climbing fast, leaving Earth, back in stealth mode. We should be mostly invisible. Plus, we're leaving this atmosphere quickly, heading toward the Earth's moon, about twenty-five thousand miles away. We will be there in minutes, accelerating the entire way, now already at sixty thousand miles per hour, maybe hitting five hundred thousand miles per hour about the time we pass the moon. Regrettably, it will be possible to see our engine blast, a thrusting fire stream visible from Earth. With this kind of acceleration, we will have a tail blast about two thousand miles long, getting longer as we gain speed.

At some point Anna and I need to get out of the SUV and head for the control room, the ship's center of operations—really my office, or the captain's bridge. I need to be patient now, need to let Anna have a chance to calm down a little, sort this out mentally. I want to show her so much, as I know she will be amazed once she has a chance to explore my world. The captain's bridge is where we can see outer space ahead of us, all 360 degrees, the total surrounding field of space for thousands of miles. To see it for the first time is breathtaking, almost supernatural, certainly incredible.

CHAPTER 11

CYCLONE'S INTRODUCTION TO ANNA

The *Cyclone* has no visible openings, no real windows, just sixteen round crystal eyes looking like six-foot portholes evenly placed around the hull, eight of them up front and then another eight at the back of the ship. These are the ship's eyes, looking everywhere, in all directions, then relaying back the 360-degree view of space to the ship's captain's bridge, showing up as real-sight visual displays, very detailed, with long-range telescoping when requested. It will show thousands and thousands of miles in great detail on a six-foot-high, half-inch spectrum plasma screen wrapped around on a circular room wall. It shows the entire 360-degree range, all directions around the ship, and an outside view of space in every direction. All views are in perfect focus, with a full-color spectrum, magnified when needed, better than your own eyesight and three-dimensional. It helps me a lot, and it is my design. I am a visual kind of guy.

The captain's bridge is in the top of the forward part of the ship, also redesigned by me. It is hard to describe the look. It might be compared to a modern US Navy battleship bridge, with smooth light-gray walls and a grated floor, with heavy captain's chairs that look like big leather sofa seats, comfortable, ten of them spaced apart in a semicircle. They are designed to look to the front or, swiveling, to view the six-foot plasma screen wrapped around the entire room, with each seat swiveling 360 degrees to see the outside panorama. The room is ten feet tall, eighty-eight feet in diameter, bending in front as a curved arc and as part of the total circle, then sixty-two feet in forward-length diameter, thus more of an oblong.

There is little equipment in the room. Instead there are ten large floating, transparent five-foot-square visual screens that change shape depending on need. They will expand and show control boards, graphics, instrument readings, propulsion systems, navigation, weapons, ship operation conditions, all red- and yellow-lighted data, some green meters. They are all displayed in front of each seat and floating to where you need them, presented for easy use and the controls triggered as you think about them. The floor and ceilings have partially hidden storage compartments; otherwise, it's mostly clean lines, with no structure other than regularly spaced handholds, several cabinets, a few tables, and one hidden bathroom tube. The room is functional and certainly not cozy.

The room also houses the brains of the *Cyclone*. It has four large floating live artificial intelligence entities and, for want of a better description, live cyber-computer beings, not organic, no physical bodies. They are more like clouds of pure energy, just boundless intelligence. They are weightless clouds floating about the room, moving as they want, using the power of magnetism, maybe eight feet high and four to five feet wide, constantly changing shape and colors and brightness. They are the full range of colors, sparkling pinpoints of light and the entire spectrum of light, coming from billions of biosynthetic neurons all connected by sheer energy and by a powerful self-created magnetic field.

They are not human yet are close to human in their own way. They really are ancient alien beings, maybe better than human.

I have initials for each: K-HO, M-HO, F-LA, and G-BE. I have known them since 1945, when I became the Consortium's military commander and the *Cyclone's* captain. They came with the starship, have been on it since its birth. They are my friends, as we have been together all these years. We are close comrades or, better, more like siblings. We are also telepathically in sync. They are my backup team, a fantastic resource. As long as I am on the *Cyclone* or in laser-wave distance, which is a long way, we are linked mentally.

They operate the *Cyclone*, as they are its brains, its operations processor, and its memories. They also increase my mental horsepower dramatically. The aggregate of their beings are the *Cyclone's* identity. Their mental ability combined is beyond comprehension, as their massive databases are collected from the entire universe. To keep the ship running, they have daily responsibilities: keeping and updating the ship's log, the navigation system, the piloting, the maintenance warning system, the communications system, life support systems, energy creation, the ship's conductor of daily activities, the operational data bank, historical archives, the weapons systems, operating the propulsion control, the security system, and all calculations and formulas. They also control everything else.

There is one real amazing reality, which was hard to get used to in the beginning. We are more than close, more than working companions. We are in one another's heads. We are all symbiotic. They are the *Cyclone's* multiple mental resources. The aggregate result is the *Cyclone*, the best starship in the universe. I am the *Cyclone's* captain and linked to it mentally, closely telepathic. We know each other's thoughts. The *Cyclone* follows my directions, although we have arguments. Even though these factors are powerful influences internally on the *Cyclone*, it is still synchronized as one entity, which is the *Cyclone* persona. Yet the *Cyclone* must accept my final decisions, my free will, as I have final say and accountability. Those are the rules.

⊶ ⊷

I am looking at Anna intently, wondering how to help her transition to this new reality.

We are still in the truck, and I can feel the effect of the lack of gravity; we are weightless, having left Earth's gravitational field. This is usual for me, weird for Anna. I know she must feel uncomfortable, and I wonder about her. She is floating in the SUV's seat, the belt holding her from floating away. She looks like she is going to be sick, and I know she is worrying about what to do if she throws up.

I ask her, "Are you OK? Do you understand about the loss of gravity? You're feeling sick, aren't you?"

She's looking at me with great fear in her eyes, totally pale. She says in an anxious voice, almost a whisper, "I understand you without your talking. You are in my head, and I can feel it. How much do you know about what I'm thinking? Are you human? Are you an alien? How did you do that? You don't work for NASA, do you? Where do you come from? *Who are you?*"

I am not sure how to respond. Honesty is good.

"Anna, I don't know where to start. I am from Earth. Yes, I am human, or mostly human, although older than you think. I can explain more as we get to know each other. Interestingly enough, I am telepathic, part of an enhancement. As you know you are also now telepathic because you are on this ship. You hear my thoughts, as I hear yours. It was necessary for you to be enhanced, too. It's so you can communicate with the crew. You have been given a communications enhancement. It is not harmful, almost invisible, and similar to what you would call a little computer module. It happened as we boarded the ship. It's a tiny drone I call a slip, and it was inserted behind your temporal lobe and another one in your frontal lobe. That is what gives you my thoughts, as I hear yours, and I feel your emotions. I hear only what you want me to hear. The crew and the ship can hear you, too, when you direct your thoughts to them. Otherwise no one on board would understand you, nor could you understand them."

Anna does hear me in her mind. She is wondering if I am hearing the massive feeling of terror in her head. One good thing, it has cured her stomachache; she no longer feels nauseated, just scared more than she thought possible. Not throwing up is good. She is shaken, not sure what to say or think, but no spoken words are needed. This could not be happening to her, she thinks. Could her thoughts be heard? What are the chances of being on an alien starship? This is so way out there. Then there is me. Who am I?

I am now apprehensive, looking at her and nodding, saying to her, "Yes, Anna, I can feel or understand your questions, and yes, it is a bizarre feeling. You will be amazed as you use it. Believe it or not, you will get familiar with it, and you will love it. Anna, please understand, it is for your own good. You are not on Earth anymore. There are several challenges facing you; communication is just one. Are you able to deal with the loss of gravity, no weight? You are not getting sick? Are you breathing comfortably? The ship will provide you with the correct oxygen levels automatically, meant just for you."

Anna does not respond, just looks away, trying to figure out what to say or, in this case, think. She is trying hard to feel comfortable with this and with me.

I can feel her sense of vulnerability, her confusion, her fear and anxiety. She will sort it out. I force myself to be patient. She needs time to adapt, to gather her courage.

Finally she looks back at me, saying, "I think I am beyond getting sick, or I would be sick, although it's hard to get my balance. I'm OK as long as I have something to hold on to, not free floating, then it's really easy to feel sick. I'm also trying to get a handle on this telepathy thing. I am really trying hard not to panic!"

I know I can pull more from her mind. However, the slips are instructed to give her privacy and to protect her. The two slips are watchdogs, making it difficult for her to get in trouble on board the ship and to protect her from any unforeseen enemy when we are back on Earth. Life may change a lot for her.

The drones, or the slips, will give me notification if she is in trouble, depending on how far she is from the *Cyclone*. No question I now feel a great fondness for her. I know this is for her own good, yet I feel guilty about hiding from her this possible need for protection. I am somewhat surprised by my feelings, and, unfortunately for me, I feel very protective of her. I am responsible for these events and not sure what will happen now. This is not a good sign for me. It is getting complicated. This has never happened before. There are severe consequences to ending up close to her—for both of us.

Anna finally looks directly at me with her big blue eyes, with a calmer expression, not so pale, informing me mentally using thought projection, "I think the slip thing in my brain is really eerie and not high on my list of good things to happen to me. I am OK for now. I can't feel anything strange, and nothing hurts. I think I'm all right. I don't feel threatened. In fact, oddly enough, I feel safe with you. I hear your words mentally, and then, the good part, I feel your emotions without your words, and it feels nourishing. I can't explain it. Actually it's comforting, really quite awesome. I also know you're human, a man. I feel it from you." Anna blushes at this, looks away, and smiles at the same time.

I smile, too. She is regaining her confidence. I feel what she is feeling, something I have not felt in many years. It feels good and makes me wonder.

Anna interrupts my thoughts, asking, "You are human, yet where are you from? This starship is not from here. Who are you? You are the ship's captain? Why are you here, and are there more of you? What are we going to do now, and when are we going back to Earth?"

"Anna, I can explain everything. Do you have a couple of days to spend some time on the ship, travel, see some of the solar system? Do you have time for an adventure? You will be amazed."

She starts to answer but stops. A worried look comes over her face, then she blurts out, "Oh my gosh, my mother!" She reaches for my arm, looking at me. "Henry, I just remembered, we're supposed to be at my parents' house. I need to make a phone call right now. They'll be worried. Do you have some way I can call them before they start to think they need to call the police? When are we going to be home?"

I'm thinking this is more of a problem than Anna thinks, as a phone call transmission from the *Cyclone* from out here, now six hundred thousand miles from Earth, has a good chance of being picked up by some government, and they will wonder. We went beyond the Earth's moon some time ago, heading for Mars and picking up more speed fast. I need to make that call quickly, before we are beyond our ability to patch into a cell-phone network. I know I really can't say no; her parents will be worried. And what could happen from one phone call? *A lot!*

Yet I say, "Anna, just use your cell phone. The *Cyclone* will patch you in. It will be a little fuzzy, as we are a long way from the United States."

Anna looks for her purse in the SUV, and she sees it is floating with all the other stuff. She grabs it, takes out her cell phone, and dials, and it rings. Her mother answers. Anna looks at me and smiles, whispers, "Thanks!" then says into the cell phone, "Mom, yes, this is Anna. Sorry for not calling earlier. I'm going to be late getting there, a couple of days late. I just wanted to call and let you know and tell you not to worry." Her mother says something, and Anna replies, "I know. I should have called, and I needed to tell you I'm with a friend, actually a guy friend I'm traveling with. He wants to show me some scenery on the way, some really interesting *out-of-this-world* sights." She smiles at her own pun, then a pause. Her mother is talking. Anna continues, "Yes, you will meet him, and you will love him. Is it OK if he stays with us?" Another pause, and Anna blushes, saying, "He's just a friend, and yes...yes...I think he is special. I will see you in a couple of days. Please call Nikki for me. She will be worried."

Anna laughs and looks at me. I shake my head and smile. I realize I love her laugh. She is looking at me, laughing and smiling a big happy smile. She says to me, "This is so weird, yet I know you will like my mother!"

I smile and actually feel happy, a rare feeling for me. I am beginning to feel like a normal human again!

CHAPTER 12

CHINESE/RUSSIAN ARMY DEPLOYMENT

While Anna is talking to her mother, the *Cyclone* feeds me a disturbing surveillance report on the mass of troops in Siberia that I spotted on my flight over Russia. To my amazement, it is enormous. There are 8,587 army divisions there, including 995,651 tanks; many more helicopters, missile launchers, and artillery guns; and many thousands of troop trucks. It is a mega massive army of both Chinese and Russian troops, about fifty-five million soldiers, mostly Chinese. They cover 280 square miles, all hidden from over flights by the dense woods and clever camouflage. They seem to be using some kind of massive video projection, giving the illusion of trees where there are none.

The real shocker: they are only about 150 miles from Alaska. Why are they there? What the hell is going on? They could be in Alaska in one day with all those troop trucks. The report also mentions that three Chinese aircraft carriers, plus two Russian carriers, have been deployed within three hundred miles of the Russian coast, near Alaska, within the last twenty-four hours. My flight over them must have motivated them to move forward with their plans, concerned about the element of surprise. Worse than that, there are several Russian nuclear-launch submarines moving into the North Atlantic Ocean, not far from the United States.

What a mess and impossible to fathom! How could they move so many troops and keep it secret? I know the United States does not know about it, as the *Cyclone* hacked into their systems, seeing everything they know. Is this the beginning of World War III? Why would the Russians and Chinese do this? Because we hacked into the Chinese classified data systems, I now know there was significant army-troop growth and large troop movements by rail and ships over the last three years, all going to Russia. There were also many meetings with the Russians, the Mexicans, North Korea, Pakistan, and Iran.

The logical guess is they are preparing to attack the United States. Could be greed or survival, maybe desperation? The United States has lots of things these other nations want, including huge resources and money. Why not take them? Why else would they be that close to Alaska with such a large mass of troops? Using a lot of troop trucks and tanks, they could pour fifty or sixty million troops down through Alaska and Canada, sweeping down into the States, using the interstate road network. Why do they think this is necessary and that it will work?

Still, how did they put that many troops there without the United States knowing? What else is going on? How do they feed them? Do they think the US Army is currently vulnerable? Is troop strength low? No boots on the ground, no civilian militia, maybe depending on technology only to defend the country. The Washington civilian leaders might have the foolish belief no country would ever attack them. This belief is contrary to what the histories of the populations on Earth have always demonstrated: war is the path to power and resources.

Surely the United States has seen these troops from their spy satellites. The CIA must know about this. Did the CIA people get paid for their treason, hiding the knowledge about the troops? Who else was paid off?

There could also be more military assets somewhere else for them to be that strategically daring, to concentrate so many troops in one spot. What else could be going on? Have the Chinese or the Russians brought nukes or chemical weapons in secret into the United States, maybe over the open Mexican border? Is the Mexican government part of the treachery? Maybe a deal was made, or maybe the drug cartels are doing it, their own deal. Maybe there are troops in Mexico, too. A second front makes sense.

Maybe they start out by planting microburst bombs close to the power plants and then destroying power lines, resulting in no electrical energy in the United States. Use cyber attacks to cut off all e-mail, and then destroy all cell-phone communications. Afterward there is complete chaos, then a coordinated military surprise attack. Are there more countries allied to Russia and China? Maybe other enemies are part of it: Iran, North Korea? The Russians and the Chinese have obviously made a deal. Who else is part of it? The Russians would be easy to talk into this.

For one reason alone, they could be convinced to have Alaska back and all that oil. Russia sold the United States the Alaskan area in 1867 for $7 million. Many in Russia think the czar was a fool. He lost a large asset, selling it for pennies, and was hoodwinked by the United States. They have always wanted it back. Now they may have that opportunity; maybe China has agreed to give them Alaska for their help. They would get the oil, too.

My guess is that it is possible their own populations do not know about the potentially coming military conflict. This is one of the advantages of an autocratic government: dictators don't have to report to anyone. Have the Washington politicians provided a reason for the Chinese and the Russian leaders to attack, something they could use to justify a war to the rest of the world?

Why? The world economy is in trouble. Maybe money lost from countries not paying their debt? Maybe the Chinese government feels threatened. Are they afraid the United States is defaulting on their debt? It was not good my last time there. Maybe the States' large debt is getting larger. To the Chinese it has always been a problem. A big problem if maybe they think they will not get their money back. It is possible the Chinese have no faith in the United States' ability to control their national debt, thinking the States will choose to print money instead, thus paying them back in cheap inflated dollars. Billions of dollars would be cheapened, the world economy thrown into chaos, and the value of their loaned dollars destroyed, making the Chinese leadership look like fools to have loaned so much money to the United States. Yes, it is a good excuse to go after US resources.

The more I think about it, the more anxiety I feel. Historically the Chinese and Russian governments have never been high on the United States; they still remember the Cold War years. They would be delighted to support an attack if it worked in their favor. Do they have respect for the Washington politicians? Politicians who might sell their loyalty, betray their country? Do they think Americans will not fight for their country, too busy on Facebook, playing video games, or watching TV? Do they consider the United States weak and vulnerable to attack?

The US government maybe thinks naively that they are respected by the world, surrounded by nations who want the status quo to stay the same. Thinking they want to support the US way of life and goals as the United States stays democratic, a free people, and well off. Then maybe they are foolish by thinking other countries are not envious of the United States' prosperity, the taking up of so much of the world's resources by a small population. The United States doesn't know, never suspects the contempt or understands another country's jealousy of the United States, the lust for that wealth and those resources.

The media in the United States could be feeding them superficial nonsense, no real information about reality, lulling them into a false sense of security. Using ugly stories to divide the country, they create hatred among cultural segments, exploiting the ignorant; worst of all, backing poor leaders. Are the young grateful, and do they appreciate their right to be free, the right to own a gun, to vote, to pursue happiness? Could the US government be overconfident, maybe arrogant, thinking they have many friends and allies, maybe assuming the world knows the United States is too powerful and too important to ever be attacked?

What could be motivating the unbelievable possibility or delusion of starting a major war? What could be worth starting all the destruction and suffering of war? Who would win?

It is easy to think this out, and the numbers are scary. The fifty-five million troops attacking would be overwhelming. As 90 percent of them are Chinese, it means the Chinese could primarily occupy the United States after the possible war. They do have the population numbers to make occupation successful. The Chinese population is about 1.4 billion, and with only 5 percent in the military they could have seventy million troops. Ten percent would give them 140 million troops. They have the numbers for a very strong occupying army with little strain. The surplus of males because of the nation's previous years of female population control helps, too. The male soldiers are without mates and may be looking for females. There are a lot of females in the United States. Plus, the Chinese troops are more or less expendable as far as the Chinese economy is concerned. They are not needed on the mainland. Better here.

The US military forces would have a tough time using nuclear weapons on such a large mass of enemy troops spread out so close to home. They could also destroy much of Canada and the northern latitudes of the United States. Radiation fallout would be terrible. Nuclear retaliation from China or Russia is an issue, too. Fear of that probably would prevent a US nuclear attack on the Chinese mainland or Russia. The Chinese could trade cities one by one with the United States, nuclear missiles back and forth, the destruction awful yet worse for the United States, as it has fewer cities to give up. Could we trade Atlanta for Beijing and so on?

Thus the troops on the ground are critical. What does the United States have in ground troops that are in the country? Just guessing, maybe about a million or less who can actually fight. Maybe four thousand tanks that are usable or maybe fewer, yet this is questionable, depending on their condition and age. Plus, could they be utilized where needed? How many attack helicopters or fighter jets are in the country, not deployed overseas?

If the regular army or the National Guard fails, can a civilian militia face off with the attackers, maybe using guerrilla warfare? Thus the question, how many people or patriots have guns, and will they defend their country? How could they fight tanks and assault weapons with shotguns? Do they have courage and the firearms expertise? Are they willing to sacrifice their lives for freedom and their country?

I am overthinking this. There must be an explanation; it's just not possible for this to happen. Why would the people of this planet risk it all?

Unfortunately there's not much I can do, nor much I want to do. I have seven days left for my visit to Earth and am not in my jurisdiction, nor is it my business, per my employer's instructions. Plus, solving the problem or the possibility of a third world war is complicated, way beyond what I am allowed to do here. The fact that this might happen is one of the reasons the Consortium is not interested in adding Earth to their membership. Surely the

CIA or the NSA knows about this, and the United States is prepared for a possible attack. How could they not know? Are they so overconfident or too arrogant to be on alert, not looking for possible enemies? Or did the Chinese pay off the right people or use blackmail on them from data they hacked from American personal computers?

This is not my problem. I have been looking forward to this visit for ten years, and meeting Anna is an extra blessing. I will follow the events in Russia for everyone's sake and help if I can, although it cannot become my problem. I am not sure if I should tell anyone, but not Anna or anyone right now; for me to scare and panic a lot of people would not help the situation. I need to check it out more. It's just too hard to believe.

The other puzzling thing would be the transporting of that many troops without anyone knowing. How could this be? Then there is feeding them. Is it possible the Chinese troops had passage to Russia by ship? Maybe that is the real reason the Chinese built their massive cargo ships. The same cargo ships used for Wal-Mart products. Ships that are capable of carrying almost forty thousand cars or nine hundred million cans could maybe carry one hundred thousand troops per trip. If you had forty ships traveling four thousand miles round trip at twenty miles per hour, thus able to make the trip three times a month, that's twelve million troops transported in a month. No one would notice, as there would be nothing strange about these massive ships working their way north toward California, just going a little farther up to the Bering Straits near Alaska. The tanks, helicopters, and trucks may have been hauled by rail overland through Russia. Maybe they are using Russian tanks. Maybe they are Chinese tanks that look like Russian tanks.

Go figure! I saw some of these ships as I passed over the straits. I wonder what they carried.

Anna is looking at me, wondering what I am thinking, probing my mind. She is learning fast, developing her telepathic skills, and she knows I am worried.

I respond, "No fair, taking my tricks and using them on me!" I laugh and tell her I will explain to her soon about a bizarre problem. For now we have a ship's tour to finish.

CHAPTER 13

THE CHINESE PREMIER AND HIS GENERAL CIA'S SECTION 58

At the same time, a large Chinese military jet is taking off from Moscow, a big Boeing modified to be a flying command ship, with a very sophisticated communications capacity. It is heavily armed. Several fighter jets are escorting it. Three Chinese generals and numerous support staff are on board, the plane heading for China to meet with the Chinese political leadership. All the critical people will be at this emergency meeting.

General Ling, the Chinese supreme commander, is currently talking to the Communist premier of the ruling Chinese party by a secure phone connection on board, saying, "We do not know what has happened to us, neither do the Russians. We were attacked, suffered serious casualties, maybe one hundred thousand hurt or dead in a matter of seconds, then it was gone. No trace of the attacker and not sure what happened or even what it was. Our guess, it's just some kind of huge military fighter jet. For sure it was much more extreme than any known aircraft. Not possible, yet it happened."

Premier Wu-Tong asks, "Have our troops been discovered by the United States? It should not be. It would be difficult for them to discover us with all our precautions. First of all we have paid off all the right technicians working with their surveillance equipment, the staff people and critical CIA management, too. We have also used blackmail and kidnapping to obtain cooperation. Plus Russia's space station is manipulating their satellite feeds after our hacking into their systems. Currently no one can fly recon over Russia without being shot down. Villages in Russia near the encampment have been evacuated, thus no one is there to spy on us."

General Ling continues, "Unlikely, yet maybe we have been discovered. If so our attack plans need to be triggered now, before the element of surprise is completely gone. Or worse, we will be attacked again and totally destroyed. What hit us we have little defense against. We could have been annihilated, millions of troops, and we are still vulnerable, just sitting there in one concentrated location. We need to move out, spread out. We have no clue where this thing came from or what it is or whether it will attack again, maybe tomorrow. We are vulnerable, and we just have guesswork."

Premier Wu-Tong responds, "You and your generals got us into this. You will give us a new military solution immediately, as you need to resolve this issue. Our plan was supposed to solve problems, not make them worse. Let me remind you, you are currently scheduled to attack the United States on August the first, with the ground and weather the most stable in Alaska and Canada. The trucks and tanks should be ready. General, as you know, the people of China need the rice and grain from the world's greatest farming area. The Midwest and Southern states are critical, as this farmland in the United States is vital to our feeding our 1.4 billion people. If they irresponsibly print currency to avoid paying their debt to us, it will destroy our ability to do business with them. We will lose millions of dollars in our loans to them, the cheap dollars in trade for our more valuable yen, deliberately done to cheat us. We would be foolish to ever do business with them again. Yet we need to buy their grain. We always are looking at possible starvation with our huge population. We will not let this happen."

The premier is getting excited, intense. In a louder voice, he says, "We also need their corn, pork, beef, coal, timber, aluminum, natural gas, and oil. We need their technology. We also need the United States to pay back our loans in full, not in mega-inflated dollars valued at half of what we loaned them. The United States has a small population, maybe 350 million people, yet monopolizes more food than they need. They have a small military in terms of actual troops, just a few divisions that are spread thin. They are a divided country and are poorly managed. Always with the left against the right, the political leaders can't make hard decisions. We have always said freedom and democracy do not work. The United States is a house of cards and will come apart easily. We also have plans to offer the president a chance to save his people. We will make him president for life for having his troops stand down, saving many American lives. It will be business as usual. Wall Street will be fine. Everyone will keep their jobs. We think he will take the offer. Of course the Congress will be eliminated, as will the Supreme Court."

The premier laughs, saying, "They will keep their fast food and movies. They all are spoiled by their wealth, which they don't deserve. Too much freedom, too much TV, too much Internet, and too much Facebook! We will save the country. You can do this, General. Get it done. Attack!"

The premier, in a low, threatening voice, says, "General, we anticipate a report from you within two days giving us your revised attack plan, with a new timeline and a new immediate attack date. You need to be back here in China with your officers, as you need to make your presentation to the entire leadership. You know the fate of China and the fate of the entire world will rest on our complete success. You need to be successful, or we all will suffer, you especially. Make arrangements to get here as soon as possible. Also, there is one more thing. As to your speculation, tell me, what is your real guesswork for the origination of this attacker? You must have some ideas."

General Ling hesitates. Then, in a low voice, he answers, "You don't want to hear this. You will scoff or just ignore me."

"General Ling, give me your thoughts immediately. I will decide their value."

"All right. Just between you and me, this situation is impossible. It could not have happened. We know there is nothing in this world that could do this, no known weapons or aircraft. Our intelligence gathering is excellent; we should know. Maybe the United States has a weapon we do not know about?"

Premier Wu-Tong quickly retorts, "If so, and if this was their weapon, then they know about us now. We have to move quickly if you are right. You need to attack soon, before August first, in a few days, maybe early next week."

The general continues, "Premier Wu-Tong, there is something else I should say, although it is difficult to mention. There is another logical explanation. It is strange for me to even think this, much less say it out loud, it is so bizarre. Premier, you may not want my guesswork, as weird as it sounds, and you are rational to ignore me or laugh at me. Maybe I am crazy, but there may be another answer. This ship or weapon might not be from this planet. It may be alien, something from *out there*, a far advanced weapon from outer space, off world. It travels at speeds we only dream about, so fast we can't see it. The other reason I say this is we do have some proof. It is because of the type of radiation measured from the tail thrust, fallout remnants on the ground surface underneath, material coming from this aircraft. The results are unknown on this planet, and there are no aircraft that use this fusion propulsion. Also, I do not think we have any real defense against it. We have real problems if it comes back. In fact everyone on Earth has an issue if this is true."

The premier does not respond. He is speechless, in total shock. Finally he whispers, "General, tell no one until we talk next. We cannot turn back now; we are beyond that point. Pray that you are wrong."

＊⊷ ⊶＊

The CIA headquarters in Langley, Virginia, is a big place, not really a place of laughter; many serious people work there, with many heavy responsibilities. At this moment, John Jacobs, chief of Section 58 on the third floor, west wing, has a department of six people in a state of confusion, including himself. He is in his office looking out on the parking lot, trying to mentally sort this out.

He thinks, *Some real ET activity has been verified.* The first verified report came from a navy aircraft carrier that has confirmation from photos from a nose camera of an F-16. One of their planes ran upon a real UFO off the South American Pacific coast, just over the Mexican border. The video shows an aircraft that looks really big and weird, not something ever seen on Earth, moving very fast. They think it's a good possibility it is extraterrestrial. No question, inspecting the film, it is an alien aircraft. They thought Section 58 should know about it, as they are the experts on extraterrestrials, and their function is to evaluate all possible UFO contacts. This is not business as usual. The navy thinks this is the real thing. They also saw something big coming in a couple of nights ago from outer space. They're saying there could be real issues. *It's time to focus.* He thinks. *This may be a national security threat.*

John Jacobs is a careful man, yet he is thinking since there is real evidence, what does he do? As he has done many times before, he gazes out of his office window, thoughtful, contemplating. The US Air Force has also reported images captured: UFO photos, pilot visual reports, and infrared heat scans plus satellite warning alerts. Some showing something hitting the Earth's atmosphere hard, penetrating and traveling really fast, images immediately captured by lots of military posts all over the world. Scientists have reported strange images, too. The NSA and NASA have it all recorded. They are saying the real wake-up call is the radiation—lots of nuclear evidence, very hot and a lot of it, all coming from this UFO, or maybe more than one. Everybody, including the president, wants a report...*from me, now!*

He remembers the most wacky part of this: as everyone is also curious about the second NASA report. That NASA scanners also picked up a very sophisticated laser-type beam, like a radio wave yet much faster, coming from outer space, at least six hundred thousand miles away. It is super sophisticated, advanced beyond our wildest dreams. The waves come from an object moving away at a high velocity. It then patched into a cell-phone tower, which is impossible; then there was a four-minute phone conversation at an American's home, a Senator Jordan's house in Richmond, Virginia. This is quite impossible; however, after much investigation, looking at satellite communications, looking at possible other alternatives, even checking with other countries, plus checking the cell-phone companies, it is not only possible; it happened.

He thinks, *It actually has happened. It is confirmed!* It seems to be an ET communication from some kind of spacecraft. This also has been given to Section 58 to figure out what it is and where it came from.

John is feeling both terrified and ecstatic; he is thinking he might screw this up, yet he's happy he will be taken seriously now. No more jokes about his "Ghostbusters department." Lots of good stuff is happening now. The lighting up of half the world

at night is a real mind bender, and then the sightings of a supersonic craft blasting across the Pacific helped a lot. Not illusions;
all confirmed. Calls were still coming in from other countries.
Some of the calls have come from people who are frightened,
certainly not bogus; this is real to them. Some of these things
have happened before, in years past. Nothing ever came of it.
Finally maybe there is a chance at the real thing. Yes…could it
really happen? A real alien contact!

The other strange thing is they have the phone conversation
on tape, caught as part of an FBI wiretap on the senator's phone.
The FBI has been investigating the senator for some time regarding his unusual financial arrangements. He has large amounts of
money and stock in an offshore captive that sometimes is funded
by First Excalibur Bank, an international bank closely linked to
Iran. The bank also is rumored to launder money for organized
crime. The problem with the senator comes from his pushing to
allow two large airlines to merge, mostly financed by Excalibur.
The silent ownership of the bank seems to be Iran. He also has a
huge block of stock in each airline. It seems to be too convenient
for the possibility of letting Iran control one huge airline flying
in and out of the United States and other Western countries. If
you use your imagination, it does not make for sleeping well at
night. Unfortunately the FBI has little information or they are
not forthcoming. However you look at it, it doesn't look good for
the senator. He also has some real dangerous friends, not the
kind of people you cross.

This phone conversation apparently took place between
Anna Summers and her mother, the senator's second wife. Anna
is his stepdaughter, and they are close, per the FBI. She made
the call from six hundred thousand or so miles away—from deep
space—to her mother to say she was going to be late arriving
home.

I guess so, thinks John. *She is heading in the wrong direction, leaving our planet at a very fast speed, three times the distance from the moon.* Did aliens abduct her? Or maybe this is a Hollywood publicity stunt. Anna is a rather popular movie star, successful, maybe up for an Academy Award. Maybe she rigged this somehow. How crazy is this? However, it is what it is. *I guess we need to find out everything we can find out about Anna and where she is.*

John hears a knock, and the door of his office open; he pauses, looks, sees his staff assistant, and smiles. He is always glad to see her. She has helped him so many times, always has his back.

He welcomes her with a big smile, "Amanda, I wondered what happened to you. Do you have the daily briefing report? Thank you for putting up with me lately. I know I have been a little intense!"

She laughs and says, "Yes, John, I have your report, just like every day at this time, and good to see you, too. Let me know if you need some help on your big report; I have some time."

He laughs, too, says, "You will be the first on my list."

She has known him a long time. She is amused as she has never seen him so excited. All this ET activity has him pacing back and forth in front of his only window, overlooking the parking lot. She is happy to work for him. He loves his work, and he is a true patriot. She drops off his daily briefing report, leaves it on his desk, and picks up his outgoing mail and his empty coffee cups. She watches him for a few seconds to see if he needs to talk to her.

She thinks about how all those who know John Jacobs know he is a serious man yet sort of weird. He is made fun of behind his back, ridiculed for his nerd status and laughed at for his ET views. John thinks there is an alien behind every bush. He has raised up the announcement of aliens being here so many times that he has no credibility with the White House or many in the science community. He is a true believer. And he is right this time. She is sure of it. She knows he is proud to be the section chief of the ultra top-secret Section 58, the watchdogs for ETs. He is responsible for investigating and defending the United States from extraterrestrials. These are the aliens, as in other-worldly beings—yes, like in *War of the Worlds*. Finally he will be respected. Amanda is so happy he may finally see some success. She smiles and closes the door as she leaves.

John hears the door shut and wonders what Amanda thinks of him; he is proud of her; hopefully she feels the same. He is grateful for all of this, finally after all these years, thinking they both may have their moment in the sun. This might a chance to learn from an advanced civilization, another species. His life could be validated, the right man at the right time, and he con-templates: *I am fifty years old, happily married, with five great kids, not expecting to be exceptional or certainly not famous or anything other than a bureaucrat. I am glad to have this job, glad to be married to a woman I love. I have been lucky in my life. It has always been my passion to make the first ET contact. However, I never thought it could happen. Never in this lifetime. Yet now I might be in the middle of it.*

Just thinking about how dangerous this might become for ev-eryone scares him; it's a real possible threat, not only to him but also to the whole world. It is hard to comprehend.

Right at this moment, John is also starting to have doubts. Could this be more than what he can handle? How many people could be hurt if he fails? He may be thrust into something really perilous and incredible, and he needs to give it everything he has in him. *My marine training needs to kick in. I have to do this right for family and country!* Still, it is normal to be really scared right now, and he feels it; he is scared. What if they really are hostile aliens with advanced weapons? If he were captured? John will be glad to go home tonight; he needs to share all this with his wife, top secret or not. She will help him figure it all out.

Driving home, he is having awful butterflies in his stomach, causing cold sweat and nausea. After dinner—he didn't eat much—and after the kids are in bed, John and his wife sit down at the kitchen table. He gives her a glass of wine, her favorite, and tells her they need to talk.

He declares, "Judy, I have a real problem. I can tell you only part of it because it is severely classified."

He tells her as much as he thinks he can, careful about the top-secret classification, as she knows he took an oath, and he does not want to freak her out. He simply tells her that for the first time in his life, he feels afraid and maybe will not be able solve a big work issue. She has to worry about the kids, and he knows she also worries about him. He does not want this or to talk about it too much, as it might panic both of them. He knows she sees it. He tells her he does not want to worry her. She listens, smiles, and goes over to him to give him a hug, trying to reassure him. She kisses his cheek and tells him to take one step at a time. She tells him many people are part of any crisis management; he is never alone. He can do it. He is a good man, and she loves him.

He feels better. He thinks, *Thank God for Judy.*

Driving to work the next day, he rethinks the whole thing. He and his section have always believed in extraterrestrials. They know it is just a matter of time before a visit, and all experts say it will not go well for the human race. This does not have to be true, as the ETs might be friendly. If they are talking to Anna Summers and maybe the senator's wife, how bad can it be?

If so, maybe there is an alien ship with Anna on board, and she just called her mother, who just happens to be a US senator's wife. It is a friendly conversation. Just crazy, yet why not? Or it has to be some weird explanation, can't really be what it looks like. Impossible. *When I tell the guys at the White House, they'll think I've finally lost it.* Naturally they will have a good laugh at John's expense.

CHAPTER 14

TOUR OF THE *CYCLONE* AND SOLAR SYSTEM

I look at Anna and say, "We need to head for the control room, the captain's bridge. Just follow me. You need to use the handrails to push yourself through the ship's passage tunnels, as you cannot walk in this mostly weightless world. There is much to learn. Going to the bathroom is one challenge for you; eating is another."

I smile, excited, "Anna, you may have never had the opportunity to learn so much so quickly. I am sorry. I know you did not plan for this when you got up this morning. I also know I need to get you home within two or three days. We do have enough time to show you the sights, truly fantastic and worth seeing, and a freak opportunity for you to see the Earth's solar system! I am delighted to show you all of it or just part, depending on how much time you have available."

Continuing, "The planets are easy to reach for sure within this solar system. Other stars and their planets are much farther. Maybe someday when we have more time, we can also beat a path to Alpha Centauri, the nearest star system to this one. To reach Mars we have about fifty-five million miles to cover, going on to Jupiter, another 350 million miles, then Saturn at 450 million more miles, next Uranus, Neptune, and Pluto, or thirty-five hundred million more miles. You don't want to know how far we need to go to make Alpha Centauri. The Proxima Centauri is twenty-four trillion miles away, and we need more than a couple of days. Needless to say, we will be using all eight cylinders to reach the outer layers of this solar system. What are you up for?"

Anna looks at me, a puzzled expression on her face, and says, "Henry, this is a little bit overwhelming. I have no clue what I want to do. I never thought I would have these kinds of options and am still not sure I am not dreaming all this. I'm game for whatever you want to do or whatever you want to show me. I have only a couple of free days."

I beam. "Anna, I am going to show you some remarkable things, whatever we can squeeze into forty-eight hours. Let's go for it! We'll light up the afterburners. Let's check out Mars, maybe Jupiter, Saturn for sure! You'll be impressed by what the *Cyclone* can do. Ask anything you want, and be prepared to be delighted. No person on Earth has ever seen what you will see. You will have stories you will want to tell."

Intently looking at Anna, I pause, thinking and knowing I need to warn her, and then continuing, "This is critical. A problem I just realized. Promise me, this all stays between you and me. It is dangerous for you to ever talk about me or this trip. It could be life threating for you. I think you understand?"

Anna looks back, bewildered but finally nods her head and says, "Yes, I think I understand. It's the alien thing?"

"Yes, it is the alien thing," I respond.

We continue to make our way up through the ship, pulling and pushing off the handles, gliding easily. I am watching Anna slowly getting the hang of the free-float, which is not easy, but she adapts quickly. She is a good athlete. She makes it work for herself. She is actually graceful and looks incredible. I am just now realizing how really gorgeous she is, truly a stunning woman. This is the only human female who has ever been on the *Cyclone.* I wonder what the *Cyclone* thinks of this. The telepathic response is immediate, and I have to laugh. The *Cyclone* really likes Anna, maybe thinks she is a kindred spirit. I smile at her, feeling pleased.

Anna looks back at me, knows I laughed, and looks at me, responding with a smile, "You cannot hide your laughs, as I am telepathic with you, or did you forget? Are you laughing at me? Remember, I am new at this, just learning the ropes."

I respond with a chuckle and say, "No, I was not laughing at you. I am in total admiration. You're very graceful when you move, and I'm glad you cannot read all my thoughts. I was thinking you are really a beautiful woman—maybe the best-looking woman I have ever seen."

Anna is embarrassed. "I don't know what to say to you, Mr. Starman, except thank you. I have a feeling you have not seen many women while being locked up here in this ship. I am still glad you approve." She smiles. "I have questions: where are we going, and how big is this ship? Is there a ladies' room? Do we get something to eat? What do you do for fun on board? Is there an activities director? Do I get my own bedroom, or are we roommates? Are there movies? And, by the way, you owe me an explanation about all of this. This is not the usual kind of job description. Do they give you a paycheck?"

I can feel the humor and warmth coming from her, and it really makes me feel good. It brings back memories of my youth, at home with my family, laughing and kidding one another. I can remember how wonderful those days were.

I look at Anna seriously, then smile, saying, "All are good questions. Before we talk about it, I need to know your specific plans this week. Where do you need to be and when? When do you have to get back to your parents', the exact time back to Earth?

Anna says, "I need to be in London in six days for the premiere of my movie—a really important obligation for me—then back at my home in LA in about eight days. So I could spend two days with you here, a couple of days or more with my parents, then head to London for a day and then go back to LA. By the way, my plans include you, as I want you to come meet my parents and stay with us at the farm. You will love it if you like trees, fresh air, green grass, rolling fields, and horses. I can cook for us. I am a great cook. We will both have some R-and-R time."

Anna beams, looking at me. "Are you not on R and R, coming from some galaxy out there in the universe to be back home for vacation?" Laughing, she says, "I'm more perceptive than you think, and yes, I do know you are beyond my reality as I know it. Maybe it's all a weird delusion and I will wake up. I don't care. I still want to spend time with you and find out all you can tell me about your life. I know you are not of this planet, and I feel fine with that, not sure exactly why. Please tell me everything possible: who you are, where you come from, the works!"

Looking away, thinking, then looking back at Anna, I say, "You will have it all, more than you want is my guess. Let's go up to the captain's bridge, settle in, and have something to drink, and I will start from the beginning. Remember, what I tell you and what you see is never to be repeated. If what is happening to you became known and believed, especially by your government or your military, it could be harsh for you."

Anna just stares at me. "Henry, I know, and I will be fine. I keep secrets. Plus, no one would believe me."

We now make our way up the main tunnel, looks like a hallway ten feet wide, all softly lit, reflecting off the dull silver walls. We pass crew members, and they acknowledge me as usual, with our common salutation: "*Calabra*," which means, "May the divine light embrace and guide you." I explain to Anna what it means, as it refers to God's light. It could be compared to an Earth person saying, "God bless you" or "Godspeed."

The crew continues to greet us.

"Good to have you back, Admiral."

"Captain, how was Earth?"

"Glad to meet you. Calabra, Anna."

"Welcome aboard!"

I introduce Anna as much as possible. She is astounded, as none of the crew members are human. Some look similar to humans, as they are my synthetic clones, part of the military brigade, who are very human in appearance, although most of the ship's crew are aliens from various worlds. I think that none are frightening to look at, yet maybe a little strange for Anna. For me they are just different.

Universe citizens come in all shapes, colors, and sizes, a lot of variety, yet I think all look sophisticated and intelligent. None look like monsters. All have eyes of some kind, maybe perception radar points like eyes, and some are more attractive than others. Yet each one is priceless, mentally brilliant, with amazing life stories and interesting backgrounds. Anna says thanks to each, and with every welcome greeting, she smiles a warm smile and acts pleased about the greetings and introductions. I am really proud of this crew. I know each of them well; they're all part of this great ship. Anna has adapted, too, and does not act shocked or afraid—maybe a little pale, yet she is into it. I am thankful.

As we make our way, I explain to Anna that we have already traveled about ten million miles since we left Earth. I tell her about the *Cyclone*'s propulsion using hydrogen fusion or nuclear energy. The *Cyclone* is currently running at a slow speed, probably half the speed of light, about 350 million miles an hour. I need to kick it up a couple of notches if we are to see this solar system in our time frame. I explain to her the *Cyclone* uses three propulsion systems in three stages: hydrogen fusion rockets, external pulsed plasma propulsion, and a dark-energy hyperdrive. The hyperdrive uses massive negative dark-energy creation, which is also the same energy that gives the *Cyclone* its antigravity capabilities. For example, we use it when traveling on planets with heavy gravity issues, allowing us to hover or float in midair. It also takes immense energy to travel effectively for just short distances in space, as we need to be running about seven hundred million miles an hour, or just under light speed, which can be done if carefully navigated.

Anna asks, "Is this all dangerous? Is the speed an issue?"

I smile. "Anna, you just asked two very large questions, which means you are going to get your first tutorial session on starship travel; please stop me when you have had enough.

"Yes, starship travel is dangerous, very much so, to answer your first question about the danger, which is constant, every second a problem. One big difficulty, there is no atmosphere. It is a vacuum. The universe is not easy, much more than just dangerous. Most critical to us, it is a hostile environment for all living creatures, especially if you are human, as you are made of carbon, hydrogen, and water. It is not a forgiving place; you either freeze or evaporate in the heat. Yet we have many tools, and we have the technology to resolve most issues. As long as we are in this ship, it protects us or is close enough to enclose us with shields. Or by using our protective suits outside the ship, we can survive. Not a chance otherwise. First of all, the temperatures are extreme both ways, very hot or very cold depending on the time and place. The human body can't survive either. Then the radiation from all the stars, meaning all suns in the universe, is off the charts at times, which means certain death. The Earth's sun supplies lots of radiation, and it is a hot place, too. The sun's core temperature averages about 5,770,000 degrees—hell-storm hot!"

Continuing, I say, "There are a lot of stars, trillions of them in this galaxy alone. If you took every grain of sand on Earth and multiplied it by one million, it would be less than the number of stars in the universe. Yet, amazingly enough, the total physical mass of all entities in the galaxies is only two percent of the universe. The universe is mostly empty with no safety net. *There is a lot of nothing. There are no lifeguards to protect you.*"

"Anna, as you know, outer space is a vacuum, has no air pressure, which also makes it impossible to survive without a suit; death is quick, within ninety seconds. Your body decompresses; the liquids and gas in your body simply vaporize, giving you about ten seconds of consciousness. In addition, as there is no air to breathe, there is the suffocation problem. There is also no gravity, thus no control of your movements without some kind of propulsion, thus you drift off, maybe pulled into some kind of gravity field. One thing that might be interesting to you is there is an odor in space. You can't smell it until you are back on board; it comes from the dust on the suits. It smells like a badly burned steak or welding fumes. The dust is composed of burned carbon particles, probably stardust left over from the Big Bang. There is also no sound in space because there is no air, which is needed to have sound. There is total silence out there, only the sound of you breathing."

"You asked about our speed or velocity being an issue. Let me explain. Because of the long distances, a critical hazard of starship travel is the massive speed needed. Hitting things becomes a problem. We need a shield to deflect the objects we hit, as we are going at millions of miles per hour. These objects can be real starship killers, even small ones, some just the size of a coin. We need and have a bumper, so to speak."

"The *Cyclone* has been building a front shield bumper in the last two hours, starting as soon as we left the Earth's surface. The ship uses water with a synthetic mineral, making a type of ice mixture that becomes frozen hard, sort of like an asteroid surface, which is mostly ice. We do so by creating a bumper that looks like a long funnel torpedo made of ice. Our spraying out ice crystals for miles in front of us creates it, going on constantly until we are completely encased in ice. These ice crystals are manufactured internally in the front hull's broad spear. The crystals are ejected forward out the nose, entering space at 350 degrees below zero. No fluid will exist in space, as it vaporizes instantly; yet ice, or water in solid form, is compatible. It makes an efficient practical bumper for the *Cyclone,* and when it's not needed it is easy to shed—just warm it up. When it returns to liquid, it vaporizes into space and is simply gone."

Continuing, I said, "The only exception is when we are traveling hot, close to a Sun, then we use our colossal solar shields, made from our security grids, created by the energy from the same Sun we are passing, the one creating the heat.

"When we are iced up, we look strange, as we end up having a fifty-mile, or longer, pointed ice shield, in the shape of a funneled spear in front of us. It makes us look like a miles-long spaceship or a very long, slender asteroid. The *Cyclone*'s navigational pilot keeps us from hitting big things. However, when traveling at high speeds we will hit small things hard and fast. The ice shield deflects and absorbs the shock, resulting in a safe journey for us.

"Another real problem for the *Cyclone* is not the speeding up but the slowing down. It takes millions of miles to get the speed up. It also takes millions of miles to bring it back down, which is always an issue. We have many times used the gravity of large passing planets to slow us down."

"Building speed is a big deal. Usually the *Cyclone* starts its acceleration progression by shooting forward on billions of horsepower from the fusion rockets, the blasting force produced by controlled nuclear explosions. It creates a powerful pure-white thrusting fire stream that is thirty-six thousand degrees—nuclear hot—with a dangerous tail four thousand miles long behind us, sometimes longer. We are building speed, and then the plasma generators hit out. They fire our nuclear laser particle weapons backward, releasing explosions equal to thousands of nuclear bombs. This shoots back additional blinding light waves, brighter than the sun, a megaforce tail maybe five thousand miles long, thrusting backward, doubling the *Cyclone*'s forward speed."

"The last jolt of propulsion forward is our negative-gravity drive, a hyperdrive using gravitons, the same energy particles that create black holes. Using extreme gravity, we compress atoms tighter and tighter, resulting in the creation of titanic high temperatures, causing atoms to fuse together and releasing massive amounts of energy. We will also bend space with extreme gravity using the extreme energy we created. We are creating a deviation, a black-hole corridor in space, a ripple that we slide through, then no fire tail, no light or sound. The ship is invisible at such enormous speeds, much faster than light. To oversimplify the concept, bending space is like the reaction you get when you put two magnets together positive to positive, impossible to hold together. They strongly repel each other. The *Cyclone* uses gravity in the same way but on a massive scale to force a bend in the dimension of space."

Anna has a funny look on her face. "I don't understand. How do you travel faster than the speed of light? My understanding from my college physics class is it is impossible, as the weight increases dramatically approaching light speed for all objects. Time can also change."

"Anna, you're sort of right. The speed of light can be nature's speed limit. The key is energy. Gravity is God's energy machine. Across the universe all mass is moving, organized by the laws of gravity, much of it at massive velocities. The universe uses mammoth amounts of energy, yet amazingly enough, it is in mathematical equilibrium. We alter that equilibrium, creating negative-gravity energy. That power changes the rules, so we can open corridors. This is a simplified answer."

Anna does not look convinced, more like confused.

Continuing, explaining further, I say, "OK, I admit I'm not much of a teacher. It's not easy to understand. We overcome inertia with the forces of this negative gravity, pulled forward by the massive energy from our dark-energy drive, where we actually alter gravity, or your college concept of weight. We use the gravity as the gravitons are charged or the defined weight of it is actually reversed. Then, by using this massive infinite energy, we can travel faster than the speed of light, first by using the progressive acceleration then also, at the same time, creating a black-hole corridor or a created path, as I said, by punching a hole in the fabric of space. This hole has no light, as light particles are also sucked in by the gravity, and is also free of objects we might collide with, the objects there are reduced to molecules, reduced by the enormous gravity in the hole and our destruction avoided. The result is we travel or develop an aggregate speed of billions of miles per hour; the longer our distance, the faster our speed. We also use the measurement of the length of time from the beginning of our trip to the actual time traveled rather than current time at the end location, thus the real length of the voyage. There can be time-gap adjustment or an alternate-reality time, to adapt to the current time at our destination. Time can be an issue. Maybe think of it as complicated jet lag. It's mind-blowing, but traveling on really long-distance trips could have a finish time before the time we started, achieved at our destination point."

Anna asks, "What about this trip?"

"Not a problem on short trips. For example, the nearest star to Earth, other than the sun, is Alpha Centauri, which is twenty-four trillion miles away. Without the dark-energy drive, it would take us four and a half years to get there traveling at light speed. By using all three propulsion drives in stages, finally in the gravity drive, we can do it in sixty-six days. We use another day to loop back slowing down, then some time to look around. Finally we head home, taking the same trip back in the same sixty-six days."

"Anna, it is extraordinary. Even after many times, I am always thrilled at the startup of the first stage, then the escalation of speed. First there is a growl, as the engines warm up, then turning into a thunderous roar, the terrific vibration, the first surge, the earsplitting explosions, the blinding light. Then there is a surge again. Finally, you feel no sensation of speed. With the blackout and total silence, we are now between dimensions of time and space using the hyperdrive."

Anna and I have finally made it to the captain's bridge, and she seems disappointed as she looks around. I surprise her as I light up the 360-degree visuals, and, as planned, Mars is right in front of us, coming close. I execute a low-altitude flyby, making her feel like ducking. It is totally spectacular. We see the unending red, rocky desert-looking terrains, sky-high mountains, old riverbeds and miles deep canyons or even larger craters, a massive unending horizon, a dramatic sunset with gigantic red dust storms below. The planet is impressive in terrain and color, magnificent, and the feeling of speed is terrific as we eat up the surface below.

Anna is impressed, maybe awestruck, trying to see it all, excited by this massive planet she has never seen, enthralled that she is actually seeing a vision no human eye has ever seen in person, and amazed by the velocity of our flight.

Traveling thirty-eight thousand miles per hour, we are in the middle of it, flying close enough to make it easy to see everything, even if fleetingly. Anna's eyes get larger, and I can see the sight amazes her.

I explain, "The atmosphere, or air, is thin here, mostly carbon dioxide. There isn't much friction, which allows us great speed without turbulence. Mars is small, about half the size of Earth, the gravity about half, too. At this speed we will soon be beyond

Mars and heading for this solar system's biggest boy: the massive Jupiter. It is twelve times bigger than Earth. We are maybe four or five hours away from it."

Anna is deep in thought, trying to take all this in, impressed by everything, maybe even entranced. Yet she still feels some real fear. Who has built this ship? Not humans. Aliens? She thinks she could be in trouble. The starship thing is truly overwhelming. She is also thinking she is crazy to be here. How could this be happening to her? She feels the need to reassure herself, to think positive thoughts: *Life has always put me in the limelight. In the past I've been given amazing opportunities. I have always felt ready for anything, always confident in my strength, and I have always been smart enough to achieve success.*

She again feels overpowering anxiety, and then the fear is there. Then she starts to panic, her stomach flutters, and she thinks, *This is more than anything I could have ever imagined, maybe more than my capacity can handle. Maybe much more than my confidence will carry. Can I do this? Who is Henry really? Should I be doing this? How much trouble can I get into? A bunch!*

She recalls moving through the tunnel, meeting one of my soldier clones, friendly to her, looking like me in an odd way. She could communicate using telepathy, talking about the ship, saying hello, all clear as day. Yet he did not feel human, not like me. He was alien. She could just feel the difference. It frightened her. Nothing had ever prepared her for this, and she felt sick to her stomach. All of it is incomprehensible when she thinks about it. *No one on Earth knows I'm here. No one on Earth has done this. I've made contact with an alien civilization. Damn, I think I am in real trouble!*

Yet Henry is amazing, she thinks. He is some kind of superman, a creature from the heavens and way beyond her capacity to understand: his life, the *Cyclone,* the visit here from out there, coming from outer space, coming from other alien worlds. The universe is here now. It is all magic, some kind of dream world. All hard to take in, yet life will never be the same for her. She is sure of that; also there will be big changes for every man and woman on Earth. Henry does not realize it yet. There is no turning back for him. She knows his life will not be the same, either; she is absolutely certain. She can feel it. *There is no going back for me. I need to face this.*

She thinks of Henry, his smile, his laugh, and his kind eyes, which makes her feel better. Now calmer, the stomach flutters are gone, too.

She knows she needs to see everything. It seems really important to Henry for her to see his life. All of this is astonishing. Seeing other planets in this solar system is impossible, yet here she is. Everything seems so close and so clear; colors are so vivid. Looking farther into space, the night stars look as if she can touch them.

I am motioning her toward the ship's captain's chairs in front of the screens. There are several she could use; two are a little smaller, build for a petite frame.

She looks at me and thinks, *How do you sit in these chairs?*

My eyes are smiling, looking at Anna, trying to sit in the weird ship seats, confused. I am not able to contain my amusement and start laughing. She is holding on to the chair, floating above it. She can't figure out how to sit in it with no gravity. The seat is flexible and will automatically contour itself to Anna's body, a perfect fit. I motion how to pull into the seat, and I tell her the chair does the work.

"Just let it help you," I say. "It will also automatically wrap you with featherlight, silklike strap tethers and then will hold you in comfortably."

I think, *It is hard not to enjoy every minute with Anna. To be with such a beautiful, charming woman is a delight and a blessing.* Feeling a wave of gratitude, I say a quick prayer of thanks.

As she looks out into the vastness of the universe, up on the ship's screens, she is feeling overwhelmed again. She now looks at Henry with a homesick look on her face. She feels the concern and the awful anxiety about being so far from Earth.

She inquires, "Henry, where is the Earth? Can we still see it?"

I smile again. "You can still see or make out Earth off in the distance. It looks tiny and somewhat insignificant, just a bright bluish light point now. Yet look at it magnified. It is still a colorful blue and white. We will be back there soon. Not to worry, Anna. I feel your fear, I know you are homesick, and you will be fine. You are capable of great feats, and you are more than ready for this."

I highlight Earth's location on the screens for Anna, pointing to it, enlarging it, as it is hard to see at 418 million miles away.

She smiles.

CHAPTER 15

ANNA

"Anna, I need to introduce you to G-BE, F-LA, M-HO, and K-HO, you might say the *Cyclone*'s computers, although they are really ancient beings, the brains of the ship, and my very good friends, like very old uncles. Please don't be shocked, as you might scare them; they have never met a human woman in real life, although they know the concept and know you by reputation. They are not what you are used to in your expectation of a computer." I laugh. "First of all they can be emotional at times and opinionated. You can talk to them using telepathy, as they are telepathic; however, they will not talk until you do."

Anna is looking around for them. I call for them, and then they materialize out of thin air, really dazzling, showing off. Each is a cloud of a billion colored-light pinpoints, like fireworks without explosions, G-BE in front, F-LA and K-HO to the left side, and M-HO on Anna's right, floating silently, startling her into a big yelp.

I say, "Anna, sorry, I was not sure how to describe them. They are pure energy, magical, like a big network of electric neurons connected. However, you cannot see the connections, as there are billions of them so tiny you would not know they are there.

All four are integrated, making them the sum of their parts. They are really one even if separated, kind of like the frontal lobes of your brain, left and right yet one brain. Please tell them about yourself, and they will return the favor. I know they already like you."

Anna is a little bewildered, not sure what to say. She looks at them, smiles, and says, "I am Anna Summers and glad to meet you. I think I have it right. You are G-BE, F-LA, M-HO, and K-HO. You are not what I expected, and I am really impressed. I am amazed you operate the *Cyclone*. I am no expert at this—it's a first-time experience for me. I just got up this morning thinking it was another same old normal day on Earth, and here I am in deep space, checking out the solar system. And now I am looking at four beings that look like computer angels without wings and are telepathic, yet surprisingly enough I can now be telepathic, too, and we are going to have a telepathic conversation."

Anna laughs. "Who would think this could happen? Out of curiosity, I have to ask, do you guys have families, babies, like little computers maybe? Do you ever leave the ship? How old are you?"

There is a long pause, no response.

I look at her. "Anna, this will be a little strange for you. They process information and events differently from a human. I think before they will open up to you, they need to know who you are. They crave your personal data; you are then official in their memory banks. You are of great interest to them, as you are a female me, part of my species, and you also can reproduce. By the way, they know something about you, as we have integrated communications; or, simply put, they hear my thoughts, and I hear theirs, too. We are sort of like kindred spirits.

"They are also part of my command structure, keeping track of me, operating as my support staff, and following my commands, sometimes offering me really good advice. To answer your questions: actually they do reproduce but not like we do. They just clone another like themselves, create synthetic neurons, energize it, and feed it with data, lots of it. They are thousands of years old; not sure who originally built them, and they never leave the ship. I am not sure they can survive off ship. They do not know, either, as they have never left the ship; they receive their energy from it. The *Cyclone* is very old, too, although updated. It has been around awhile, I think for many, many centuries."

Anna looks at each of them and nervously says, "All right, to start out, I am a twenty-eight-year-old female, born in the United States, just a young thing, no boyfriends, as I am too dedicated to my career, and I love what I do. I am an actress, as you may know. I am hoping to achieve great success in my field, an Academy Award maybe. My stepfather is Senator Sam Jordan; my mother is Linda Summers Jordan; and my biological father is Mike Summers, who is also an actor. I have a younger half sister I love dearly, Nikki Jordan.

"My birth father has not had much success in his life, drinking too much when things went poorly and now working as a waiter in a fancy restaurant in Chicago. My fame has helped him, and I bought him a condo in downtown Chicago, which he is ecstatic about, not thinking he would ever have a place to live other than a cheap apartment. The restaurant makes a big deal out of him because of me, and I stop and eat there when I am in Chicago. They have my photos on the walls all over the restaurant. They are my biggest fan club. The food is wonderful. I am taking Henry there when we are back on Earth.

"I also have a charity foundation I am very proud of. I set it up to help support children born with no homes—kids not in foster care, just on the streets. We supply a safe place to stay, meals, and guidance. It never has enough money; it's a constant challenge. There is a lot of suffering on planet Earth. Maybe I can get a contribution from you guys. Still not sure who everyone is here or where you come from and really not sure I want to know.

"My favorite hobbies are many: reading, as I love books; cooking, as I love to have dinner parties; and all outdoor sports, such as horseback riding, tennis, swimming, boating, skiing, and running. I like to dance, too, and I love music.

"I live in LA, or Los Angeles, California. Maybe you've been there. I have a place there on the ocean, a large estate. It's beautiful. I love it. I also spend time at my parents' farm in Richmond, Virginia, a great place. I ride my horse. I also run many miles on the country roads. I am a real competition runner, too; I have competed in several charity marathons, and though I actually never won, I bring publicity to the events, as I am a celebrity. You probably don't understand the concept of being a movie star."

"On Earth people are slightly crazy, and they follow my every move because I have been in a couple of movies. Guys take photos of me everywhere and sell them; newspapers write about me. I have even met the president of the United States. What's hard to understand is I have done nothing to be worthy of the fame, yet it is fun, and I get free tickets to everything. The downside of it is the real crazy people I meet, and then I have to have security people to protect me. Maybe you could help me on the security stuff, some ideas. I bet you have real humdingers, some *out-of-this-world* stuff."

Anna breaks out laughing and looks at me. I can't help it; I start laughing, too.

G-BE, F-LA, M-HO, and K-HO start talking all at once, thanking her for her background data, asking Anna if she wants to know more about the *Cyclone* and where we come from, maybe more about our home planet and the rest of the universe we cover, maybe also about the Consortium of Civilizations, about my function, who I am in the whole plan and how civilizations throughout the universe depend on me. Anna's head is spinning as all this information starts downloading into her brain telepathically; I feel her alarm, and I soothe her with a happy thought: my memory of her sister meeting me, her smile. I share it with Anna. It helps her, and I feel a thank you coming from her.

Anna then learns about the part of the universe we know. Not all the universe is known. And she hears about the Consortium. She learns about me, even the World War II stuff, although I was not excited about her learning my real age versus the age of this body. G-BE, F-LA, M-HO, and K-HO are surprisingly forthcoming, and I have no idea why. Actually I think it is overkill on their part, and they know I am not that pleased with them for giving so much detail since it is overwhelming to Anna.

They go into the immensity of space, the galaxies, the planets where life exists and doesn't exist, the political structure in my world, the overall leadership, and my role. They tell her we are from the world called KA*AM, which is the English translation, and it is 1,758 trillion miles from Earth. She learns about the clone soldiers, the starships, the military guardianship, the Consortium's laws of the universe, and the elders, my bosses. They explain the committee of elders, guys thousands of years old who lead our part of the universe, more or less, what we know about anyway. It's a big place. They even tell her about Gabriel, my very good friend, my mentor, whom I report to, one of the head guys in the Consortium. They explain Gabriel has been like a father to me and helped me through the years when things did not go as well. He was there to see me through it. To my surprise they also say Gabriel will probably want to meet her.

I am not sure how Anna will take some of this information. There have been some real enemies through the years, dangerous beyond comprehension, and I think they were all evil, or at the very least I can say they did terrible things to a lot of beings, made a lot of lives miserable. Of course I think they deserve what they received from me, and thankfully I can say they are all dead, or most of them are not around anymore to cause trouble. Yet still a few are out there, still doing terrible crimes. Unfortunately my old friends explain my role in detail to Anna—the policeman thing, the commander of the entire Consortium's military, the guy who has lots of responsibilities and challenges.

I am starting to understand F-LA, G-BE, M-HO, and K-HO; they are either recruiting her or warning her off. I guess they sense a female of my species who is interested in me, and they are giving her the whole story. They know I am not happy with their performance, and they start to apologize to me without Anna knowing they are concerned about my feelings.

Fortunately Anna cannot handle the information download anymore, looks at me, and shakes her head. She says she is too tired to receive any more information, truly overwhelmed and dazed from all of it.

She pronounces, "I am hungry! I have go to the bathroom. I'm tired. And what time is it?"

CHAPTER 16

DAY THREE

"Anna, I am sorry for all of this. I know it's too much for one sitting, and you must be starved. It has been a really long day, as in Earth time, it is three in the morning now." I am thinking, *Day three for me.* "Please follow me. We have a galley, and they can fix you anything you want, including Earth food. I changed the menu years ago, could not stand the stuff they called food. This is better, although maybe not perfect. As for the bathroom thing, you can use my facilities off my cabin. Since I have lived here for years, I am used to it, not sure if you will feel the same about it. You may not like it."

She looks at me with an odd expression. Surprisingly, I am not sure what she is thinking.

"Anna, I apologize. Relieving yourself of fluids aboard ship is not easy because of the lack of gravity. As you can imagine, the use of a bathroom in outer space is much different, as we are weightless most of the time. There is no flushing the toilet here. I will have to show you. It is a suction thing, easy once you get used to it. Don't be embarrassed. I can help you. You have to do what you have to do."

Anna smiles and looks at me. "I have heard every line in the world, but *let me show you how to use the bathroom* is brand-new to me!" She laughs and says, "Big guy, I think I can figure it out. Just show me the facilities."

After a brief training overview, Anna masters the process, and afterward she says it was not that difficult. She smiles and says she did not need my offer of assistance; she can do the starship stuff.

My personal cabin is a small room, dull-gray walls, fourteen feet by twenty-eight feet, which is huge by starship standards. I have some comforts, as I can eat in here, although there's no real furniture—no bed, no pictures, yet a few soft chairs for reading platforms, a big magnet desk and lots of side cabinets to hold things like clothing, and everything is locked down. I do have my many precious Earth books secured in wall bookshelves. I like old-fashioned books. On the port side I have two torpedo-type holes that are little bedrooms, both with sleeping bags. It has a simple bathroom facility for bathing and for the rest of my needs, also a little round room. All fluids are recycled.

I also have a full communications center, which is always on, giving me visuals of what is going on everywhere in the ship and in all directions outside the ship. It shows me everything in three-dimensional images. Other beings calling in are displayed visually, in hologram form, suspended on the starboard side of the cabin. I can also pull up a real-life display of the entire universe if needed, showing the locations of all Consortium fleets. Condensed news briefings are always available. I usually have hologram staff conferences daily, some with virtual reality. With the sophistication of the *Cyclone*, anything is possible when reaching out to other worlds and other starship fleets.

We have dinner in my cabin. Anna is learning to eat in no gravity. We are both tired after a long day. It is about four o'clock, early in the morning using Earth time. Even tired she is charming, and I love watching her every move. I know the ship is still heading for Jupiter, originally about five hundred million miles away, now maybe twenty million miles away. We will be there in about two hours, as we slow down to make the interception. We need to sleep and might have to orbit Jupiter until we wake up. I will show Anna Jupiter and tour around the ship tomorrow, introduce her to more of the crew.

"Anna, the sleeping arrangements are not like bedrooms, more like sleeping in a torpedo tube in a submarine. I point toward two, four-foot portholes about six feet up on the wall. You have a big comfy sleeping bag in there that you get into, holds you down, keeps you from floating away. My cabin only has two tubes. You are welcome to either one. We have nothing else. I am sorry."

"Henry, I am sleeping in your sleeping bag with you. I may look like I am brave and have it all together—not so! I am really scared, more than I have ever been in my life. I am over my head beyond belief. I understand only half of what's going on. You are the only real human on this ship, and I am not straying far from you. You have a sleeping buddy whether you want one or not. This is so surreal; I think I am in a movie."

I am startled learning about her fears and more surprised about her proposed sleeping arrangements. I never thought I would be sleeping with Anna tonight. And it will be really close and intimate. What could happen? I am now worried about me, as all of a sudden I feel a lot of anxiety. This is really new for me. It has been many decades since I slept with a woman. Yet I think, somewhat reassuringly, I am sure we will be both be asleep quickly. In the next few seconds, I realize I am in big trouble.

Life is sometimes not predictable. It is hard to believe yet I am looking at Anna undress. I can't take my eyes off of her as she slowly takes her clothes off, each piece floating away in the no gravity. I suddenly realize I am not used to the bodies of young women or the underclothing they wear. She leaves on her gray T-shirt, which is clinging to her almost visible breasts, displaying her nipples as hard and extended. She is almost naked except for a little white-lace panty thong. As she moves to the sleeping tube, I get a good look at her bare bottom, as several times she bends over to maneuver—just maybe, I realize, a couple of times for me to see.

Surprisingly, she is giving me a perfect view of her, and she is flawless. My heart is pounding, and I feel awkward, embarrassed, yet really aroused, feeling my face turning red from my thoughts. She ignores me, pulls herself into the bag, laughs, and says to me, "Henry, hurry up. I am exhausted."

I undress and am with her quickly, and I feel her warmth immediately. I love her scent, sweet and salty and delicious. I feel her body intimately close to mine, touching in all the right places. Her skin is soft. I have not been with a woman for seventy-two years, not since 1942. I am very much aroused and just thinking about how unexpected this is. Incredible! What can I say? I love feeling this way, so human, so truly magical.

I am too excited to sleep, my tiredness gone. The telepathic connection between us is boosting the emotions, and now I feel my wild, surging hormones. I am hot all over. I am in way over my head.

Anna is suddenly not that tired either. She is breathing hard and rapidly, her face flushed, and she is eagerly kissing my face, then my lips, caressing my face and murmuring my name. She is saying it is OK, that she wants me, then moaning, opening her legs, pressing her hips, rapidly pivoting her pelvis back and forth, with a very wet mound pushing up and hard against me. She says she needs me now.

I can feel her heart pounding, hear her heavy breathing, and her excitement is exhilarating. I am overwhelmed, trying hard to steady my nerves, trying to remember what to do and contain the force of my passion, too. I am trying not to manhandle her, not to hurt her. I try to slow down, not hurry, stay gentle, yet I can hardly control the flood of emotions and the massive physical urges. I am astounded by this and even more so as I feel her emotions telepathically. I am ecstatic, as I know she feels me mentally also. The physical intimacy and mental awareness are somewhere between ecstasy and sublime. We are together as one mentally; the intimate awareness of her emotions is extraordinary, wonderful, like nothing I have ever known!

I finally remember what to do; some things come naturally. To my great excitement, I am truly surprised by how I enjoy the job of stripping her of her thong and T-shirt. I am delighted in the intense pleasure of feeling her body, teasing her, petting her. To my joy I can sense what she likes best, and I am using my fingers to tease. Her desires become more urgent, and she becomes even more eager, hungry, needing me, wanting much more. She is magnificent. Her body is gorgeous. Her breasts are perfect and reacting to my touch. I am starting to enter her, my thrusts deep into her, becoming fast and hard, and she is meeting me, thrusting up and down with me. I am intimately part of her as she uses her legs, wrapped around me with the power to clasp me tight. It is beyond belief! She is demanding yet submissive, and she surrenders to the sheer joy and ecstasy. I fill her needs more than once. I feel her elation and pleasure each time. The thrill of her completion is astounding as I can feel it, too. I never knew how good it is to be human until this moment.

Afterward I am exhausted, yet I feel like I could conquer ten worlds. Let's say this hour rocked my universe, changed the course of my life. I know Anna felt it, too, although she is now fast asleep in my arms. My mind is thinking again, and I am wondering if I could have gotten Anna pregnant. A little late to think on it, not sure I am even capable of it. My DNA is not the original I was born with, and I may not be able to reproduce. This has never come up before. Too late to worry now.

We sleep a long time, maybe eight hours, and I usually never rest for more than three or four. We fall asleep spoon style and wake up the same way. Anna gets up and uses the facilities, and coffee is automatically ready. I smell it. Coffee is my one true pleasure, and it is real Earth coffee; I bought it at Barnes & Noble when I was there. I had put my purchases, including the books, on the ship's tender right before Anna picked me up, for delivery to the *Cyclone*. Even though it's served in a bottle, it tastes the same. I give Anna her coffee, and she tenderly smiles at me, looking rested and happy, floating close by, holding a handle, wearing only her T-shirt and lace panties, watching me intently. I am the happiest I have ever been, and I do not want the moment to end. I dread the issues of my leaving Earth. I have no clue what the future holds for us; I wish to be part of Anna's life, although that's probably impossible.

We chat some about little things, about her family, her friends, her life. I love hearing it. It is delightful.

After several minutes pass by, I smile, looking at her, and say, "Anna, I could stay here with you forever, yet we should get going. I have much to show you. How about a quick tour of the *Cyclone*? And then, believe it or not, the planet Jupiter is waiting for us. We are above her. We have been orbiting her for a while. You will like seeing it."

I continue, "We also have to do a workout. The lack of gravity will damage your muscles quickly and harm your internal organs unless you exercise. It is critical we work out every six hours, or you will deteriorate badly. I am more used to it and have adapted. We have a whole selection of workout machines, including a dance machine you will like. We have some gravity in there, too. This room has been given gravity to help you work out and give your body functions a chance to act normal. The *Cyclone* can create gravity when needed, sometimes in certain rooms and sometimes in the entire ship; we rotate to create gravity. Also, if we are accelerating or when we create centrifugal force, there is some gravity."

Anna smiles and nods her head, saying a good workout sounds fine.

We eventually head for the captain's bridge. I take the long way around to show her around some of the ship. I want to introduce her to the crew, too. I know the *Cyclone* wants her to look around, for some reason glad she is on board, and I think Anna feels it, too. She is looking everywhere as we float through the ship's hallway tunnels, pulling on handholds and gliding our way forward.

She is focused on everything she sees, asking interesting questions: "How does the ship supply oxygen? Where are the engines that propel it? How do you cook? What makes it stay up, floating, just suspended? How many people on board, or should I say beings? Are they all aliens? Where do they sleep? Is there any recreation—movies maybe? Do you have weapons on board? How fast does it go, and how far am I from my Earth right now? Do you own a home? Are there other humans like you? Is it like Earth where you're from?"

Then she looks at me intently. "Henry, have you ever been married?"

I laugh, then respond, "Anna, these are all good questions, and as you spend some time here and see part of our daily operations, you will learn everything about us. One answer for you is that I have never been married. And unfortunately we have no Earth movies. However, we do have virtual reality that seems really real, and some of it will be what you call movies. It gives you any story plot needed, and any recreation or any training you want, for example, all sports: tennis, swimming, snow skiing, basketball, even mountain climbing. Basically the *Cyclone* supplies everything we need. It maintains oxygen by recycling our air and is able to produce oxygen. It makes our food by transferring energy chemically, yet it looks and tastes like good food, sort of healthy. I insist on regular food for myself, like bread, meat, and eggs, just like on Earth. Everyone here, besides us, is fed per his or her nutrition design package."

"Everyone breathes like you and me. There is some variation, as it is a mix, which is adjusted by the ship for each of us, created chemically as you breathe. Only you and I were born on Earth. There are no other real humans besides me that I know about—actually none anywhere in the universe. Only on Earth."

"We do have a brigade of military troopers on board that are my clones and about forty percent human, sixty percent synthetic. They can also hibernate when needed on long trips. The rest are from several different civilizations throughout the universe. There are thousands of separate distinct civilizations out there. These are the ones I know about, that fit in here. There are more."

CHAPTER 17

KA*AM, HENRY'S HOME PLANET

Anna asks, "Henry, how about your home planet? I'm curious where you come from. Please tell me about your home—I think you called it KA*AM?"

"Anna, be prepared, as you have asked a huge question with a long answer. First of all, the universe is gargantuan, mostly just space, not much mass. As you know, for traveling across it, it's much more than immense, more than vast, maybe immeasurable. My home is really the *Cyclone*, because of all the time spent on the move. Yet my planetary base of operations is my second home, about one hundred and sixty-five light-years away, or nine hundred, eighty-eight trillion miles from here, actually in another galaxy. Yes, as you know, it is called KA*AM."

"You cannot see it from Earth. It is unknown to you. Everyone there lives in a moisture-soaked atmosphere almost like Earth's, yet some big differences. You could call it air-water. KA*AM's mesosphere, where you can still call it air, is a hundred and twenty miles out, much farther out into space than Earth's, which is fifty miles into outer space. KA*AM's air is much heavier because there is more of it and more moisture, much more than Earth. The water in the moisture is heavy. KA*AM's atmosphere is about six thousand quadrillion tons of weight, with KA*AM's gravity easily holding it in place. This is a lot heavier than Earth's air. Earth's atmosphere has a weight of 5.5 quadrillion tons or about a thousand times less."

"Our sun is also much smaller and not as bright; thus the atmosphere must retain the solar power or we would be excessively cold, not able to survive. I can breathe almost normally there, as I have become used to it. The oxygen content is similar to Earth's, yet there's much more moisture, thus the air is heavier, making it harder to breathe. The heavier density also holds the sun's solar energy, or more simply explained, it stores the heat of the sun. The temperature and weather are moderate, mostly comfortable, never really cold, no snow, and never really hot. Crops grow the entire year. The weather is mostly controlled by us, using gravity for manipulation of the wind and moisture."

"The gravity is about the same as Earth's, and the planet is about the same size as Earth. However, we can adjust gravity slightly, just enough to change wind patterns, making it possible to cool or warm the moisture, enough to change weather patterns, creating better efficiency using the sun's heat."

Continuing, I say, "Anna, the population is very diverse. Some beings come from other worlds and stay. They look nothing like the way we look or even like the local population. In my opinion they all are handsome in their own ways. We have land farms and freshwater farms, yet no saltwater oceans, or beach terrain, like you know from Earth. It is mostly tropical but has none of Earth's species, nothing like Earth's plants or animals. The food is mostly manufactured from plants and something like Earth fish, many varieties, and it is quite good. The issues of eating nutrition pills never caught on, although every century or two someone promotes it. Simple old-fashioned prepared food works best, as sitting down together is a wonderful social event. There are the old ways of eating, too, cooking from scratch. Those who prefer it live that lifestyle, left over from past traditions."

"There are lake farms everywhere. They grow delicious water plants and many tasty water organisms; some are what you might call fish varieties that are farmed extensively. The menu results are wonderful. Like on Earth, our traditions ask that meals are a family time, and sometimes meals are prepared by the families for other families. Mealtime is an important social event, part of our culture, even if served professionally. No one is ever hungry on KA*AM, and there is no poverty. Everyone has a place and a purpose. The family is more critical than the individual and last for many centuries."

I smile and look fondly at Anna. "I know you are curious. I have never told anyone about KA*AM. It is hard to describe— better that I give you a vision of it. Anna, please just relax, trust me, and let me into your mind completely—"

Before I can finish, I feel Anna's instant fear and see panic on her face.

"No, Anna, I promise it will not hurt, and I won't look around in your memories. They are totally off limits."

Anna gives me a concerned look, showing somewhat less fear, and then she finally smiles, nods, and closes her eyes. I slowly fill her mind with my mental vision of my adoptive world and friends. As I push into her focus, I feel her relax. It plays like a movie from my memories, and she closes her eyes, her face completely blank. She actually has a very serene look as my memories download to her; maybe she feels my pleasure, as she even smiles at times. She sees a happy place. She sees my adoptive home world and feels many of my fond memories. She is looking at a world covered by hazy, thick moisture vapor everywhere, like a light fog, as you can see through it, plus many low-lying white clouds, yet some sunlight filtering in. She sees many strange, tall, bright, and colorful dazzling cities coming up through the clouds, reaching high up into the blue skies.

The tall, mirrored skyscrapers are massive, towering way above the clouds, reflecting and absorbing the bright-silver sun rays, yet constantly changing colors, like many rainbows, magical in appearance, and collecting the sun's power as they are really colossal solar panels. These skyscrapers are many miles high, penetrating into outer space; most of them are almost 130 miles tall and sometimes thirty miles wide. Small passenger airships are coming and going between all smaller buildings, with much activity everywhere. All production and manufacturing are done in these buildings. They are massive inside, millions of square feet.

Anna hears Henry saying, "The silver exterior on the buildings are really massive, extremely effective solar panels, as the buildings are above the clouds. They supply all the energy requirements needed."

Then, way up, above it all, the starship spaceports are located on top of the tall buildings, 150 miles high, extending into outer space. Beyond them, miles above, in outer space, are the massive starships being built by hundreds of huge drones. These starships are hundreds of miles large. Several are in various stages of production.

The spaceports are the ones where the larger cargo starships are approaching, some many miles long and just as wide. They are docking, letting off passengers and cargo. There is one special building, taller than all the rest, splendid in appearance, actually surprising in its sophistication. This is where the *Cyclone* comes in to dock, which is always a big event with the entire population watching, the anticipation of its arrival a national pastime.

She sees there are beings everywhere, all in a hurry, all shapes and sizes. There are probably some that are different species. Most of them, the main population, are small, three or four feet high. Surprisingly enough they are very good-looking to her. They even look familiar to her: friendly and happy. They are marvelous! She feels at home, feels their warmth, and even misses them. *Impossible.* It must be Henry's feelings coming through to her. She feels Henry's fondness for them.

Her vision moves on, as if on a bird's flight, moving quickly over land. She is looking down at many massive high, dark-green mountains protruding from the vapor-dense clouds, then narrow, deep, dark valleys thick with fog partially covering many crystal-clear, fast-moving rivers, looking dark green, with rough white currents. And then, surprisingly, she sees many bodies of water with many oversize islands that seem unending, comprised of lush green landscapes shaded by masses of vegetation suspended in air by trees spaced evenly across the land.

Then she sees the massive dark-emerald-green tropical forests covering the swamps and thousands of five-hundred-foot-tall ancient trees everywhere, yet spaced evenly, looming up out of the clinging fog with more lush vegetation suspended from most of their branches, hanging down like a woman's long hair. Flowers and fruitlike objects are many, with wonderful colors, not like Earth plants or colors yet marvelous. Lakes are also everywhere, also spaced evenly, and many look like farms, as about every inch has either seaweed-type crops or enormous fish beds populated with thousands of things that look like small fish. Some look like silver sardines; others look more like wiggly things. Anna wonders what they taste like and thinks this must be a great source of protein for the population.

Low, light fog clouds, absorbing the sun's energy and protecting the surface, are moving in the light breeze and are everywhere, streaming like water flowing in a river. Yet there is bright sunshine above these fog clouds, and it filters down to the land, providing the energy it needs to sustain life.

The land area seems equal, about 50 percent solid ground and then the rest scattered water, yet no saltwater oceans and few individual houses. It is a mixture of thousands of islands, with swamps and freshwater lakes everywhere, two or three miles apart, yet all are spaced evenly. The water is part of everyone's life. There are some large buildings on stilts in the water and then many massive tree houses high in the large limbs, looking cozy. The buildings are similar to Earth structures yet composed of a synthetic material and smooth, with no angled corners, only rounded edges. They are all shades of green and blue, as if they are camouflaged to melt into the trees or landscape. Fog hangs everywhere, yet many gaps let the sun shine through.

Anna marvels, as this world is beautiful in its own way yet completely alien, populated with these handsome beings that are definitely not human to her and definitely another species. The colors are also wonderful here, constant rainbows, and lush, dark-green landscapes, really dark-blue water, next to land of a fertile, almost black dirt, growing odd-looking, leafy plants, which are deep green. There are also ancient granite mountains in the distance, wrapped in fog, backed by deep-blue skies, not anything like Earth, a much darker blue sky. All the mountains are massive, blue gray and dark green, snow-tipped white, high above the surface of the ground, which is covered by a heavy, moist atmosphere of fog-like clouds, also clinging to the trees covering the sloping sides. Higher up, way up above the mountains, above the steep cliffs, thick white clouds are billowing everywhere, thousands of feet above, much higher than Earth clouds. She wonders if there were ever storms or violent winds in the past, as it's rare to have light breezes only, especially with so much heavy moisture. There are currents, and she can see the effects. She can see the air moving like real rivers of water, as it is saturated with so much moisture, like a thick fog flowing, dripping with water.

Anna looks up. The vision is done. She is exhausted and also excited, her emotions in turmoil. She laughs and says, "Henry, Hollywood needs this! It is astonishing what you did to me. It is incredible. I can't describe it. It's really amazing and unnerving at the same time. It is like watching a movie in my brain except the colors are so clear. I can smell the forests, hear the rivers, see all the white clouds, feel the coolness of the moisture in the air, and I feel your presence and the warm feelings you have for those beings, especially all the little ones. They are so small; they look like slender fairies, so beautiful, so graceful, with large noses with big nostrils and very large soft-brown eyes, like the kind eyes of deer. They have gorgeous facial features, so refined and so human, too. Their slender, long legs and arms are wonderful. Magical! I think their hands and feet are webbed, yet the fingers and toes extend beyond the webbing; the fingers are so delicate, long, and slender. Some have long, beautiful silver hair on their heads, or maybe light blond, and their hair sparkles when they move. Their clothing looks silky, flowing with their movement and blended colors. Their skin looks soft, colored by white, brown, and silver freckles, like a fawn."

She is wondering, *They are quite amazing. Who are they? Can they fly like fairies? She thinks she saw them flying. Are they fairies? Are they Henry's friends? Is Gabriel there? Are there different sexes, like on Earth? Does Henry like it there? Do they eat like we do? Do they have children like we do, get pregnant and have babies and raise them? Does Henry have a home there? And good friends? They are so different from us yet beautiful in their own way. Do they have vehicles like we do, like cars, although I saw none? How do they get around?*

Laughing, Henry responds, "Anna, please hold on. They do not have cars, and use power beams for small trips. The longer trips are in tunnels under the surface that are like subways except there is no gravity, and the tunnels are more like tubes that go everywhere, air-powered. The speed is really fast, and they are safe, and they also keep the surfaces of roads clean. They are underground as they conserve land for other better use."

Continuing, I say, "There's a lot to talk about. You asked if I have many friends there; yes, some are good friends. They are a lovely people, and they are called *Allos*. They are part of a large race spread over several worlds, many billions of them. They are like us yet not like us. First of all they can swim well, especially because of their webbed feet and hands. They also can fly short distances, as they have small wings off their arms and legs. The heavy water-saturated air helps them fly, and there is a little less gravity there, too. Plus their filament wings will extend, expanding from their arms and legs, looking like Earth bat wings and only spread when needed. They are very light, thus they are quick. They look like fairies when they fly or similar to fast-moving butterflies. I have wondered if that is where we got the myth of fairies on Earth, maybe coming from seeing the Allos that have visited in previous centuries. Who knows?"

"Yes, they have children, yet not like we do. There is no sex mating like we do, and they do not pair off like us. They have large family groups, and the children are hatched, not like birds but more like clear fetus sacs they can carry and nurture, mostly kept in a safe spot for two years. The fetus sac comes from the designated mother, conceived by mental melding of the family; they all contribute DNA for the reproductive process. The child is a product of the entire family, DNA designed by the family, and raised by the family group, normally forty to sixty members living together, sometimes more. New members, other than children or those not related, are invited into a family by the elders, depending on circumstances."

"I am part of a family the elders invited me into; I am still a member and will always be part of this family. I cannot contribute DNA to the reproduction process. However, I am considered a provider and nurturer plus I have specific responsibilities."

"The Allos mostly live forever. They are immortal, and except for being killed in accidents they keep living. Thus a family has only four or five children every fifty or sixty years. A child takes about fifty years to be raised. Most of them are very old in Earth years. Some are ancient, yet all still look very young because they do not age as we do. They are slender to the point of almost being fragile. They are much smaller than us, averaging four feet tall; some are five feet at the tallest possible height. Their skin is a light color, soft to touch, and they have two sexes like us. The females have light-brown eyes mostly. The males always have dark-blue eyes. The differences between the sexes are small, unlike humans."

"Anna, you are right, their head and facial features are very refined, pleasing to look at, I think beautiful like angels. Their voices are also angelic and in perfect harmony, having a broad range of sounds. When they communicate by song, it is with rhythm, like poetry, sometimes communicating in remarkable lyrics when using their voices, telling a story. You can also hear it mentally, as they are telepathic, therefore guaranteeing little chance of miscommunication as you feel the words and the emotion. Deceit is not possible. You can hear their thoughts and ideas, yet they can also speak well vocally, sometimes using both together when talking. Their mouths, lips, and faces are without flaws, just exquisite. They can sing together perfectly. I could listen to them singing for hours!"

"As for intelligence they are just brilliant, beyond interesting, witty, fun, and just delightful. It is like listening to the conversations of the angels of God. You can't get enough of it."

"Anna, I confess, I love them because they have very similar emotions to us and even better than us, better than any culture I have met in my travels. They are always of high character. They are wise, kind, and compassionate, never malicious or causing harm if it can be helped. None are on board the *Cyclone*, as they do not harm others. The *Cyclone* is a military starship created to do what military ships do. Although they built the *Cyclone* thousands of years ago and they currently maintain it, they are not a warrior species. They do this for all the fleets, all military starships, constantly updating them, building new ones, making them better. Yet they are never the soldiers. They are nurturers, the teachers, the engineers, the leaders, and the creators."

"They have me for their military needs and my many clones. It has been that way for sixty years. I am not sure what they did before me. It might have been another me, someone like me. They don't respond to this question, not sure if they ever will."

"Anna, I will never achieve their knowledge or skills, as they are much further down the road on the evolution path. Their race is many millions of years ahead of the human species. They must think of me as a primitive specimen from a lower species. I am not refined in their way, as I have deformities in their eyes. Plus, I am physically huge in comparison to them. They may see me as sort of a brute. I may be even overwhelming to them physically, maybe repulsive. Yet I am part of their family. Over all the years, they have stood by me, accepted me. They have been loyal to me and have cared for me as I have cared for them."

"Maybe at times they find it difficult to bring me up to their level. Their thought process is far advanced, yet they do not criticize me. They smile and are always patient with me. They treat me as an equal, with much respect, and have been very kind to me from the beginning, completely open; they have taught me so much. I live because of them, and they are my benefactors. They have given me almost unlimited resources. I have total respect and love for them. I would give my life to protect them."

Anna, with a perplexed expression on her face, looks at Henry and says, "The Allos are immortal and look so young. They remind me of you, Henry; you look so young. I know you are much older than you appear, and it occurs to me that you might be like them, immortal. If it is OK to ask you this, are you immortal, Henry? Do you ever get sick?"

I am surprised, as I never thought of myself in that way. Technically I am not totally immortal; however, I know it is much more complicated than that. The clone thing would freak her out. I am not even comfortable with it. I need to explain the other thing, though, and this is my chance. She needs to know about herself, too. I cannot put it off any longer.

I smile. "It is probably a good idea to talk about this. It is hard or too complicated to explain the whole biological process. I will try a short version. I'm not even used to it yet. I've been enhanced genetically, which means I'll have a real long life. I'm not really sure how long, maybe at least two hundred years, maybe much more. The real problem for me is if I am killed in the line of duty. I can be killed; I have no real immunity there. They could then use my DNA to recreate me. You know about the concept of clones. The problem is memories, my experience, and values— or who I am. These do not transfer without the original model. You have to be alive, with a functioning brain. The second problem is who you are, your identity. As you know, the first ten years of a human child's life is critical to their character. Plus, all the experiences in your life make you who you are. After living several hundred years, you lose some of your early memories. These memories do not transfer to a clone. You also start to forget more as the years pass. After a few hundred years, you change a lot; you're not the same being. You do get smarter, yet there are some real issues. You must clone before you get too old, to save those early memories."

Anna nods her head. She has that confused look, a little dazed, like she does not believe she is here.

"Anna, there's more. Part of my enhancement needs to be explained. I was given an internal medical repair kit. That is the best way to explain it. You know about drones. You know they can be very small, like the size of cells. I have been given a drone medical cell package, as I carry these cells in my body always.

My body nurtures these cells, as these are organic, yet they are drones. They are different from my other cells. These drone cells are intelligent, like little computers. They can think. These little satellites wander about my body fixing things, flowing in and out of problem areas. They diagnose the problem, then repair and fix. They repair severe wounds immediately, destroy invading diseases, even replace missing limbs with aggressive cell generators, engineering the rebuild, and turn water into blood as they need it. They also help prevent old age. I will stay younger much longer, extending my life by many years. They monitor all life cycles, including food intake and air breathing. They will alter or reject any poisons coming into the body, either by stomach or by the lungs."

Anna still looks perplexed, staring at Henry, starting to talk, then pausing.

I am watching Anna. I raise my eyebrows, concerned, and smile a tender smile, with soft eyes. "Is this too much information?"

Annoyed, Anna exclaims, "Henry, I understand what you're saying, but you can be too much at times. Did your mother ever tell you that?"

Continuing, she further explains, "This is wonderful for you! It's amazing, and I'm happy for you. I wish we could sell this on Earth. We would be rich and help a lot of people, although I'm sure doctors and hospitals would complain. Actually I wish we could just give it to the people of Earth, as they sure could use this. It would prevent a lot of pain and suffering, especially in children."

Anna is eyeing me, has a look like she might cry. She looks away.

I am alarmed. "Anna, what's wrong?"

She finally looks at me, and I see her tears. She explains, "Henry, I know this sounds silly, and I don't know why I am acting this way, so irrational." She pauses. "It occurs to me that you will outlive me by a long time, and as silly and stupid as this sounds, I miss you already."

I laugh, then smile, saying, "Not a problem. I have wanted to tell you, but I was afraid you would get spooked or become angry. When you came on board, you were given my same medical drone package. It is in you now. You never felt it. I had to do this to protect you. On board you have no immunities to any on board illnesses or possible radiation or injury. You could be dead by now if I had done nothing, and I am sorry I did not tell you sooner. You now have this medical repair kit inside you. You do not feel it, and you will never know it's there. It's for your own good, and it added at least two hundred years to your life, maybe a lot more. You will still age, yet much slower and look younger for a long time. We will be the same as we age."

Anna looks totally freaked, like when she came on board. Her eyes are big again, moist, ready to cry, and she is breathing fast.

I am stunned and quickly react. "Anna, it's like a fancy vaccine; think of it that way. It's not a big deal. It really is a good thing, better than health insurance. Don't worry. I can extract it when we are back on Earth if you prefer. Please, I'm sorry!"

Anna stares at me as if she just came out of a coma, then finally talks in a whisper: "Henry, it's a fantastic gift. I don't know how to thank you enough. It's like a gift from God. I'm more than pleased. I am astounded and grateful. You have changed my life for a long time, protected me from much pain and suffering over the coming years. I don't know what to say. With all my heart, thank you!"

"Anna, thank God you're OK with it. You're welcome! Remember, it doesn't make you immortal; you can still be killed. You still need to be careful. I wish we could do it for everyone on Earth. It is more complicated than you think. Never tell anyone. Your body is not quite the same, and no earth doctor would understand. No one can know this, please, for your own benefit."

CHAPTER 18

GABRIEL

Anna and I are eating dinner and talking in my cabin. It is pot roast night, made like my mother would have made it; and, I prepared it, even with gravy. We have wine. I think this is good. Anna seems happy. I have finished and am drinking my third glass of wine.

I look at her seriously, considering, and then say, "About your question about Gabriel. He's hard to understand. He's not like us or any species I know of. Maybe *supernatural* should be part of his description. He is also kind, thoughtful, generous, and wise. He really is beyond belief. Yet he is different from all others; the first thing, he is ageless. No one knows how old he is, just older than everyone, although there are elders that are ancient. The second observation, he is magical, maybe like Merlin in King Arthur's court."

Anna laughs. "Henry, you do not need any more wine, and I thought I was losing it; tell me no more."

I respond, "Wait, give me a chance. For example, you didn't see Gabriel in the vision I gave you, right? He does not translate well that way. He is so far advanced. I cannot transfer memories about him. Everything about him is, as you would say, top secret and classified. He is not like anyone. I think he's from another ancient species that no one knows; amazing as this sounds, he may be the last of his kind. It's difficult to comprehend. I think he may be millions of years old. He is very powerful and respected by all. When asked about his age, he does not respond to the question or talk much about himself. He just says, 'It's complicated.'"

Anna looks surprised and shakes her head. "Henry, I think I've passed into another dimension and wonder if I'm going to wake up and find out this is all a second reality. Should I be afraid of Gabriel?"

"No, Anna, it is not that way. You have nothing to fear. I've felt close to him from the beginning, and I'm sure he will be delighted to meet you. I can't explain it. The best way to understand him is just to think of him as you would a very old elder in a very old church. He is more like a mentor to me than my boss. I like to think of him as the archangel in our Christian Bible. I think it says, '*The Archangel, Gabriel, as picked by God as the head of his angels, shall descend from heaven with the cry of command as the trumpet of God.*'"

I pause, then serious, I look at Anna. "It makes me feel better about some of the things I have to do. It helps to think I might work for an archangel, as a little divine help is most useful in my line of work. If he is not the archangel, he should be. He knows everything, has guided me and taught me most of what I know; I mean the impossible stuff. First he gave me the starship technology, then the universe; a really complicated subject, a reality almost beyond my comprehension. He has shown me the way to deal with so many different cultures, then the solutions to control or destroy our enemies, plus the forecasting of future probabilities and looking at the game of life philosophically. He also taught me to know my limitations—and everyone else's."

I continue, "He gave me the *Cyclone*, a gift beyond measure. Also, Gabriel is miraculous to see, bigger than me physically, or I think so, like a father figure. Wise and old is the aura he projects to me. It seems spiritual to me. The weird thing is he appears to those who look at him as the image they feel the most comfortable with. He makes the beholder feel safe with his appearance. He might even appear as a woman to you. Gabriel radiates warmth to me, makes me feel instantly at ease, which I think would be the same for you. He has been my guide and my boss all these years."

"Also, Anna, as hard as this is to believe, this means no one feels or sees the same image. It depends on you, what you need to see. I always see an incredibly wise old man, soulful and sad, and sometimes I feel blissfully happy when I am with him. Unfortunately this is not so good if you're an enemy of his. Then the opposite occurs. He is the most fearful image the beholder will ever see, a glimpse of hell. I think there is a good chance you'll meet him someday. He will be delighted with you. I want you to meet him, Anna; you will love him."

"Henry, to be honest, meeting Gabriel scares the hell out me, no humor intended. Just warn me when he's coming to visit. By the way, just how did Gabriel teach you all that you know, the starship stuff, the languages, bringing you up to the level of intelligence equal to their civilization, their technology?"

I shake my head. "I'm sorry about not making you feel good about Gabriel. That's not my intent. He has been very kind to me, taught me patiently. As you would guess, my knowledge was like an infant's at first in comparison to theirs, with no starship expertise, less intelligence, less wisdom, and no knowledge of their culture."

I continue, "The learning process is much different from the human process. The best description is a download of data you might do with your PC, which is only one-dimensional whereas my downloads, many of them, were multidimensional. The data I received was a complete visual, in color, even with sound, as if I was there. This included the depth of emotions, sorting or ranking the importance of the emotions and the data. Thus the pain, then the joy, the whole experience of their knowledge and culture were given to me. Even more, there were values, character, history, politics, languages, social views, and technology."

"The information and process transfers were massive, and, as strange as it sounds, it felt like I was listening to music during the hours of transition. It was pleasant, inspiring, stimulating, although I was extremely tired at the end of each session."

"I went through a mental transformation. My process of analyzing problems and creating solutions is much different from human or what I used to be. Because of this I have a much more sophisticated thought process, yet it's still a small percentage in comparison to Gabriel's. I am smarter because of it, thank goodness, yet I am still human."

"Anna, I feel all the same things you feel: frustration, sadness, happiness, despair, anger, passion, love, and desire."

I smile, pause, look intently at her. "I am still human, especially those emotions regarding my mating instincts."

Anna and I are looking deep into each other's eyes, wondering. We both are really serious, then we both blush...Then we both smile...Then we both laugh until tears come to our eyes.

CHAPTER 19

STARSHIPS AND SPACE TRAVEL

I smile a tender smile, looking at Anna, as we clean up the cabin from the meal, and say, "Enough of that. Let's continue the ship's tour. We can finish later. It won't take that long."

Anna nods her head, visits the head, or bathroom, combs her hair a little, puts lipstick on, then looks at me with a smile. She pushes herself in the no gravity, jetting herself across the room my way, forcing me to catch her. We both laugh.

As we head down the corridor, I explain the *Cyclone* is very small by starship standards, as many ships are miles long, like large cities built into a starship, some as massive as 650 miles long, like the big cargo starships. The *Cyclone* is five miles long, a couple of miles wide, and about a mile high, weighing thirty-four billion Earth tons. It is truly a miracle of technology built centuries ago, a military ship to provide guardianship and protection for trillions of beings across the universe. It has been my real home for years.

In addition it provides room and board for 514 souls, including eight-two on the starship crew. It houses a laboratory and clinic medical staff of twenty-eight; a support crew of forty-four workers, including military; a commanders' brigade, including officers; and a total of 360 troopers. The ship is a complicated maze of passage tunnels, connecting rooms containing the operations machinery, massive hydrogen fusion reactors, antimatter operation equipment and dark-energy-contained materials, antigravity energy generators, warp engine drives, polarized magnetism generators, massive electrical panels, solar energy conversion panels, communications and security shield energy panels, and massive energy weapon systems with operations control. There are assorted rooms for crew, equipment, weapons, supplies; also pipes, various control rooms, landing cargo ports with two ship's tenders, and some extremely sophisticated flight accessories; and then general storage. I mention that Anna's SUV, the one she rented, is in one of the landing ports.

Anna asks me about the rental car and I respond, "It's probably best we have the crew drop it off for you, using the *Ship Tender* tomorrow night, after dark, make it ready for an early morning pick-up in Richmond, maybe in front of the car rental branch there or close by their offices. I will have my law firm, Lindemann, Noakes & Beagle in New York, call them and handle it for you, including any extra expense due because of damage from the accident. They can rent another car for us at the same time, drop it off near where we are meeting your parents, at the restaurant, unlocked, and leave the keys under the seat."

Anna looks at me, laughs, and says, "That sounds good. And really, you have a law firm?"

I laugh and say, "You never know when you'll need a good lawyer."

I realize Anna has now seen most of the ship. To my pleasure she has been interested in most of it. One area she was most curious about was in the armament storage locker. The dog soldier suits—that's what I call them—are stored there along with our normal armored suits. We go back and look at them again. They do look strange. She asks about them, and she is not unfounded in saying they look like werewolves. They are frightening even hung up, with no one in them.

I respond, "Anna, you're right. They really do look like Earth movie fantasy werewolves, and there are a hundred of these armored suits. When you wear them you look like a huge vicious dog or a wolf that can stand up, or maybe like a massive Hollywood werewolf, and for good reason. They are designed as camouflage for what they really are—a serious deadly weapon— when worn by a soldier. The soldier is completely immersed in the suit when he enters it from the back. The suits are actually copies of a ferocious animal called a *hiyack* on an off-world moon, in a solar system in another galaxy. Hiyacks just happen to look like werewolves."

"The flexible synthetic suit has an armored hide that is covered with short brown-red fur, and it is impenetrable, as it has a sophisticated security shield. The suit provides powerful synthetic muscles that attach, adding to the soldier's strength, and jet propulsion drives for short low-altitude flights. It has wonderful and accurate laser guns positioned on the forehead, shooting wherever you look. It protects you from all weather, has a communications package, and lets you run upright on two legs or, for increasing speed, on all fours with a maximum speed of 145 miles an hour, with the legs in an extended mode, making them longer. It works on any terrain, carrying up to three hundred pounds of equipment in Earthlike gravity. It is eight feet high when worn, normally increasing your weight to 460 pounds if you weigh 180 pounds."

"The suit provides some serious metal alloy talons on every gloved paw, like a cat's claws, that can extend several inches and can grab any surface, making it a superb climber. The head and mouth are large, with large lion jaws that are powered by hydraulic force bars, extremely powerful, with large razor-sharp teeth, including long fangs that can tear off a head. It cuts through anything. It has two large devil-red eyes, like cat's eyes, set into an armored vision mask capable of night vision and with magnification for long-distance sight. The head is also a helmet with a closed air system with recycled atmosphere air, also capable of underwater use for three hours."

"More critical and dangerous, and what I call its main weapon, is panic. It terrifies most of our enemies. They panic or lose their resolve. Wearing this suit gives you a fierce appearance, with gruesome sound effects. You can roar loudly, louder than any Earth lion. It terrifies an enemy. Any enemy soldier or civilian that is organic carbon based has real problems standing up to dog soldiers. They scare me."

"Anna, I know you probably don't like this part of the *Cyclone* or this part of me, and I apologize for this. However, as you know, we are primarily a military vehicle. The universe has some of the same issues Earth faces. We defend civilizations from the same evil that exists everywhere. All beings with free will are vulnerable to evil."

Anna does not respond, does not know what to say about all of this. She just shakes her head.

I tell Anna we also have silver-metal-armored spacesuits covering us completely when outside the ship, used on the ground or outer space. They protect us from radiation, supply air, resolve severe temperatures, and provide weapons and a security defense field. We have powered propulsion, too, limited range yet effective.

We are headed for the captain's bridge. Jupiter is waiting for us, and we are still in orbit over her. As we go into the room, the visuals are up, and I can see Jupiter below us, mostly white in color, mostly a hydrogen atmosphere, thirty-five-thousand-feet deep, huge streaks of various colors over this massive planet. G-BE, F-LA, M-HO, and K-HO are all here. They acknowledge us, and they want to go on, as Jupiter is old news for them. As

Anna stares at the panorama in front of us, I tell her the *Cyclone* is moving about twelve thousand miles per hour and has just passed over 88,846 miles of surface. Jupiter is eleven times larger than Earth and rotates at twenty-two thousand miles an hour, about twenty-two times faster than Earth. Thus we are seeing the surface at thirty-four thousand miles an hour, ground velocity or the total aggregate speed, as we are traveling against the planet's rotation.

Also Jupiter's day is ten hours long, not twenty-four hours like Earth's. Jupiter has sixty-three moons, some of them more interesting than others. I tell Anna when we have more time in the future, we can explore them more closely. The gravity on Jupiter is two and a half times greater than on Earth. It pulls on the *Cyclone*. It actually may have captured its moons the same way as they passed by; they may even be former asteroids that are now moons. Our individual weight is two and a half times more, too, which would cause a lot of strain if endured for any length of time.

"Anna, you asked before, and to answer you, we are now five hundred fifteen million miles from Earth, and it is now eight o'clock your time in the second day on board. We probably should end our trip out now and head back, as you said you have only three days. We are too close to Earth to use our warp drive, and the right speed on the fusion drive is limited because of the time it takes us to slow down. So we will start back at about one hundred fifty million miles an hour, end up averaging about fifty million miles an hour because of trying to slow down, taking us fourteen hours to be back on Earth. We need to slow down in the last eighty million miles coming in to Earth at a much slower speed. We will lock into an orbit and then land the ship's tender where we can rent a car and get you to the restaurant. You can make lunch with your parents and still be in the third day of our adventure. What do you want to do, more adventures in space or home tomorrow?"

Anna looks at me, smiles a big smile, and responds, "Henry, the trip into the solar system is awesome, not my normal date with a guy." She laughs. "Sort of an *out-of-this-world* experience, no pun intended. And I do want to try again later, if you are willing. However, I do need to get home. I want to introduce you to my parents. Come to lunch with me tomorrow. And it's my turn to have you stay with me. I also want to take you to London as my date to my movie's premiere. Then I want you to come to my home in Hollywood and meet some of my friends, maybe come to a couple of functions with me. Don't say no. You'll enjoy it."

I shake my head, knowing this is a bad idea.

"Please, Henry, come with me!"

I am thinking this is way more than I ever thought about, and that is the problem: I am not thinking. I am in some kind of daze—captured, I will admit. I know what meeting the parents means; even a stupid guy knows that. No wonder the human species continues to grow. Now is the time to cut and run, just need to say I can't; we go our separate ways. It's the best thing to do for both of us. I am bad news for her in a lot of ways.

"Anna, you are wonderful to invite me. I'm sorry, it's not possible, and there are some things I need to do here before I can leave. I'm really sorry, I need to…"

The look on Anna's face is awful, and to my surprise she starts to cry. She looks away. Her tears are my defeat. I can't do it. There is no question I'm going with her. Anna may regret it later. I already regret it. This is probably not wise. Yes, she has me.

"Anna, please, I can change my plans. Yes, and thanks, I want to meet your parents, see their home, and go to London with you and see your home, too." I dread saying this, but I continue. "Anna, you know I have to leave. I'll stay as long as I can. I want to spend my time with you. I know you might not like this situation, but it's not my doing. I will have to leave."

Anna looks at me soulfully. "Henry…" There's a long pause. "I don't want to cause issues for you. I know your life is really complicated, and I have no idea how many responsibilities you have. I'm overwhelmed by all of it. You need to do what you need to do. Yet I want to be with you. I can't help it; I'm sorry."

"Anna, I have to admit, it is really complicated on many levels, yet no matter how complicated, I also feel the same way. I'm sorry, too, as you may regret ever having met me at some point."

"Starman, I am one step ahead of you. I know this is not a normal relationship. It's all crazy. I'm not even sure it's real yet, that it's not some kind of dream. Really, I have no idea what I'm doing, just following my heart and praying we have some time together. I do know you've been here before, on Earth, and you come back now and then. We can see each other, or I hope this may be possible."

Anna continues, "Also, I do know how you feel about me, as I can read your mind, thanks to you. By the way, you hide very little. Now, I think it's time for dinner and your bed. I'm looking forward to both."

CHAPTER 20

ENEMIES OF HENRY

At the same time, unknown to Henry or anyone back on Earth, in the Pacific Ocean, deep in the Mariana Trench, at about thirty-two thousand feet in depth, sitting on the bottom, is a massive starship, considered a battleship, as more military than not. This considerable amount of water effectively hides it from everything, including the *Cyclone*. This ship is not part of any consortium or from any civilized world, far from it. They are nomadic, no world to call home, more like pirates living off what they can steal or extort from defenseless worlds. They prey on the weak, traveling thru the galaxies looking for off-world civilizations with primitive technology. There is always something they can use; kidnapping and extortion are favorite tools to obtain it. They usually leave the civilizations devastated, and then move on to the next victim, even after the ransom or tribute is paid. Currently they need fuel; specifically they need nuclear fuel and a lot of it. The city-size starship requires huge amounts of energy to power it.

This ship is about two miles high, thirty-eight miles wide, and sixty-four miles long, a black rectangle with a long front bumper as a deflector, yet graduated forward, like a blade six-teen miles out, running along the entire forward end. It is a huge city, an entire civilization on board with eighteen thousand aliens. Henry has chased this ship before. They know who Henry is, having escaped him on a couple of occasions. They always stay out of his way, out of the normal starship pathways, locating in some backwater planet like Earth and latching on like a parasite.

Overall, Earth may not have much for them, not anything of real value, with the big exception of nuclear energy, which is starship fuel and of great value. They are waiting for the right time to strike Earth, searching and taking anything of value they can find. Besides nuclear supplies they are interested in rare minerals, all metals, chemicals, and any other usable resource, anything they can use or sell. They know the easiest way to motivate Earth governments to supply tribute is to take wives and children as hostages. They are now preparing their ship for a large volume of humans, which they will capture, hold hostage, and trade for nuclear energy or anything else of value. They are preparing their ship to load up fifteen thousand humans. They know even if Earth does pay the ransom, they never return the hostages, no matter their promises. Not a happy ending.

They also know Henry was here on the planet briefly, and then his ship was gone again. They recognized the *Cyclone*. They saw its signature briefly three different times: once as it came into Earth's surface running hot, then once again close to the planet, and then again before it blasted back out into deep space. And now the *Cyclone* is back, coming in fast.

Not sure why Henry is here, but they will do nothing to draw his attention until they figure out why he is on Earth again and with only one ship. He could not be looking for them with just one ship. If he is here for another reason, they might be able to catch him by surprise and destroy him and the *Cyclone*.

If an ambush is possible, they will go operational. If it does not work out, they still have a chance to escape Earth. It is all depending on what the *Cyclone* does in the next few days. If necessary, they know they might have to fight their way out, and they are fully prepared for and delighted by the prospect of killing Henry and the crew. Henry without a backup fleet is a pleasing thought, and to catch him not paying attention and to ambush him would settle a lot of scores.

They have to figure out a way to ambush the *Cyclone*. One strategy is to attack Earth with their smaller deadly planet-surface fighters, called *wasps* by Henry in the English language. Their attacks would keep Henry busy, then they would use the main ship to toast him with their massive fusion weapons from behind, trapping the *Cyclone* between them and Earth. Still, Henry and the *Cyclone* are unpredictable and dangerous. As a further precaution, these nomads have sent an emergency beacon drone into space to alert the other six starships in their group, all part of the same civilization. The nomads have requested they come to Earth to provide military support against Henry and his crew, and to come immediately.

⊨≪+ +≫⊨

Back in Richmond, Virginia, Senator Sam Jordan, Anna's stepfather, is having dinner with Luca Deforleo, a longtime wealthy supporter and the boss, or the don, of the largest organized-crime syndicate based in New York City. The senator well knows about Luca's background and Mafia ties; however, the relationship between them has always been discreet and goes back to the senator's days in Chicago, when he was just starting his career. He has made a lot of money partnering with Luca over the years and has been careful that the deals are on the legal side of their syndicate. Most of the joint ventures have been real estate in New York City and the stock market, certainly nothing illegal.

This last deal is not the norm and not what the senator wants to be involved in, as he told Luca before, actually several times. Now it looks like the merger Luca put together with two large airlines, combining them, is much more dangerous than their normal business deal, and to his shock he is in the middle of it, no doubt about it. He became alarmed, actually angered and afraid when he saw his annual report showing huge sums of cash showing up in his offshore captive and then corresponding purchases of stock. He has hidden money there for years, making him very wealthy, mostly from Luca's deals. His business arrangements with Luca usually end up with a lot of money being earned and showing up there. This time, however, Luca has gone too far, unknown to the senator until now. The captive has been buying large shares of stock in two airlines. Luca has been using the stock proxies to make a merger happen, and now he expects the senator to make sure Washington stays out of the way and approves the merger, as the FAA would have agree to it.

What has terrified the senator is the possibility that Iran is behind the merger with their cash, then using front companies, like his offshore captive, to buy huge shares of stock in each airline. Their partnering with Luca is for him to provide the muscle of organized crime plus the payoffs that may be needed to make it happen right under the noses of the US government. The senator knows this is happening, as he knows the bank involved on the financial statement is First Excalibur Bank of New York. He knows about Excalibur because of the FBI national security briefings to the Senate indicating the bank is a front for Iran, doing Iran's bidding. If the link to him is discovered it will be awful, even worse for him than for any elected official involved with a conspiracy. He will go to jail for a very long time. The FBI investigates all of this daily, looking for public officials tempted by foreign governments. The senator now realizes he currently could go to jail for fraud or maybe even treason if discovered. What a mess!

The senator and Luca are at an Italian restaurant on the Upper East Side in New York City; they have just finished dinner and are on their third drinks, making lots of small talk. The senator is thinking how Luca has been very charming tonight, which is not easy for him. The seventy-year-old Italian Mafia killer is never pleasant. He is a big man, stocky and overweight; muscled; with big, powerful hands; bald; a scarred face; and ugly beady eyes. He never had a good bedside manner. He is usually vulgar, smells like cigar smoke, and is sadistic and cruel. He delights in torturing the waiters whenever he and the senator have dinner together, making dinner disagreeable. He always brags about his exploits, proud of the terrible things he does to people who get in his way. It is hard to spend time with a man like this.

Even worse is how he has become so wealthy. There is no telling the money he has made in the heroin business. He and his people have made a fortune over the years in the drug trade. Then there are the huge profits from the human trafficking and prostitution he oversees, using his thugs to do his dirty work. The senator feels the awful anxiety he always has when dealing with Luca, and for the first time since he's been associated with this ugly man he actually is physically sick with fear. He has been thinking about and dreading this dinner meeting for a week.

The senator, with a worried look, is anxious to speak after all the small talk. "Luca, what have you gotten me into? I know about Excalibur Bank, the Iran connection!"

Luca smiles. "Senator, Sam, please, you are not to fear. Of course there is some risk. However, all the right people have been considered and paid off. All of it is hidden. The airlines need this, and you know it. Both airlines will go broke if this does not happen. The merger will save them. Money is money. Iran's money spends like anyone else's. You and I will make a fortune the legal way, just like the banks and hedge funds have done for years. They actually invented it, the easy way to make money. You have to admire them for it. I could not have done it better. Senator, let me remind you, you will make a lot of money. You have done well by us in the past. Right? Just do your part!"

The senator responds, "Iran is not your normal partner. They are a terrorist government outlawed by most of the countries in the world, including the United States. They are a military threat, and they use assassins when they have issues. They could smuggle nuclear bombs into the United States using those planes. They are dangerous bedfellows, and I can be investigated if this blows up."

Luca is angry, leaning forward, with a snarl, exclaiming, "Senator, stop complaining. We will take care of you!"

The senator just gives Luca a defeated look, a sad, painful expression, and does not reply.

Luca actually smiles, even friendly, then responds with a normal voice: "We are not lightweights in this area. Enough said. You know what to do. Senator, by the way, I have something completely different to ask you. I have another proposal I would like you to think about as a personal favor to me, something really critical to me, good for you, too."

"My son Anthony, is turning thirty years old, and his mother and I wish to see him married. I know your daughter, Anna, is twenty-eight, and I have seen her in the movies and I know she has done well. You must be very proud of her, as we are of Anthony. He is very good-looking, as is Anna, and he has expressed an interest in her. His mother and I would consider it a special favor if you would arrange a date with Anna for our son and foster the relationship as much as possible. Your future and mine are linked; let's become real family. I cannot tell you how important this is to us. He is a good boy."

The senator is visibly shocked. "Luca, this is a complete surprise. I have no control over Anna. She is self-supporting, actually wealthy, a celebrity, and she says she's not looking for romance. Her career is critical to her."

Luca smiles. "Sam, I understand. It's just a date. They're both young. Who knows where it may go if given a chance? Surely you can arrange a simple date."

The senator, with a superficial smile, says, "I will explore this with Anna, but as you know, she is my stepdaughter, and she has a mind of her own."

Luca looks hard at Sam. "Senator, over the years I have not asked much from you personally, and we know each other very well. You know what I am capable of when I need something important. I also know all of your secrets. You have gained much from our relationship over the years, and I want this to happen. I hope you understand me. Let me make it clear to you: my son is my son, and I will do whatever I have to do to make this happen."

Luca gets up without a further word, looks at his two bodyguards, two big thugs waiting at the door, and nods at them. They follow Luca out the door.

After Luca Deforleo walks out, the senator sits at their table not moving, physically nauseated, and trying not to vomit. He always knew over the years that this day would come, and he would pay the devil his due. He knew what was going through Luca's mind, and it was not finding a wife for his awful son Anthony. Sam knows Anthony, in and out of trouble for years, more sadistic than his father, narcissistic to the extreme, cruel, and using up girls, the prostitutes working for him, like throwing a daily newspaper into the trash can. Even more disgusting, he is involved in human trafficking.

No, Luca is more cunning than that, Sam reasons. *The safe way is to kill me after this is done,* he thinks. *No evidence back to him.* Yet Luca wants to find a reason for not killing him, to continue to use Sam as long as possible. He needs to find something to tie Sam down, yes, by using his daughter. Otherwise, he knows if Sam is caught, he will ask the US attorney for immunity. And get it just for ratting on Luca and his thugs. No, before that happens it is much smarter to kill Sam, maybe make it look accidental, maybe even kill his entire family in case they know about his dealings with the Luca Deforleo mob. Probably it will be a car bombing or maybe the house. Of course his family doesn't know about Luca, yet he will kill them anyway.

However, the senator thinks, Luca may prefer a second way, a better option for him and Sam. He thinks if Sam's daughter is married to his son, he holds her hostage, and they are all one big happy family. Anna is beautiful and a famous actress, which will please Luca and his son. Then when she has children, she will want to protect them. Luca controls her and Sam. The senator knows if he rats on Luca, he hurts Anna and his future grandchildren. God only knows the abuse she would receive from Luca's terrible son. Maybe even beatings or worse if Sam doesn't behave. Luca figures Sam could never rat on him and will continue to do his bidding because of what would happen to Anna. How on Earth can Sam tell Anna this, then face his wife? If he ignores it, they're all dead. What can he do to get out of this mess?

The vision of Anna being married to Anthony is ridiculous. Maybe she will have some ideas to solve this awful threat? Sam is ashamed to tell her, and his wife will think he is an old fool, or worse. He does not blame her. "I am an idiot!" he declares under his breath. Oh yes, tomorrow, he just remembered, he is having lunch with Anna and his wife. He has been looking forward to it; now he is dreading it. Wait. Maybe he should put off telling them, as Anna is bringing a boyfriend. Sam thinks his name is Henry, someone special she is excited about, probably some famous Hollywood actor. And he remembers Anna wants him to stay with them at the farm for a couple of days.

CHAPTER 21

EARTH AGAIN—DAY FOUR

The *Cyclone* is about forty-five thousand miles out and looking at the moon orbiting on this side of Earth. The navigational challenge is the simple fact that Earth is a moving target. It is traveling 67,108 miles an hour orbiting its star, the sun. Then, to add to the problem, the entire galaxy is also orbiting at a massive speed, averaging five hundred thousand miles an hour as it moves through space. Then, a further complication, the Earth is spinning at 932 miles an hour. The moon is very close to the planet, with all its massive craters, gray and foreboding, looming over the Northern Hemisphere, its gravity slowing the *Cyclone* down. Henry is thinking once again he is coming into the Earth's atmosphere so fast it will light up the sky when he hits. He knows he can be noticed by maybe 10 percent of the Earth's population when the *Cyclone* hits the atmosphere so fast, maybe this time around forty-five thousand miles an hour.

Yet there's no time to waste, as lunch with Anna's parents is set at a restaurant in Richmond about four hours from now. The *Cyclone* already burned off the frontal ice shield three hundred thousand miles back. It looked like an asteroid breaking up, hopefully not noticed by anyone paying attention from Earth.

Announcing the *Cyclone*'s presence so many times just causes ramifications, none good. And worse, although it is necessary, Anna makes another cell phone call to her mother, asking about lunch, where to go, the time and place. The FBI and the CIA will have fun figuring this all out. Henry smiles as he thinks about this and then about Anna. He needs to wake her up and make her breakfast.

Not too far from Richmond, back at CIA headquarters in Langley, there is a lot of activity going on. There is more breaking news. Finally, thinks John Jacobs, along with the best minds at Section 58, there is some definite and maybe real evidence of ET activity in the United States and maybe worldwide. Sitting in the CIA's largest conference room are the three staff members on his team, two agents from the FBI, one colonel from the air force, and a staff assistant from the White House to advise the president of whether this is worthy of his time. He knows they are all skeptical behind his back, maybe even worth a good laugh or two. He will show them this is the real thing. Actually, now that he has some real evidence, he's a little frightened of what to do next. There is no textbook on this, and there will be really heavy ramifications if it's not handled right.

He starts the meeting by saying there is a top-secret folder in front of each of them with a briefing on some outer space activity in the last thirty days that looks like ET spacecraft. He says, "You all have probably read about the ET activity in recent magazine and newspaper articles—the lighting up of the night skies. And there have been some new eyewitness reports. You are probably thinking, *More of the same old stuff.*" He pauses to build a little suspense, looks around at everyone, his excitement growing. With a strong, confident voice, he says, "Ladies and gentleman, not this time! This time it is different. Yes, now we have verified communications coming from deep outer space. It's impossible that they came from any Earth craft."

Now everyone in the room is staring intently at him. He has their attention.

"There have been sightings that were verified by radar and radiation monitors. Our satellites have also picked up proof of a spacecraft coming from deep space at speeds impossible for any Earth craft. We have other sightings, too. Witness statements verified a UFO. Several car passengers in Virginia saw a UFO off of Interstate 64, and it was at the same location where our jets were scrambled because of another massive radar signature. They, unfortunately, were too late for contact. It vanished."

John continues, a little embarrassed, "Another report in front of you includes a bizarre twist. It's almost impossible to believe. The most interesting UFO event that has been verified is the one about Anna Summers, the Hollywood actress. She has called her parents' home, using her cell phone, from outer space."

Everyone in the room laughs. Jacobs, not fazed, says, "By now you have seen the first transcribed conversation in your briefing folder. Please look it over. It is real. Another call happened late yesterday. The second transcribed phone conversation is in your folder. Both were from Anna. Yes, the Anna you know as the movie star. Yes, she is the stepdaughter of a US senator, Sam Jordan. She made two phone calls from outer space, the first from six hundred thousand miles out, the second from several million miles out, not that far from Mars. These calls are verified by several sources. We know they happened! The craft she was traveling on during the second conversation was calculated to be moving at about a hundred and fifty million miles per hour, many times faster than anything we know about, and moving away from Earth. As you can see in the transcripts, not much was talked about. The second call was to arrange lunch today with her parents. She is bringing a boyfriend."

He continues, "By the way, we have put the whole family on surveillance—wiretaps, everything we have as a resource. The senator, as you might not know, is already on surveillance. The boyfriend we know nothing about, although we just started checking him out. Maybe he has something to do with the alien connection. We will know more after their lunch, as we will have several surveillance teams on it. We will get photos of him, maybe even talk to Anna and find out if she was abducted. This is being handled carefully, as there may be alien oversight of her or maybe all of us. There is the possibility we accidentally made contact with an alien. It does not seem possible, yet we have some real concerns. The ramifications could be dramatic, as you can all imagine."

"The last item is a big one, and really bad news for all of us. One weird thing happened, real breaking news for all here, extremely frightening for me and really strange. We think there is now a possible threat to our national security. We think our checking these cell phone calls, checking the data route to find where they came from, led them back to us. Incredible as this sounds, we think this alien ship knows who we are, and it is now in our systems. They routed back to us using the same path, sort of a flashback stream, and hacked into our databases within seconds. It went right through some very sophisticated firewalls quickly. Our software protection and our virus defense had no barricades to stop them. We think it is currently pulling data from us, meaning coming from the entire US government; and, roaming through our systems wherever it wants to go, including all top-secret classified stuff."

"Now the real scary part: we can't shut it down. It is in our systems and will not allow us to shut it down. We even cut the power, yet everything is still running. I'm not sure where or how it is getting electrical power. Actually it doesn't matter now, it's too late anyway. They are with us, penetrated everything we have in place. We're trying to figure it out—who they are and what they want from us."

"Gentleman, even worse, they are not hiding from us. They know we know they are checking us out. We know data is leaving us and going to outer space. This is my final proof that this is real. We are in the presence of aliens, and they are checking us out, and they know there is nothing we can do about it."

Jacobs looks at the people around the conference table, who are all in shock, pale, and with real fear on their faces. No one is laughing now. All were expecting an easy day, not an extremely complicated day, as it is now. All now have to brief their bosses, all thinking they are telling their spouses even if they are sworn to secrecy. All are thinking everything they know about life has just changed.

⊷⊶

Unknown to Henry, these aliens on the bottom of the sea are thinking about a strategy to attack him, allowing them to proceed on their Earth plans. Henry is in the way of their plans. They know they are a serious threat to him, even more since his last encounter with them, as they have recently obtained more sophisticated technology: weapons equal to those of the *Cyclone*. Unfortunately for Henry, as Henry was on Earth, as of now, they might have him with the element of surprise. Just waiting to ambush him, and if successful, everyone on this planet would suffer. Earth would be without his defense. They know they just need to patiently wait, making preparations to attack, in their massive starship, their battleship; and, stay hidden, deep in the Mariana Trench in the Pacific.

They hate Henry and everything he stands for. They blame him for the politics of the Consortium, which considered them criminals to be arrested or destroyed at any opportunity. The truth was they had few options other than their current source of revenue. By pirating nuclear capacity in off worlds, they can almost meet their energy needs, but they always need more. They also are experts at extortion, kidnapping, and stealing anything that has value. They take and sell minerals and scrap metals, creating valuable element compounds needed by wealthy civilizations. They are pawnshop dealers and peddlers of stolen goods, selling throughout the universe, murdering most of their victims. Rarely do they give mercy.

As far as they are concerned, Henry's death is long overdue. If he does not know they are on this planet, a trap or ambush has a good chance of catching him unaware. Yes, a chance to destroy the *Cyclone* and Consortium captain, Henry Johnson, would be a fortunate turn of events.

They are preparing their lighter attack ships, going up to patrol the surface, careful to stay hidden. These spacecraft fighters are good for confronting anything, with especially vicious weapons in short-range battles. They are eighty-two feet long, dull black in color, and difficult to see in black space, with small upfront windshields and fourteen-foot wings on both sides, a dorsal fin on top, sleek and very fast, as propelled by huge fusion rockets, attached underneath with support arms. They are not manned with organic pilots; instead use deadly efficient, intelligent robot pilots. They are deadly machines using direct fusion weapons and incredibly hot lasers. Just one can destroy every army or air force on this world. The pirates have 284 of them on board and are now preparing ten of them to do stealth reconnaissance; if there is no *Cyclone* or other Consortium starships, they may go ahead and attack Earth. There must be something here they can sell, and they will also take as much nuclear energy as possible. Caution is the priority right now. There will be many issues if they end up in a confrontation with the *Cyclone*. It will take every weapon they have to destroy the *Cyclone* and then make a fast escape, head to a far corner of the universe, as the Consortium fleets will try to hunt them down. If caught by them the revenge will be brutal.

CHAPTER 22

MEETING ANNA'S FAMILY

I am currently in a strange environment, one I've never encountered before. I am not at all confident in these surroundings. In fact I am feeling really vulnerable. I am a long way from the world of starships right now, feeling both physically and mentally challenged. I am completely focused on Anna's parents, who arranged this luncheon at a very expensive restaurant in downtown Richmond. My mission is to make a good impression and the possible results seem problematic.

I think, *A good war is easier than this.* Anna's parents are tough, giving me a hundred-question overview. They want to know all about me. *How did I get myself into this?*

Both Senator Sam Jordan and his wife, Linda, are charming, and they are paying a lot of attention to my answers. Both of them are looking me over head to toe, asking me many personal questions. They both are really intent on finding out about me, not easy to avoid. The senator asks if I am with the military or have military experience, as I certainly look military. Anna said the best way of handling my current occupation status was to be honest, as the senator might check me out, and Anna feels honesty is always the best way, even if, as in my case, it's unbelievable.

I think maybe Anna is naïve, or at the very least, too trusting, but it is impossible for me to tell her this.

My other problem is that Anna does not know, nor do her father and mother, anything about their being the target of FBI wiretaps and surveillance. They are clueless. But I know a lot about the senator now; the *Cyclone* has uncovered many issues with him and his dealings with the Deforleo crime family, plus some serious illegal Iranian connections. I might be able to help him with some of these bad guys, although he is in a real fix, with no decent options left.

For today the *Cyclone* can block the CIA/FBI surveillance; plus maybe I can try to explain as much as possible to her parents. Not the whole story—best not to freak them out. I can make the CIA/FBI equipment not work just for today and blank out the camera shots, giving no information from us. However, I will not stop the FBI's continuing investigation into the senator's possible criminal activity in the past or future, nor will I tell him about it. Although I have decided I will insert the recognizant slips into the brains of all the surveillance team here today for some reverse surveillance. They will become my eyes and ears without them ever knowing it, and I will know who they are as individuals. The only effect they will feel from the slips inserted into their frontal lobes is a slight headache and some weird dreams when they sleep. Slips will be inserted into the senator and Luca Deforleo as soon as possible, too.

For the first time in my life, I have a critical personal dilemma. I am leaving in six days; my ten days will be up. Because of Anna I am thinking I need to change my life's direction. Who would think this could happen, and so fast for such a major life decision? The *Cyclone* thinks I need counseling. I'm going to attempt to retire from my position, although I'm not sure about telling her about this. My intentions may not matter, as there is a good chance I will not be successful. My retirement is complicated, to say the least. Heading back, when I am in face-to-face communication range, I will speak to Gabriel. I will tell him my story. I am unsure how this will go with him—probably not well.

I dread leaving Anna, especially if I cannot make it back for another ten years. She should not have to wait for me. That's not going to happen; it's not fair to her. I have to try to do what I can for her before I go back on duty and am gone. Of course there is the issue with all those troops in Russia, too. Not much time to do anything.

Also the *Cyclone* warned me about our communications breach by the CIA infiltration, Section 58, all because of Anna's phone calls. I arranged a return penetration into their IT systems, which gave me specific information about the FBI and the CIA. I know they are investigating this lunch meeting today. I need to know a lot more about Section 58 at the CIA. I also need all the FBI information about this whole mess. I especially need to know about the Iranian threat, and I want to know how far the corruption goes in the US government, maybe right up to the president.

The *Cyclone* will use thousands of our reconnaissance slips to enter and pull information from data banks both artificial, as in computer systems, and organic, meaning people. Unfortunately, entering organic means penetrating human brains and probing memories and following the conversations of US senators as well as officials from the Pentagon, the White House, and other branches and departments, as many as possible. I also want to know what's going on at Excalibur Bank, in the Deforleo family, and in the Iranian government. The *Cyclone* will deliver the slips there, too. The top guys at both places will then become very helpful to us. I am not sure why I feel so compelled to interfere in a situation that is none of my business.

Back to lunch with Anna's family, as I need to focus on how to make this work. I am thinking about how to answer the minefield of questions as the senator continues to interrogate me. Mrs. Jordan, Anna's mother, is much nicer, asking the usual things: about my parents, family, friends, where I grew up, how I met Anna—nice questions. Mrs. Jordan is a slender, attractive woman in her late fifties. She is not tall, has beautiful blond hair, is very well dressed, and looks as if she has seen a lot in her life. I like her. Anna looks like her. I think she likes me, too. I smile a lot, which is easy to do with her. I try to be charming and answer most of her questions. She does tell me this is the first time Anna has brought a male friend home.

Anna is quick to rescue me when she can break into the flow, using her newfound telepathy skills to coach me, keep me focused. The waiter comes again, thankfully breaking the attention away from me. Anna orders for both of us, saying the club special is great; this is of interest to me, as I have never had one. The blessings with Anna are the new experiences coming every hour. She excuses herself to go to the bathroom, and to the surprise of her parents she kisses me, smiles, and tells me to behave when she is gone.

The senator is now ordering lunch, too; after drinking several drinks, he orders another. He's definitely a bourbon guy. We all have ordered lunch. Anna is back, and I am not sure what to do about the senator, as this is so personal for me, dealing with Anna's family. I really don't want to disappoint Anna. She reassures me mentally, saying I'm doing fine. I decide to tell the senator we should have lunch again sometime and get to know each other better. I tell him I can try to answer some more of his questions as best I can under my circumstances. I just tell him I was former military, classified operations, not much I can talk about, and currently a type of military consultant. I tell him that as we get to know each other better, I can give him more detail on his questions.

As we continue with lunch, the senator all of a sudden glares at me and says roughly, "I don't want these evasive answers. No BS! Do you work for the CIA or NSA? What do you really do for a living? Are you solvent, and what are your intentions with Anna?"

I am concerned by his directness and hostility. I look him straight in the eye, penetrating, and firmly say, "Senator, in your situation, with Anna as your stepdaughter, I understand your anxiety. I will tell you I am very wealthy; actually I have many times your wealth. And I know everything about you. And I mean everything. As to what I do for a living, it would be dangerous for you to know what I do. It is also way beyond your comprehension. At some future date, not long off, we will have a long, very complicated discussion. As for my intentions with Anna, they are straight from the heart. Very simply, I care for her!"

The senator is really shocked, can't hold eye contact with me, real fear and anxiety in his eyes. This is not what I intended, although it is probably impossible for me to have a relationship with him knowing what I know. Yet I want to help him for Anna's sake. I look to see if she is angry with me because of the exchange. I am surprised to see she is angry but not with me. She is angry with her father.

She is obviously upset with him and blurts out, "Dad, just slow down. I've brought Henry to meet you and Mom because he has become important to me. I know you and Mom must be surprised, as this is the first time I've brought someone home. Yet it is what it is, and I would appreciate less hostility."

Anna's mom, although visibly stunned, is trying to make amends, saying she is glad Anna finally brought a friend home; it's about time. Actually I am surprised, too. I made my statement of my feelings without thinking, and I am really relieved Anna feels the same. All of this is happening so fast, way too fast even for me, yet as Anna said, it is what it is. We just have to make it all fit.

We all look at one another, and Anna's mother breaks the silence when she smiles and says, "Well, Anna, I guess that answers the question about how serious you are about Henry. And Henry, the senator and I open our home to you and insist you come out to our farm for the next few days and stay with us. I know Anna is planning to stay with us, and I'm sure you will have a great time. What do you like to do for fun? We can plan to go out for dinner. You also will have a chance to spend time with Nikki, Anna's sister. Anna doesn't know this yet, but I just found out she's coming tomorrow. She wants to see Anna and you, too, Henry."

Across the room, John Jacobs is looking at Henry sitting at an adjoining table on an outside patio. He is monitoring the surveillance teams at the restaurant. He can't believe the cameras are not recording, and there is no sound from the microphones placed everywhere, even under their table. Thus nothing has been achieved at the lunch, where there is a chance for some real intelligence. Anna and her family had a nice little reunion, and nothing worked; all their equipment was blocked, no evidence of anything.

John knows for sure this is more than coincidence, yet it would seem some really sophisticated electronic blocking is taking place. He doesn't have a clue how or from where. If it is not an ET event, it could be the Mafia trying to protect the senator, although if they know about the FBI investigating him, they might have some more sinister plans for him and his family. The only good news today is the senator called Luca Deforleo in New York by cell phone about thirty minutes after the lunch, from his car while driving to his Richmond home. The conversation was recorded. Nothing interfered with this wiretap this time.

The conversation was about the lunch. Apparently the senator thinks Anna's new boyfriend, Henry, is some kind of military intelligence agent and wants Deforleo to check him out. The surveillance teams agreed that the boyfriend looks real military and maybe is a former SEAL. He is definitely not a guy you would take on without a lot of serious backup. Interestingly enough, Deforleo also mentioned Anna to the senator and said to him this problem with her boyfriend is all the more reason she should marry his son Anthony. He wants the senator to help Anthony get to know Anna. The senator responded this would never happen as long as Henry is around, as there is no question Anna is serious about him. Deforleo laughed and said that is not a problem. He asked the senator if he had brought up the suggestion of a meeting with Anthony, and the senator replied that it was impossible with Henry visiting them. Deforleo suggested to the senator that he tell Anna that Anthony is coming to LA in a couple of weeks, and he would consider it as a favor to a very old friend if Anna would show him around Hollywood and LA.

Deforleo assured the senator that Anthony would take care of Anna and not to worry about Henry. He would take care of Henry; no worries about that. He asked the senator how long Henry is going to be at his Richmond farm. The senator thought two or three days. Deforleo asked the senator to call him back, to check on Henry's activities, find out when Henry would be planning to be outdoors, maybe when Henry runs if he runs or takes a walk. What does he do in the mornings?

Jacobs wonders if he should warn Henry that his life is in danger. No, the surveillance team will be there, and he will bring in two SWAT teams in addition, knowing an assassination attempt on Henry is going to happen, probably when Anna and Henry take their run in the morning. *We should help keep him alive,* Jacobs thinks, and they will stop a hit if they see it happening. Henry will not be easy to take down. This is getting really complicated.

And who is this Henry? He does not work for any intelligence unit they could find, or the CIA, as no agency here has any knowledge of him. Might be for a country overseas. Russia? They could find out nothing on him anywhere; real spooky. He does not exist, absolutely nothing. Maybe black operations of Mossad of Israel?

Anyway, John is tired. He needs to go home, see his wife and kids, get a night at home, some real sleep before the early morning activity at the senator's farm. He is thinking about the best thing that ever happened to him, which is his beautiful, loving wife, Judy, his college sweetheart, now married thirty wonderful years. He is fifty years old, in the CIA all his life, joined right out of college. He is also lucky as she still loves him. Now, after all these years, she has a reason to be proud of him. He has real news to tell her. He finally is at the right place at the right time and can do something for his country and finally make her proud of him.

When he arrives home, the house is dark, and the kids are in bed, maybe Judy, too. He goes into their five-bedroom brick colonial by way of the kitchen door. They have lived in this same house for twenty-five years; it's in a nice neighborhood, even better with just five years left on the mortgage. They just need to get the kids through college and married off.

Surprising him, Judy is still up, reading on their living room couch under one small reading lamp. She looks up, looking tired, and smiles warmly. "John! Good, you're home. It's late. How is work, and how are you? I was getting worried. I have hardly seen you this week!"

He leans down, kisses her, and, with a loving gaze, smiles. "Honey, I am so sorry. How are you, the kids; everything OK? I apologize as I have not been much help around here lately. I will make it up to you. This stuff at work has taken me for a spin."

Judy responds, saying, "Yes, you do owe me; come in the kitchen; I will fix you something to eat. Do you want a drink? Tell me what is going on while you fix yourself a drink."

"There have been some new developments in this project I've been working on, real remarkable things. I never tell you about my work, as it's classified information. However, this is different. You need to know this, especially if something happens to me."

She looks up at him with a worried look on her face. "John, are you in danger? Are we all in danger? What about the kids?"

"No, we're fine for now, yet I see some serious stuff coming. Never in the history of the world has this type of stuff happened. I think it's coming. I can feel it. I should not disclose this for many reasons. You cannot tell anyone, absolutely no one! Please, I want to tell you, yet no one must hear this."

"Judy, do you understand? You cannot divulge this to anyone."

She has an upset look as she intently stares at him. Seeing her tired, frightened husband, she is totally baffled. She whispers, "Yes, I will tell no one. You have my promise."

"Honey, you know what my section does. You know no one ever takes us seriously. Everyone laughs at us." He pauses and looks at his wife, then continues. "Well, it's hard to tell you this, but I am dead serious. It's finally happened. We have real contact from an alien life form. I think there are spaceships currently here on Earth, verified proven contact, and they are not from this planet. I'm not sure where they're from. We have alien visitors, and they're not trying hard to hide from us. They're even checking us out. Even crazier, I feel odd, like someone is watching me, and I am afraid. For the first time, I am really afraid. They have to represent a civilization far older, more advanced, as they have starships that come from trillions of miles away, and they are not human, although they may look human."

"I just know we will have an event sometime in the next few days or maybe in the next few weeks. I think life will change on Earth as we know it." He looks at his wife in silence, with a foreboding expression, certain finality on his face. She stands, says nothing, and goes to him, wraps her arms around him.

⚔ ⚔

Anthony Deforleo just got off the cell phone with his father. He is thinking his father is normally a pain in the ass, but for a change he is on to something really good. He is working on his senator friend that they own, to help Anthony out. He is trying to hook Anthony up with the senator's stepdaughter, famous, gorgeous Hollywood actress Anna Summers. Yes, she is somebody he would love to train, make a good girl out of her. Maybe he might get his chance. He laughs, an ugly look on his face. He's never been a kind man; his laughter is something to fear.

Anthony knows he first has to get some things done. Lot to do. Plus he is short three guys, so he has to do some of this work himself. Three of his best guys are gone; the whole crew just disappeared. Marco, the crew chief, never reported back, and he had some good things going. Not a good sign in this business. He will find out what happened to them, then, time for payback; if someone was behind it, they will suffer plenty. Strange, though, no one knows anything, no sign of them.

No matter, his father told him another shipment of girls is to be picked up in the Ukraine early the following morning. Time to call his pilots, take the corporate jet, another long trip. Yet an enjoyable meeting with some new girls waiting for him, time to train the innocent ones, young girls between fifteen and twenty, just the right age to break in, their total surrender to him inevitable. Their pain is his pleasure, slowly breaking them down, and then teaching them the skills of prostitution

216

and sexual slavery. He prides himself on breaking their will in four weeks, then they are making him money, with several tricks a day. Each girl averages $3,000 a day in revenue, six days a week, for about $72,000 a month minus $6,000 a month in total expense. This leaves $66,000 a month in profits, thus each girl is worth much more than half million a year. They are good for about six years, and then he sells them at auction for around $50,000, depending on their looks and ages. If not sold, they are eliminated.

What a wonderful moneymaker. His father finally admits it is the best source of revenue they have and all because of Anthony. It is better than selling drugs; there are no turf wars. The number of customers is unlimited, too, as there's a constant demand. They have gone national, with girls set up in every state. He is even leasing the girls out monthly and always with plenty of blackmail possibilities. Truly a great business, and there is little risk of going to jail. No girl ever testifies. He laughs.

Everyone knows how well Anthony trains his girls, and a GPS chip is embedded in each of them, so they can never escape him. The chip is embedded under their scalp during the plane trip to the United States, when they are initially drugged. They land on an isolated and unknown landing strip in northern Minnesota. They end up in a warehouse not too far from the airstrip, also isolated. No one hears their screams. The training methods are perfected through a lot of experience. They all give in sooner or later. The drugs help, too; cocaine is the best controller. We use shots of hormones to help make sex addicts out of these girls, as they are young and vulnerable to the effects. It is helpful in their line of business.

They also learn about the leather belt. It will be used a lot during training and as a weekly reminder as the months go by. It is amazing how well it works across their bottoms, leaving no marks on their faces.

Sometimes, after they become working girls, one is enticed to escape just so she can become an example to the rest. Anthony enjoys these moments immensely, savoring them, torturing her in front of the rest, a slow, painful death. Killing one every so often keeps them all in line, culls out the losers, too. It helps the attitudes of the rest. They are willing to please customers with any fetish, never a complaint. Anthony always enjoys doing quality control. He again laughs to himself.

The girls are so pretty, young, and sweet when they get on the plane. They come from villages located all over Europe and Russia. They can speak a little English; still they know how to giggle and laugh as happy, young girls do, when going to fulfill their dreams. They are excited and so proud about being selected to be models in the United States, to make more money than they ever dreamed about, to receive their visas. Amazingly enough, sometimes their parents actually deliver them to the corporate jet. Also proud of their daughters although the mothers are crying at letting them go; tears pour; promises to write home are made. They sacrifice as a better life beckons for their daughters. They are told the immigration process will be done for them— another lie. If they somehow escape, they are deported back to their homeland. If they are lucky enough to make it back home, they are too ashamed to tell anyone of their deeds.

Damn, Anthony thinks, *life is good*. He's making big money. Now this Anna Summers thing. His father finally did something right. Who would think, him and Anna Summers? Wow, great bragging rights, and she is hot. He knows exactly what to do with her when his chance comes. She will never know what hit her until it is too late, and then she will know a real man. What a stroke of luck, a chance to get in Anna Summers's pants. Life does not get much better.

CHAPTER 23

DAY FIVE

I was up and ready to join Anna for her morning run on the farm. She insisted she needs it to clear her head, and she agreed I could run with her as long as I can keep up with her. Just no talking!

The events of yesterday are still on both of our minds. We came back to the farm after lunch and spent some time touring the place, checking the horses and looking at Anna's favorite hunter-jumper, a large chestnut quarter horse called Misty. She shared many favorite stories about growing up on the farm, telling me about her friends, explaining about her sister and school, and then talking about her acting. I loved listening to her. I am glad I am here and that she feels the way she does about me, although neither of us brought this up. Too many minefields and issues about me leaving, not good to talk about this now. We agreed, later, after the farm visit, we will talk, before I head out on the *Cyclone*, back to where I came from.

Dinner with her parents last night was much better than lunch. The homemade dinner, prepared by Anna and her mother, was excellent. The senator was not drinking as much as he did at lunch. Then the evening was finished out with us playing bridge. I learned the game long ago, during my college years in Bloomington. It was a truly a delightful evening. This may be my best trip back ever; it's truly a good life to be a human.

Then, two in the morning, the *Cyclone*'s report on the CIA activities came to me, including the CIA download of the senator's conversation with Deforleo and a briefing on the Deforleo crime syndicate. Everything was thoroughly reported, including the Iran connection, which is, by the way, a real US security threat. How could Anna be related to the senator? He is such a cheat. Well, that's not right, as I now remember what Anna said. She is his stepdaughter; although she is close like a daughter, they are not blood related.

Now I know what Deforleo is up to regarding me. His plans for Anna are disturbing and arouses an annoyance in me that reveals more about me than him. I am also a little surprised that I am a target and that the senator knows about it; so much for making a good impression on Anna's stepfather. It is much easier to counter them knowing their plans. He has managed to put together a twenty-man team of professional killers, some Mafia but mostly an Iranian military hit squad. I am surprised he can do this so quickly. I am not anxious, just surprised I am a high-priority target. The *Cyclone* will be here as always, up above, close, maybe eight hundred feet, with all its killing power. It will know where every Iranian soldier or terrorist is positioned and every Mafia thug by their heat signatures. Yes, Iran's military intelligence and Luca will be introduced to an enemy they have never experienced before: lethal, ruthless, accurate, and, even worse, completely unknown to them.

I am thinking Anna should not be in danger from the hit squad, as she is not the target. It would be better if I could talk her out of running this morning—better not to take chances with her life. I know they will try to use snipers against me, an easy hit, as they think I am not aware they are here. Regrettably for them, I will know exactly where they are, as the *Cyclone* will spot them and take them all out in the same second. They will be vaporized at fifteen thousand degrees, no bodies or weapons left, including hitting their command vehicle and three cargo vans parked two miles from here. I know they came in at night, set up at daybreak, and arranged eight snipers hidden in the trees. Six more are scattered behind trees as backup guys, heavily armed as a plan B, and four of them are stationed in a communications van, with two standing guard. It really is professionally done. It is remarkable Deforleo could put this together and find out about Anna running with me, or my running with her. I am an easy target. It had to be the senator tipping them off.

The farm is a beautiful place. Anna was accurate in every way when she first told me about it. First of all it is large, two thousand acres, with several streams running through it, many trees, and pastures with white fencing. The land is mostly rolling hills with a few meadows, full of wildflowers. The scent of it all is fantastic—the fragrance of freshly cut grass, the wildflowers, the bubbling creek, and the trees, even the wildlife. The sounds are comforting: the water trickling over rocks, songbirds singing, trees rustling in the breeze, and horses grazing on the grass, making munching sounds as they greedily work their way through the fields.

It is a working farm: breeding, raising and selling stock. There are eight full-time hands maintaining the grounds and horses. Two of them live on the farm, in small houses not far from the main house. Also, the main house, the senator's home, is magnificent, right out of a movie about the South or Virginia. It was used in a film years ago, showing a huge Southern plantation home at the end of a long lane, with a big front porch with pillars and a circular driveway also connected to a back lane, with large well-kept horse barns plus a grand six-car garage.

Anna and I are going running on the farm and it is perfect. Horse trails through the woods make good running trails. The weather is just right, with blue skies and a cool morning breeze. Anna runs six miles most mornings, and as we run together today I stay close. Because of my benefactors, my running range is many miles more than a human's range. Per my DNA enhancements, I also run with great speed, maybe hitting forty-five miles an hour and continuing day after day, stopping only for minimal nourishment and a little sleep. Yet it is still hard work to cover those long distances. My running with Anna is not work, just pure pleasure. Just seeing her run is wonderful. She pays no attention to me. She laughs at me when I mentioned her not running today, and she took off. She is graceful and an excellent athlete, and I pushed to catch her.

⊶ ⊷

Jacobs knows the CIA and the FBI are also at the senator's farm this morning with three four-man teams, all heavily armed yet no match for Luca's hit squad, which is already in position there as well. Jacobs is heading up his team and can see most of the hit squad snipers in the trees, not that hidden and arrogant because of the high ground and there are so many of them. The number of Luca's men, so many, shocks Jacobs. They look more like military black ops, really well armed: sniper rifles, grenades, RPLs, and large-caliber assault guns.

Jacobs thinks, *I need to find another line of work. This is way too dangerous for a man with so many kids.* At the moment he is also wondering if he will see his wife tonight. She will be lost without him. He is now frightened by the possibility of losing all his men, thinking they're all good men with families to support. *How could Luca put such a large, heavily armed hit squad together so quickly and position them here at the farm for an ambush?* It looks like at least twenty heavily armed men with automatic military weapons, looking like real elite commandos. They set up their positions like military, not Mafia guys. Jacobs shouts at his guys, warns them to find cover. They run, spreading out and trying to find defensive positions. Unfortunately Luca's men have high ground in the trees.

No way can we win this, thinks Jacobs. He knows he could lose his whole team. What a terrible way to end his career.

Each side has spotted the other. Jacobs's men try to set up their positions. Neither party is sure what is going to happen. Jacobs guesses there will be an immediate attack from the other side before he can get more backups, thus preventing reinforcements. He has already called everyone he knows for immediate aid, and he needs some SWAT team guys fast, lots of them. Police, too, whomever he can get here as soon as possible.

How could I have been so stupid to end up like this? Jacobs wonders. In that instant he can see the snipers lining up their shots on his men. It all happens so fast. "Damn them. Damn Luca!"

Then, just as it looks like World War III will break out between them, in an instant the snipers are all gone. They disappear before Jacobs's eyes! Even though it's impossible, it happens, and it occurs instantaneously. It's almost like individual explosions timed at the exact second, or maybe more like many strikes of lightning hitting at the same time yet much faster; then shock waves afterward like thunder. The trees even burn after the strike, black from the heat. Jacobs cannot believe his eyes. The snipers all just vaporize in a fraction of a second and all at the same time. Just gone! It looks like the killing strike turns all of them red hot, and then they are dust or more like smoke in the wind. Jacobs and his men run out, looking for some clue as to what happened. Nothing is left of the shooters—no weapons, nothing. The only evidence is the scorched leaves, a terrible smell, and darkened grass below the hit. Every one of them is gone in exactly the same second. It cannot be; it's impossible, yet it happened.

Jacobs is speechless. His mind is in a state of disbelief as he tries to figure it all out. Then the state police arrive, sirens on. Then more backup from the FBI. The local police arrive, followed by the local sheriff. And then Anna and Henry come running up as the senator and his wife drive up behind them. The farm crew shows up. It is one big mess. Jacobs dares not mention the failed hit on Henry, yet he has to say why all this happened. Yes, the FBI and state police are here at the farm. What to tell them?

The total disappearance of the hit squad needs reasons, but that will have to wait for now, as there is no real evidence: no bodies, no anything, no explanation. Even though Jacobs and his men saw what happened, it would have to be kept in-house for now. A forensics team will be arriving soon. He will cover up what really happened. He will explain they were notified of an immediate terrorist threat to the senator and his family. One break is this is an excuse to meet the principals of his investigation, as they are all here. He would like to know a lot more about Henry, maybe even more at another time and place. Something is not right with him. Jacobs needs to find a reason to arrest him and get some answers. Close surveillance is needed for sure. For now he will just tell everyone it was a false alarm. They had notice of a plot, probably false, against the senator and came out to check it out. Nothing to it. No terrorists showed up. Sorry for the scare.

Henry and Anna have about ten minutes with John Jacobs. They tell him their names and say they know nothing about the threat. They are shocked that a terrorist group would threaten the senator and glad they have the government to protect them. Henry cannot help but like Jacobs. He likes his basic honesty; he's a good man trying to do the right thing. Jacobs is tall, middle-aged, decent-looking although with some extra weight on him, balding with gray hair, and he takes his job seriously. Henry knows Jacobs is married with five children and is a good father, also living paycheck to paycheck. It is interesting that Jacobs is really curious about Anna and him. Henry knows Jacobs knows a lot more about the situation than he lets on, enough to be afraid. Henry is glad the *Cyclone* was able to save Jacobs and his men. Henry needs to continue to keep track of him, know what he is doing, and maybe even protect him. He already knows what Jacobs is thinking, as the *Cyclone* inserted a slip into his brain the previous day at the restaurant. Henry knows all about his family, too, including their problems.

Anna excuses both of us, telling Jacobs good-bye, thanking him, and we head back to the house. Walking slowly, Anna starts talking: "Henry, the last four days have been a roller-coaster ride—you and me, then my life turned just crazy, and then this. I think Mr. Jacobs is not telling the whole story. He brought a lot of armed men out here without calling us, and he looked spooked, like he's seen a ghost. His hands were shaking. There's a lot more to this. My father and mother are really upset, too. I have never seen Dad like this; he is not himself. He looks so old and tired and...*afraid*."

She continues, "I wish I knew what's going on. I know you don't need to hear this family stuff, and it's not usual stuff for me, either. I guess I've been sheltered. Dad has always provided me with security, has security guys here at the farm and pays for them even in LA. I have a security service there mostly because of the paparazzi. They drive me nuts! Of course with you around, I don't need security. By the way, we have to come up with a better cover story than you being a grad student in political science at Indiana University. My friends will never buy it. Seriously, Henry, I never believed it. I doubted you right away. The ex-military story you told my dad is much better."

I look at Anna walking beside me, still sweating, her blond hair a mess, wearing a sweatshirt and really short shorts, wedged a little into her bottom because of the running, looking great. She is just a gorgeous woman. Never underestimate human hormones. I feel like grabbing her.

Instead I smile at her, responding, "Anna, truly I thought it was a great cover story. I have used it for years, even have false records planted at IU admissions. The theory is I should not be a glamorous person but rather under the radar, nothing special to cause someone to think of who I might really be: an eccentric guy from outer space."

Anna says, "Henry, it's a good thing you have me to coach you. First of all, you do not look like a student, not even a little. Actually, you might scare the hell out of anybody when you don't smile and use that stare. It's scary even for me. You look all military, like Special Forces or a SEAL, or maybe a tough professional football player. It's your eyes. Henry, you could kill with your eyes. I can't explain it, and I figure it's in your past. You have seen some really bad things. You are not much of an actor, either. Go for a story that is extreme military. Maybe you were in the French Foreign Legion. No one knows those guys; they're just scary guys, too. Some truth helps make your story more plausible.

"By the way," she continues, "you scared the hell out of my father, and he does not scare easily. He wants nothing to do with you. Mother likes you, thinks you're sweet and good for me, will protect me from the bad guys in the world; she thinks you are very handsome, too." Anna is blushing now. "My sister thinks you're awesome and wants to know you much better. And what was the talk with my father about you being wealthy? Maybe you're really a rich space pirate taking advantage of a little Earth girl."

I laugh. "No, I am not a pirate. The money I have was gold originally, from one of the worlds we were on. Some worlds have lots of it, as common as dirt. Actually this planet is the only planet

I know of that treasures gold. It's easy for me to be rich here on Earth. I had a law firm handle selling the gold when I brought it here years ago. They work with my bank and oversee my holdings here on Earth. I wanted to mention them to you, too. They're coming to see you next week, after I'm gone. They'll call you. Please see them as a favor to me. The attorney's name is Mark Beagle, and he will call you, will come to LA to see you. He and his firm represent me here. They may be able to help you when I am gone, and you will find the conversation interesting."

Anna looks at me and says, "I don't know why I'm surprised. It sounds like you. Like I said, it's a crazy world we live in, and I will be happy to talk to him. Although I am not interested in you leaving so soon, and maybe I can change your mind. We will need to have a serious discussion."

We head out at a fast run, and back at the house, we undress and shower together. We are doing most everything together now; we are inseparable. I am really dreading our parting. Next week is coming too quickly.

I smile at Anna, looking down at her, enjoying her being bare, both of us in the shower together, holding each other. We are enjoying the warm-water spray, looking at each other, locking eyes, taking it all in. I am loving all of it: her scent, her warmth, the intimate physical contact, her closeness, tasting her as I kiss her, feeling her breasts against me, her nipples stiff. It is hard not to become excited about human life. I love it, and Anna loves it, too. She is flushed, excited, and aroused, her arms around my neck, tenderly moving closer to make herself available. She has that look of submission on her face; she is mine to take. She closes her eyes and bends her hips into me, spreading her legs wider and wider, arching up, then slowly moving her pelvic mound up and down. She presses harder against me, moving faster now. She is breathing heavily, wrapping her arms tighter around my neck. She then lifts her body with her arms, with my help, bringing her pelvis up to me higher, wrapping her legs around my hips. I have slipped into her before I can take another breath.

I am holding on to her bottom with both hands, controlling her, lifting her up and down for deeper penetration. She is all mine, her moans of pleasure motivating me further. I am feeling a wild, primitive lust, moving hard into her, and her submission is amazing to me. She matches me with her own hard thrusting, both of us now frantic, moaning. We also both mentally feel the fever, her mind to my mind. We are both as one, an intense fire building up, more now, then way beyond control, wild and hard, then her total surrender into an explosion of ecstasy. I hear and feel her crying my name in an emotional outburst of sheer delight. My mental and physical explosion happens in almost the same second, and I am in the world I want to be in. It is wonderful, beyond my wildest dreams. To be human is fantastic!

We dry each other off, and then I lift and carry the naked Anna to the bedroom sofa. She is totally spent, her submission to me a total turn-on. She is glad to be in my arms, smiling, humming my name lovingly, and saying how blessed we are. Then she falls asleep in my arms. We are like that for the next hour, covered with a blanket. I am the happiest I have ever been in my life.

Anna wakes up, still curled up in my lap like a little girl, and then looks at me with a big grin, jumping up, saying, "Starman, it's probably time to get going. We both need to get dressed. Nikki is coming in; she'll be at the airport soon. By the way, we're all going out to dinner tonight with my father and mother and Nikki, too."

Anna continues, talking fast, "You met Nikki, remember? Susan's roommate and my sister? She's great fun, and she will laugh at our being together. I am picking her up at the airport today; you don't need to come. You probably have things to do anyway. I can only imagine what might be in the universe-problems job, waiting for your response. Scares me just to think about it! Nikki and I will have lunch together and catch up. You know, sister talk. You have the entire afternoon to do your thing. Then I think we should head out for London tomorrow and attend my movie premiere, with you as my date. You will need a tux. Then, in a couple of days, we'll go to my place in Hollywood. I want to introduce you to my friends and cook meals for you. Is this still OK for you?"

I smile and just look at her, thinking, *Never underestimate the power of the human female.*

Then Anna grins. "Henry, if it's not OK, too bad for you. You're still going. We'll pack tonight. Do we take the *Cyclone*, or do I need to call the airline?"

I laugh and reply, "We take the *Cyclone!*"

⟫⟪

John Jacobs is back at Langley, thinking that all hell has broken loose. The phone has been ringing off the hook ever since the event at the senator's farm. His report was clear and factual, and a forensic team from the FBI was out there, too. The site was clean, undisturbed; their report backed him up. They also had checked a military satellite, pulling the infrared photo scan of the area from the exact time. It showed the shape of a massive invisible aircraft of some sort that was hovering high above the confrontation. It also clearly showed a massive radiation shot of fifteen thousand degrees or more in a split second, simultaneously hitting all the locations of the shooters. They must have been totally vaporized, as there were no bodies. This was a really serious weapon using massive energy. Nothing like this existed on Earth. Yes, this really was alien, the real thing. Finally no one was laughing at him.

The White House was briefed, including the National Security Council. The president gave Jacobs the green light to use all resources to figure out what was going on. No contact was to be made with an alien civilization without discussion with the president.

Of course, thought Jacobs. *What if I get a phone call from an alien? What do I do? Tell him I'll get back to him?* Actually he would like to thank them for saving his life, as Deforleo almost ended his career that day and could have made his wife a widow. He severely underestimated Luca Deforleo.

The following morning Jacobs would need to follow up on his wiretap on Deforleo, extend it to all his family and known associates, the bankers, too, and follow up on the twenty-four-hour surveillance on Henry and Anna. He had a crazy thought: could Henry be an alien? He looked normal, like a military guy, and did not fit the profile. Neither did Anna. Henry was charming and hard not to like. Anna certainly did not look alien. She might be a movie star, yet she is really nice. He actually likes them both, a nice couple, and they were good together. Learning more about both of them should be interesting.

At the King Georges Café in Richmond, Virginia, the two sisters are eating lunch, happy to be together. Nikki is looking at Anna, trying to eat her club sandwich and keep talking at the same time. They have been talking nonstop since Anna picked her up at the airport. She has brought Anna up to date on her recent activities, telling her she loves her classes and knows she will be a very good doctor. And then reading the tabloids that are talking about Anna with a new boyfriend, a Henry Johnson, spotted together in a restaurant looking very cozy. Anna laughs, saying it's nothing, yet Henry is at the farm, and all of them will be having dinner together, as a family, that night at a nice restaurant.

"Anna, come on, quit stalling. Tell me about Henry! I can't believe you've fallen for him. You just met him a few days ago. It's impossible, yet I definitely see it in your eyes when you talk about him. They really light up. You're flushed, and your face glows big time. No question, you are in love. Give it up, girl!"

"Nikki, I don't know what to say. It is crazy, and you would never believe me. Henry is much more than he appears. I am talking earth shaking and world changing, nothing like you could ever anticipate. No one has a clue just looking at him. I don't know what to tell you or what I can tell you. I think I'm hallucinating just thinking about it. It's overwhelming, surreal; it changed my life forever. I am not sure about love, although this could be a real possibility. I have never felt like this before. I feel it necessary to be with him every minute. Is that love? I miss him even now. I know it is stupid and senseless."

Nikki, excited, exclaims, "My God! Please tell me everything. What has happened? Is he some kind of prince? Is he in the CIA? Maybe he's a government assassin like James Bond. Is he a billionaire? Are you having sex with him? I know you are. Tell me!"

"Nikki, much more weird than all of that, it will astonish you, if I can get you to believe it. You have to keep what I tell you secret. Tell no one; swear it. Lives are at stake. I am not kidding."

"Anna, seriously, is this for real?" Pausing, she sees Anna's expression. "OK, then yes, I swear. I will tell no one. I swear it!"

"Nikki, for you to believe this, I have to start from the beginning, from our first day together until now; otherwise it is unbelievable. I don't believe it, and I lived it. Are you ready? Keep an open mind, and don't say anything until I have told the whole story. You agree to this?"

"Yes, I agree. Please tell me. The suspense is killing me!"

Anna goes through the whole thing, every event: their argument while driving, the car going over the cliff, the starship, the solar system, staying on the starship, the tour of the ship, the telepathy, and a condensed version of their couplings. The visions of KA*AM and talking about the other worlds and the aliens are a shock. Her words sometimes widen Nikki's eyes, causing a few groans and a few tears, some of it causing her eyelids to flutter, maybe a couple of looks of fear plus real concern, and then some fast breathing at times. Her face flushes with excitement or maybe astonishment.

Anna asks, "Nikki, do you have questions? Do you believe me? Are you afraid? What do you think? Do you have any advice?"

Nikki is pale, no expression. Nothing. She tries to talk, can't, pauses, shakes her head, and then finally, slowly breaks into a big smile. "Anna, it is incredible, unbelievable, mind bending, and I do believe you. You are the only person I would believe with a story like this one. When I think about my meeting Henry, before, at our first meeting, I could not understand my feeling then. It all makes sense now. His eyes are so penetrating. No one I have ever met has eyes like him. It's like he can read your thoughts. No wonder. He probably was reading my thoughts. Anna, there might be a lot more about him than you know. You need to be careful. This is one for the history books and much more significant to me as I'm your sister."

"Anna, I should not encourage you, yet you know I like him. It's hard to believe, yet in a strange way he reminds me of you. He also seems lonely, sad, too, very kind, and really miraculous, just like you. Intuitively my feelings are telling me he is a good man. And for sure, like every normal man I know, it seems he certainly likes sex!" They both laugh.

Nikki continues, "He is what you say: awe inspiring and definitely intimidating. He is certainly different, more than unique, not like anyone on this planet, to say the least. Anyway, for what it's worth, I approve, as long as you stay on this planet."

Anna laughs.

Looking at Anna with a loving, tender smile, nodding her head, Nikki goes on: "Yes, Anna, I like him, and I think you can trust him, if you can trust any man. And I really like that he makes you happy, more than I have ever seen you." She laughs. "He is really hot, too!"

Anna smiles and tears come to her eyes. "I love you, Nikki. You always know what to say, and you always have my back."

Nikki responds, "I wish I could do better. I don't know what you should do about all this. I have no real advice for you. This is way too much information for me to respond to. This is way beyond the world as I know it. You are in uncharted territory and you have not known him long. I have to think about this a long time. You're right, this is life changing, totally astonishing. Please be careful."

Anna, her face serious, says, "I know it's unreal, totally outlandish. It is surely not your typical, normal relationship. I may be in way over my head, and there may not be a happy ending. It is so complicated."

Nikki responds, "The question is, what are you going to do? What if he asks you to come with him? Will I see you again, and where would you go, out there in the universe? How can you be sure you really love him in such a short length of time? This is totally crazy. And you don't have to answer this, but do you think Henry is an alien?"

"I don't think so. I don't know what I'm going to do. It's too soon to seriously think about it. I know Henry is not an alien, not totally, or at least not in the normal way. He is mostly human, yet there are some good alien things about him, not weird, just good things. The telepathy is definitely good." Anna laughs. "I'm not sure where the sex is coming from, but that part is outstanding!"

She pauses, intently looking at Nikki, and smiles. "Nikki, you will love him. He is like an angel: kind, compassionate, strong, fun, charming, loyal, smart, and sure not boring. He has a lot of responsibility, too. You cannot let on you know about him. Promise me again. It is actually dangerous."

Nikki responds, "Yes, yes, yes. I promise, and I do understand why. It is scary to think about it."

⊷⊶⊷⊶

Back at the farm, the senator is trying to figure a way out of making the call to Luca; he does not want to talk to him, although he knows Luca is waiting for his call. He dreads the reaction he will get from Luca. The situation is bad as well as tragic. He has failed a lot of people and he is totally boxed in, with no options.

The senator could tell Anna cares for Henry and wishes with all his heart it could be different. However, Luca will never give up. He will kill all of them, including Henry. He knows telling the police would not be great, as he would end up in jail. Somehow Anna must be made to understand. He will call her next week; tell her how bad it is for him. It will not be a pleasant call.

He has to call Luca, needs to get it over with, another nasty call. Before he can dial the phone, his special office phone rings. It's Luca.

Luca asks, "This phone you are using is still secured, encrypted? Yes, good, I am not sure what happened out there today. Do you know anything? Why was the FBI there? What the hell happened to our people? No one returned, no word from anyone. They're just gone! The Iranians are crazy, and they don't trust us. They are saying we betrayed them, killed their people. They want to know what happened to the bodies. They want to know what happened. Who is this Henry? Where is he now? You say they're going to London? And then they're going to Anna's house? When will they be there?"

"Senator, we are both dead. All of us are in our graves if we don't figure this out. If the Iranians don't kill us outright, we will suffer an even worse fate. They have nuclear bombs positioned in several major cities in the United States, and it will not take much for them to become desperate enough to blow up a few US cities, start Word War III. Believe me, they are freaking nuts and trigger-happy, too. They also have a lot of troops over here, maybe a couple of divisions hiding in plain sight. They've come over the Mexican border and mingled in the US population. Who knows what they are up to? They are wacky. We just need to go along. There is no other choice. They are even saying they have the Chinese and Russians backing them."

"They say they want this deal with the airlines to go through. They want access to air power to break the economic embargo and prevent future embargoes, also to bring in critical stuff: technology, military stuff, more guns and ammo, and maybe smuggle cocaine out, export terrorism and arms throughout the world, and whatever else they want. Who cares? I don't. I just want to survive, as should you."

"I promised them the airline deal would happen; and Sam, if I have to, I will kill you and your daughters and your wife or anyone else. Senator, you can't find a hole far enough away to hide in, and it will not be a quick death. Don't screw this up."

"By the way, Anthony will call Anna in a few weeks. He is flying to LA in our corporate jet. Make sure she sees him. Make sure they have mutual open calendar dates. Anthony can be persuasive. I told you they need to end up married. Say nothing to the FBI. Do you understand, senator? And don't worry about the FBI; we have people higher than them. They can be handled."

"Sam, remember, I have Excalibur Bank as a partner, with plenty of cash. These bankers have lots of friends in high places, higher than you, senator, people who will do what we tell them. They have already been paid off. Do what is right by your family. They do not deserve to die because of you."

CHAPTER 24

JACOBS—SECTION 58

The *Cyclone* catches this entire conversation between the senator and Luca and relays it to Henry immediately. Henry calls John Jacobs as soon as Anna is gone. The *Cyclone* patches Henry's call directly into Jacobs's office, shutting down all monitoring devices hooked internally to his phone and securing the line.

Jacobs notices no ID on the call, strange, but answers, "John Jacobs, Section 58, to whom am I speaking?"

Henry replies, "John, we met yesterday out at Senator Jordan's farm. This is Henry Johnson."

Jacobs is astonished and stammers, "Yes, Henry, I remember you. Actually, I wanted to talk to you more. However, now is a bad time. I have to leave now, to meet my wife at the hospital, as I am picking up my daughter to take her home."

"John, actually this conversation between you and me needs to be done immediately and away from your office. I will meet you at your house in one hour. Do you have enough time to make it there with your daughter at the hospital?"

"Yes, but I am not sure about this. My family is my private life."

"John, I know all about your daughter Kati. I know about the terminal diagnosis of Hodgkin's disease and all you and your family are going through. I am sorry for that, yet I have good news for you. When you get the results of the latest treatment today, you will find out she has no signs of Hodgkin's. It is gone—a gift from me. Now, I need a return favor. Not a big one; you will not have an issue. I will explain more when we meet at your house. Can I see you in one hour? Can you make it?"

"Who are you, and how do you know about my daughter? What are you talking about, curing my daughter?"

"You will find out when you are at the hospital."

"I don't understand—" The phone goes dead.

At the hospital John and his wife hear great news from the doctor. Kati is well; the test results show no traces of the disease. She is more than healthy; there are no signs of ever having had any issues. Her body is perfect. They are all ecstatic. John is wondering how this could be. He remembers the conversation with Henry. It has turned out to be true. The Hodgkin's is indeed gone, much to the amazement of the doctors. All say it is a miracle.

On the way home, John explains to his wife all that is going on—the suspicion of the alien contact and all the events happening on Earth. The first possibility, Henry Johnson might be an alien, then telling her all the confidential stuff, plus his last conversation with Henry. He tells her Henry saved Kati, then about the return favor, Henry's request for a favor from him.

Judy is quiet, only staring at John, turning pale, with a look of fear and worry on her face.

Jacobs says in a worried voice, "Judy, I'm not sure who Henry is." He pauses, then continues, "I am beginning to think he really is an alien. He will be at our house soon. There is nothing I can do to prevent it. Maybe you need to be somewhere else. I can drop you and Kati off, although she is asleep in the backseat now. What do you think?"

Judy responds in a firm voice: "John, please pull the car over. You need to look at me."

After the car stops on the shoulder of the road, John stares at Judy, afraid of what she might say. She is staring back at him intently.

"John, finally I understand why you have not been sleeping at night. This is inconceivable! Our entire world may change with one conversation, the conversation you are about to have in a few minutes. It is unbelievable and totally incredible, yet I believe you. I think it is happening. There is nothing you or I can do, much less the entire world. Every person on this planet will be affected in some way, all depending on what happens now. You are in the middle of it. It looks like God has appointed you to be part of this first contact with an alien civilization. It is terrifying if you think about it too much. I have confidence in you, John. You will do the right thing; you always do. Have faith, as this is your moment."

She continues, her voice now firm, "Think about it. If Henry actually did this for us, it is a miracle, and we should thank him with all our hearts. If he needs a favor we should help him in any way we can. He saved Kati! He must have a good heart no matter who or what he is. I am coming with you. We will thank him together."

She laughs. "After all these years, maybe this is your day, John. You will meet and talk to an alien!"

She is smiling, looking intently at John. "Really, John, what does he look like?"

Looking back at her, also smiling, he says, "He looks like a normal guy, maybe more like a military guy, not like an alien, and I think you will actually like him."

When they arrive home, leaving their daughter in the car, they look around, look down the street, walk up the driveway, and peek in the backyard. Both are relieved. Maybe Henry won't show. Then, to their absolute shock, the most astonishing event occurs, an event out of the movies. They look up: a spacecraft comes down out of the sky, moving fast, and lands in their backyard. It is a really tight fit, but it comes down easily, without issue except for some air turbulence.

There was only a little turbulence, mostly a few trees bending over from the force of the hot air, yet no real loud noises. The *Ship Tender* slips down, its weight on leg pads sinking deep into the yard; otherwise, there is not much yard damage. John and Judy are not sure anyone noticed other than them, although every dog in the neighborhood is barking. John thinks the neighbors wouldn't believe it anyway; hopefully they are all at work. The Jacobs just stand there in the driveway, confused, not sure what to do. This thing in their backyard is truly weird, without question an alien vehicle, sizzling with heat, and with no windows, just several hatches.

A hatch opens on the *Ship Tender,* and Henry is quickly down on the ground, walking over to them, saying hello, smiling, thanking them for meeting with him, just like everything is ordinary. John collects his daughter from the car, and they all go into the house, the daughter still sleeping. She ends up in her bed for a nap. They all meet up back in the kitchen, standing around the table. It is cozy, and there is a coffeepot on the stove, the burner still on low. Judy takes a cup off the counter, pours coffee into it, almost takes a sip, then changes her mind, looks at Henry, and then offers it to him.

He smiles at them and says politely, "Yes, thanks. I love coffee the way it is brewed here on Earth. It smells wonderful."

John and Judy are both standing there dumbfounded, not sure what to do or say and a little dazed.

Henry smiles. "You have wonderful children and much to be proud of. It is never easy with a large family. I know all about them; in fact, I have been briefed about all of you. I know the other children are not here; they are in school now. Thank you for meeting with me on such short notice. Please, let's sit down. I can tell you about myself, answer some of your questions. You have nothing to fear. I admire you for what you have done for your children."

After sitting down at the kitchen table, Judy, a little nervous, responds, "Mr. Johnson, thank you. You are very kind to say this. We love all of them dearly. They are great kids; always try to do their best. We've been blessed with such loving children." She pauses. Tears are coming to her eyes, yet she holds back. "John said you saved our daughter. I don't know how; I can only say we will all be grateful our entire lives. You may not have children, but you probably know what this means to us." Tears come to her eyes again. "Bless you for doing this."

Henry responds, "You are welcome, and I am glad I was here to do it."

"Judy, John, you both need to know something. What I am going to tell you is not easy to understand, but it's critical that you do exactly what I tell you. Kati will be different now, health-wise, which is mostly a good thing. You have to take my word on this, although it will be hard for you and especially your medical professionals to believe. Not only will she not have Hodgkin's, she will be immune to all diseases. She will be able to heal all wounds, even regenerate lost limbs. She will live longer, too, also look younger. Good or bad, she will possibly live to age two hundred or longer. She eventually will have to hide her age. She will be smarter, maybe genius level. Please tell no one other than her and only when she is old enough. Do you understand? Tell no one. It is dangerous for her to ever tell anyone. Do not let any doctor examine her or take blood from her. They will never understand it and will want to study her. Her blood heals wounds quickly—a dangerous thing for her if anyone finds out. The chemical content of her blood has been changed; any lab will see it. She will never need one of your doctors again. Never let anyone take her blood for lab work."

Judy gasps; her face shows amazement; she exclaims, "Yes, yes, we will tell no one. Are you sure about this? It is unbelievable, amazing. We praise the Lord, and we thank you. I think I understand what you are saying. I think it is a miracle. We will do whatever you want. No doctor will ever see her, no lab work ever. We are grateful to you for saving her life and extending her life, giving her this gift. Can we help you in any way? Can we include you in our prayers?"

John is staring at Henry in awe. "Your technology is much more advanced, although I'm not surprised. Are you immortal?"

Henry smiles, looking at Judy. "Yes, certainly, include me in your prayers. You can help me that way. Thank you for asking. More specifically, I think John might be able to help me in a mission."

Judy says, "One question, if I can ask, why are you here? Are you visiting Earth with some mission? Where are you from? Who are you? Not to offend you, but John thinks you may be an alien, which now seems to be an obvious conclusion, the correct observation. I am beginning to think you're an angel sent here to help this world and our daughter."

Henry laughs. "John is sort of right, and you are asking good questions. I am from a long way from here, trillions of miles away. You do not know the world I am from. You cannot see it from here. I am visiting—sort of a vacation, and I will be gone soon. As you can see by looking at me, I look like you. I am originally from Earth. You have nothing to worry about, at least not from me, and I don't consider myself an alien."

John is now really nervous, fidgeting, not knowing what to say. He blurts out, "I have a lot of questions, too. I know you're here for a reason. You want something from me. First of all, before we talk, will our discussion be of a confidential nature? Is it OK that my wife is here?"

Judy says to John, "I can answer that question. I think I should check on Kati, and I think this should be between just you both. This is part of your job, John, and I don't want to get you in trouble. We can talk later." She looks at Henry. "Mr. Johnson, is this OK?"

"Yes, and please call me Henry." He smiles at her. "Judy, it has been a pleasure meeting you."

"And you, too. I hope everything works out. If you need something or maybe a drink, more coffee, please let me know. Thank you again! It has been an honor and a privilege to meet you. My husband is a very good man!"

Henry smiles. "I know that, and it will be fine. Don't worry. It will all work out. And Kati will be fine."

Turning to John I say, "There will be no secrets between us. However, what we talk about is very confidential and totally secret outside of you and me, and maybe we tell some things to your government. You will have to be careful about what you say to your CIA comrades, the FBI, and others. They all can't be trusted as some of your people are traitors. I know this will cause a problem for you, as you may not believe me, yet it has to be resolved. Actually many lives are at stake, and we must do this correctly. By the way, this building has been swept, and there are no listening devices here. Go ahead and ask your questions."

"Henry, I know we may have traitors in our government; can you tell me who? Also, if I can, I'll ask one really big question and then some small ones. Who are you really? I knew you were an alien, even suspected it before. You look and seem so human. How did it happen? How many of you are here, and why are you here? I find it hard to believe you're here on holiday. There is too much going on around the world. And you say lives are at stake? What do you want from me? What do you want from us, the people of Earth?"

"John, I will try to answer you. Although some of what you ask is complicated, not sure we can cover it all today."

"I'm captain of the *Cyclone*, a military starship coming a long distance, actually from another galaxy. I am originally from here, many years ago. I look human, and I think I am still mostly human although changed in many ways. Too complicated to explain. One issue for me is I am here for only a few days. My visit here has no official authority, personal reasons only. The United States is in a dangerous situation. I have information I just cannot ignore. It is information you need for your survival, and I know now you do not have a clue."

John is still really nervous. He frowns. "I don't understand. What do you need to tell us, and why do you need to reach out to me only, as without question, this is an official contact? Why not contact the president of the United States? Really, all things considered, I'm a nobody."

Henry is staring at John with penetrating scrutiny. "Not to me. Listen closely. As I said, everything we talk about regarding me personally is strictly confidential. No one else, except maybe your government, and only on a limited basis, should know about me. I do not trust everyone in your government. *I do trust you.* Your country has some corruption issues, and some of your countrymen have been paid off. You would say they are traitors, and you're right, they are not working for the best interest of the American people. There is a reason you don't know this; whoever these people are don't want you to know."

"John, I have known who you are for a while. I know everything you know and everything your government knows, and I have decided you and I need to be friends. Does this work for you, our collaboration? Can you keep most of who I am between the two of us? I will be totally honest with you, and I expect the same from you."

John almost faints. He feels lightheaded, and he is shaking all over; he feels a lot of anxiety sweep over him. He is speechless; he can barely think, and he stammers, "Yes, I can work with you. Are you saying my country is in danger?"

"Yes, your country is in mortal danger and not from me. Let me explain. The first issue: yes, I am off world, from another galaxy, a different solar system. Even so, you can trust me. It will be hard because I am from another civilization that is not human, and I am not like you, and you have many doubts. You know I came in on a starship, just visiting for now. Yet I have not harmed you. I am no threat to Earth, and I know of no other threat from any other aliens. I am on your side. I think I am mostly human, and my roots are here. I am originally from here. The second issue is the fact that I care about Earth and its future, and I want what is best for you. Can you understand this? Yet I can speak for the aliens, as I am one of them, permanently linked to them forever."

John, with a confused expression, exclaims, "I don't understand you completely, but don't worry, I am satisfied you mean well toward us. More importantly, the question about our survival is really more critical. How are we in danger? Why did you call me, and why did you want this meeting?"

Henry answers, "John, there are some things that might happen in the future that might be dreadful. It is confusing at this moment, but I will explain it to you. Your government, and maybe the whole planet, has a real problem. It is all your own doing. Not you individually but rather several governments who are to blame, including your government. Many have caused this situation, and it is serious. You have a bit of a mess. First of all I want to relay to you a phone conversation between Senator Sam Jordan and Luca Deforleo, both of whom you know. I picked this up today. I know you did not get this with your wiretapping equipment because of my security drones blocking your wire, protecting my conversations and thus the senator's, too."

He continues, "You will find it of great interest. It is authentic. You are welcome to use voice analyzers to verify the content. I will download it to you, into your CIA database. By the way, you are the only recipient of this recording of the conversation. Please use it carefully. Do not trust too many people. Be careful how you use it, as it might become dangerous for you. I think you personally are in danger from a lot of sources. You are picking up more enemies, but that's too complicated to talk about now. You will figure it out, those that I know are traitors in the CIA are listed on your computer, protected by your password. To help you for now, I have put you under my security shield to keep you alive. This is invisible to you and lethal to your adversaries. For now you are under my protection."

John is stunned, not sure what to say. Before he can react, he starts to hear the conversation between Luca and the senator as it plays in his head, as if he is hearing it. He is shocked that he can hear it mentally, and then even more by the bad news: "Iranian nuclear bombs are here in the United States. Could this be possible? Iranian troops are in the United States? Two divisions? Lord, that's really bad!"

After the recording stops, he blurts out to Henry, "This is awful. Is this really true?"

"John, I think you immediately need to do something about the conversation you just heard. You and your government need to resolve it, as it is a dangerous national security threat. I think you need to find out what you can about the bank they mention, First Excalibur, as banks are clever and camouflage themselves well. You need to know who is getting paid off in the US government, as the bank has been making payments to certain individuals, coming from Iran and their allies. You have some traitors who have been paid a lot of money. They are shrewd, influential, and dangerous. That is why you personally must be careful."

"John, I have more bad news, and I am sorry to tell you. It is much worse. You have another awful problem that is part of this whole mess. The most dangerous threat to your national security may not be the bank or Iran, although Iran is certainly a loose cannon and a menace."

"You need to immediately—I mean right now, within the hour—scramble some aircraft out of Alaska and do reconnaissance flights over Western Russia, in Siberia, not far from Alaska. Look for large masses of troops, millions of Chinese and Russian troops. Do the same in Mexico, the Yucatan Peninsula. Look there for more Chinese troops. I don't understand how China was able to put so many troops in Russia and Mexico without your government knowing it. They are certainly a threat to your national interests, as I think they are preparing for an invasion of the United States."

John looks like he is going to vomit, his face pale, responding. "We knew the Russians and the Chinese had signed a pact to become partners in event of a war against one or the other. As allies they started the war games in Russia, where they and the Chinese troops practiced working together. We knew there were troops up there, just never imagined how many and that they could be a real danger. Who would think they would dare attack us? Why would they do this? Why did we not know? The CIA should have known. Were they paid off, and were our military people paid off, hiding this threat to the United States? Do you know?"

Henry answers, "You have my list on your computer. You must be careful who you trust. As I said, you have traitors, and you now must go to your highest operational military defense level immediately, whatever that is. You have people in high places that were blackmailed or paid off; all to help the Chinese cover that they're massing troops in Russia. Your troops should be readied to go operational in the United States and look to defending your borders. Talk to the Chinese and Russians fast, within a few hours, as you may be at war if you can't talk some sense into them. My advice is to be persuasive, maybe compromise, yet be firm enough to resolve your issues."

"The president of the United States has a lot of resources. Let him know about all of this right now, and then he needs to do something immediately. You do not have to contact me; I will know when you know something. If you need to talk to me, I will know and will contact you. By the way, you cannot counter my systems or activities or successfully investigate me, so don't waste your time trying. I will get back to you. John, be careful, and good luck! I am not interested in any other contact from the United States other than from you."

John sits there for a few minutes after Henry has left, thinking, *Holy hell! I have to call the president or maybe his chief of staff. None of this is good, not with this kind of message, and I will be going over all the chains of command. Yet Henry said to call the president immediately.*

John is thinking, *Yes, I will pass on his message, directly to the president, this alien starship captain's message of warning. Henry actually said some really scary stuff, critical to the United States. Millions of troops off of the US border. Damn right, I am calling the president*—John thinks—*using his classified phone number*—the national security phone number—*to warn him and the country of an impending attack.* John hopes Henry knows what he's talking about as he dials the passcode into the phone call to the president. He never in his wildest dreams thought he would use this number. Crazily enough, it was given to him in case of an alien attack.

⇒+ +⇐

I am out the back door and up into the *Ship Tender,* quickly heading back to the farm. I have just enough time to make it back and dress for dinner.

Anna is back home with Nikki as I am coming in. The *Cyclone* is above us unseen at two thousand feet, and the ship's tender is back in the hold. Anna and I both dress in a hurry and we are in the car heading for dinner at a very nice Chinese restaurant in Richmond. I am thinking, *I'm not sure how popular Chinese restaurants will be in the future.*

The senator misses dinner. I am glad to have dinner with just Anna, Nikki, and their mother. I am not interested in the senator and don't really know what to say to him. I am sorry for Linda, his wife of many years; she does not deserve the result of his sins, as a lot of grief is coming her way. I am not sorry for the senator. He deserves his fate.

All evening I am delighted by all three of the women. Nikki is fun. Her stories of her and Anna's childhood adventures are hilarious; the two of them are obviously close, both are fun, and both like to experience the world. They both absolutely love people and life. Nikki will make a great doctor, as she is brilliant, easy to talk to, and cares a lot about people.

Anna's mother asks me to call her by her first name, Linda. She is charming, too. It's easy to see how proud she is of her daughters, and she is very supportive of me as she speculates about me as a possible mate for Anna. She asks about my opinions, what I like, and what my family is like, and she and I agree on almost everything. I think we have the same basic values. We really like each other, and I think how blessed her daughters are to have her as their mother.

A wonderful evening! On the way home, Nikki squeezes my hand, eyes moist, saying she is so happy to see Anna and me together. She says Anna has never been happier, and she is good for me, too. We are a perfect fit, she tells me, and it's obvious to anyone close to Anna. She hopes we stay together. It's hard not to love Nikki. She even looks like Anna—she has the same eyes that light up when she smiles. She is also petite, although with longer hair and a darker complexion than Anna's. Her figure is slender like Anna's, but she has smaller facial features; she's just a stunning-looking girl. Or, better said, she is a beautiful, charming woman.

Unfortunately there's one issue: when we're leaving there are lots of photographers. Someone tipped them off about Anna. I forgot about her celebrity status. My photo is taken many times. I need to stay out of any confrontation with the photographers, so I just smile and hope nothing comes out of it. I ask Anna.

Anna says, "No way!" The tabloids will want to know all about me, Anna's new boyfriend. She laughs. I worry. It could be a real issue for both of us, much more than Anna knows. The publicity is foolish for me, yet I have allowed it to happen. I am tempting fate.

We pack to leave that evening. Anna's family thinks we have a commercial flight out. Saying good-bye is tough; even the senator is nice. He loves Anna; that's plain to see, and he is emotional about her leaving. Of course I know why. Yet there is a true closeness in the family, especially between Anna, her mother, and her sister. They are affectionate and pleasing to one another, and I cannot help feeling the same toward all three.

CHAPTER 25

PREMIER WU-TONG AND GENERAL LING

Premier Wu-Tong is waiting. The entire command of the Chinese central party is in the room. Twenty-two of its most powerful members are there as well as the number two deputy premier in command and the third deputy in command behind Premier Wu-Tong. They are all there, sitting next to the premier; all are waiting for the military.

The generals finally come into the large conference room, six of them, the most powerful military men in China's history. They represent the entire leadership of the massive military forces of China, the largest army in the world. They bow to the premier; they then bow to the rest of the group, and they each sit at the end of a huge mahogany conference table, looking directly at the premier.

General Ling, the supreme general and commander of all the military forces, does not sit. He stands, with a severe expression on his tired face. He bows and starts to speak. "I apologize for the delay and asking for this evening meeting. I know you are all tired. We wanted to give you this report yesterday. We had difficulties in getting here—we had a long flight, as some of us came from Russia. There were also issues in traveling because of damages to a number of our helicopters and the chaos from the results of attack in Russia.

"I know you are anxious for my report, as I have asked for this emergency meeting. There is some real urgency. I asked for this meeting because I want to immediately trigger our previous plan, not wait for the scheduled August date. I know August was chosen because the weather will be the most decent in Alaska and Canada, and it was the right decision at the time. Troop trucks and tanks move over dry land much faster than on mud."

"Things have changed. Because we were attacked this week, sustaining damages, injuries, and casualties, about one hundred thousand soldiers in total, we now have some critical issues. The problem is we are not sure who attacked us. The surprise factor is essential in attacking the United States. Now someone knows about those millions of troops there. Whoever attacked us knows about us. When we are concentrated in one location, our troops are in harm's way. We cannot afford another attack; we could lose all of them. Upsetting to us is the other issue: Russian radar and their defense systems saw nothing coming in the last attack."

"I have asked our Iranian allies if they know anything. They are at a loss to explain, completely baffled. The Russians, our other ally, know nothing, have no clue. Our Mexican ally is panicked, knowing nothing about the attack in Russia, and want to back out of our deal with them. They think it was the United States, and now they know. They are complaining a US backlash would be most harmful to them, a military attack likely, if we are discovered. They would be caught with fifteen million Chinese troops in the Yucatan Peninsula waiting to move up into Texas, saying it is impossible to keep them hidden if someone is really looking and saying there is the same problem in Russia."

General Ling continues, "Iran is ready to move. Their atomic weapons are in the United States and placed in the locations as planned. The nuclear blasts will take out at least six major cities, maybe more. They also have ten power plants ready to be hit. They have two divisions of their Special Forces in the United States, brought over the Mexican border and now mingled into the US population. They are heavily armed. Of course discovery is always an issue. The sooner the attack, the better it is for all of us."

"There is no reason to wait any longer for North Korea to decide to join us. Their delay in responding is answer enough. I think we should attack next week, as early as possible. We'll start moving troops toward the borders of the United States. The Iranians will take out the cities with small nuclear bombs and they will attack the power plants with troops. They will also take out the cell-phone centers using micro-energy bursts, or just bomb them. Several dams will be targeted, causing floods."

"We take out the Internet with an attack of multiple viruses. We will neutralize it completely. No e-mails, no communication. And with no electricity, there will be total chaos in the United States, as that means no food, no gasoline, no banking or purchasing, and no communications."

"Most of the media networks will be taken over by Iranian commandos, and they will broadcast the Chinese people's message. They will be told that the citizens of the United States will be treated well, as able to keep their jobs, their bank accounts, and their churches, and they will be able to take care of their families, just as before. No real changes!"

"In our newly revised plan, we should be operational by the sixteenth of June, with some troops in the United States. The attacks will be starting on the fourteenth of June. By the eighteenth of June, at least half of our troops will be in the country, about thirty million. The other thirty million will be there by the twentieth. We have lots of trucks, trains, and ships to carry them. Troops will be coming up from Mexico and from Russia by way of Alaska and Canada, also entering all across the California coast by ship. The United States has a superior interstate road system, which we will use. We expect minimal resistance. New York City will already be gone, destroyed by a small Iranian nuclear bomb."

"Per our communications plan we will blanket the rest of the world with e-mails, breaking news bulletins, press conferences, all on the seventeenth, explaining why we were forced to do this. It was necessary to prevent the United States from driving the world to an economic depression so bad there would be millions starving. The US printing currency at their current rate would destroy the world's currency values, devastating the world's ability to feed itself and plunging us into a deep international depression late next year. The United States has effectively defaulted on their debt to the world and to us by recklessly printing currency, creating cheap dollars and predictable hyperinflation. This is a deliberate act of dishonesty to cheat the Chinese and the world of their loan repayment, paying back in dollars worth half as much. This is an act of war. It is a complete lack of responsibility, and steps had to be taken to prevent this catastrophe.

"We will also offer a deal to the president of the United States on the twentieth, offering to make him president for life. If he takes it, he will report to the Chinese government, saving his life and the lives of many thousands of his countrymen. We think he will surrender and tell the US troops to stand down. The US Congress will be discharged and the members taken prisoner along with their families. Democracy will be dead, yet the country will live on. The troops and citizens of the United States will pledge an oath of loyalty to China. All those who oppose us will perish. Eventually seventy million Chinese and Russian troops will occupy the United States after sweeping down from Alaska and over Canada. Another fifteen million will come up from Mexico. It will be over quickly. Do you have any questions?"

All those sitting in the room are sober, deep in thought; none responds.

Finally Premier Wu-Tong stands up. "General Ling, thank you for you report. You are saying if the United States knows about us, they will bomb our troops before they can move? What about nuclear missiles attacking us?"

General Ling nods and responds, "Yes, we predict they will bomb us if they find out. If we do not move out soon, it might become a severe problem. Our critical issue is we need to know who attacked us this last week. Who has seen us? Are they coming back? Was it the United States?"

"Once the army is deployed, we should be fine; the plan will work. The US knows we will fire nuclear missiles back at them if they attack our cities in China. After our troops are spread out, no longer in one concentrated position, it will also be difficult to bomb them, and we would retaliate with nuclear weapons. After the Iranian nuclear destruction they have fewer cities to give up; they will not want to give up any more cities in a nuclear trade-off, so it's not a real option for them, as they would cease to exist. We would end up with a smaller population, yet we would survive. We all need to have a future."

"*I think no nuclear weapons will be fired at us!*

"As long as we get our troops on the move, spread out over Canada and the United States, victory is ours. If this happens, we think, the United States will give in, fold, as it is the smart thing to do. Yet if our army is caught in one small location, as it is now currently encamped in Russia, all is lost. If we are discovered there before we move out, the United States will fire at us. They will use small nuclear bombs on our troops and we will lose all of them. We will not be able to go on as planned. We will not use nuclear weapons, no retaliation from us, unless they fire on us, at our mainland. Other than that, there is no reason; it has no purpose; we have failed in our mission."

The general continues, "Our critical issue now is who knows about us. We do not know who attacked us, no clue; our speculation is frightening. The attack was very effective, power-ful to say the least. It is incredibly dangerous for us right now. If the same weapon comes back, we can only assume all our troops will be killed. We have no choice other than attacking the United States as soon as possible, before anything happens. I need your agreement to trigger our immediate attack, not wait for August, attacking on the fourteenth of June."

Suddenly the door to the room opens. An army captain enters, comes to attention, salutes, and stands there stern and rigid. All are intently looking at him, with worry or concern on their faces. Only something critical, bad news, would cause this interruption.

Annoyed, the premier harshly asks, "Why are you interrupt-ing us?

"Premier Wu-Tong, you have an urgent phone call on your personal line from the president of the United States. Do you want to take the call?

CHAPTER 26

LONDON VISIT—ANNA'S MOVIE
PREMIERE DAY SIX

Back on the *Cyclone*, we have a late drink in my cabin, before we head out. It is hard not to tell Anna about the possibility of World War III and all the crazy stuff going on with the Chinese, the Russians, and Mexico. There is nothing she can do about it, no reason to upset her before the big premiere. I am left to worry about it. I think I can help the United States; however, it is in their court; I am a visitor with no passport.

Anna tells me the next day's plan and my part of it as her date. We are to be in London tonight, although really we are there early morning because of the time change. It is late evening here now. We are five hours behind the London time, in the US Eastern time zone. The actual flight is about fifteen minutes. Then we drop down in the night, early morning, about 5:00 a.m., using the ship's tender, and discreetly land in one of the many parks, the one called Regent's Park.

The trip was easy; the landing in the park was unnoticed in the darkness; we quickly walk out, end up on a main street.

There are few people up that early in the morning. We grab a cab, as we are staying at a fancy hotel near Leicester Square in

London's theater district. We check in at the Ritz; Anna's staff has already arranged reservations, adding me, too, per Anna's request. I am to stay in her room. We both are sleeping within minutes of arriving, both of us exhausted.

At an early breakfast I meet her personal staff, consisting of three people: Jill, her secretary; Yonetta, her events planner; and Frannie, her everything-else girl. They are all sweet girls, smart and loyal to Anna. They are all smiles with me.

Her business manager, Sonny Lauyans, is in and out. He seems to be a good guy—smart, certainly charming, and good-looking like most Hollywood people. All are impressive, very nice to me, and say nothing about my staying with Anna. This event is a big one for publicity, the London premiere of her new film. She is required by contract to be there, and I can tell she loves it; she is glad to be part of it. Actually I am happy to be part of her life, better off than I have ever been.

Yet this activity is problematic for me, as it provides way too much exposure. The first problem is the *Cyclone*, as it will always provide me security and now also for Anna. It is always hovering overhead, whether I want it or not. If an issue comes up regarding security for Anna or me, my concern will be overkill by the *Cyclone*—literally. I can only pray nothing happens. And it is not that hard to figure out the *Cyclone* is up there above us. Some military satellite could easily spot it. It is one thing to be moving and quite another to be sitting there like a duck in a pond.

I have not been to London except during World War II, and it is much changed. It was not fun then, and my memories are not great. World War II was mostly misery. Anna wants to show me around before the evening premiere, and it should be fun this time; there's a lot to see. London is exciting to see. We do finally leave the Ritz and take a cab. Not surprisingly, there are photographers, and many photos are taken. I'm not sure what to do, although the *Cyclone* thinks I have lost it, thinks I am brain dead, tells me I am asking for a lot of problems. I don't care. I want as much of this as I can get. To be with Anna now is terrific. The problems will have to be handled.

London is spectacular! Anna knows it well; we see it by a limo, rented for her, and with a driver included. We see the Tower of London, the Queen's Guard, the River Thames, Saint Paul's Cathedral, Big Ben, Hyde Park, and the National Gallery—all great, especially sharing them with Anna. Her delight is infectious. I have never felt so glad to be alive. How could you not be grateful to be a human, a gift from God, then so blessed to be here on Earth, to enjoy a life here in the splendor of this planet?

Unfortunately there is not much time left on Earth for me. It is day six, four more precious days remaining.

Of course Anna is recognized everywhere, and I am now recognized as her boyfriend. Many questions are asked by many reporters at the press conference, which is held in the huge lobby of the theater, as scheduled before the beginning of her movie premiere. Anna answers them all. I sit with her, proud to be with her. She seems to know all the reporters, and they are friendly to her. More important are the big producers or directors. Then there are also wealthy men, many celebrities, powerful executives, and well-known politicians. Some are really Anna's friends, and some act like they're her best friend, and are acting only, not friends, not sure of their real motivations. All are curious about me. Some like me, and some don't, and some are contemptuous of me.

There are some who are more handsome than others, and there are also many powerful men after Anna, who hoped to be her date tonight and to bed her before dawn. Especially James Algeir, a famous Hollywood director, who is good-looking and wealthy and who has come just to see Anna. He is a former boyfriend who does not think *former* applies to him; he pesters Anna, and I know he previously abused her physically. He is still trying to bully her. I know this by Anna's thoughts, as she unknowingly lets a little out when she sees him, a fear of him. He has helped her career, and he thinks she owes him. He makes my blood boil.

I think about what I want to do to Algeir when searching his mind for his real agenda, and I discover an ugly man: narcissistic, selfish, self-centered, and not good for Anna in any way. I have the *Cyclone* put a probe reconnaissance slip in his brain, as I have a feeling he and I will meet again. The *Cyclone* will keep track of him until then. The next time will not go well for him if I have my choice. However, I try to be nice to him at Anna's insistence. He could hurt her career, and I am here to support her. He does not appreciate me or show me any respect, as he does not consider me either wealthy or powerful. I am just in the way.

Surprising to me, I notice everyone else, including some of my competition for Anna, are careful with me, cautious, maybe a little concerned. Some are afraid, although I have no clue why. My story is always the same: talking about being ex-military, did classified stuff I can't talk about, evasive otherwise, and I live a boring life, just not much to talk about.

It's getting worse. Now, everyone I meet is nervous with me, some more than others; there's just a lot of real anxiety. I know there is some extensive surveillance going on by a lot of governments, all undercover. Not sure if they know about one another. I think there are ten or more groups here. The *Cyclone* identifies each, and all are tagged with reconnaissance slips. All the publicity and letting myself be exposed has led to this, stupid on my part, and my conversation with John Jacobs will come back to haunt me. I know the United States, Britain, Mexico, Russia, and China have people here watching me, all within two hundred feet. Who would think I would be so popular? They must be stepping over one another. No wonder people are anxious.

Anna has no security detail; she refused it, says she has me. However, there are no incidents, and I know why. We are subjects of heavy-duty surveillance, especially by the British and American intelligence services, both working together. They are really everywhere. They are also our security team, although they don't realize it. They are watching us and looking at whoever might be a threat, too. I also have reversed the surveillance, putting reconnaissance slips into their brains; every single one involved is tagged this way. I know what they know, and I know why they are intensely curious. I now know there is another reason they are all here—something planned. I should have known about it but did not know until now. It was predictable though, and smart.

The *Cyclone* will keep track of them and us. The *Cyclone* is also hacking into the British government data systems; we will know all they know very soon. If there were an attempt to detain us, all involved would be incapacitated by the *Cyclone*. Of course the *Cyclone* is the ultimate security team, so it's impossible to hurt us with it there on top of us; there would be severe consequences for anyone who would try. There are also a thousand drones or more, or slips, all around us, invisible, all with the capacity to kill quickly.

Anna's movie is fantastic, and she is perfect! Afterward there are a lot of excited people all congratulating Anna, talking about an Academy Award for her, saying how impressed they are. She is absolutely charming, gorgeous, the definition of glamour; I think she is incredible. She also keeps constant tabs on me, making sure anyone important to her meets me. For some reason she acts very proud of me and is excited about me being there, treating me as a celebrity. Her eyes are on me when I am not looking, and I know she is falling in love with me; all who see her know it, too. I wish I could be equal to her. I have not done much on Earth to earn her pride. I hope I don't screw this up.

Unfortunately it is hard to avoid my situation as an alien visitor on this planet. Constant security issues are not pleasant, as there could be errors, like killing someone by accident. There are over one thousand security reconnaissance slips here, all armed, all around us now and during all events. The *Cyclone* is absolutely paranoid about security for Anna and me, and I'm paranoid about the *Cyclone*.

Fortunately Anna has no clue, and I hope it stays that way. I need no threat to her or me that would force a defense, messing up her evening. I actually think I am the one overwhelmed, as I want this to work out for Anna. Her success has become my success. Our relationship has become too close, and the *Cyclone* knows it, as I do. We are both worried about my leaving on the tenth day. The *Cyclone* constantly warns me I am in over my head. I have met my match with Anna.

I know Anna well now, as I have come a long way over the last three days. We have talked about everything, like we are two school kids: her family, my family from years ago, having and raising children, her friends, some of my military life, Anna's work, her chance at an Academy Award, taxes, destiny, life, and death. We do not talk about my leaving. It hangs over our heads. I know Anna thinks I will stay, and yet it will happen. I leave after the tenth day. I'm not sure how to fix it.

As a professional soldier, a violent death is always a given, to die with honor the main criteria. I never planned for a real life. You just accept your destiny. Although I could never describe to her how much I care for her, she is all I have missed all these long, lonely years. Until now nothing has meant much; it has just been hardship and duty. Now even little things with her are great. The meal she put together for us in my little ship's cabin, a real treat done with limited gravity, was wonderful for me, as it was just to be with her on the *Cyclone*. She will be a wonderful mother someday; if only it could be different, and I could choose my life, marry, and have children. Maybe I can do something special for Anna tomorrow, maybe a real spectacular adventure, maybe take her on the *Saber* for an extra spin. We could use it for the trip to LA after London.

Finally, when alone, walking, leaving the theater, smiling at her, I say to Anna, "First of all I think you are awesome, an incredible actress, and I am humbled you chose me as your date tonight. I think tonight is one the best moments of my life. Thank you for letting me share your success. I hope I can do something for you to equal it."

Anna actually glows, her face flushed, and she laughs, smiles, then tenderly looks at me. "Henry, you have no idea how happy you make me."

Per Anna's agent's scheduling, we walk down to one of the larger after-premiere parties to have a few drinks, meet people, and promote the film. It is not far, held in a fancy London pub, centuries old, a watering hole for the rich and famous. It is impressive—oil paintings on wood-paneled walls, everything centuries old. Soft classical music is playing in the background, and even the scent of the place is comforting: good smells of food, wine, beer, old leather chairs, and old wood. The massive old oak tables over old polished dark-wood floors, with large silver candleholders as centerpieces, are impressive yet inviting. The huge extraordinary main dining room is full, with standing room only. Many big Hollywood people are there, including numerous beautiful women, talking and laughing, all saying hi and congratulations to Anna.

My buddy James Algeir is there, and he tries to get Anna's attention. She ignores him. The bar area has some room left, and we head there, as I want a drink, specifically a Maker's Mark, Kentucky bourbon, one of Earth's treasures. Anna has only water.

I also get to meet more of the important people: Hollywood directors, famous old actors, producers, agents, attorneys, big corporation CEOs, and then there are all the charming celebrities. None of them can figure me out, and I know they wonder why Anna brought me. They are all thinking I look military, yet I have no rank. Why did Anna bring this nobody when she could have brought so many really important men?

One surprise is the prime minister of England, who no one expected to be there, and he is impressive and friendly, as he comes in, shaking hands with some surprised celebrities. After a few hellos he comes directly over to us with a couple of security guys following him. He makes a point of meeting me. His defense minister is there, too, just appears, and a couple more military types, probably generals not wearing their uniforms. All introduce themselves to us. Then, out of nowhere, two Chinese generals are there, too. Also, another surprise, as it looks like two Russian generals want to introduce themselves. These generals are uniformed; lots of metals, serious-looking guys and their security guys are here, too. They are intense, covering up some anxiety or maybe fear. What do they know? I tag them with reconnaissance slip drones. Actually I don't have to, as I realize I already know the answer to why they are here, confirmed by the *Cyclone*. They all know about the troops in Russia. They also know about me, know who I am. I can feel their fear, close to terror, afraid of the unknown, meaning me. John Jacobs has been busy. Who else is coming? It is getting crowded.

I smile. Yes, there is Mr. Jacobs walking toward me. He looks sheepish as he shakes my hand. He looks at Anna, smiles, shakes her hand, too. "Anna, congratulations on your movie; we saw it in the United States. My wife loved it and says you are splendid in it—she thinks Academy Award greatness!"

Anna beams, responding, "We meet again, and I am sure it's not a coincidence. Mr. Jacobs, thank you for liking my movie, and your wife is someone I want to meet."

Stepping away from my new friends and Anna, taking John with me, I smile and say, "John, you arranged all this? I think the United Nations is here, all these powerful men in one place. You worked hard to get this done."

"Yes, sir. I apologize. The only way to avoid World War III is to get these guys together. They are here because I told them you wanted this meeting immediately. Right now, get it done while you are here, in London. I knew you were coming here, as I called Anna's mother and she said you were going to the premiere of Anna's movie. I knew or hoped if we all showed up, you would give them some helpful direction. Their fear of you got them here fast. No one else could do this. I think they will do whatever you tell them. They are all totally freaked out by your presence here on Earth. I am trying to save us all. Please help us. Please go along with my telling them you called this meeting. I think you have their attention."

Then, to my surprise, out of nowhere, the Chinese premier is in front of me, shaking my hand, bowing slightly. The Russian president is next to him, reaching out his hand, too. Then, turning, the Mexican president reaches out and shakes my hand, and, amazingly enough, the president of the United States is looking at me, smiling. He steps through, introduces himself, like an old friend, smiling.

Now, Anna is standing there next to me, real surprise on her face, and I can see, she is not sure what to say.

All are looking at me, after introducing themselves to one another. Security guys are now all over the place. There are a million police cars outside, having just appeared out of nowhere, officers in SWAT uniforms all around the square. The Russian president, in English, breaks the silence, by saying good things to Anna, complimenting her on her film and how beautiful she looks. She is now next to me tight, moved in much closer. I think she is guarding me, or maybe I am guarding her? They all then join in, saying how lovely she is, and the Chinese premier tells her in excellent English she is invited to come to China as his welcome guest.

Then they all look at me at the same time, as if rehearsed, the British prime minister then asking if it would be possible to talk to me alone. Then looking at Anna, asking if she would be kind enough to lend me out just for a few minutes, for a short meeting.

Anna is mostly speechless and alarmed, as is the entire Hollywood crowd. The place becomes quiet from the previously loud buzz. Security guys from several countries are everywhere, all packing weapons. This cannot be a coincidence; something big is happening right now, all while they are here watching. Some really big political guys representing the leadership of the largest countries in the world are here meeting Anna. Who would think Anna is so important? They came a long way. It is an astonishing thing to see; however, no cameras are allowed to take photos, and no photographers are here. Some rough-looking men, including the prime minister's security team, all wearing guns, have taken all photographers away; the police then arrest them outside. Police are now standing guard around the pub; actually, everyone notices a lot of police are still arriving. There are many police cars everywhere, lights flashing. No one is allowed to leave the pub.

The people in the pub are not moving anyway. They are more than curious, amazed to see such powerful men all in one place, right here, right now. How could they find out the reason? What could be going on? How did Anna's publicity team manage this? This is a long way from normal; something big is going down, especially with all this security. It is more than unusual to see the premier of China in public, much less in London. This could not be because of a movie opening. All are thinking the same thing. History is happening right in front of them; just what history is the question.

They realize, one by one, it is not Anna the heads of state came to see. It is her date, the ex-military guy with no job. He is the one this select crew came to see. Thus the question, who the hell is he? You could see easily that all these important world figures are all being really careful with him, almost like he's some really significant person they are trying to please, waiting for permission before they speak. They can see the security guys and the police are really afraid of him; none of them will make eye contact with him. These tough guys are really fearful of him, staying clear of him. Wow! Who is Anna's date? Everyone in the pub, without exception, is wondering if they should be here or not. Is this dangerous? All know some kind of event is occurring, and they can say they were here. The question is, what is happening? Could this be life threatening?

The president of the United States asks Henry if he wants to go outside for some privacy. Surprisingly enough, Anna, hearing this, immediately says, "No, you will not take him out of my eyesight. This party will not be interrupted by this meeting, either. You can find a couple of tables in the bar, sit down, and have drinks."

She looks at them and says she will be close, excuses herself, says she needs to mingle. She looks at me, saying she will be back to check on me. I smile. These guys do not intimidate her.

There is nothing they can do as I comply with Anna's wishes. I shrug and say the bar is a good place; we can take a couple of tables. Several tables are shoved together. After we all sit, the area around us is cleared out. No one is allowed inside the room, not even the bartender. Security guys are on guard at the entrances and behind us. John Jacobs stands behind me.

The Chinese premier, looking tired from an all-night flight, bows to me, then sits down. In excellent English he asks me if I will be offended if he is candid and if he can ask a few questions, which I do not have to answer if I choose not to. To clarify the situation, he says they all know a massive camouflaged starship is above us as we talk. They are quite sure I can do anything I want to them or to this world, without any recourse. They know I am military, not an ambassador, and they know I am alien. Would I tell them where I am from, and do I come in peace? They know I am telepathic, and they will not say anything or think anything other than the truth and hope I will give them the same respect. They do not want to offend me. Is it appropriate to ask questions? How long will I be here? Why am I here?

Making eye contact, I look carefully at each of them intensely, making them all really nervous. I can see my eyes frighten them, maybe too much penetration, as I am probing their minds and seeing if they are honest or if this is an ambush, their purpose malicious. I want them to feel my mind probe to warn them against doing anything foolish. It also covers the reconnaissance slips as they enter their brains without them feeling it. I need to know what they are thinking and who they are, their basic character, and their plans for the future. I certainly feel their fear. They are close to panic as they feel my presence in their minds, the telepathy acknowledged.

The *Cyclone* knows everything that is happening, including there being a lot of military security outside, with several streets closed off. The *Cyclone* has the brigand ready to go within seconds. I am told, "All weapons are operational; defense shields are up; thousands of extra drones are also deployed." The *Cyclone* also warns me, "None of these men can be truly trusted. Strength and power is all they respect."

I finally smile, looking at them, my friendliness catching them by surprise. Making eye contact again with each of them, I reassure them. I need them to calm down, to reduce their fear. I start talking, a calm voice, as soothing as I can make it.

"To answer you, yes to all of the above. However, I am not here officially. This visit is more like a holiday, and I'm like a tourist. Yet, as you know, I am fully prepared to defend myself if needed. You are right, you are not equipped to contain me, and you are, even combined, no match for me. You think I know much more about you than you know about me, which is correct.

I do not want to be a real threat to you, nor do I have political aspirations here on this planet. However, while I am here, I will not allow major military actions to take place. I have come trillions of miles, and I will not be here long, only a few more days."

The Russian president says, "Mr. Johnson, do you have a military title we should be using in addressing you? Also, I want to apologize for our involvement in the reckless Chinese venture. We know you know about it, and we were foolish. We are standing down. It will not happen again."

"Yes, I understand. I am titled as captain because of my starship. However, in your terms I would be an admiral. I know you are curious but afraid to ask me. The answer is I have fourteen billion troops under my command, over four million starships, and keep the peace over a third of the universe, inhabited by trillions of beings. Please call me Captain Johnson."

Premier Wu-Tong again asks to speak. I nod, and he responds, "Captain Johnson, I apologize about having to ask you this, yet I must. We think it was your ship that attacked our troop encampment in Russia. Was it?"

I make eye contact with him. "Yes, it was; however, it was not started by me, and it was no more than a little skirmish. It would seem, because of a brief flyover, I was attacked. I did return the attack only lightly. If I had really attacked you, there would have been no one left alive, over fifty million troops gone in an instant." Harshly staring at him, I ask, "Do you have an issue?"

I pause to see if there is a reaction from him. He says nothing. He just stares at me, with no emotion; he has a great poker face. I know differently, as I feel his anger at my comment, blaming me, the internal rage from his failure to take down the United States. His humiliation from the event is disastrous. The fear of losing some of his strength, his power, is the real issue. He probably has lost face with his comrades. He could still be dangerous. I feel it in him. He is looking for another way to redeem himself with his comrades, searching for another way to take down the United States. It is time for me to remind him, to humble him; I have to change his mind or kill him right now.

I mind probe him, talking to him and projecting my thoughts into his brain. "Premier, I understand your anger. It could be much worse, as you could die right now, a heart attack, and I could annihilate your country!"

He is shocked by the penetration of my thoughts into his head. I give him a mind meld, showing him the very real vision of millions of his countrymen dying in agony in a few seconds' time, fire everywhere, total destruction of the entire country, with no one spared. He can't breathe well now as I slow his lungs and heart down, lowering his blood pressure, preparing him for a cardiac arrest. He is starting to feel acute pain in his chest, his heart starting to protest; he wants to vomit from the fear. He is not young, and I have to be careful not to kill him too quickly, by going too fast. The vision of the annihilation of his entire country might be his last thought. He has seen a brief glance of hell. He is terrified, shocked, turning pale, fading fast; there is now real pain in his chest, and he wants to come up for air.

He stares at me, and he whispers, "Captain Johnson, please, I beg you. I have done you no harm. Please, I apologize for my arrogance. Please save me. I was only trying to feed my people, as we have lots of mouths to feed. I will not go back on my word. We will not start a war, I promise."

I restore him: he gasps, takes a deep breath of air, coughs, his eyes wide, fear in his face, his skin pale, now breathing fast, trying to catch up.

Staring at him I ask again, "Premier, do you have an issue with me?"

Once again, catching his breath, with normal breathing, he says, "I apologize. I am sorry if I offended you. No, certainly not! Please, Captain Johnson, forgive us; we understand, yes, we were wrong to attack your ship. We sincerely apologize. We were also wrong to plan a military venture that would do so much collateral damage. We wish only to thank you for ending a bad decision. The United States has our agreement that we will bring all of our troops home, including the troops in Mexico. We have only one request. It is only fair. We would like your recommendation to the United States that they pay our loans back with our currency, at the value of the money we loaned to them."

I look at the president of the United States, making eye contact. "I agree. I highly recommend it. The United States will pay the Chinese back with currency of the same value that was borrowed."

The president nervously nods his head, swallows hard, as we lock eyes; he is saying, "Yes. Yes. We can work it out. Yes, we agree; it is not a problem."

The president is thinking, *There definitely will be no issue from the United States. He saw the Chinese premier, and it looked like he was going to have a heart attack. He's sure Captain Johnson had something to do with it. He could not hear the premier respond, as he is mostly whispering; yet the premier's look of terror is convincing. Crossing the alien would mean severe consequences for all of them personally. No question his eyes are scary, not human, a predator. It feels like he is in my brain.*

The president looks at the Chinese premier, saying, "Yes, the United States will comply with China's terms."

He thinks further, without comment, thinks: *Even though it will be the end of my presidency. The political fallout will be terrible, as the austerity economy will be awful. Budgets will be slashed, government jobs lost. Paying it back is a lot harder than borrowing it. The higher taxes will go on for years. I'm toast.*

"Thank you, Mr. President." I respond. Then, looking at all of them, I say, "I know you all have lots of questions. To answer you further, I know most of your concerns, and yes, there are lots of worlds with large populations. You are very small and primitive compared to most of them and centuries behind in comparison to their technology. Fortunately, you are off the beaten path, thus you are protected by your obscurity. You also have some limited protection from my fleets."

The British prime minister asks, "Captain, please, two questions. You look very human. Do all aliens look like you? Second question, do we have reasons to be afraid of what's out there, a possible threat to our world?"

"I am originally from Earth, and I think of myself as human; however, I admit I have been rebuilt a couple of times since my birth, thus I may not be totally human, yet I claim my roots from here. My looks have not changed since my birth right here on this planet. There are all kinds of species across the universe, all interesting and wonderful in their own ways. Few are similar to this species; none look like humans, nor do they speak Earth languages—not even close. Your second question is more complicated. Yes and no, there are threats out there. This world has little to offer to other civilizations, thus nothing to attract them to come here. Currently this situation offers you some protection. I see no reason for you to know more, as there is absolutely nothing you can do about it. Just keep your own house in order.

"To answer more of your questions—and as you know, I hear your questions mentally, and I can feel your concerns, and many questions are coming from each of you. You are all thinking there are critical questions that have to be answered."

I laugh. "Please relax. I'm sorry I have made you anxious. At this moment you have nothing to fear from me. You have lots of questions, and they are all good; most are the same. I will go through them one by one. You will then have your answers."

"First of all, you have never been alone. You have been visited many times over the centuries. Many cultures out there are millions of years old, having developed centuries ahead of yours; you are young in comparison, still in your infancy. Remember, the universe was created billions of years ago."

"No, I will not meet with you again unless there are issues."

"My ship is called the *Cyclone*, and yes, we came a long way to get here, many trillions of miles, beyond your comprehension. It is a military starship, capable to do whatever is needed, and we have no plans to attack you."

"No, I want nothing from you, and no, you cannot visit my ship."

"I cannot give or sell you starship technology. You have to earn it. How can you earn it? You already know the answer. Just think about it. I would be the first to have you join our ranks. I am one of your protectors."

"Anna is a good friend and under my protection. She is not part of my operations; she is an Earth person. She is not an alien. I have just met her and her family."

"Yes, I am leaving, and yes, I do plan to come back, not sure when."

"Yes, for now, you do need to keep me confidential, a secret. Do not tell anyone about me or these conversations for your own good. You are not ready yet to talk to the public. Keep working together; stop wasting money on issues that bring no results. Focus on nuts and bolts: feed people, educate the kids, value honesty, value life, stop those who hurt and kill, take care of the planet, and reduce your military. Just do the right thing! No excuses. Other civilizations are watching you. You have a lot to do. If you work together and help one another, you may have a chance."

The president of the United States asks, "Are you part of some governing body that is universe-wide? How many starships are here?"

"Yes, Mr. President, I work for the Consortium of Civilizations, to which many thousands of civilizations belong. It stretches over all the known universe. There is only one I know of, and this is the Consortium, creator of the laws or rules, and I am charged with the enforcement of their laws. I hope to see Earth as a member of the Consortium someday."

"Your second question, I will not tell you how many ships are here, and you know the overall total number of ships."

"I have one question for all of you: where is Iran in all this? They are not here at this meeting. Are they still a problem? How about Mexico?"

The president of Mexico immediately stands up. "Captain Johnson, I am ashamed about our part in this Chinese aggression. I apologize, and I welcome you to this planet. I am truly sorry it is under these circumstances. We regret we were ever a party to this event, and we are pleased it turned out like this. We were bullied into participation. Please accept our apology. We invite you to visit us; we would be delighted to show you our wonderful country."

"Mr. President, thank you. Maybe someday a visit will work." Then I look at everyone and ask, "How about Iran? The nuclear bombs?"

The president of the United States looks at me, then glances at the rest and says, "I am sorry to report they, meaning Iran, have not responded to any of us, even though they know the situation. We don't know what they are doing."

The Chinese premier joins in. "We are very concerned about Iran, and we take no responsibility for their actions. They have ignored us completely. We have told the United States everything we know about what Iran has been doing. We will do all we can do to correct the situation. Any help from you will be appreciated."

"Yes, I will help. I know what you know, and, if needed, I will be there. As I said, the discussion here today needs to stay with us only. Do not reveal anything about me, who I am, or why we talked; this is for your own good."

I sense Anna coming over. I catch her scent, as her real scent is great, and I smell her perfume, which is even better. It is delightful. She is really gorgeous, and everyone's eyes are on her; it's hard not to stare at her. She is looking at the group, then at me. She smiles at them. They all start to stand.

Anna looks at me, saying, "Henry, are you finished? It's time to go."

I also stand up. "Guys, solve your problems, and I will keep in touch. Be careful that you do what's right. It was good to meet each of you. I wish you no harm. You have my best wishes for success."

They all stand up, hands out to shake, thanking me, all talking at the same time, inviting me to come see them, all saying they would like to talk a lot more. They would be delighted to take suggestions. I smile and then start to shake hands. I pay special attention to Premier Wu-Tong, thanking him, saying to him, "Premier, in the coming years I look forward to the leadership in this world that China will provide. You are a truly outstanding people."

Afterward, leaving quickly, Anna and I are outside, walking down a sidewalk, moving away from the pub. We are savoring the warm air, a summer evening in London. Feels good to be out, and Anna is holding my hand, saying nothing, just smiling up at me. We walk. It is good to just walk the tree-lined London streets, wandering slowly on the wide sidewalks, looking in the lighted store windows, checking out the other walkers. In return they check us out, as we are dressed so formally from the premier, looking like we are important. Many recognize Anna. We feel happy with each other. We don't talk; we just enjoy each other's company.

I feel the *Cyclone* two thousand feet above us. I know there is concern that Anna and I are exposed, and I know there are thousands of drones around us, invisible and lethal. We are safe.

After a while Anna says, "Did you solve the world's problems back there? You had the right guys."

I smile back at her. "Anna, it's impossible to solve those problems. They are like quicksand—the more you do, the more complicated it gets. By the way, are you ready to go to your home in LA? The *Cyclone* is now six hundred feet above us, following us, ready to take us wherever we want to go. Also, I have a better idea of the travel plans to LA. Let me take you there on the *Saber*. It's much smaller than the *Cyclone*, as it is an attack ship. It is my personal attack and reconnaissance ship, uses fusion rockets, powerful and very fast. You can drive it if you want. It is a real thrill. It is one of my most favorite things."

Laughing, she says, "Henry, just another typical boring date with you, and it sounds great! You know I have never piloted a plane in my life, much less a military craft."

I do not respond, as at this moment I am admiring Anna, gazing at her. She is very alluring in the half light of the evening lamplights, like in one of her movie scenes.

I continue to gaze at her, reflecting, *Anna looks seriously beautiful at this moment, her stunning dark dress, lightly sprinkled over with a little glitter, the thinness showing every curve, the light silkiness of the fabric moving with her body, flowing with the breeze, the hemline slit in several places, part of it traveling high off her knees, showing a lot of her long, slender legs. Her breasts are firm and teasing, almost visible through the light, thin dress, as she wears no bra, and she looks at me with her dazzling eyes, a coy alluring smile, humor on her face. She is definitely looking up at me in a flirty way, in a sexy way, and it is magical; she is doing it all for me, and this coming from a very gorgeous famous movie star. She is also kind, intelligent, charming, humble, and loving. What a divine blessing. Calabra.*

She is also now laughing at me with a wonderful laugh, finally saying, "Henry, I can read your thoughts without even using telepathy. I do look good. It's my job. And by the way, you look great in a tux."

I smile back at her without saying anything, just continuing with my observation. I am thinking she has a great sense of humor, too. She is truly lovely inside and out, and it's hard to take my eyes off of her. It is also difficult in this world to be an ambitious woman of strength and still have her straight-up honesty. I am humbled to be with her. She is extraordinary, a splendid being, none equal to her among trillions in the universe. Thank you, God, for this treasure! May our fate and destiny tie us together.

"Anna, I wish I could do more for you. One thing I could do for you is give you flying lessons before you take over piloting the *Saber* tomorrow. If you are willing, we leave first thing in the morning, maybe right after a quick early gym workout on the *Cyclone*. What do you think?"

Anna shakes her head. "If you think I can do this without killing us, I am game to try; the *Saber* sounds exciting! Just remember, this is all new to me. It scares me to just think about it. I have to trust you, Henry."

She continues, "Anyway, it is such a wonderful evening. The moon is out, the air feels so refreshing, and you said you are rarely in London. Rather than take a cab back to the hotel, let's take an open-air bus back. The open top on the second story of English buses is very fun; the big red buses have been traveling London streets for a hundred years. It's an awesome way to see the sights. What do you think?"

"Sounds great, and it's exactly what we need to do! There's one going our way over there. Come, give me your hand. We can make it."

We run to make the bus and are almost there as it goes on without us. Everyone on the bus is yelling for the driver to stop, as they recognize Anna. They are all saying, "That's Anna Summers, the American movie star. Wait for her!"

We jump on, pay the driver, and climb the steps. Everyone is laughing, and many ask Anna for autographs. She stops at each person and smiles, signs whatever they give her, and writes a little note, hugging each person. We finally make it to the top of the bus, up a small stairway. We find a seat toward the front and cuddle up together. Everyone claps when we settle in. Anna smiles and pulls my coat over her shoulders to keep warm. She waves at everyone, grins, and snuggles in under my arm. A couple of teenagers then come up front looking for seats, bouncing around, as the bus is moving. They manage to jump on a couple of seats close to us. The first girl asks Anna for an autograph, and while waiting she asks me who I am, which movie star. I laugh and say, "I am no one."

Anna loudly declares, "No way!" Smiling at me, she says, "He is the Starman, known throughout the universe. He's going to be the leading man in a new movie coming out next year about a starship and space travel. I hope to be the leading lady. He already is my leading man."

I laugh and say, "Anna, remember, it is supposed to be a secret."

Someone in the back yells, "What is the name of the movie?"

Anna grins at me and yells, "It's called *The Sword of Gabriel*. It will be a fantastic movie, with lots of action and a superhero." She pulls herself up to my ear and whispers, "The best cover story is a real one. A movie is more believable than the real you. You can keep your secret, as you say, and hide in plain sight. Actually it would be a good movie. You could play yourself, and I know a good leading lady. For that matter, I know who could finance it—you!"

I am nodding my head, laugh again, and say, "Yes, you are brilliant!"

Anna beams back, pleased that I am pleased. It helps the pain, as she is actually feeling some real anguish, with the dread of knowing my time is almost up; it's been a fast six days. She is thinking so much happened so fast; impossible, yet it did happen. The last few days have changed her life direction so quickly, as if she has been waiting for this, her real destiny. Her fear of losing me is intense.

This has been an awesome day thanks to Anna. The open-air bus ride is terrific. We see London's shopping areas, where lots of shoppers come from everywhere in the world, as well as some magnificent centuries-old buildings, all lit up, the tracks of the past and a lot of historical facts. Anna explains everything, the history of each building with the lives of people living in those times, as they are the ghosts of centuries past. She details all of it as we go, and it's captivating. The flickering streetlights and the warm breeze in the cool night air are delightful, as is my date with this wonderful, bright girl, a gem worth a thousand worlds. We are close to the hotel after getting off, waving good-bye to all our new friends, and then we take a brief walk. We pack, check out, duck out the back door, and, after a short, fast walk, meet up with the *Cyclone*'s ship's tender in a dark corner near the woods in Hyde Park. It's a fast lift up to the *Cyclone*.

⊷⊹ ⊹⊶

When Henry and Anna walked out of the pub, a shocked group of people stood there staring at them leaving, all wondering who Anna was with, this mysterious stranger all the world leaders came to talk to, her holding his hand. She was obviously enamored with him. He was impressive, to say the least, looking more like a gladiator in a tux, not an actor but the real thing. His eyes are remarkable, penetrating, like he sees everything. The heads of state were so deferential to him, actually fearful, anxious, trying to please him. The security people all gave him a wide berth, clearing a path for him through the crowd, as did the police outside. They all knew something they were not telling, as if they knew who he was and were frightened by knowing it.

After he and Anna left the heads of state, the politicians said their good-byes to one another, and their security teams accompanied them to bulletproof limousines. None were talking, deep in thought, all contemplative of what just happened. They all were nervous about this new future; the time was finally there to face up to beings on other planets. All were thinking there could be real issues. The big one question, could there be alien oversight, which could be dangerous, or maybe something even worse? This all has to be kept a secret, really secret, no media. They all wondered how Anna plays into this. She and Henry are definitely a couple. Could she be an alien, too? Hard to believe; what do they know about her? What if something happens to her? Would she talk to them, tell them how this all happened? Will the US president find out about her role here? How much does Captain Johnson know about each of them?

And then the other issue: what were the Iranians up to? Will they cause a crisis? Do the heads of state really want to ask Henry Johnson for help? What would the aliens do to humans on Earth if they don't do the right thing? What about this Consortium? Is Henry originally from Earth, like he says? If so, where was he born, and does he have family here? Can the heads of state trust him, or was he built to look like humans to make it easier to trust him? What does he really want, and how bad could he be? Absolutely no one there at the meeting wanted to find out; fear is an awful thing. The odd thing is each of them could still feel Henry's presence remaining with them, like being haunted by a ghost. This was not comforting to think about, with awful possibilities. They all were thinking they should have found another occupation.

As we are climbing up to the *Cyclone* on the ship's tender I am also recalling the memories of the day. I have one strong specific memory of the meeting, not a good one, an event that happened afterward that I am not sure I should follow up on. I do not tell Anna. She would not be happy.

I think I even might have gone too far. Some human emotions are fire starters. The emotions of jealousy, male testosterone rage, and the matching adrenaline rush are totally new. The only person I looked at when leaving the pub was James Algeir. I know he gave Anna a hard time when I was occupied with the group. I could hear his thoughts and Anna's, too, as he belittled her new boyfriend, then asked her if she's just plain stupid. He was almost physical with her, yet he restrained himself, looking over my way to see if I was watching. He threatened that he would ruin her career and tell the tabloids about their sex life, and he had photos. She warned him that he was in way over his head and to shut his mouth fast for his own good, then walked away. It triggered me. I could not help it.

When we left I made sure James Algeir could feel my anger in his head as I stared at him, probed his brain, scorched his mind with my rage, threatened his sanity and life. As Anna and I had walked through the pub's door, him staring back at me, our eyes had locked, which caused him to urinate, his eyes becoming frantic, and hands trembling, as he is not too sure of his sanity, feeling totally horrified. I also told him we would meet again; to his shock he heard my words in his brain, felt the painful probe. I left him with the slip in his brain. I hope we meet again.

CHAPTER 27

DAY SEVEN

Anna is up, drinking my Earth coffee from a sealed cup, secured to the wall using one foot behind a handle, as there is no gravity. She is adapting quickly, smart girl. I also know she is happy; I feel it. Last night went well; the movie premiere was a huge success according to all the morning newspapers. Anna checked most of them and has already talked to her staff. Nothing was said about my meeting with the group, although there were lots of photos of Anna. She also had called her mother and sister last night, as we orbited Earth on the *Cyclone*. We both worked out in the little gym early this morning; it felt good for both of us. We ate a meal I prepared, my Spanish omelet, which I think I invented. It has everything in it, plus the kitchen sink.

I remind Anna we are taking the *Saber* to LA this morning; she will have a chance to pilot it, too. She looks at me with wide eyes, some fear, yet excited, and says, "It scares the hell out of me just thinking about it. Although I think I'm completely irrational, flying a supersonic military rocket ship sounds like fun, while I must be crazy to do it. My problem is I think I would follow you to hell and back, and I hope I'm ready for this climb-the-mountain adventure. Let's do it. Although, Henry, please remember this is my first time for this kind of thing; don't let it kill me!"

The *Saber* is mega-advanced technology. Actually I only half know what it's fully capable of. For one thing, although I did not tell Anna this, as she will soon find out, it does not need her or me to pilot it. It is completely controlled by its own brains, a thought process way beyond me, with its own survival skills. It is a being with an opinion, like a living, breathing predator, like riding a living thing linked to your brain. Although I am the captain, I am not sure who controls whom; it's like riding a tiger. You live in the moment, only a partner in the adventure. Yet I truly love this craft. It is more than a friend, and it is the ultimate thrill.

I have loaded it with my favorite music, telepathically linked to my brain and now Anna's. When traveling fast or in combat, I love the Rolling Stones blasting away—calms the nerves. As a military attack ship, it is well armed, and it can kill almost anything in its way; in my many previous battles, it has always prevailed. At times it has scared the hell out of me. It uses directed-energy weapons: fusion high-temperature streams (sixty-five thousand degrees), particle beam shots, long-distance intelligent drone nuclear rockets traveling at light speed, massive electromagnetic area radiation, heavy-gravity force fields, and forty-eight individual extreme laser cutters used as strobe rapid-fire weapons.

The *Saber* has my own additions, too. I installed old-fashioned P-51 Mustang "stick between the legs" controls for the pilot and the copilot, strictly for the fun of it. At the speed this thing goes, it is impossible for a human to control it; you have only microfractions of time for steering adjustments, and it's just not possible with slower human reflexes. The *Saber*'s intelligence, or the ship's brainpower processors, control the ship at high speeds, following my directions. Megasupersonic speeds are too fast for even my reflexes; by the time I reacted to the visuals, we would be dead. Even though the *Saber* pilots without me, it reacts to my thoughts telepathically with one exception: it lets me drive up to ten thousand miles per hour or at any lower speed, as I can handle the lower velocity, and I use the pilot stick. It can raise the hair on your neck, as it is terrifying to watch the ground flash by during low-altitude runs, just a blur, and also more thrilling than any roller-coaster ride.

The *Cyclone* is now orbiting above Earth at a high altitude, running twenty thousand miles per hour, just barely into outer space, about 135 miles up, over a bright-blue Earth sky, as it's now early morning and mostly good weather. Earth is below in all its splendor: blue oceans, green and brown continents, mountains, and white billowing clouds. We are over Canada, just entering, now over the border, heading due west, having just passed over the North Atlantic Ocean. It was dark blue and frothing with large swells due to heavy winds on the surface.

Anna and I pull ourselves into the *Saber*'s big, comfortable captain's chairs and strap in well. I check Anna's straps, and while leaning over her I surprise her with a forehead kiss to reassure her. She nervously smiles at me and says she is ready, although I see the fear in her eyes, and her scent is thick with adrenaline. The ship is ready to go, all hatches closed, fueled up, fully armed, navigation in place.

I open the *Cyclone*'s outside doors, causing some thin, cold wind to rush up into the hangar bay, as we are too high for much atmosphere. I trigger the *Saber*'s release, the locks disengage, and the *Cyclone* drops the *Saber* out of its underbelly down toward Earth. We are free-falling with the gravity, no power, dropping for three or four minutes, sinking down into Earth's atmosphere, gaining momentum as we plunge. We say nothing; just enjoy the spell of this magic, viewing Earth from this elevation, completely silent. Then we hit the top layers of Earth's atmosphere, the sound of more wind, a little bouncing with the turbulence and moving at a speed of nineteen thousand miles per hour.

I can hear Anna's thoughts as she projects to me: *It is impossible not to believe in God when you see this. Henry, it is beyond belief. The Earth's horizon with the reflection of the sun off the atmosphere is magnificent, all golden and just magical. Then looking beyond into black unending space, we are so insignificant. Yet I feel connected, like I have purpose, part of God's plan. When I am looking down at Earth, I feel comforted, our Mother Earth as far as I can see, a land full of colors, with the deep greens of the massive forests, the blue rivers, gray mountains covered in white snow, then the massive dark-blue oceans below the snow-white billowing clouds, and the world spinning around. It is truly splendid and beautiful, a gift from God.*

Anna pauses, looks at me. "Henry, you are a wonderful man, thank you for this."

I smile, and she blushes as she feels my answer, as I am thinking about her—another blessing from God.

We are still plummeting in complete silence, no engine thrust or sound. We hear only the concussion of rushing wind against the hull, getting louder as we drop deeper into Earth's atmosphere. There are many colors of dazzling light around us because of the air friction against the hull. It slows us down; the air around us is getting hot, reducing our speed from nineteen thousand miles an hour to ten thousand—still swift, about thirteen times the speed of sound or a Mach 13. The speed of sound is around 760 miles per hour, depending on the density of the air. The silence is gone, replaced by the thunderous noise of the air hitting us hard.

Anna is all eyes, really excited, looking at Earth below, then she looks at me like a kid, smiles a big smile, and does a thumbs-up as we drop. Then I smile and do a thumbs-up back, also excited.

It is time.

I ignite the rocket fusion burners, pure nuclear power, really hot, much advanced over anything seen by Earth scientists.

It growls for a couple of seconds then explodes like a massive thunderbolt. We make a massive jolt forward, surging with the blast then surging again, pinned into the seats, exploding thirty miles forward by a huge fired blast tail behind us, now under full power, thrusting forward, both of us pressed against the seats. Then, with perfect timing, the Rolling Stones booms out, and Anna looks at me laughing. We have dropped down over the dark-blue Atlantic Ocean blasting east, the wrong way, away from Los Angeles.

I telepathically tell Anna we're going the long way—around the world. She nods her head, and I feel her excitement. We're going to go around Earth, first over England, heading across Europe and China, then over the Pacific. We will be there in Los Angeles in about two hours, as we are taking it slow, the scenic route at low altitudes. I take the *Saber* down low, mostly under radar, still running at ten thousand miles an hour, real low at just two hundred feet above the ocean. The sensation of speed at this low altitude is incredible, plenty of turbulence and wind—like riding a comet, bouncing with the airstream. The water below is coming so fast under us, it's a blur, and the *Saber* is booming out massive shock waves.

We blast out, surging forward, pressed hard back against the seats, with thirty-nine thousand degrees of heat blasting out the rocket burners behind us, causing more massive turbulence as it whips up a huge mass of frothing water for a hundred miles back, a tail that is three hundred feet higher than sea level, almost like a circular typhoon, part steam, part wind velocity. It's amazing to see, even for me.

I am sure the world is seeing us by satellite and radar, maybe a few ships here and there, since we're hard to miss. I just don't care at this point, as I am living day by day, wanting to give Anna a thrill. I know no one can figure it out anyway, as the speed is faster than anything Earth has seen, much faster than a bullet and not easy to visibly make out. I am also making sure I am staying out of cargo-ship routes. I know there will be some sightings, and the *Saber* will create some excitement when spotted in that one split second as we blast by anyone out there. The front hull is hot too, as the friction is on fire.

We are over England, and I'm putting on the brakes as much as possible, coming down to three thousand miles an hour. We can't see much of the scenery, as we are moving too fast for the human eye and too close to the surface to see much, so I climb to 4,800 feet, still dangerously low, and I ask the *Saber* to watch for other air traffic. We can see the countryside now, charming villages, curving roads and cars, lush green forests, streams and pastures. Anna is taking it all in, moving with the music of the Rolling Stones, and definitely having fun.

The *Saber* is not in stealth mode and has a serious tail blast. I am concerned about radar or satellite scans, as we are not invisible to Earth's technology. Although, more important, I just don't want to hit another aircraft, nor am I interested in a missile chasing us. Unfortunately we are also letting out some sonic booms and shaking some windows, making it unwise to accelerate without climbing. We see rolling farm fields, green and lush, and small villages here and there; and then, in about a second, we cross over London at ten thousand feet up. I hit the gas, running eight thousand miles an hour, and take a sharp climb over the English Channel, banking to the starboard, up to forty thousand feet, heading east to Europe. I drop to ten thousand feet again over Normandy Beach, cross France, and then head south, climbing again up over the Swiss Alps, heading southeast and over China before we realize it.

Anna is having a parallel-dimension experience, a two-for-one thrill, both good and bad. I can feel her wonderment of it all, as she has never been in a military jet, and the sheer impact of the ride is awesome; however, when you have not done this before it is also terrifying, not that she would admit it. Thank heavens we are not in combat. I can feel she is having fun, a big thrill. Maybe Anna would want to pilot the *Saber* for a while.

I know I need to be more careful about this flight, as the showing off to Anna has alerted ten countries. It would be impossible not to see us, not only visually but also with both radar and the huge heat signature. We are moving much too fast to be caught, as nothing on this planet could even come close. Yet that is exactly the problem, as it means they know this ship is not from Earth, which sets into motion issues for everyone. Lots of sightings are trouble for me. I still can't help myself, and I think I should let Anna feel the *Saber*; that means giving her the control stick and letting her pilot the starship.

"Anna, are you ready? Do you want to pilot the *Saber*? You have the copilot stick. It's easy; the flight computer will correct you if you stray off path or get in trouble. The *Saber* will engage you mentally when you take the stick. It will know your thoughts; think your flight, and then it happens. Use the stick, as it helps you project your thoughts to control the flight. The stick does nothing to guide the *Saber*, it just helps your mind focus. Remember, just relax. The *Saber* reads your mind to know what you want instantly. It's easy."

I hear her thoughts and reply, "Don't worry, you can't fire the weapons by accident. Push the stick forward and you dive, backward you climb; pull right and it will swing right; left is the same. Just do a little at a time to get used to it. Your speed is adjusted when you squeeze the stick handle; the harder you squeeze, the faster it goes. Press the button on top, and it locks in that speed. As I said the flight is following your thoughts; the stick just helps you channel your thoughts."

Anna looks at me—excited, not afraid—and is ready to fly the *Saber*. I feel her emotions, and it feels good to have her next to me. She laughs, yells, "Geronimo," takes the stick, and immediately accelerates, surging forward. With some g-force we climb quickly: the speed is twelve thousand miles per hour, then quickly to twenty-five thousand miles per hour. We are now at thirty thousand feet, climbing to forty thousand feet within a second. We are over the middle of China, and Anna dives, dropping to a ten-thousand-foot altitude and slowing down once again to seven thousand miles an hour, giving us a chance to see the country. The Great Wall passes under us, and we see many little villages. They are all pleasing to look at, and it's certainly a big country. Of course we are booming out air concussions.

Anna has leveled off at five thousand feet, and as we near the Pacific she hits the pedal again and boosts the speed to fourteen thousand miles an hour, climbing fast. She's having a great time and looks over at me every so often, smiling, needing confirmation she is doing this right. I nod and say, "You're a natural, and the *Saber* likes you. Take us to LA; the flight processor will give you the navigation."

I lean back and let Anna feel my confidence in her. I enjoy the Rolling Stones music, feeling the power of the music and also the *Saber's* power as it flies faster than a bullet, faster than lightning, like riding the wind.

We are now at twenty-four thousand feet of altitude and running sixteen thousand miles an hour. I tell Anna we are over the Mariana Trench, the deepest part of the Pacific Ocean, thirty-two thousand feet deep. She nods her head and is just starting to look over at me when—

Ga—baaammmmm—mmp—mah—wup!

We are hit hard. The pain to our ears is instantaneous. It's a massive ear-splitting explosion! The *Saber* is blasted off course, rolled over from the blast surge, the concussion terrific, now in free fall, then again...

Booom—booboo—ga-bang!

Another huge hit. Then more. It's all around us, more mega-deafening explosions bombing us, our ears exploding with pain. The *Saber* corrects itself violently, plunges right and drops down, then accelerates with a roaring blast, massively surging forward due west, then straight up, then plunging down. Neither of us is prepared for the thrust, and we are violently jerked back as we are rocketing up again, pinning us violently to our seats, the force of gravity painful.

The rocket's fusion reactors are all screaming, thrusting out, with more massive surges forward, and even more explosions are all around us, punching us. The noise is deafening, as the weapons of the *Saber* are now all firing back, so fast it sounds like multiple Gatling guns firing at the same time, just ear-splitting rapid fire bursts, overwhelming to all the senses.

The *Saber* is shuddering with massive vibrations from the power of the torque as it twists and turns. The g-force is unbelievable, more than I have ever experienced in all my years of battle. The sky is lighting up for miles from the full fusion thrust, causing a blast tail coming off the *Saber*'s burners like fire from hell. The stream is sixty miles long and eight miles wide, striking the Pacific Ocean. The airspace over the ocean is consumed by a scorching fire, temperatures around thirty thousand degrees, more like a torrent of continuous nuclear bombs going off, creating massive windstorms of steam over the area, looking like a hurricane that is blasting upward.

We are in combat, and I don't know who this is attacking us, trying to kill us. It cannot be Earth craft; this is much more lethal. Some powerful enemy has ambushed us. How stupid to be caught like this and maybe kill myself and Anna, too!

I realize the *Cyclone* is now coming fast for us, as it was instantly alerted and has started firing its weapons toward our attackers. It crosses California at thirty thousand miles an hour, still accelerating, lighting up the night sky there, terrifying the entire population with the fire-stream thrust tail and the blast shocks of the massive nuclear-fusion guns hammering ahead, firing at the alien ships. As the *Cyclone* comes for us, it's causing multiple massive sonic booms from the accelerating speed, thunder shaking the Earth like an earthquake.

The *Cyclone* has discovered the enemy and is detailing to me that there is a massive civilization military starship in the Mariana Trench, protected by billions of tons of ocean water and well-armed. It has ambushed us using its attack ships, which I named wasps in a previous battle fought with this same ship, which escaped me then. The wasps are smaller than the *Saber*, deadly, though, and we are severely outnumbered. They are all around us, coming out of the sea. They are firing at us, and the *Saber* is defending and firing back, trying to use its speed to escape and the hot tail thrust of thirty thousand degrees to burn anything behind us. We are leaving Earth, blasting straight up. I can see more than four wasps still tracking us, and then they all evaporate into nothing as the *Saber* leans starboard, the fire stream hitting them. The *Cyclone* destroys several more of them, instantly vaporizing them, as it is now close enough to accurately target them and fire at them successfully.

Many more suddenly appear out of the sea.

"Damn it!" I am swearing, raging, and ready for them. We come back to Earth accelerating, diving straight for them, hitting them with fusion guns, firing thousands of strikes a second, like strobe lights on steroids. Even more wasps hurl out of the ocean, hard to count. They're rising up out of the sea, coming from the mother ship. The *Saber* is vaporizing them with the fusion guns, yet some escape. I need to sweep them again. The *Saber* climbs again, making a wide bank to portside, ascending at the same time.

The massive full blast from the *Saber*'s fusion reactors becomes a sweep, like a broom. We are spiraling up, the ship's sizzling tail burning straight down into the sea, the fire stream 125 miles long, six miles wide, composed of pure nuclear blast, thrusting down into the ocean at fusion temperatures, reaching the bottom, deep down. The mother ship feels the heat and starts to burn, yet not enough; it returns fire with heavy nuclear weapons, hot fusion-burner streams exploding out of the ocean meant to hit us.

The *Saber* is again quickly accelerating away from Earth, trying to avoid the massive nuclear bursts coming directly from the mother ship, hotter than the sun, aimed at the *Saber.*

Once again the massive tail thrust of the *Saber* burns straight down into the sea, thrashing the enormous enemy starship with the blast pressure and tons of scalding water, a fire heating miles and miles of ocean, billions of tons of water converting to scalding steam. Down deep on the bottom, the mother starship tolerates the heat and the radiation. The *Saber* is now twenty miles above the Earth, out of range of the mother ship's nuclear weapons; it's still too deep in the Pacific. Yet the *Saber* is preparing to return and will join the *Cyclone* to destroy this alien enemy, this vast battle starship. Now they need a plan.

The *Saber*'s brainpower has had control of the ship, fighting for survival and demanding the great speed, then all the twisting and turning, plus accelerating at incredible speed and changing altitude. It's like riding a roller coaster from hell, at times bursting out into space above the Pacific, finding and killing the enemy wasps at every turn, tracking them down, killing them. They are no match for the *Saber,* much less the *Cyclone,* also hammering them.

The *Saber* is currently talking to the *Cyclone,* which is below us at an altitude of four miles, still twenty miles west of us, circling. The *Cyclone* says we need to kill the enemy mother ship. I dread this resolution, yet it's the right response, meaning I have no other choice. I order it; the *Saber* immediately heads toward

California to get out of the way, and I create a firing solution for the *Cyclone* with an interception point.

Knowing this navigation point, the *Cyclone* proceeds to set up the bomb run, climbing, blasting straight up into outer space, directly above the enemy starship, forcing it into a defensive mode to deflect the massive heat from the accelerating *Cyclone*, which is using its huge fusion reactors to thrust the enormous heat down into the depths of the ocean, again vaporizing billions of tons of water. Steam explodes upward at a mile a second, and there's a tremendous deafening sound of massive pressure, the hot air hitting cooler air and exploding, making thunder a thousand times louder than normal. The *Cyclone* needs to position itself for the attack, miles up into outer space.

Because of all of this, there are massive lightning strikes and huge storms everywhere, expanding out quickly to a hundred-mile radius and farther, with wind gusts as severe as any hurricane, grotesque in appearance. The millions of tons of scalding steam are moving high up into the atmosphere, covering Earth at a high altitude. The storm's velocity is more than a thousand miles an hour and high above Earth, over fifty thousand feet, too high to threaten the surface or its inhabitants. However, the entire planet will soon be totally covered by a dark, heavy cloud layer loaded with moisture. It will take a couple of days for it to clear; it will be a rain-filled world for a while, with widespread flooding.

Tonight will be a good news night for the TV networks. All of this action is very much visible for miles. How will the networks explain this, or government officials, or scientists? Of course the distinguished group from the London pub will speculate, my new high-level friends will all wonder.

The *Cyclone* has disappeared into outer space yet it is still blasting the ocean at depths far down below, vaporizing more of it with its long propulsion tail, now many miles away; as there's just that much power hitting the surface of the ocean, equal to a many atom bombs, beyond comprehension. However, this will not kill the alien starship down below. It severely feels the heat and the radiation yet suffers no real damage, nor can it fight back at these depths. Yet it cannot risk coming up to the surface to do battle unless it is forced to ascend. The huge starship will die only with a direct hit. It needs to stay underwater, as the massive depth of the ocean protects it.

I know this starship. It belongs to the Seatisveres, a nasty, mostly nomad civilization not acceptable to the Consortium, considered an outlaw civilization and unfortunately they have starship technology. Their original home world is mostly uninhabitable because of their greed, misuse, global neglect, war, extravagant waste, and pollution. They are like locusts, or maybe pirates, destroying whatever they touch. They are my sworn enemy, and we've fought before. There are, all together, seven of these city-starships, each a military battleship, traveling as a fleet. These are massive ships with entire cities inside, more military than not. This ship is separated from the pack for some reason. It will be hard to destroy, dangerous, too. It needs to have a direct hit from something big—our negative dark-energy beam would work. One large issue with using this weapon, however, is a big problem, that it might cause more collateral damage than Earth can handle; it might destroy Earth.

All this brutal combat has happened in a few short minutes, and I just now have a chance to look at Anna, as I am suddenly feeling something is wrong. To my total shock, I know there are no brain waves coming from her, then feeling the terror and desperation of knowing she is not alive. I see her sitting next to me slumped over. I realize she is not breathing. What happened? She is dying, only seconds left. There is blood on her mouth and nose, and she is blue all over. I know her drone medical slips are working, though, I can feel them inside her, frantically repairing the damage, trying to get her lungs to breathe.

Oh my God! The gravity pressure, she was hammered by the massive weight caused by the Saber's surges in altitude.

She has never been in combat; the g-force was incredible. She must not have been able to handle the extreme gravity weight caused by the *Saber* accelerating, and her heart stopped, permanently damaged.

I have killed her!

I jerk out of my harness although the *Saber* is still moving fast, preparing to position an ambush on the Seatisveres' starship. I grab on to Anna's harness. I am giving her mouth-to-mouth resuscitation, breathing into her lungs, and it is not working. I scream mentally at the slips in her brain, as for both of them to help, one needs to move to her heart and electrically charge it. The other one needs to spark the brain with enough electrical energy to start her lungs, force them to expand, drawing in air. The heart needs to start moving blood, as the slip does the job—*bam!*—the electrical charge hits her heart. It happens. Now she has a pulse; she is coughing and coming alive. Her medical drones, with the help of mine, are quickly repairing her wounds, repairing the heart muscle, stopping the hemorrhages. Her ribs were broken in several places; the lungs were pierced, then much too much bleeding, now all being repaired by the drone slips. She's breathing and her pulse is better. She will make it.

Thank you, Lord!

She is beat up some; I can see some bruising where the harness fits. She comes to. Her eyes are panicked, then she vomits, and I have some gravity to work with, as we are not in space or free float. I catch it mostly in my hands; use a urine disposal unit to get rid of it. She is coughing. I clean her up as much as possible using some ship's cleanser and wet air wipes to wash her face and throat. She's weak.

The thought of having almost lost her horrifies me; no question in my mind, damn...damn...this was a major screw-up by me. I couldn't lose her this way. I am trying to recover from the shock. She looks at me; the slips are back in telepathic mode, and I am reassuring her, my loving thoughts and tenderness flooding her, soothing her: "I am here, and I will protect you."

She looks up at me, tries to respond, coughing, then blurts out, "Henry, what happened? What hit us? I don't remember much after all the explosions. Lord, I feel lousy, sore all over, just awful, feels like someone beat me up. I hurt everywhere. My mouth tastes terrible."

She looks out at the massive turmoil of the black storms and asks, "Oh my God, did I cause this?"

I smile, so relieved, and respond, "Anna, no, no, you did not cause this. It's really good you don't remember much, better not to know. You missed a war with another starship, an old enemy of mine hiding in the Mariana Trench. They ambushed us, with a lot of fireworks and noise. I think it's almost over. It almost killed you; the gravitational pull stopped your heart and broke some ribs. You came out of it. You will be OK. I am so sorry!"

I remember what's happening. I stop looking at her and look ahead. "Just look out there. I hope you see our victory coming, although it's not a great day for me. I never saw it coming, a bad sign. It was a close call and my fault. Never should have happened." I look at her, feeling awful, disappointed in myself, wanting to make it better. "I am sorry, Anna. This was not the joy ride I planned."

Anna looks worried. "No, I feel bad but not that bad. Does anyone know about this, like Earth people?"

I answer, "Unfortunately the whole world knows. And it's not done yet; let's hope my plan will work. Say a prayer, Anna, for our success."

The *Cyclone* is three thousand miles from Earth, far enough away to make the shot. It loops back fast toward Earth, accelerating to forty thousand miles an hour and blasting a bright, spectacular tail of nuclear propulsion fire thrust at least five hundred miles long behind it, back up into outer space. It starts its bomb run to deliver its death black-hole shot, an almost invisible negative-gravity stream of power, pulsating, then creating the severe gravity of a space blackhole that will implode a planet or star. We have chosen this strategy because we have nothing else that will work.

The beam takes massive negative energy from our dark antimatter generators and then creates the tremendous gravity needed. The *Cyclone* has aimed it at the Seatisveres' starship deep down in the dark depths at the bottom of the Mariana Trench. When it hits the starship, the suction of the gravity will start to fold it up like a crushed paper plate, destroying it within a couple of minutes. Then it will continue to do much more; it will continue to expand, the massive gravity pulling in more, destroying this part of the world, then pulling all of it inward, us too. The Earth will just disappear; end up the size of a golf ball. We are dead, too. We are too close to escape it, and I can't reverse it.

If I don't use it on this ruthless starship, these repulsive, true cannibals, worthy of death, will stay in their ocean parking place, safe from attack, using the Earth as a shield. If they kill us, Earth will be ravaged, then sucked by this parasite. We could run. We could make an escape, come back with a Star Fleet VII, the fleet that's nearest; however, they would be gone by the time we got back, and Earth would be severely damaged or destroyed and plundered by that time.

The *Cyclone* triggers the negative energy stream. The plan is only a short burst to scare the enemy starship, then hold off to see if it runs. The first burst is so powerful; I can feel its pull on the *Saber*, now many miles away. My boss, Gabriel, will know about it, as he always knows when I use this weapon. He will ask me about using it. The entire planet will feel its energy when it starts to hit; then, if it's continued, the Earth will disappear, pulled into a black nothing.

The Seatisveres' starship has only two real options: escape from Earth now or be destroyed with it. I think they will think it is better to go by fighting their way out. I also know they are extremely vulnerable as they power out of Earth's gravity, since they are massive and heavy. The *Saber* is ready and waiting to spring the ambush, in stealth mode so it can't be seen, on the coast of California now, as the huge enemy starship takes the first and only real option: to escape. The *Saber* will run at it and fire when the starship is nineteen thousand feet up, just the right altitude for the Earth's air to help it burn. The hit will self-combust around the starship, and the oxygen will bring the heat up to three hundred thousand degrees, an incendiary hit. The *Saber* will use a fusion reactor gun using a sort of nuclear gunpowder. The *Saber*'s one huge blast must hit perfectly, and it must breach the starship's powerful security field. We will have only one shot; it has to work, or we face their deadly return fire.

The *Saber* signals that the Seatisveres' starship is up and out of the water, accelerating quickly, with massive blasting, on its way to outer space. I order the discharge, and it is triggered. It instantly streams out of the *Saber* like a massive lightning megabolt, visible for thousands of miles, sheer massive heat and energy, enough to power the world. It instantly jolts the *Saber* into a lower speed like a brake, slowing us down from sixteen thousand miles an hour to six thousand in a second. We are heading straight for the starship, still firing. I'm not sure what will happen, can't see the starship clearly with all the moisture and debris from the previous detonations and still a long distance from it. I think it's a hit; we are miles from it but closing in fast.

I look at Anna; she is looking at it, too. She felt the ship jerk with the stream shot, slowing us down, saw the massive hot fusion-bolt stream to its target, all coming from the *Saber.*

Yes...yes...I can see it. The huge starship has taken the hit, the firestorm making the ship easy to see. It hesitates, rolls over, starts to fall back to Earth, and then explodes into a fiery mess, vaporizing in the extreme heat. It's colossal; the gigantic fireball explosion shoots miles up into outer space, probably can be seen for thousands of miles, and the wind concussion is considerable as it sends a shock wave out, moving hundreds of miles an hour, fortunately much less when it hits the California coast.

We bank a hard right, turning away from it; the air concussion hits the *Saber*, causing us to jolt and lose two thousand feet in altitude. The *Cyclone* is gone now, done its part of the plan, blasting off and covering thousands of miles, now going after any active wasps. It turned off the negative-gravity stream as soon as the big starship started rising from the bottom; otherwise we all would be dead.

It's been another close call, a terrible victory. There is no pleasure in this success. I know we have not heard the last of the Seatisveres. There are six more of the civilization starships, all battleships, somewhere out there, not far. They usually travel together like a pack of wolves. They will eventually know what happened, and with my current luck they probably will be coming back to Earth for revenge. Maybe they will go on, not bother Earth, and come after me instead. I need one or two fleets to find them and a fleet to protect Earth. This, unfortunately, is one more reason I have to leave; I must go back and apply to bring Earth into the Consortium for their protection.

Regrettably, I know all eighteen thousand souls on board have perished. Some of them were normal, not evil. Even if they wasted lives in ill pursuits, not all deserved this fate, and their children on board did not deserve this. I feel their deaths and regret it happened; this feeling is something I live with constantly. It always comes after a battle; can't avoid it, like some kind of self-punishment. It is a sad day for the Seatisveres and me. At least they died mercifully quick.

Unluckily, the explosion was so large it paused the Earth's orbit a fraction—not a lot, thankfully. It also shifted the world's axis a little, which caused a small movement in the Earth's crust or shifted the top layer a little, causing small earthquakes and tremors over the world. It's bad, yet it could have been much worse.

At the site of the starship's destruction, the blast was equal to a 50 megatons atomic bomb exploding at nineteen thousand feet up, where the shock wave dissipated, thrusting up into outer space and no damaging radiation from the blast. It was also too high for any resulting tsunamis, nor did the ocean blast from the *Cyclone* cause tsunamis.

Yes, thanks to divine providence we are alive, undamaged. So is the world, thanks to the *Cyclone,* the *Saber,* and thank you God for saving Anna. I know she now wonders about my real life and me. I feel her doubts, and it brings me much sadness. I rarely bring happiness to the beings I come in contact with—ask the eighteen thousand I just killed.

For the Earth the most significant result of all of this is that over the next few hours, the world becomes dark, almost night, as a heavy cloud cover spreads out over the land and oceans. Heavy rain and some flooding occur everywhere across the world, even rain in the deserts. It comes from vaporizing trillions of tons of water, all of which rises into the upper atmosphere. Nothing like this has happened since the age of the dinosaurs. There were floods then, too.

The heat resulting from the battle explosions warms California by ten degrees, and most of its residents come out to see where all the fireworks came from, looking toward the west. During the battle they could see massive star-bright explosions, flashes, and massive thunder, the firestorm thrusting way out into outer space. The power from the energy lit much of these outer limits of Earth. It was like a thunderstorm the size of Texas. The lightning strikes looked like falling stars—big ones!

I look at Anna, feeling awful. How bad can it get? I say to her, "I'm sorry you had to be part of this; you ended up being part of my world, the bad part, and I'm not sure how I can make it up to you. My world is terrible at times; the violence is never acceptable. Fortunately we survived. I know we're late in getting you home; I am so sorry. We're now heading to your house in L.A." I try to joke: "Hopefully we'll be there in time for you to get your newspaper."

No comment from Anna, just silence. It was a bad joke and the worst timing.

I am worried about Anna. What could she possibly be thinking? I know she is alive as I can feel her mind.

"Anna, we need to find out tomorrow how your fellow citizens are receiving all of this, maybe catch the news. They may not be too happy with all of this? There may be some real issues."

"Are you hungry? Are you feeling better? I know you took a real beating. Although it sounds crazy to ask you after all this, is there anything I can do to help? I can get you something to eat or drink, now or in the morning. Tomorrow morning we could have coffee and read the newspaper, have breakfast, relax, no starships. We will be human. I will even make you breakfast."

No answer. I look closer in the dark, the cockpit red-lighted, and I see she is asleep. She has not been listening to me, must be worn out from the near-death and the entire trauma, all my doing.

Then she wakes up and shakes her head, looking at me, also looking really tired, says nothing, then goes back to sleep. The *Saber* is moving fast toward California. Not sure this all went well. Not sure what California looks like, and not sure anything is open for business. All the water and debris from the resulting storms will cause issues. There will be a lot of rain and moisture covering the Earth for several days. Anna is now back to sleep, half-curled-up in the chair, beat up, and exhausted. I slow down, reduce the *Saber*'s power, no rush now. I have to make a phone call, too.

CHAPTER 28

REPERCUSSIONS

B ack in Washington, DC, the president, the vice president, the CIA chief, Section 58 staff and John Jacobs, the FBI top guys, the National Security Council, the Senate Oversight Committee, key congressmen, all high-level generals of all the services, and all the cabinet members are crowded together in an emergency meeting in the secure room under the White House. The president is explaining what has happened, bringing everyone up to speed, briefing them.

The president was on the phone earlier in the night with the leaders of other countries, mostly allies, all in a panic about what had just happened out in the Pacific Ocean. He had called up the military and put them on continued high alert, depending on events and investigation of the whole affair. It was coincidental that they were already on high alert and have already been in high-level meetings.

All know about Iran and the bank payoffs. Most of the traitors employed by the United States government or the military have been arrested and are pointing fingers at their fellow conspirators. The FBI and the military have also rounded up many of the

Iranian soldiers, who are now behind walls in a military prison, being interrogated. The hunt is on for the nuclear bombs.

They all found out who Henry Johnson is, which shook everyone. The long-awaited alien contact has actually happened.

China has confirmed they believe Henry Johnson is an alien, the real thing, no illusions or fabrication. His military starship is advanced thousands of years ahead of us and impossible to defend from any attack coming from it. Earth totally vulnerable. They agreed to stand down, bring their troops home. The United States promised to pay the Chinese back every cent in their currency values. No war needs to happen, thank God. It was too close a call.

Russia and Mexico also apologized. Neither of them could speak for Iran. Both were thrilled yet apprehensive about meeting with the alien, this Henry Johnson. It is a moment in history, changing everything. They have many questions. It is hard to believe; yet they all think it is real and a possible huge opportunity. Who would think this could happen in this way? Henry has answered many questions; everyone is now concerned about the future dealings with nonhumans. All wonder about Henry Johnson. No question, they are fearful of him, and they do not trust him, yet, maybe a link.

The president says, "I do not consider Captain Johnson human, not with the telepathy stuff. I felt his mental probes and know he could read my thoughts. Since the meeting we have asked one another about feeling weird, not comfortable. All of us agree the uneasiness started at the meeting with Captain Johnson. He may have been built to look human to gain our trust, yet we can only hope he really is on our side, as he is originally from Earth, and we believe that's not a fabrication. Some understanding from him would be most beneficial, and maybe he would actually help us."

The president told them about the London meeting with Captain Johnson. He says it is extraordinary that such a secret meeting was held in public—so confidential and classified yet held in London in a pub. Even more surprising, all current issues were resolved, including a possible World War. It was really odd, very last minute and amusing, as no one was too sure Mr. Jacobs had told Henry Johnson they were coming. The leaders of several major countries were all there, confused and in panic mode.

The president laughs and looks at Jacobs. "Well, John, I guess we all know now that Henry didn't know about the meeting. It certainly shows some courage on your part! Good work, we all owe you as you may have saved the world, as we know it. Also, what is this Anna Summers thing? This Hollywood star is with Henry Johnson, in some kind of relationship? The commander of billions of troops is visiting here, coming on a military starship from trillions of miles away, and now it seems, dating her. Go figure. How did Anna meet him? How long has he been here? How old is he? If he leaves and something happens to Anna, what will he do? Would Anna talk to us? She must know a hell of a lot about this alien civilization. The two of them look like a couple, but how close are they?"

"Another crazy coincidence is Anna's stepfather, Senator Sam Jordan. This is another problem, as he is in big trouble. Between his relationship with the Deforleo crime family and then the Iranians using him, charges for treason are possible."

"And now we have this massive firefight in the Pacific that happened between aliens. Why? What does it mean for the future of Earth? Was Henry Johnson there? He must have been. Did he survive? Ten million phone calls or more—most did not get through; lines were jammed—were made this morning, asking us if the government knows anything about this obvious alien activity."

"Everyone called to this meeting today knows about the massive military engagement over the Pacific and knows it was not of this planet; no question, there were aliens in battle, and they may be here now, still here on Earth. I waited for Section 58 manager John Jacobs's completed report before I called this meeting together. He is the point man on this and has personally met with Captain Johnson on several occasions.

"John, please tell us what you have."

John stands up, handing out his written report copies. He looks serious and tired.

Looking out at everyone, he starts out by explaining the state of affairs. "There has been confirmed possible alien spacecraft activities around the world over the last few days—an aircraft moving at supersonic speeds spotted in China, Britain, and France and across the United States. And apparently there has been a major firefight over the Mariana Trench in the Pacific by massive aircraft, probably ships that can only be spaceships with technology not of this world. The result was a terrific demonstration of their technology. Mega-energy direct-fire weapons were used, much more sophisticated than any known Earth weapons, which included nuclear-fusion guns and lasers. All are unknown weapons here, equal to a hundred atom bombs going off at the same time. There were possibly some dark-matter gravity weapons used also."

"No one knows the results of the battle. Who was in it? Who was the victor, and is it even over with? No one knows yet the resulting total collateral damage to the world and to the United States, but reports are starting to come in. The navy has ships out there now examining the area, looking for debris, checking for radioactive waste and other damage. Fortunately we have no indication of radiation fallout. The dark-cloud layer over the world currently is weather related, and one result of the battle, plus the violent rain and thunderstorms across the world; and another, the frequent and severe lightning. The Pacific is a mess of heavy, choppy seas; there have been hurricane-force winds at times. Flooding is becoming more of an issue as the hours go by."

The president interrupts, "John, please skip ahead. We need to know about Henry Johnson."

John nods his head, and he is thinking, *here goes*, pausing, intently looking at everyone, as he stands there at the lectern. He hopes he does not screw this up. He had a call from Henry Johnson, his second call, and Henry was clear on what he should say and not say. Henry was also clear to make sure that his name is to be kept confidential, nothing going to the media and the public. Henry said he would know all that was said, which alarms John. He has to get this right.

"Gentlemen and ladies, I have an interesting report. Take the facts for real, as I believe they are authentic. As all of you know, we have had the London meeting with Henry Johnson and re-solved a possible World War III situation with China, Russia, and Mexico. Iran was not there. First of all, let me warn you, all that is said today is top secret, classified, never to be repeated to either the media or the public. Also, Henry Johnson's name is to be kept strictly confidential. Are we all in agreement?"

All nodded their heads, serious expressions, agreeing wholeheartedly.

"Gentlemen, I have received two phone calls from Henry Johnson—one yesterday and another one today, about two hours ago, which I will report on these discussions. Before I do this, please think about the situation. Strange as this sounds to those of you who know nothing about him, I believe Henry is half-hu-man, part of our world, and yet half-alien, thus not part of our world. This could be good for us. He is our bridge to a new real-ity; he can help the aliens understand us, as he will help us un-derstand the aliens. I think his possible relationship with Anna Summers helps this, too."

He lets this sink in, looking out over many concerned faces.

"I am not sure about the planet he comes from; it's just a long way from here. He could be a replica to make us feel more comfortable, less fear. Yet I think he is telling us the truth; as he says he is from Earth originally and was rebuilt, now half-alien, or part alien. We need his help as we are vulnerable."

The president interrupts, asking, "First question: is this information in the report in front of us accurate? Has everyone read this?" The President is looking at all of them.

"Yes, Mr. President, I believe it is one hundred percent correct. I am sure he is part of an alien civilization from another galaxy. I have seen and know of recent events, which are all in the report in front of you. I think he really is a commander of many military fleets spread throughout the universe. I say this because he says he is, and I believe him. I think this is true for a lot of reasons, all listed in the report. Believe me or not, he is here. Per his words, I know he knows about all the recent activities and knows stuff about us in a way only an alien would know about—weird things, like everything we think about and everything we have that is classified. He knows about this meeting today and will know everything that is said or even thought about. He is completely telepathic. I think all the beings on his ship are telepathic and communicate that way. All are aliens, not from here."

"They have all our databases, everything, and I think they can shut us down anytime they want to, even our military systems. So far they have supported us in all we have done. They have proved not to be our enemy. They have been here a long time, too, years of looking us over, coming and going without our knowing. He also says he is leaving in a few days, and I think is he is being truthful."

"He says the firefight over the Pacific was as we thought: a battle between alien starships, and he says he was the winner. He says this enemy was our enemy, as they were what we would call pirates and could have destroyed Earth as we now know it. He says this specific enemy ship was destroyed; however, Earth is now known by other worlds because of this battle. He says he thinks we will need the protection of the Consortium of Civilizations, or we could eventually perish by some other rogue starship. He says he works for this Consortium that controls the known universe, and we need to apply for membership."

John looks up, and everyone is looking at him in disbelief, like he is a crazy man.

"I know this is hard to comprehend, and believing it is difficult; however, it is all we have, and it fits our current situation. He also said we might not be accepted as a member of this Consortium. He says we have no other option. We need to try. Hopefully we will not be refused."

"If and when inducted, we will be given the rules or laws to follow, and we can also then trade with other worlds, and we will be given the chance to buy starships of our own. The Consortium laws are somewhat simple but strictly enforced. Of course there will be changes; however, in the end, he says, we will be happy to be part of the Consortium. For example, war between our country and other countries will become impossible, as all wars will be taboo, or if it happens it will be a very short war, quickly ended by the Consortium. The leaders involved would be held responsible with penalties. The Consortium has a legal process, which would address issues between countries with lawyers and judges. Disputes would be resolved fairly with due process."

"Another example of change is there will be almost no crime. No one will ever be without nourishment or shelter, and there will be tremendous enhancements of our technology. Additionally, social concepts with appropriate applications will be vastly improved. It will become impossible to hide from law enforcement or not to tell the truth. Our judges will have the use of mental probes, like the ultimate lie-detector test, keeping everyone honest and accurate. By the way, there is some kind of universe policeman appointed to us that enforces the laws between the worlds. We will also have an appointed representative from Earth who will be our representative in the Consortium's Congress if we are accepted."

"He says he will follow up with more details after the approval of Earth's application to the Consortium. And yes, I know what you're thinking: this is crazy, unbelievable, no documentation or any proof of this information being real. How do we know he is telling us the truth? The answer is, we don't. I am not sure of anything except he has no reason to lie, and something big happened over the Pacific Ocean last night. Those of us who have met Henry believe this. The president will vouch for him, too."

The president stands up, then steps back to the lectern. "Gentlemen," he says, as everyone starts talking at once. "Gentlemen! Please be quiet. John, we have to have some verification. How do we know if any of this is true, if there really is a Consortium?"

"Yes sir, I told him the same thing, and he said we would have verification, as of right now, here at this meeting, that we would all believe."

The president, startled, is now suddenly tired, drained. What now? He is starting to feel fear again, looking at everyone in the room, then saying, "John, are we in any danger here?"

The room is completely silent; all have looks of worry. The Secret Service guys pull out their weapons, saying nothing. Then a marble-size little drone satellite just appears in the room hovers in front of them. To everyone's shock there is a voice in everyone's minds. Everyone looks at one another and realizes they are all hearing it, hearing it mentally, and panic is starting to set in.

At first the voice is really eerie, yet it becomes nice as everyone becomes used to it. It is calm and charming, giving a feeling of warmth and happiness, like going home for Christmas and sitting in front of a blazing fireplace. It feels so good; it feels almost religious, yet not spiritual, more like yoga serenity, much better than any church service. The crazy thing is the voice is clearly understandable in their minds, as in thoughts shared, like hearing a voice that feels comfortable, like coming from an old friend. The voice is saying, "Do not be afraid. I have news. The news is good. You will have new friends to meet. All will be well. You will be happy with all of this."

The voice then announces, "First of all, I apologize for any fear I have caused. The drone you see is a communications slip, one of many, allows me to speak to you. You may know me; my name is Henry Johnson. I know you mentally as you hear my words. Just relax, and you will feel my emotions. I am here to calm you and answer your main questions. Am I real, and am I honest? Will you be harmed in some way? The answers are: yes, I am real, honest and no, you will not be harmed. I am here representing the other civilizations of the universe, and I welcome you in friendship. I wish you no harm, and I want to introduce you to our group, or, as we call it, the Consortium."

"It is populated by trillions of beings throughout the universe, spread across the expanse of space—some in your galaxy and some in other galaxies trillions of miles from here. You are not alone and never have been. You are living in an old world, in an old universe over ten billions old, in a very young civilization, and you are also an outlier. This is because of your location in the universe and the lack of starship technology. Until now you have not needed us, as you're an unknown off-world civilization; our connection was probably not in your best interest. But that has changed. You need to be part of us now. You are at risk. We can help you."

"First of all we are a kind civilization, nonthreatening. We believe in right and wrong, just as you do, yet we are more advanced than you, as our civilizations are much older. We believe in a common creator, as many of you do, and the concepts of love and honesty are critical values for us, too. And even though you do not know us, we know you well."

"I wish to be of service to you; and, as in your world, we have a procedure that makes these kinds of changes easier to bear, as change causes concern for good reasons. I will apply for your entry into the Consortium of Civilizations if you wish to join us. It is fair to warn you there are issues throughout the universe, and your entry into our group will bring you many changes, hopefully many good things, and protection from many future difficulties you may know about and some you are not aware of at this time."

"For example, there are criminals causing problems in the universe, as in the recent battle over the Pacific, which you know about. With our protection you will be insulated to some extent, and you will have peace and prosperity as your new future unfolds. I feel your thoughts, and no, there is no going back if you are approved. This is because you will not want to reverse course. Many wonderful things will occur in your future with the Consortium."

"You know I am here, and what I say is true, as I am part of you. You can feel my honesty. We are linked mentally. It is hard to hide the truth either way; you need to be honest with me, too. As soon as your membership is confirmed, you will move into the Consortium jurisdiction. Although you will move into this new culture, it may take years to achieve true membership or for you to catch up. It will be a passage to a new renaissance period for your civilization. You will be delighted with it!"

"When you are accepted, you will be also part of a new world order on Earth. It will be better for all populations, especially the poor countries, as no one will be hungry ever again. And to answer your questions, yes, you will like it, and yes, there will be changes. And yes, you keep your job, and yes, your life will be mostly the same. The United States will exist as it does now. Yes, there will still be elections, and no, there are no hidden agendas. No, we will not enslave you; you will have free will and freedom. Nor will we ask you for money, and no, no fees or taxes, no gimmicks. Yes, you can travel to other worlds, and yes, there is a cost for the tickets. No, I do not know how much—it's too complicated to tell you how it works."

"As for the planet where I come from, yes, it is a long way from here, trillions of miles. Yes, there is a starship here, and yes, it is military. No, no more battles that I know of. No, not sure how long the approval will take or how long it will take to find out if you are not approved. Not sure, not a concern for you now. We have to push forward and make our case to the Consortium."

"Sorry, I need to go. Think about joining the Consortium. Create a detailed list of questions, as I will help and advise you. John Jacobs has all you need to apply. Do not wait too long. I will be gone, yet John Jacobs will know how to contact me."

"You are welcome. Thank you, too. Let me know what you think might be harmful. Keep my identity secret from the public. It is premature to tell anyone about this. It would be dangerous. You will need to contact the other world leaders. It would be better if they understand and agree. I think they will want to be part of it, as none of them will want to be left out. There will be a plan of action created, and many more of us will come to help you reorganize. It may take a lot of time. Good-bye and, as you say, good luck."

With that, the drone is gone, no feeling of his presence, no mental connection. He is gone. They all feel loneliness, an empty, sad feeling, and all missing the comfort of the voice, then a feeling of loss. Really weird.

All present remain speechless, total silence, looking at one another, their faces white with total shock, overwhelmed, and their energies totally drained. The knowledge of what just happened is beyond reality, a massive change in the possible future of every person on Earth. The president can hardly talk, ends up whispering, "We need to keep this quiet, and no one outside this room needs to know. We need to digest this, meet again tomorrow. I will notify you about the time of the meeting. I know you have lots of questions."

Looking at the chief of staff, the secretary of defense, the head of the FBI, the head of the CIA, then the generals and then the navy admiral, the president declares, "We need to find the Iranian nuclear bombs, or we may have nothing to talk about."

Then he looks at Jacobs. "John, you and I need to talk."

CHAPTER 29

ANNA'S HOME AND LIFE IN LA—DAY EIGHT

B ack in LA. I land the *Saber* partially over Anna's swimming pool, smashing a lot of concrete with the weight and then taking up the entire backyard of her house, a big estate, just enough room thankfully. Although I knock down one fence, some concrete, and destroy a lot of lawn, the house is OK. I will need to fix the damages. I turn on the camouflage shield and put up a defense grid around the house. I can only hope her neighbors do not see anything and call the police; I'm not in the mood for a police visit. After all I have put her through, I do not want to wake Anna; I just carry her in, still sleeping, from the ship to her home.

I am lucky to be here, as just to find the house was a challenge; I found it only by Googling it, using MapQuest. Crazy world. All this technology, and I have to Google Anna's address to get directions. But I have made it here, and I have no right to complain. It must be eleven o'clock or so, late at night, and it's been a long, hard day. Anna's housecleaning service and security team know she is coming in tonight, and she told them earlier today they would not be needed. The *Cyclone* is overhead again, hovering four thousand feet up, in stealth mode, watching and providing information and security.

Anna's estate is outstanding: large, luxurious, well done, classy. I can't help myself; I just love it. Looks like a great place to live. I am proud of Anna; she keeps a terrific home. The lights are already on, and I have the security drones sweep over the house, my drone slips that now travel with me everywhere, looking for any threats. I'm not surprised; they disable numerous listening devices hidden in the house. The FBI or somebody has been busy. I know the *Cyclone* has set up a perimeter around us, thus we are shielded and guarded with some serious weapons plus wall-to-wall surveillance. No one is coming in here, including FBI or any agency or any alien threat. A security grid is over the top of us, too, which can't be penetrated by anything known in the universe. One can never be too careful. I follow the ninety-nine percent rule, which is that ninety-nine percent of the time life is somewhat predictable; however, it's usually the one percent that gets you.

I find Anna's bedroom, carry her in, and put her in her bed. I need to undress her, put her in a nightgown, something she can sleep in. I feel her pain, looking at her bruises, feeling guilty and responsible. I look for and then find a white silk nightgown; she is half-awake now and totally exhausted. She undresses, and I help her put on the nightgown, after which she crawls under her covers and she is asleep immediately. I gaze at her for a bit, then kiss her on her forehead, whisper, "Sleep well, Anna," and turn off the lights.

After I close the door, I realize I am way too wound up to sleep. I look around and then decide to tour the house, sort of a reconnaissance. It is huge. It's a beautiful home—it looks like Anna's home. There are charming rooms everywhere, an in-house theater, a gym, a massive kitchen, and fireplaces throughout. It is all gorgeous. She has many photos of herself everywhere with beautiful, glamorous people, many other stunning women, and many really handsome men all looking great. They all look like they are in love with Anna. She has many trophies and awards; some are from the many charities she has supported. Her movies are successful, many framed newspaper articles on the walls, showing major hits; and, she is a true celebrity with photos from the all the talk shows. She has a wonderful rewarding life with many close friends. I am impressed, and not surprised.

As I think about it, I am not sure what I have to offer her. How could she be proud of me when she has so many truly elegant people around her? She has a perfect life now. She is talented, famous, beautiful, accomplished, and wealthy. Her friends would feel sorry for her for considering me over all her famous suitors. I'm not even sure I will be here much, maybe never; maybe I'll never be able to retire. The alternative is not good, as she would hate living on a starship, and the loneliness would destroy her. It is impossible. An alien world other than Earth would be even worse; she would have nothing she loves there. Humans need humans, as I know so well.

I am now on her second story, standing on the huge covered balcony overlooking the ocean. Even with a heavy cloud layer and rain, I enjoy an outstanding view. I am angry with myself and feel sad, too, disappointed in myself for letting this happen. She deserves better. I feel like a fool. It is better for her if I leave, although I will give her my best these next couple of days; it will be my short moment in the sun and real happiness for me. I will also try to protect her from her enemies, even if she does not know it. She does not know about the senator's friend Luca and his son Anthony, two real criminals. Might be the only thing I do that is to her real benefit, take care those two.

I am such an idiot, clearly selfish, doing nothing more than looking after my needs, my ten days of fun. Her life is superb without me; it would be even better if she'd never met me. I was warned.

Since I can't relax, too emotional, distressed by my lack of judgment, I need to do something. I decide to take a run. I need to do a hard run to work off the aching sadness and the day's stress; it has not been a great day. I put on a baseball cap from Anna's closet, then some sweats and running shoes I find in the guest room closet and head out.

I hardly need to worry about security for Anna, as there is my drone security team, plus so many CIA, FBI, and NSA guys around Anna's house they are stepping on one another. They are trying to hide from me as I head down the street. I am running in the rain from the storms I created yet making a good pace, maybe twenty-five miles per hour. The run feels good, my muscles stretching out, needing the workout, my strength returning with each stride. I know my detail of FBI guys will be hard-pressed to keep up with me, and I know the *Cyclone* is also moving with me, leaving the *Saber* back at Anna's house to protect her. I quickly run about ten miles and decide to stop at a late-night bar all lit up, big neon signs, easy to spot on one corner. I cross over to it. The neighborhood is rough but perfect for me. I could use a drink and I love Kentucky bourbon. Time to medicate my depression.

I go into the bar soaking wet and sweating, no surprise, looking like I have been running in the rain. I look around, not too many there. It is late, and no one pays me any attention. In one corner there are three big guys, well muscled, long-haired, with their dates—young, good-looking girls, with some class. I am surprised they are here with these guys, at this bar. Not much brainpower there. The girls have on short skirts; they're sexy girls yet intelligent. One smiles at me. There are also a couple of guys at the bar, half-drunk, and another older couple at a far table.

I sit at the bar, ask the bartender for a Maker's Mark on the rocks, a double. He looks at me, hands me a towel to dry off, laughs, and in a British accent he says, "You must be from Kentucky? Maybe Fort Campbell?" He gives me my drink.

I smile. "Thanks! Yes, I am from Kentucky and I know Fort Campbell. Have you been there?"

He shakes his head no and looks at me real serious. With a strong British accent he exclaims, "You need to get back there. It's not safe here. The world has become a dodgy place today, especially here. Can you believe what happened over the Pacific Ocean? Did you see all the fireworks? It wasn't far from here. Half the world lit up. The Pacific looked like a fireball! It's a lot more serious than the government is saying because they don't say anything, just smoke and mirrors. Totally dodgy! Thousands of phone calls, all the TV networks asking; the president and the military say nothing. I know why. It's all rubbish! They're scared of what they think it really is, aliens, and they don't have a clue what to do about it. I know what's going on; what do you think?"

I laugh; tell him I have no clue. I take a drink of the bourbon; feel the warmth as it goes down my throat, enjoying the taste and the comforting scent, an overall sensation that feels good. I also love the warmth in my belly and I feel the strength of the drink. Nothing like being home. I ask the bartender, "So what is going on?"

He looks around as if someone might be listening, then he stares hard at me, troubled, his eyes bloodshot from too little sleep. "The aliens are here! They're all around us, might even be living in this neighborhood, maybe disguised to look like us. They were out there in the Pacific today, practicing with their weapons, getting ready to take us over, kill all of us. Yes, quite lovely! Maybe they will freeze us, save us for dinner for their long space trips or some kind of bloody thing. We don't have a chance.

If they can come from millions of miles away, they have technology way beyond us, and they want something. There is some reason they're here. It's—"

He stops talking. We hear a woman's pleading voice, stressed and garbled, causing both of us to look over at the three big guys at the table. It is the same girl who smiled at me. One of them has her by the hair and is pulling her head back, trying to force her to drink from a bottle. She is crying, choking, trying to resist, pleading for him to stop. Her blouse is ripped, her hair a mess. He is much stronger and hurting her, and he is relishing it. The other two guys are laughing, and the other two women look frightened, yelling at him to let her go.

The bartender looks displeased, staring at them yet saying nothing, then looks at me and says, "They play NPL football with the LA Chiefs and will break up the place if I call the police or say anything to them. They can't handle the booze, and always causing trouble."

I laugh and say, "I'm glad I'm here to help you. No reason to call the police. I can do better! I'm in the mood, too."

I hear the *Cyclone* in my head, warning me to be careful, asking if I need more drones. I ask if there is anyone outside the building on the sidewalk. I hear a negative.

I immediately walk over to the big guys' table, before the longhairs can react. Barely stopping, I grab the table, gripping one side hard, then lean way back, swinging it farther back, then lurching forward in a massive jerk, throwing it forward hard over their heads, straight through the window twenty-five feet away. Since it is a big wooden table, it takes out the entire window and a big part of the wall. It makes a huge explosion of a lot of glass, wood fragments, drywall, window framing, and lots of dust. It leaves a large gaping hole looking out onto the wet night, with streetlights visible. It also makes a lot of noise on the outside street, like an explosive going off, as it lands on the sidewalk.

Everyone drops back, stunned; there are a couple of loud gasps and one short scream.

The football player with the woman's hair in his hands has let her go, staring at me as if he can't comprehend reality, standing there with a panicky look. I help him keep thinking that thought, as I step over to him, grab his hair and part of one ear with one fist, pulling him closer. His resists by pulling back. My other hand grips his jaw; he stops resisting, afraid I will crush his jaw, his eyes tearing up from the pain, although I am trying not to actually crush his face, careful as I can be, considering the situation. He is on his knees now. My eyes are penetrating his eyes, and his brain feels my thoughts, asking him if he feels sick. I tell him he should be ashamed. He will apologize to the girl, plus pay the bartender for the hole in the wall, and I probe his brain to make sure he agrees; he feels the terrible pain of his mind reacting to the probe, now terrified. He urinates in his pants and then starts vomiting. I push him down, drop him to the floor. He down on all fours. He can't stop vomiting, dry heaves, moaning, and sobbing.

Looking at the rest of them, I smile and politely ask the girl if she is OK. She nods her head, sort of a shocked, dazed reply, and her eyes really big. I ask her if it is all right for the FBI to haul these guys off, as the FBI will be there in about two seconds. She just stares at me.

I look harshly at the other two guys, not surprised by the horror in their eyes. They are terrified of me, hearing my voice in their heads. I tell them they are going to enjoy the next few hours of being interrogated by the police, NSA, and FBI. I look at the other girls, saying to them they might not see these guys for some time. Do they mind? The cavalry is coming, the *Cyclone* tells me.

They all stand there thunderstruck, and I am moving again. I am walking over to the large opening in the wall, looking out at the sidewalk. Before I step out, six big guys, some in black

SWAT-team uniforms, plunge through the bar's front door and are now all around us, guns out, a couple of assault rifles, too. They are all yelling at us "FBI! Get down on the floor!"

Everybody does except for me. I quickly step outside through the new wall hole and I am gone before anyone has a chance to react. I run hard in the rain for Anna's house, knowing the *Cyclone* has assigned twenty drones to provide me with security. They will scout ahead and also cover my retreat. I am back at Anna's home in about twenty minutes, finally exhausted and anxious to get some sleep.

⊷⊹⊶

The FBI security team is delighted that there was no confrontation with Henry Johnson, just three drunken football players—although they will not be playing much football in the near future, as they will be held in custody to prevent them from talking about Henry. The rest of the people in the bar, including the bartender, and the girls, will face confinement, too. Now is not a good time to have loose lips. All the FBI needs is a panicked population thinking the end of the world is here. Aliens are on Earth. No human could have thrown that table through the bar's wall. Henry Johnson might think he is human, as he looks human, but he is not human. The FBI can only hope he has a little humanity left in him.

CHAPTER 30

LOS ANGELES—ADVENTURES

I end up falling to sleep out on Anna's deck, close to the *Saber*, in a deck chair next to her pool and under a large canopy, as it is still raining. I slept there all night and I am delighted to wake up to the smell of coffee and Anna standing there beside me with a cup.

I look up, and she is smiling down at me saying, "Here you go, Starman! You need this. You certainly had a rough day yesterday, taking care of business. You look worse than I do, and I look bad. When you take a girl for a wild ride, you mean it. I have more bruises than I thought possible. Luckily for you they are in places you cannot see, hidden by my clothing. The tabloids would love to print 'New man in Anna's life beats her up. See her bruises!'"

She continues, "Henry, did you get anything to eat last night? I was dead tired and was not much good to you. I feel a lot better today. I heal fast now, thanks to you. I am remembering only bits and pieces about yesterday, and I'm not sure I want to read the newspaper today. I remember a whole lot of stuff about what happened to us, stuff we Earth people might find terrifying to know. The really alien stuff, like the *War of the Worlds* stuff. By the way, where is the *Cyclone*? I see the *Saber* parked over my pool. Aren't you clever? Is the *Saber* OK? Damages? The *Cyclone*'s not injured? Are you OK?"

Smiling, looking at her fondly, I reply, "Anna, thanks for asking. We are all well, all survived and mostly recovered. The *Cyclone* and the *Saber* are fine, their wounds repaired by now."

More serious, unease and concern on my face, I continue, "I am delighted you still have your sense of humor. It was as bad as it gets yesterday, and I thought I might have lost you at one point. I am so sorry about it. It's not what I had planned. I had a few bad moments of real dread, as you were hurt badly. I would not blame you for being furious with me, as I put you in harm's way."

Anna looks at me, leans down, and kisses me on the forehead. "You protected me, as usual. Let's go out for breakfast. I know a diner close by, and I am starving. Unfortunately we have to disguise ourselves, otherwise lots of people will be hanging around taking photos. And no starships; we just ride bicycles. You can see the neighborhood. Are you up for some normal life, big guy?"

I laugh and say, "I need a shave and shower, and I'll be ready to go. Not sure about the disguise."

Anna laughs. "I need a shower, too, and we can save water if you don't mind washing my back. I have something you can wear. The security guys leave clothing here. You are my new security guy!" She laughs again. "You think you're up to it? We might need that army of yours. I meet all kinds of dangerous people every day."

The shower is great and the bike ride perfect, although riding bikes in the rain is rather unusual. However, the warm rain feels good. The cloud layer is heavy, with constant rain, resulting from last night's activities. We each wear a black military-style rain poncho from the security guys' lockers. Underneath Anna's poncho I get a glimpse of her small shorts and a sweatshirt over a sports bra. I have on my own jeans and a sweatshirt, as I elected not to wear the security guard uniform; it was a little too small to fit me.

We are at the diner after a thirty-minute ride. The place is full, and Anna is recognized immediately, with some smiles and a friendly "Hi, Anna," all showing more real affection than not. It is not an issue for her; she is all smiles. Everyone looks me over carefully, curious about who I am. Maybe somebody famous?

Also, I know something Anna does not know. We have lots of company: FBI, Secret Service, NSA, Section 58, and LA Metro. The guys and girls are all there; actually they are everywhere, with several teams. Must have followed the bikes. I know they are posted here and there around Anna's house, as part of their surveillance. They are trying to blend in, seem like regular people.

Of course the *Cyclone* is overhead and knows about the surveillance team, and I have been half listening to their communications back and forth. The *Cyclone* blocks any surveillance listening to our conversations thus they cannot hear us. Interestingly enough, John Jacobs is heading up the teams. He is more important these days, the man of the hour. I am thinking Anna and I need to have dinner with Jacobs and his wife. I just need to make him more comfortable with all of this. I wonder if he would go to work for me?

I have a couple more days to enjoy being with Anna. I need to let the CIA, the NSA, the FBI, and the rest solve the senator's issues and the Mafia problems plus the Iran threats—that's their jurisdiction for now. I need official approval of Earth's membership before I can become more involved. I think it's time for Earth's entry into the Consortium; my reasons are all valid, and I think Gabriel will agree this time. After last night's meeting, the president and his staff know my position is to help as much as possible. The *Cyclone* has sent my request to Gabriel for Earth's entry into the Consortium. It is now more critical because of the enemy Seatisveres' starship being here on Earth and attacking us, and then me destroying it. The real fear is the other enemy starships out there somewhere, the rest of the Seatisveres' battleships. Are they heading for Earth?

After Earth's approval I can ask for retirement, and maybe Anna will consider me husband material. I don't want to lose her. I know she has expectations, wants children; maybe living in this galaxy is one, too. Surely this will work out. I can only hope it is our destiny. I will not bring her misery if being with me means that, or, even worse, her isolation, living without her friends and family. I know I am leaving in two days without her.

The restaurant's breakfast is generous, and it is great fun being with Anna; of course, it is always fun being with Anna.

She is laughing, saying, "Henry, we have to talk out loud, the old-fashioned way; we need to use our lips. Someone could notice we just look at each other and smile, no conversation. It looks odd. Too much telepathy is a bad thing when people are watching us. When I'm in public, there's always somebody observing me, even taking pictures, and now you, too. I am sorry for that."

Anna does not know the half of it. We are also under constant surveillance by every government agency in the United States and most of the world, if they have the opportunity. The *Cyclone* is always there, too.

I start talking, telling her I am having a great day. She hears me, laughs and says I have a great voice, like an actor. I ask about acting, and, with her intently looking at me, with a serious expression on her face, she responds, "Acting is a wonderful occupation and tough, no sissies for sure. You take great risks and go for it. I've worked hard, been lucky, very blessed, more fortune given to me than earned. Yet I have not been happy. I am lonely. Henry, we are alike; you are so lonely, too. I feel it. We are kindred spirits, and it is our destiny to be together. You know it. It is what it is. Do you understand me? We need each other."

I am surprised. As usual Anna is one step ahead, and no question she is right. She could make me a happy man, more than I have a right to expect.

I respond, "Anna, I agree. I understand. Yet I have to get permission to leave the military. To leave the Consortium is no small thing, not the same as quitting a regular job. I have some critical responsibilities that are hard to comprehend; I am needed, and I have to do a transition without interruption. I am not free yet. It is much more complicated than you understand. I can only say I promise I will do my best to make it happen."

Anna pleads, "Henry, if you ask me, I will go with you when you go. We can ask together. I will live with you. You just have to ask me."

I look at her, my eyes moist, and say, "I would give anything for that, to have you with me. I could never ask; it would destroy you. Ship life is not this life. It is only duty and hardship, dangerous, with few comforts, lonely beyond belief, enough to test your sanity. The loss of gravity over a long period would permanently harm your body. I love you, and I would never do that to you. Another world is not Earth; it's not human, for one, and not something you could adapt to with ease. You wouldn't want to raise children there; it's not even where you should be. Anna, you have a wonderful life here. What about your family, your mother and Nikki? For you and your children to be happy, you should be here. Earth is a wonderful place to raise children, and Anna, you do want children?"

She responds quickly, "Yes, I want children. I want your children, a lot of them, and I don't want to wait. I know we've known each other only a few days, and I know I'm foolish. I don't care. I'm going for it. I know you're right for me. You know it, too. I love you. You need to make it happen—for both of us!"

I laugh. I have lost the battle. I smile, happy to hear her say this. I respond, "I understand, I understand."

Anna also laughs and says, "Mr. Starman, forget our problems. We are going out tonight and having fun. We are going to dinner, to some parties, to meet some of my friends, maybe dancing at a nightclub, and maybe, just maybe, you will get lucky tonight. And since you're wealthy, you are paying—no Dutch treat. Are you up for it?"

I laugh and think I am already lucky. "Yes, and I think combat will look easy after tonight."

We finally finish breakfast, and Anna does the bathroom thing as I buy a newspaper, actually several newspapers. I am sitting and reading them at the table. Not great for me, way too many photos of alien spaceships. A lot of weapon firing, bright streaks across dark skies. Massive explosions lighting up half the world have been photographed, with lots of damage reported throughout the world. The resulting storms were fierce, the rain causing floods. All the news programs are covering the "alien story," with speculation and much discussion around the world about what could be happening and possible ramifications.

All governments in the world take the official position that there still is no real proof of an extraterrestrial appearance. The fear of the aliens is still awful. I wish I could reassure everyone, even if they would then know they are not alone in the universe. They are spooked by the possibility of waking up and seeing aliens in the backyard; maybe *terrified* is a better word. There is not much I can do to help Earth until I have Gabriel's sign-off. They need to be inducted into the Consortium; only Gabriel and the leadership committee have the authority to accept Earth into the family of civilizations. Even in the most advanced culture— who would think?—there is still red tape, procedures in place.

Anna is back. She sits down, picks up a newspaper, and reads the headlines. She says, "I guess all of this was us last night?" She shakes her head and looks at me. "Henry, how bad was it? Was it as close as I think it was? We were in real trouble, weren't we? I can't remember much, just that it was a horrific nightmare and I hurt everywhere."

I nod my head, looking at her, seeing her bruises, saying, "It was a lot worse than I ever thought possible. Calabra!"

She pulls the paper apart, reads more, focused on one story, then looks sad and becoming angry. She looks at me with a pained, angry expression and says, "Read this."

I read the newspaper article she points out; it is reporting on a serial killer who killed another young woman yesterday, her body found mutilated, as she had been tortured. Her twin sister is also missing, no body found yet. Her parents are devastated. Several beautiful young women have been found dead in the last year after being tortured brutally, then killed, and the killer is still killing.

"Henry, can you help her? Can you find the missing girl? She may still be alive. Can you find the awful person who has killed all those beautiful young girls?"

"Anna, did you know her or any of them? How important is it to you? Yes, I probably can find him and the girl, too, and if she's still alive, we could save her. However, the Consortium forbids me from interfering in Earth's affairs. I am pushing the issue already, and it's not a good direction for me to go; however, if this is really important to you, I will take care of it. I think..."

I pause, looking at Anna's distress, thinking this is not Anna's fault; this guy needs to be taken out, rules or no rules.

Continuing, "Actually, I detest the situation of me not helping in this. It needs to be resolved. Even if I think I might be breaking Consortium rules, you're right about me doing something about it since I can resolve it, and since I am here on Earth, I should help. Lord save us from the demons. This gruesome idiot and his dreadful crimes certainly qualify. There is enough time to take care of this before I go."

"Henry, thank God. Thank you from everyone in LA. Of the girls killed, I knew none of them. I think the paper said, he has killed thirteen young women about my age, all beautiful and accomplished, from good families. The police have no clue who could have done this or how these women were targeted and kidnapped. Please, Henry; it is a dreadful situation. For everyone's sake, all the heartbreak he has caused, please take him off our streets."

"Anna—OK—I'm your man, and I will also need your help, as it will take both of us. This is more complicated than you think, and it will be messy. We will send out drones immediately—you know, the little reconnaissance slips, thousands of them. Several will visit the last victim; there will be microscopic DNA particles from the murderer on her, maybe just several molecule-size flakes of his skin, impossible to see with the human eye yet easy for a drone. We will reconstruct him with his DNA—not real, just a computer image, yet it will be him. We will know what he looks like, his face, his body, and, more important, his aura signature, the infrared warmth each human gives out, which will identify him with one hundred percent accuracy, locating him from an overhead scan. We will use one hundred thousand drones or more to scan every foot of LA, looking for his signature. We will keep searching until he is found, taken, and then examined in our ship's lab. We have to see how nuts he is, download his memories, locate any other bodies, and try to tell those parents without them knowing about us. He will be executed and vaporized along with anyone else involved."

Pausing, then continuing, "The difficult part is understanding why he is evil. Some beings in the universe seem to be made evil; their DNA is corrupted; they are just bad. They are simply a cancer to be removed from society, expunged, no rehabilitation possible."

I reach out and hold Anna's hand, looking intently, making direct eye contact, saying out loud, "Anna, the other problem is if we find this victim still alive, she will be a mess. She has to be dealt with, maybe treated for emotional and physical injuries, and sworn to secrecy about us. We need you to help with this. She may need you. If there are issues with her, you will have to take care of it—and take her back to her home, deal with her parents, help her with a possible police statement, all without giving us away."

Anna is nodding her head. "Yes, yes, I will help. I'm sorry to pull you into this, and I will do anything you want. Are you still going to help? Can you find him?"

"Already in the works. The *Cyclone* has programmed the mission orders; the drones are on their way. It will be over within twenty-four hours. Let's hope he has not killed another woman. We will be notified when he's been caught. We should head back, as a crowd is gathering outside to see you, cameras, too."

We are heading for the bikes, breaking through all of Anna's fans, yet she signing autographs along the way. Anna jumps on her bike, yelling at me that we both need some decent clothes to wear for tonight, and we are going shopping this afternoon. She is off, heading down the street, yelling something about racing me back home. It's still raining, and she is already ahead. I am moving fast behind her, trying to catch up; I figure this is how it could be in the future, me trying to keep up with her.

Within two hours we are ready to go out. She drives some kind of sports car out of her five-stall garage, a red and fast-looking car. She is laughing and saying it's her turn to take me for a spin. I smile, open the door, and jump in, wondering if I will survive this. She reads my thoughts, and I hear hers—and her laughter—as she is exclaiming I deserve everything I am going to get. And with spinning tires, off we go. I feel like I'm in the *Saber*!

After all the shopping, I am exhausted. I've been in every store in LA and had my photo taken in every store because of Anna. I am done in, and Anna is still flying. Once home we get dressed and ready, and Anna has arranged for a limousine and driver to take us out for the evening. We are heading for dinner at a very nice restaurant, meeting twenty or more of Anna's friends, all celebrities, some famous directors, famous actresses, and corporate CEOs; all are wealthy and renowned. I know none of them, and I cannot understand why Anna is so proud of me, making it known to them she wants to introduce someone who is very important to her.

After that we go nightclubbing. Anna asks if I can dance, to which I respond yes with a laugh. Actually I can dance much better than she could imagine thanks to the shipboard virtual-reality dance and exercise program. She will be very surprised, as I plan to introduce her to telepathic dancing, which is completely synchronized. We will be together as one, in rhythm, with perfect timing to the music and very sensual, almost erotic, every primitive instinct on fire. Yes, it will be a surprise for her, and I think she will be delighted, as long as I can do it right. It will be an experience beyond belief, and let's hope a good one. Unfortunately, I am not completely sure; this will be a first time for me, too. I laugh, thinking, *I hope Anna has a good sense of humor.*

CHAPTER 31

ANNA'S FRIENDS—A NIGHT ON THE TOWN IN LA WITH A MOVIE STAR

The *Cyclone* is up above us as usual, insistent to remain close, just not that far up and lower than I want; however, security is tight now because of recent events. I can feel the *Cyclone's* presence just four hundred feet up, all thirty-four billion tons of it. Thank God no one else knows it's there. I wonder where the other six Seatisveres' civilization starships are tonight; I hope far from here. The Earth will be on their target list, now knowing one of their pack disappeared here. They would be delighted to plunder this planet. I wonder what else is happening across the universe, in my jurisdiction.

We are at the restaurant, which is not fancy, yet it has class; it's sophisticated—Anna's kind of place. Having dinner here is a special treat, as the place has a worldwide reputation for superb food. Anna warns me telepathically to be charming and on my best behavior. I smile at her with no reply.

She beams back, saying one of the guests is famous, and a wealthy actor I met in London, Ed Delaney. She dated him; he is with a good friend of hers, another beautiful, young actress. She says he is in love with himself. Her friend wants to marry him, as she thinks she loves him. He is jealous of me because he's still hung up on Anna. She does not want me probing his thoughts. For one, it's none of my business, and for another, he was abusive. Anna is questioning if I can stay calm, as she does not want him dead. Actually I am little surprised, as Anna is serious, not kidding.

I respond with a laugh, "Anna, I will control myself. I will not harm him."

I keep looking at her, and she just smiles back; she is absolutely the most awesome creature I have ever seen. She is perfect beyond words; beautiful inside and out, and I love her. I now dread leaving even more, alone, having to live with the desolation and pain of missing her. I have no clue if I will be able to make the deal with Gabriel. Will he let me retire? As a plan B, just in case, I am having my law firm put her on all my accounts and put all my holdings as joint ownership. All total it is about $9 billion in value. I will tell them she is to be treated like my wife. I hope that becomes true someday. Either way she will own what I own. If I am gone another ten years or never come back because I'm killed in some battle, or if I lose her, at least she will have real wealth.

When I sit down, everyone is sitting, talking, laughing, and drinking. It is a long, massive table, also wide, so we all see one another. Everyone at the table is impressive, more than very good-looking, really most of them are gorgeous, all smiling, some laughing. At least twenty seats are filled. After Anna introduced me, most of them have ignored me and are busy with Anna. She is in her element.

We finish eating, and we all have had plenty to eat and drink; the wine is excellent. Then, as if it's my turn to be examined, they turn on me. Anna's friend Lisa, another famous actress, asks what I do and how I met Anna. The table grows quiet, not a soul talking, waiting for me to respond. I hear Anna coaching me, hear her thoughts; she says to try to be honest as much as possible without telling them too much. Be charming!

They are all quiet, looking at me intently. I smile, laugh. "Really, I didn't mean to cause so much curiosity. I guess I better not tell any of my jokes."

They all laugh, although a little nervously. So I say, "OK, you are curious about me. Here it is: this body of mine is thirty years old; my life is a complicated life yet much of it boring; mostly I have a military background, traveled with the military more than I want, seen too much battle, hate to talk about it, been lonely most of my life, not important or famous, done nothing like you with your glamourous lives. As a soldier, honor and duty are important to me. I work constantly, and it is difficult work. Plus, my life has a lot of hardship. I do have a little money, and I live modestly. I do not own a house. I live on a ship, although a big one. And I truly think you are the most beautiful people I have ever seen at one table. I appreciate your kindness by including me tonight."

Everyone laughs; Anna is pleased.

Since that went well, I continue, "Also, I am delighted to meet all of you. Anna's friends are really important to her, as she is to me." I look at her and smile. "And I will try to be your friend in every way. I am really a good friend to have. Thanks again for letting me have this evening with you."

Everyone laughs again, and Anna laughs, too. She is pleased and looks at me with fondness. I am happy.

Anna smiles. "Henry is being modest. He is extremely wealthy, and he is actually the most interesting man I have ever met, more complicated than you would ever believe or could comprehend. I think he may be the most powerful man in the universe, and actually I know for sure he is the most powerful man in this world. And yes, I am completely overwhelmed by him. He is simply awesome! He could do much tonight for our evening if he will do me this one little favor. He has given me the gift of telepathy. Maybe he'll give it to you, too."

They all look at Anna as if she is telling a joke and they are waiting for the punch line.

She shakes her head. "I'm not joking. I know you don't believe me; you think telepathy is impossible. You'll be totally thrilled! I've learned from Henry how amazing it is. For example, you know more than what is being said, and you actually feel the other person's emotions with their thoughts. It is simply wonderful. It would be so comforting for you to feel the warmth and love coming from me and then between each other, the feelings made so clear, as you'd have no confusion, no doubts about our friendship or worry about hidden agendas. Please, Henry, would you do this for all of us?"

She pauses, looking at me, waiting for a response.

They are all looking at Anna as if she has lost her mind. I did not see this coming. I should have told Anna the telepathy thing is just for us. She is out on a limb, and she would look foolish if I do not do this. I do not immediately respond, and I can see they are embarrassed for her. I do not know what to say. I cannot have this hit NBC News tomorrow night.

I have no choice; I need to do this for her. I should have warned her—my fault.

Finally, looking at her, smiling, then looking around at all of them, I say, "Yes, on one condition, if you promise not to tell anyone. Maybe just a little tonight, for a few minutes, just to introduce you to it, as it can be spooky to have someone in your brain. Perhaps the best way for you to try this, is to have to ask for it, as this is very personal. You may not want this to happen; you may be giving up too much intimate information. If you are game for the experience, just look at Anna and think hard, with a lot of focus, and tell her mentally you want to hear me. When I feel you are really ready, you will be given the ability, as I will make it happen. Please do not fear this. It will not hurt you, although it will shock you at first. After you feel it, close your eyes, as this will help you focus; trust Anna, as she will be your guide. I will try to resolve your fear and reduce anxiety. Remember, it is only temporary, lasting just a few minutes."

"Now, please look at Anna if you want to do this. Look away if not."

They all look at one another, a nervous laugh here and there, a "Why not?" and a "Let's try it!" Surprisingly enough, each one looks at me and smiles. Then, one by one, all of them look intently at Anna in absolute silence. The woman across from Anna closes her eyes and smiles, and her face relaxes, with a happy look. Then another woman closes her eyes, then another, and finally the men. Anna is already there. My little slips have been inserted in each person's brain, and they are activated as they ask for it, one at a time. They are truly telepathic, and I am hoping I don't regret this later. I let them feel Anna's true warmth and her love as she mentally talks to all of them. She is amazing! I give her the energy and amplification needed so they feel wonderful, all coming from her love. They know this remarkable woman loves them.

I push all of them toward better feelings; too, toward the love and friendship they have for one another. I also try to block their fear and negative thoughts, the harmful, critical ones they have learned as adults. They chatter mentally, and I make sure each thought is clear, as are the feelings; the emotions, the visions, and they are absolutely loving it. It is the ultimate mental yoga, three dimensional, called a mind meld, with me as their guide to soothe their anxieties or shyness. I know Anna is wonderful, and I can't help showing my love for her. Her friends feel it, too, which gives them a real emotional high. This is the best kind of high, as love is very powerful, and it makes them all happy. It is good for all of them, inspirational, maybe spiritual, an awesome experience. All feel secure; they have bonded, and they have reached a higher level in human understanding. I can feel it from them. I feel good, too, and I laugh, thinking I need to do this more often.

I pull the telepathy slowly from them, leaving happy thoughts so as to not put them into withdrawal and the shock of losing it, which is a deep, lonely feeling. The slips disengage at the same time, leaving them. They all open their eyes at once, all with wonderful pleased laughs, joy in their eyes. All smile and talk at the same time, looking lovingly at Anna. They all have tears in their eyes, even the men, all saying, "I love you Anna, thank you!" and then thanking me, hugging me, saying they love me, so grateful for the most miraculous experience of their lifetimes. They thank me for sharing my love for Anna with them and opening up the depths of my mind to them. I am not sure exactly what that means, yet it is pleasing to me. Again, it's good to be human. Who would think?

I tell Anna I will pay for dinner. She nods and smiles; I feel her happiness, and she leads her friends out, saying good-bye to each, and each hugging her, crying tears of happiness, thanking her. I pay the restaurant tab by giving the owner a $20,000 cashier's check I picked up at a bank when Anna was shopping. I say he should keep the change, as this is much more than the tab, and he is more than pleased, maybe a little shocked by my generosity, as the bill was just under $10,000. I tell him I appreciated the private room and to not say anything to the press or anyone else that might ask about our being there tonight. It would not be a good thing, as everyone attending needs his or her privacy. He nods and says he understands, and it's no problem—nothing will come from him or his staff. He smiles and thanks me again for the money; he appreciates the generous tip.

Anna and I are now in the back of the limo, the driver's window closed, heading for some fancy nightclub the rich and gorgeous people frequent. I still feel unworthy of Anna. She went to Duke. I went to a state school: Indiana University. My parents were working class. Her stepfather is a senator. I am not talented or a beautiful person, hardly even close to glamorous. She is a stunning celebrity actress. Everyone at the dinner tonight was accomplished, charming, and beautiful to look at, and they all have real homes. I have nothing to give her; even to help her have a family is a dismal offering. I am also totally bizarre. I am a freak. No matter how lonely it is for me, I need to be fair to her, explain to her that I'm not a good fit for her. The worst of it is I'm leaving in two days. I'm not sure if I will ever be back, for many complicated reasons. And I need to tell her I love her and I am sorry, explain my situation better, and try to make her understand why I will not be coming back. I owe her that.

We are sitting across from each other. Anna is smiling, looking out the window and acting innocent yet she is very sensual. I know she is teasing me on purpose. Anna's black skirt is very short, pulled up even higher now, and I see the bottom of her white-lace panties. Her blouse is pure white silk, no bra, her perfect breasts and her nipples hard and pointed, easy to see through her blouse. I feel the effect, amazed by how powerful the human sexual drive is; the push to mate is irrational. I am not sure I can talk. I feel inadequate, for one thing, not equal to her. Even my looks are not enough. In comparison to her, I look plain. She at least likes my clothing, as she picked out what I am wearing. I am wearing gray slacks, an expensive black-leather belt, black loafers, and a navy blue sports coat over a blue silk shirt—not my normal look. Anna bought it all for me, her gift, and all of it fits me perfectly. It's designer clothing, and the shirt shows my chest muscles. It's really embarrassing for me, but Anna loves it.

Anna is looking at me seductively, smiling coyly. "Henry, thanks for that. What you did for me and my friends was awesome, and I know there were a thousand reasons not to do it. It's an experience they will remember forever, and I hope you are going to get to know some of them well in the future, maybe even love them, too, like I do. They are my best friends, or the women are for sure."

Anna smiles and says, "You know we are alone in this limo, and it's roomy, don't you think?" She laughs.

I smile and say in a serious tone, "Anna, I have something to say. Even if it's bad timing, I need to tell you, as I am not sure how the next few weeks will go. I may have issues trying to retire, and if it goes against me, you need to know why. No matter what, even if I've been with you a very short time, I love you with all my heart, and no matter what happens to me or what the future brings us you are the love of my life."

Anna's eyes widen. She smiles; her lips tremble, and tears are coming down her cheeks. She laughs and says, "Henry, I know. I feel the same about you, crazily enough. I love you, and you are the love of my life." Growing more serious she asks, "Henry, you're having doubts. What do we do? Have you changed your mind? Can I go with you on the *Cyclone*, or will you stay? Where do we live? Will you live with me? How do we stay together?"

I respond, "Anna, I'm not sure about our living together for now. Yet believe it or not, I do have a plan. Hear me out. I have thought about it a lot, and it's not great, but it's the only way under the circumstances."

"You know I have to leave. You cannot live on the *Cyclone*, as it would be terrible for you, and you have your career and a busy, happy life here. I dread leaving without you and hardly want to talk about it, yet it is a reality. The question of me being able to leave the military is the challenge. The ripples are many, with many problems to solve; the ramifications are severe in some cases. No matter. I am planning on leaving the military, retiring or resigning and then coming back. I will also push to get Earth into the Consortium, thus ensuring Earth's future and its future protection. I have responsibilities across the universe, providing the protection many need. I hope to transfer those responsibilities to a replacement."

"Anna, I need to protect you while I'm gone, physically and financially. The physical part is tough, and I will work on a plan. The financial part is easy. I have notified my law firm to contact the bank, and you will become a joint owner of all my assets; a lawyer will come see you next week to sign the papers to give you access to my assets. The law firm will work for you then; they can help you with any problem you have and provide you with as much money as you will ever need or want in the future."

"If I return, I will ask you to marry me. I want this more than life itself. If I do not return, you will have everything I have on Earth. No one will question it, as you will be listed as a joint owner of my assets. Of course there is a chance my next time back will be ten years from now, or, worse, I may never come back. I do not expect you to wait, to put your life on hold. Either way, I will notify you as soon as possible."

Upset, Anna responds, "I do not care about your assets; I have more than enough now. I will wait for you to arrange your retirement and then you will return to Earth."

"Anna, there is more than just retiring. I have never told anyone this. There is a good chance they will not let me go, and you need to know why. I am tied to them physically and mentally. If they say no, I can't leave, or at least I may not leave alive. As you know I am attached to the *Cyclone*. Unfortunately it's more than you think, as the *Cyclone*'s current identity dies without me, and the same with me. Without the *Cyclone*—I also lose my identity, who I am, and maybe my life. We are symbiotic, with an obligate symbiosis relationship; think of it as tied together with one shared soul. We have been together now for sixty years. The *Cyclone*'s personality as you and I know it would expire without me or without installing another me. For the same reasons, I am not sure if I would survive a total separation either, as it was how I was rebuilt. The symbiosis with the *Cyclone* was part of my mental design."

Now frowning, I continue, "Also, even more critical, you and I will both be vulnerable without the Consortium's consent and protection. I would attract my enemies to Earth, which could cause the destruction of you, me, our children, and maybe the entire population of Earth. I have some serious enemies."

I am looking at Anna, and she looks really angry and disappointed—the reaction I had expected and hoped I could resolve in some way. I know I am on thin ice, and this might be our last moment together.

"Anna, I'm so sorry. I have no choice. I have to leave in two days. When I reach my home planet, I will request my retirement, then sort out the issues with the *Cyclone*. I will ask to have the Earth inducted into the Consortium. I hope to come back with the means to safeguard Earth's future and ours. I do not think it will go well for us as a couple, as they will not understand my request. I must be honest with you. You know I will fight for us, yet I am not optimistic."

She is angry, intense. "Henry, your plans are *your* plans, not really *our* plans, and yes, you will come back. No other way works for me. We will not tell anyone publicly about us. And I will let you leave in three days, not two. You will be back for the Academy Awards, as you will be my date. This is not negotiable. The awards are in six months. You will be here then, if not before."

Anna looks tenderly at me. She comes to me, kneeling in front of me, holding my hands, intently looking into my eyes. "Darling, you are powerful, cunning, a commander of a huge military force, courageous, loving, and resourceful, and you can make it happen. Anything else is not acceptable; do you understand? We will live wherever you want us to live; if necessary it will be on whatever planet you call home. Yet I see no reason you can't call Earth home. I will retire from movies even if I get the Academy Award, and yes, I want your children, lots of them, and you will protect them. You also will eventually marry me. Even if you have to stay in the military, I can still be your wife. I may be your second wife after the *Cyclone*, which I accept. I do not accept the end of this relationship, as I believe with all my heart we are meant to be together." She smiles a very big smile. "You also owe me."

"Anna, yes, yes, I understand." I also smile, yet I know better.

"Henry, all right, you can kiss me."

⟫⟨ ⟩⟪

We arrive at the nightclub, and I don't want to go in; however, the limousine door opens, cameras are going off, lights are flashing, and before I know it Anna has me in the nightclub, sitting at a big table with lots of famous people, and she's introducing me as her boyfriend. She is happy, as it is her right to be, and I am glad for this moment.

She has no security team. She asks why she would need anyone if she has me, the most dangerous person in the universe, and a massive military starship overhead with lots of troops. She laughs and says, "On top of that, at least five federal agencies with armed teams are all around us. The president has less security."

I laugh! It feels good to be with her.

Anna is quite famous, and she pays for nothing wherever she goes. The nightclub is delighted she is here—it's great for their reputation—and everyone in the place acts like they know her. She says she wants to dance with me to some great music and asks if I am up for the challenge. Not sure I have danced before. She teases me about dancing in my cabin in front of an illusion, like a created reflective wall of people dancing to music. I look at her, shake my head, and laugh.

She looks very sexy and smiles coyly, moving her hips back and forth, slowly spinning around, laughing, saying we need to dance. She tells me not to pay attention to the crowd, as everyone will be watching. Cameras are to be ignored. She starts to lead me to the dance floor. The music is loud, too much noise to talk. We are using telepathy now.

I smile and project my thoughts: "I have a new experience for you, too, if you want to experiment, and if you want to risk our dignity. We can do even better than regular dancing. We are telepathic, both of us. We have the possibility to really come together in a dance no one in this world has ever done. For example, on some worlds there are mating dances that telepathic couples dance, where they mind meld, like before at dinner, yet more. It is the coming together of two beings, both physically and mentally, during the dance, both in perfect rhythm, totally synchronized as both bodies and minds are perfectly moving to the music as one. It is very sensual, primitive, and erotic. I have never done this kind of dance with a woman before, just seen it."

Anna looks at me and says, "Can we do this here? Is this music right for it?"

I say, "Yes, I think so Anna, yet I think you should pick the music. I'll be in your mind much more than ever before. I will lead you in the dance; I will be in your brain. We will really be together. We will meld into one. I think it might be scary for both of us. It's very erotic, and it will arouse you. It's on the exhibitionist behavior list, not quite having sex in public yet not far from it. Are you OK with that?"

She responds, "Sounds crazy and wild! I know I should say no. I don't care! Let's do it. I know just the song that will work. It has a lot of rhythm and a good beat, not too fast. You'll love it. It's called 'Amazing' by Seal."

Anna continues, "This is all incredible to me. I never knew life could be so good. Henry, you make me so happy, and the dance meld sounds exciting. Let's try it." Anna goes toward the DJ stage, saying, "I'll get them to play the song. Are you ready, Henry?" She makes her way to the disc jockey, smiling at him, asking him; he fawns over her, his eyes loving her and says he is delighted to play anything she wants.

Anna is back, and we go onto the dance floor. There are people everywhere, cameras pointed at us, strobe lights sparkling on and off. Everyone knows who she is, and the rest of the couples and dancers part for her, smile at her, loving her, her beaming back at them. She is absolutely beautiful, in her element, a goddess among Earth's creatures, and who is she with? I can't believe that I am with her. Does not get better than this.

I hear the music change. Anna looks at me, and I feel her. This is the right song, just perfect. It sounds fantastic; I can feel Anna's excitement, too. The beat is just right, the rhythm, the tempo, the song's lyrics; it really is amazing. The song is for Anna, although I am sure Mr. Seal, who sings it, had someone else in mind.

As we feel the effects of the song, I start to enter her mind, and she resists. I probe gently, and she gives in to me. We are in mind meld, mentally together as one. We start dancing, swinging in perfect timing, our hips close together in rhythm, our arms intertwined. We are so close, moving fast, hands locked, perfectly synchronized with the song, our bodies moving to the beat as one, changing directions perfectly, putting our backs to each other, swirling. Then we physically meld together, facing each other, locked in each other's arms, hips moving faster, totally sensual. We are both aroused. We lightly kiss. We are in perfect harmony with the music, eyes locked most of the entire dance, almost never losing connection even as our bodies move in and out, sometimes swirling yet always in sync.

It is supernatural, awesome, and magical, and even wilder— even more crazy—ten or more tiny security slips are swirling around us in rhythm with our movements, all are lit up, looking like sparkling points of brilliant lights. Absolutely magical! I am not sure why they're there; maybe the force of my mind signaled them. It's mind-bending for the people watching this, too. The intense excitement of the moment is causing my mind to fully project, which is more powerful than planned for, as I have lost some control. It is pushing out powerful mental penetrations into everyone in the room, and they are feeling my emotions through my telepathy, capturing their minds. They feel my emotions as I feel them. The raw force of my mind is incredible, and they are part of me, as is Anna.

None of the others are dancing by themselves. All are dancing with us, even the DJ, all entranced, staring at us, mesmerized, captivated in this amazing moment. They are all clapping to the beat, hands over their heads, swaying back and forth just like us, all of us moving in perfect unison with the music, all spellbound by the moment as my mind is throwing off the powerful stimuli they feel, holding them spellbound. They engage our emotions and accept us in their minds, all swaying in sync with us. They feel our sexual intensity as if it is their own, and all are aroused. It is tribal. It is primitive. It is magic! And everyone there feels it. We slow as the song slows, and it ends with Anna and me kissing deeply. I can feel her powerful sexual arousal, she feels mine, and we awaken from the trance to yelling, whistling, and clapping, laughter, tears, and smiles. They all feel our love and this primitive sexual stimulation. We all felt the dance as one, pure magic, then a group mind meld. This is new territory for me, too.

Anna laughs and says, "Henry, we have to go. This is really embarrassing, and to leave at the finale is good!" She is flushed, embarrassed by her sexual excitement, breathing heavily, feeling the passion and again saying we need to go now, right now. She says she can't stand it; she needs me right now. We need to try to make it to the limo. She says she can hardly wait. It's hard for her to walk, she says, laughing. She has never been so aroused. She might not make it to the limo. She says it's my fault, and we need to hurry!

Laughing again, she yells, "Henry, please hurry!" She grabs my arm, and we are making our way out fast, slowed down by everyone hugging, smiling, laughing, and giving us high-fives. We push through the crowd. I have to push to break through, helping Anna, although she is doing some pushing, too. Soon we are in the limo and heading out.

Anna yells at the driver to just drive anywhere and close the window between us. Then she strips, ripping off her silk blouse, then her skirt, slipping off her panties, and then helping me take off my clothing. She's breathing hard, really rushed, and we are together again, both naked, and she is very ready. Then we are in a new mind-body meld, similar to the dance before but much more physical, powerful in another way. We are moving in unison again as our bodies are intimately joined at the hips. Anna's legs are wrapped around me. She has multiple orgasms, wild and vocal. We simply wear ourselves out, and we can hardly move. We are both exhausted. I'm astounded!

We put on our clothing slowly, laughing, joking, acting like teenagers, yet we both still feel the incredible passion, still can't keep our hands off of each other. Anna tells the driver to please head home. Wow! It's no wonder humans have sex. I feel truly blessed, never knew.

CHAPTER 32

A SERIAL KILLER—DAY NINE

I t is late when we are on the way home, around midnight, yet I am not tired. We are not far from Anna's house. Going there reminds me: I wonder what is happening with our hunt for the serial killer. The *Cyclone* immediately responds, saying it's glad to hear from me, and the mission is going forward. We know who the serial killer is and where he lives, and we are on the way there now. The girl, Caroline, is still alive, thus we need to move fast. Forty legion guys in my guard are currently ready to go. They will use the dog soldier armored gear and descend to overwhelm the security guards and guard dogs using stun weapons. It will be over fast. This is overkill, as these guys could take on a couple of army divisions. Ten or so security guards is nothing.

Our serial killer is wealthy, with enough money for a lot of armed security guards. The estate grounds are high-walled, with lots of cameras, and the mansion is secluded, with a sophisticated security alarm system. There is also a large lead-lined vault in the basement, used as a panic room or, more likely, a prison for his victims. This guy's name is Sebastian Branski. He is in his midforties and made his money developing software. He is worth millions. He sold his companies and, as he said, retired to help mankind; he's now a philanthropic celebrity, with several charities and a foundation. He never married. He teaches at Berkeley part time and is good with the ladies. He meets many at charity events, which is probably where he acquires his victims. He is at his mansion in Malibu overlooking the ocean, not far from where we are. Anna and I can be there in a few minutes. I think maybe we should be there. Our attack is going to happen immediately. We have to hurry. The girl is still alive in the basement vault, according to the drones. Branski is about to kill her.

⊷⊶

It is still a basement, as it smells a little moldy; maybe it's all the stale air, even with the paneled walls and working ventilation. There are no windows; the room is private and soundproofed, quiet, with only the soothing sound of the vent fans. It is actually a real vault. Sebastian loves the room; it is a place with good memories. It looks like a hospital room, with an operating table and bright overhead lights. There are also all kinds of operating-room tools and equipment: scalpels, surgical saws, pliers, and some weird stuff—leather straps, paddles, and whips. In the corner there is a toilet and a huge sink with an attached shower. There is an adjoining room that has a toilet, too. It has a bed with attached chains and handcuffs arranged just right, pleasing Sebastian greatly. It also has a huge steel door that locks.

Sebastian is smiling, cleaning the blood off the scalpel in his rubber-gloved hands, looking down at what used to be a lovely young woman. She is now bleeding where both ears are missing, her face swollen horribly, blood everywhere. She is naked and strapped to a steel table, on her back, mouth taped shut and eyes taped open. She is still conscious enough for him, although she's close to catatonic from six hours of torture and sexual abuse. He slowly cut off each of her ears, careful not to put her into shock. He thinks it is time for her breasts. Cutting off breasts is always a delight, so sensitive and so much pain!

The girl is way past terror, now gone to a deep place in her mind. She has surrendered to her fate. Curiously enough, she is thinking of her sister, Elisabeth, and her father, her mother, of her wonderful childhood, all of them a close family. She and her sister could have made their parents proud; they both loved people and were doing all they could do to make a difference, working endless hours for good causes, mostly helping the really poor and the really sick. She and her sister tried to be kind always, never turned away from hardship. Now the sickening, excruciating memory of her twin sister being tortured comes back. She was forced to watch, vomiting from the horror, knowing her turn was coming. There was nothing she could do to help as her sister screamed and begged for both their lives. Her sister loved her, asking God to save her. Elisabeth suffered yet asked God for mercy for her sister. The sorrow and sadness were overwhelming. Did he kill her?

She looks up and sees him over her. As he grabs her face, she tries to scream. The grisly scalpel in his hand slowly comes down to her again, the agony to come again, and his delight in her fear and pain…then…

Whoosh…bam-bang!

Without warning there is a massive ear-splitting blast. An explosive detonates in the room. Sebastian instantly uses his arms to guard his face, falling back off of her, shrieking in fright.

There is another bright-white, searing heat strike, as a second thunderous concussion explodes from up above, and a second blast of dirty air full of dust fills the room. His face is mostly behind his arms, and he's looking out, his face expressing sheer terror, dirt in his eyes, both eyes big and wide, his mouth gasping for air in the dust and smoky powder, and coughing. Then…

Bammmmm...ga-bam!

A third explosive blast of air hits him, knocking him farther back, on to the concrete floor, combined with brilliant hot light, more searing heat, and deafening bedlam. The overhead lights are gone, and bright searchlights beam down, blinding to look up at, lighting up the entire room, as a violent airflow clears out the dust in the room.

Caroline is totally bewildered as she watches Sebastian eerily rise up over the room, suspended in the air. There is no ceiling; actually there is no house, just a black night sky. It's all gone. He's screaming at the top of his lungs in sheer horror as two massive furry, clawed hands have a grip on his neck and shoulders, bringing him higher into the air, propelled upward by some unseen force. Then two more hairy hands that also are not human grab his leg and the hand holding the scalpel, twisting it, the scalpel falling.

Over the room, up high, in the night's air, hovering, she sees what Sebastian has seen. She must be delusional, as she sees demons. They're everywhere, massive, eight feet tall or taller, terrifying wolf like creatures, large jaws with fanged teeth, dark-red hair, and deep-throated growling, like lions or werewolves. They have demonic red glowing slit eyes. They are now roughly thumping Sebastian, beating him into submission, forcing him to do as they want. He is screaming in pain and terror. They are putting him in a strange silver metal tube that is weirdly floating in the air about twenty-five feet up from the huge hole above her, the werewolves hovering over him. His entire body, now limp, is being clamped in, part by part, and the screaming stops when his mouth is covered by a tight black mask with breathing tubes that are connected to a small cylinder attached to his tube. His eyes are ghastly, ugly black holes, both eyeballs gone.

She is hoping for a quick death from these demons, probably the spawn of Satan coming to collect Sebastian. She no longer has the will to live; the pain of her many wounds is intense. Then, to her alarm, she is rising. She feels the fast momentum. She is surrounded by some kind of weird light, pulling her steel table up, with her on it. Then her strap ties are coming off as she is placed in some kind of strange, totally white wonderful space, on her back, floating free. She looks up and sees the most beautiful woman she has ever seen, maybe an angel, although amazingly enough she looks like somebody she knows. She hears the woman talking to her in a soft, soothing voice, with tears running down her face, telling Caroline she will be fine, fixed up good as new. The healing process has already started. She says, "Don't move."

She feels herself being lifted again, like she is floating, not sure how. A silk covering is on her, and she actually feels good, then there is a comforting blackness. She wakes as soon as she blacked out, or she thinks so, lying on a very soft bed, her face up, looking at a silver metal ceiling. She is not tired. Her body feels stimulated, no pain, feeling superb, like she's never felt before. She immediately looks at her wounds on her hands, and they are gone. The pain and soreness in her face are also gone, and there's no pain coming from her ear stubs. She knows Sebastian cut off her ears, as he made her look at each one after the mind-bending pain of his handiwork.

Her angel friend is bathing her with a peculiar-looking sponge. The woman smiles at her, saying, "Caroline, I'm almost finished. Your body has been cleansed, or almost done. And some good news, your ears are fine now." She tenderly puts the girl's hands up to her head. Caroline feels normal ears. Her ears are back, as if they were never cut off. Has this all been some terrible nightmare?

This is all impossible. For one thing the beautiful angel washing her is Anna Summers. She recognizes her as the famous movie star she loves and always wanted to meet. Maybe she's dead, and God has granted her this last wish. She asks, "Are you Anna Summers, the movie star, or are you an angel? Am I in heaven?"

Anna laughs, tears come to her eyes. "No, Caroline, you are not in heaven, and yes, I am Anna Summers. You have been through a horrific experience and have been saved by a friend of mine. You are on the starship *Cyclone*, in their medical clinic. We are orbiting Earth. My starship friends have technology we do not have on Earth. Many molecule-size drones repaired you very quickly, and you are as good as new. In fact you are better than new, healthier and with a long life ahead of you. I know it's hard to believe, but really it doesn't matter. What matters is that you are OK, and you will see your parents tonight—that is, after I finish cleaning you up. You will have one of my dresses, and I will take you to your parents' home."

"Caroline, try to focus on what I am going to tell you. You must be strong going forward, as many people need you. Your sister would have wanted you to survive. All of this is awful, totally inexplicable; it never should have happened. Yet you will eventually sort it out. The world needs people like you."

Caroline kisses Anna's fingers on her right hand, as the sponge cleanses her face, then she reaches up to touch Anna's cheek.

Anna smiles, holding Caroline's hand, tenderly looking into her eyes, saying, "I also need a favor from you."

Caroline nods her head.

Anna responds, "I ask you for both our sakes, do not tell anyone about my friends or me. It will be better for you, too. No one will believe all that has happened to you; it's even unbelievable for me to digest. No one will understand."

Caroline, now tears in her eyes, says, "Yes, you are right. Is this reality? Are you here? Do you know if my sister Elisabeth is dead?

Caroline continues, "Have you seen her? How do I know this is real? Are you really Anna? It is hard to believe. Anna Summers, is it really you. I have always loved you, and now I guess I owe you my life. This is surreal; if you're not an angel, are you really Anna Summers? Is my sister dead? Do you know?"

Anna responds, with tears in her eyes: "I am so sorry. Your sister was killed."

Caroline's despair is immediate; she cries out in misery, soulful, pure anguish; she is sobbing uncontrollably, trying to talk, cries out: "My poor sister! She was better than me. I should be the dead one. Elisabeth was so kind and good, to have suffered so badly! There was nothing I could do. I think I want to die. It could not have happened. God would never allow something so evil to occur to such a wonderful person. Yes, maybe I will wake up tomorrow out of this nightmare. How do I know if this is real? What happened to that monster, Sebastian?"

Anna leans forward and gently kisses her on the forehead, then tenderly whispers in her ear, "You will prevail. You are strong, and he did not defeat you! He has been taken care of; he will never bother anyone else again."

Caroline, intently staring into Anna eyes, says, "If it's really you, I do thank you with all my heart, and I will say nothing about you or your friends. If I can ask, how did you heal my wounds, give me my ears back? Did you actually say we're in a starship, and they're your friends? It's not possible. And what happened to Sebastian? Who were those wolf creatures? Were they real werewolves?"

Anna sits on the bed, leaning over, reaching out for her hand, making eye contact. "Caroline, yes, we are on a starship. You probably are still in shock, and it's hard to comprehend all of this. It will take a long time, and I know you will heal from your loss. You're strong. No worries about Sebastian; he paid the price for killing your sister—the asshole is dead. You will never see him again. You have nothing to fear from him, nor does anyone else. I am so sorry about your sister and what you had to see, what you went through. You will need some counseling. You know your Elisabeth would want you to go forward."

"As for your wounds, just consider the healing and the repairs a gift from God, a miracle provided by him and your new friends. Also, most importantly, tell no one; do you understand? The police will want a statement. Tell them you remember you and your sister being kidnapped by Sebastian but nothing more. You have amnesia from the trauma. They will believe you."

"Caroline, so that you know, we burned down the rest of his house and buildings. It's all gone, everything completely vaporized. Even the basement is filled in, the rest just scorched ground. No one needed to see it or to know what happened to you there. And the rest of the girls he killed don't need to be remembered that way. It is good to erase this evil. We will also destroy any DNA left, make him totally disappear. The fire was so hot, everything vaporized; there is nothing left of him or his belongings. The wolf-looking soldiers you saw are just regular soldiers wearing disguises. They saved your life. Please do not mention them to the police. Just stick to the loss of memory due to shock. They will not believe what really happened, and they will not leave you alone if you don't give them a story they can understand."

"Caroline, it's time. Are you ready to go home? We'll catch a lift to Earth, and then we travel in my limousine to your home. It is early, three o'clock in the morning, still dark; you may be hungry, not sure the last time you ate, so you'll be able to have breakfast with your parents. You are alive and in one piece. I've called them, and they are ecstatic that you are alive. They're waiting for you. They will let the police know after I'm gone. I did not tell them who I am. Please do not tell them. Remember, you do not know how you ended up at home."

She nods her head, reaches for Anna's hand, and whispers, "Bless you, and I thank you. I will say nothing about you."

⊷╬⊶

Although Anna did not know about the current police activity, Henry knew every detail. The police had been at Sebastian Branski's estate within minutes of the attack, one police car only, as the entire backup was delayed by the *Cyclone* microwaving pulses at the incoming cruisers, causing the engines to quit as they drove toward the mansion. Officer T. J. Bishop had made the call for backup, as he was already there. He was coincidentally driving by on a routine patrol and noticed some weird things happening. He stopped at the closed front gate then noticed, oddly enough, there were no security guards at the gatehouse. Looking through the bars at the long road to the mansion, it was all dark, no lights on anywhere, yet there was all kinds of activity. Security guards were lying on the ground moaning, dazed, and not moving much. There were flashes of light going off here and there on the grounds and some kind of scary, weird growling sound every so often, just scary as hell.

T. J. decided to call for backup and quickly retreated behind his police cruiser. To his complete shock, there was a series of large explosions in the mansion and then terrible-looking werewolves, like something out of a horror film, were all over the grounds, some disappearing into the mansion. Then the mansion disappeared in a massive explosion, just gone, vaporized. He could hardly breathe, as it seemed the air was being sucked up. He grabbed the bumper of the cruiser and held on, feeling the suction and a wave of hot air coming from above. Looking up, he could see what looked like the underside of a massive spaceship, maybe a couple hundred feet up. It was hard to see in the dark, but it was definitely not from this planet. T. J. then passed out from sheer overwhelming fright.

—+‹+ +›—

I'm waiting for Anna and the limousine at the all-night diner where we had breakfast previously. I've just finished a really great cup of coffee. Coffee from Earth, fresh-brewed, is priceless.

I know the FBI, CIA, and NSA guys are not too far away, watching me. I am used to them.

I'm glad about Sebastian. That was the end of a truly evil man. His download of memories was gruesome and his mind truly twisted, even more insane after the drone slips manipulated his brain into giving up his secrets. The drones used his eye sockets to come and go, extracting a lot. His DNA was examined and found to be corrupted. One good thing was Sebastian did not have children or siblings, and both his parents were dead. Death was not quick for him, as the drones did a number on his brain, and then killed him when they were done. He was vaporized, including his clothing, all gone forever. He will never hurt anyone again or use any resources for his own gain. He signed away all his assets, a new will, right before his death, authorizing the setting up a trust fund for the families of his victims, anonymously giving them monthly payments. The unsolved crimes he committed were taken from his memories and will be reported to the police and to their families; the missing bodies will be recovered from the burial locations.

Looking out the diner's window, I see Anna is here with the limousine. It's four-thirty in the morning. Time to go home and get some rest.

CHAPTER 33

THE PRESIDENT OF THE UNITED STATES—IRAN—NUCLEAR WEAPONS

A few minutes later, on the way back to Anna's house, four large official-looking black SUVs come up on us from behind. Two of them pass us, two are behind us, and, much to our surprise, they all turn on hidden blinking police lights. I am thinking, *What now?* I'm not interested in having issues with anybody. The limo driver pulls over and gets out, goes back to meet them, comes back, and says to me, "Mr. Johnson, they say they're FBI, and they want to talk to you."

I can feel the *Cyclone* over us, and I calm it down. I think we're fine, yet the *Cyclone* drops in altitude, only three hundred feet up, close enough that I can feel its heat, and can hear the exhausts; know it's watching these men. Anna is alarmed, looks at me, and asks what we should do. I say I will talk to them, not a problem.

I get out and walk back. Three are to my left, and three have come up behind me from the front vehicles. I know they will all be vaporized by the *Cyclone* in a fraction of a second if they pull out their weapons. I say, "My name is Henry Johnson. Please do not pull your weapons. I am unarmed. It is critical you do not look hostile or do anything that looks threatening. I have security here over your heads, closely watching you. Please be careful because it is instantaneous death for you.---- Do you understand me?"

They are all looking up and around, real nervous. All of them nod; looking at me, fear in their eyes.

"I am happy to talk," I say. "What do you want?"

The FBI guy nearest to me says, "Captain Johnson, we have a phone call for you from the president of the United States, and if it's OK to hand this phone to you—"

I nod, and someone hands me a cell phone. It rings, and I answer it. The president is on the call. I recognize his voice, and I respond, "Yes, Mr. President. Yes, I am Captain Henry Johnson."

"Yes, Captain Johnson. How are you?"

"Fine, Mr. President. What can I do for you?"

The president says, "I have a real national crisis. It is critical that we talk. However, what I am about to say is a matter of national security. Plus, the lives of millions of Americans are at stake. There is no time. First of all, so that you know the latest information, I will bring you up to the last hour. Much of this you may already know." It had been explained to him that I have access to all the US databases, including the encrypted stuff.

The president continues, "Unfortunately Iran has become an acute critical national security crisis, and since I know about Iran then I know about the current issues. It is much worse now. One hour ago Iran gave the United States an ultimatum: they intend to bomb Israel with nuclear warheads, with six ICBMs, at 7:00 p.m. Eastern Standard Time, which is about fifteen hours from now. They want the United States to stand down after the bombing, no retaliation and no interference, or face the destruction of six major cities in the United States and more attacks from the Iranian army. Several units of commandos have infiltrated the United States. This problem we have neutralized, as we think we have these troops captured, or they have been killed, thanks to your warning. Unfortunately, the nuclear bombs are still a really appalling problem, and the next twenty-four hours are really critical. We desperately need your help, the help you offered previously. By the way, neither China nor Russia has any part of this. It's more like a plan B for Iran."

"The Iranians have planted six large nuclear warheads to be detonated when triggered. They say the warheads are impossible to find, as they are moved every twenty-four hours, traveling back and forth, using unmarked trucks, between selected major US cities. We have been told not to warn Israel or to react to the destruction of Israel; we are to mind our own business. It is a desperate situation. Millions of lives could be lost. We are hoping and praying for a miracle, praying you will help us with a miracle."

"Mr. President, I am interested in helping you, although at this moment I have no authorization. As you know, Earth is not a member of the Consortium and officially not in my jurisdiction. I am restricted in how much I can do for you."

"Captain Johnson, first of all, we have decided to apply for membership to the Consortium if you will help us. Second, John Jacobs explained to us you have incredible weapons. He said you vaporized twenty Iranian solders simultaneously with pinpoint accuracy. Your weapons are far more advanced than ours. Our question to you is can you take out six nuclear warheads at the same moment? Can you find these nuclear warheads for us? If you can do this, would you do it for us?"

"Mr. President, yes to all three. However, I need three favors in return."

"Captain Johnson, if it's in our power, we will comply with whatever you want. You have my word."

"Mr. President, we will talk later about it. For now I have only one issue in helping you. The warheads must be activated before we can accurately detect them. They will be activated only right before they are used. Thus we have a split second to destroy them, which means collateral damage. There is no time to warn people. When we vaporize the warheads, the temperature will be close to thirty-five thousand degrees, which will explode any buildings instantaneously where they are located and all people within two hundred feet. After this is done, your people will think we attacked them. You must go on national TV immediately and explain what happened in detail and why, then explain that we saved these cities from Iran. Do you agree? Also, do not mention me. Just say a Consortium military starship is here, and you asked for help. We helped because you asked."

"Captain Johnson, I agree. What do we do now?"

"Mr. President, at one o'clock this afternoon, Eastern Time, you will call Iran and tell them they will not activate the nuclear warheads in the United States and that they will tell you where they are immediately. You will tell them they will not attack Israel and will hand over their ICBMs and the warheads. If not, Iran's leadership of their military plus all government and religious leaders in power who made or help make these decisions will cease to exist within one hour of the attack on Israel. They will be in violation of Consortium laws and subject to these penalties. Tell them a Consortium military starship is here on Earth. Are we in agreement?"

The president responds, "Yes, Captain Johnson, we are in complete agreement. I will make the phone call. What will you do?"

"Mr. President, we will be in contact. It will be taken care of. The bombs will be destroyed. Israel will not be harmed."

The SUVs drive off, and I am back in the limo with Anna. She looks at me, questioning. I look at her and give her a hard, compressed smile. "It was the president of the United States. He wants a favor from me."

I explain the situation to Anna, and she asks, "Can you really do this? Will the *Cyclone* be successful? It seems impossible. What if you fail? How many people die? I wonder if LA is a target. What about my home and my friends? Can we warn them? What about my sister and family? Henry, what do you want me to do?"

"Anna, you're going with me. Can't chance you staying here in LA. No time to warn anyone, and where would they go? If we fail then there will be total chaos, martial law, no place will be safe. We have a ninety-four percent chance of success. I think we should be able to do this, but the timing of the attacks is critical. You will be on the *Cyclone*, the safest place in this galaxy. And you might be able to help, too. The *Cyclone* might use you, might need your instincts; it might access you. If so just relax, and the *Cyclone* will do the hard part. It will be something you could do to help. The *Cyclone* will succeed. Your family will be fine."

"The *Cyclone* will position itself fifty miles above the United States and wait for the nuclear bombs to be activated. The sensors will detect the activation, and the lasers will fire instantaneously. The bombs may not be set to detonate right away; however, we can't chance it. The *Cyclone* will fire as soon as the bombs are activated or located. There are six per Iran's declaration, but they are lying. The *Cyclone* says there are nine, and we think we know which cities they're in. Unfortunately the Iranians move them daily within the cities, and those doing the moving don't know where they will go ahead of time, so we can't lift the data. We have to wait for their activation to locate them."

"Anna, because of this attack the Iranian leaders are criminals, plus fundamentally immoral, sinning in the worst way, ruthlessly killing. Their leaders have endangered millions of lives, and it truly is a rogue country. They need to be corrected and rehabilitated per Consortium laws. It would be easier for me if I had official backing from the Consortium and if the Earth was in the Consortium and part of my jurisdiction. However, I will do what is necessary. As you like to say, it is what it is."

I shake my head, thinking about what poor judgment has led to this. What if I had not been here?

I tell Anna. "Using the *Cyclone* we will take care of the issues here, we vaporize the Iranian bombs here in the United States, and then head out, go up over Iran and wait for them to start up their attack on Israel. If Iran does what they promised, the *Saber* will be ready, hovering over Iran, positioned to kill the ICBMs when they are fired off or when they are heading for Israel. The Cyclone is back-up."

"That's the plan. The *Saber* will also then continue the attack, hitting any launching pads on the ground and take out the military aircraft, military bases, radar, and communications. Then the millions of drones that have been released by the *Cyclone*, will take care of the guilty ones, the people responsible. The guilty will be all identified, as the slips will penetrate their brains. The *Saber* will activate the larger military drones to kill the identified targets; afterward the bodies will be cleaned up by our debris eater drones. All of the responsible people will cease to exist. Recycling drones or trash eaters are good at doing their job. No bodies will be left. The drones then will reboard the *Cyclone*."

Anna looks like she's going to be sick, her face pale, and she says nothing.

We head back to her place, shower, and dress, and Anna packs some clothing for the trip. She is filled with anxiety, talking about Nikki and her family, and she has no appetite, not eating anything, even knowing we will not eat for a while. She is petrified about what could happen to her family if Iran uses the nuclear weapons and trying to hold steady, trying not to be a problem, summoning her courage to face the next twenty-four hours. I'm thinking since she has known me, life has been nothing but problems for her.

Anna and I board the *Saber*, and in minutes we move up and out of Los Angeles and enter the *Cyclone*, allowing the *Saber* to refuel and rearm its weapons. We leave the *Saber* to move forward to the captain's bridge as the *Cyclone* goes to an orbiting altitude and prepares for the war with Iran. As we pass over Iran, 915,000 military drones and 22 million recognizant slips, plus 304,000 trash-eater drones are dropped silently into Iran, all armed and activated, mostly invisible to the human eye. They will be maneuvering into position, waiting for the trigger to be pulled.

Anna and I, both exhausted from no sleep last night, fall asleep in the captain's bridge chairs as the silent drop takes place.

At noon the *Cyclone* maneuvers into position above the United States, directly above the Kansas-Nebraska border. All hands on deck are preparing. Anna and I are still in the captain's bridge. All on board are on high alert, ready for anything. The *Cyclone*'s sensors are searching the continent, listening for possible nuclear activation. At 1:00 p.m. Eastern Time, the president makes his call to Iran. The *Cyclone* notifies me and gives me the details of the call.

Anna is looking at me, now awake, very worried, fear in her eyes. We are in the captain's bridge, in the chairs. She leans toward me asking, "Are we going to wait until Iran attacks, or is there something we can do before they attack?"

I look at her and surprise her by smiling, responding, "Anna, it will be fine. It will all work out. I know more than you know, as we have our own little spies. Remember the drone slips? They are everywhere, and we have had access to Iran's database for a long time, even everything that is classified. I know all they know. The problem is what they don't know; their bureaucracy is not always accurate. It is the idiot issue. Otherwise we are ready, and they know nothing about me, thus it will be a total ambush. The *Cyclone* and I have been keeping the peace in the universe for a long time. I am reasonably sure where the nuclear weapons should be and just need the activation confirmation to target them. The *Cyclone* will vaporize all of them. Unfortunately we will kill some innocent people because of the massive heat, as it will light up the buildings around the bombs. This is never acceptable, yet we have no choice, as millions more will be saved from death. Of course, a quick prayer might not hurt."

Anna reaches out her hand, and I do the same; we touch. We look at each other; neither of us needs to say anything.

At 1:29 p.m., true to their word, we know Iran has activated the bombs, and the *Cyclone* knows their locations immediately, strikes, the blast shots cause the huge starship to lunge upward, throwing us both up out of the chairs. We grab the seats, pulling in and strapping down. The simultaneous blasts caused the movement, and we both know all were successful, as Anna also hears the report from the *Cyclone* telepathically. We have discovered there are more than six bombs; there are nine, and all nine are vaporized in LA; Dallas; Kansas City; Chicago; Indianapolis; Atlanta; Washington, DC; New York; and Miami. There are fires in each city at the point of impact but no harmful nuclear remnants or radiation. Our strikes were perfect. We immediately head out, going into orbit, which will take us over Iran.

The *Saber* is already gone, having left an hour ago, and has been hovering over Iran. Where Iran's six ICBMs armed with nuclear warheads also blast off at 1:29 p.m. Eastern Standard Time toward Israel, Iran not waiting for seven o'clock. To Iran's disbelief, all six are vaporized, with no trace they ever existed.

The *Saber* continues its attack, hitting the ICBM launching pads, radar installations, missile sites, military planes, tanks, troop bases, plus uranium reactor sites, and warships. Using the fusion power shotgun weapons, the *Saber* travels at about twelve thousand miles an hour, sweeping the ground with constant hits, going from one end of the country back and forth, firing rapidly at targets, like a Gatling gun, enabling it to vaporize targets so quickly that Iran does not have a chance to react or even know what is hitting them.

It is around ten o'clock at night in Iran, no moon, and a dark night. Many of the terrified population run into the streets upon hearing the thunder of the explosions, not sure of what is happening. They are not looking for an enemy, seeing only fires exploding in the dark skies on the horizon, lighting up everything. Why would they be attacked? The *Saber* is running at velocities causing massive booms, sounding like detonations from nuclear bombs and shaking buildings like an earthquake. The targets are all military. The speed creates friction on the hull, burning air, and then an exhaust tail of thirty thousand degrees. It makes the *Saber* look like a huge comet, striking and blasting over Earth, fire everywhere. As the *Saber* dips down, finding targets, vaporizing them, the propulsion thrust tail burns behind it, causing the surface features to catch fire. Because of the massive heat temperatures, there is a firestorm, burning red-hot. Fortunately most of this happens over rural land areas, populations are less; the cities are spared the worst. The starship is moving too fast for any missile reply.

Smoke and fire are covering the country. Iran seems like a vision from hell's inferno. All the military assets are gone, either on fire or vaporized. With everyone so distracted, it makes it easy for the slips and the military drones to make their attacks, invisible and deadly, as they start their search for their designated human targets. They are extremely efficient; no one can see them as they spread through the population, stalking and efficiently striking their designated enemies. These victims never have a clue, and those untouched do not understand why they are saved. Many die quick deaths, their remains quickly consumed by the trash eater drones. The *Cyclone* hovers overhead about five miles up providing energy for the drones.

All the targets are easily identified by the slips and quickly finished off by the bigger military drones. The mission instructions were simple; the targets are those responsible for the military attack on the United States and Israel. They are many of the Iranian senior military people, some of the senior political decision makers, the Iranian president, and many in the Iranian parliament, some in the military operations staff, and some of the major elected leaders. Those who are guilty of this crime, all disappear, no trace of them to be found, forever gone. The religious leaders involved in the nuclear plan also cease to exist. All the families are left with no explanation. Their loved ones are just gone, disappeared, no trace, as if they never existed. No one knows why exactly, and in the next few days, there is no official announcement, nothing in the news. The media is mostly quiet, afraid, terrified, not sure what to say or print. Those people still alive, as they were not involved in the planned US and Israel military strikes, are just grateful to be alive.

Tomorrow the people left in government go on about their business, attempting to pull the remaining citizens together, start the repairs, rebuild the country. New people will be hired to replace the missing—a lot of new people, all younger, and there will be a much quieter smaller government, with a "no violence" policy. The next day they apologize to Israel and the United States, asking the world to accept a new day in Iran, where they wish for friendship, causing no harm to anyone. Iran announces they are a real democracy now, and elections will be scheduled soon. Amazingly enough, there is hope and optimism in the land, despite all the difficulties. Politics and disaster make strange bedfellows.

Life in Iran then goes on as if nothing has happened. Those gone may be missed, and there is great sorrow; but no one talks about them; they are officially forgotten men and women. Maybe those left are all fearful yet know it is better to forget and go forward. No one wants to think about what happened. They wonder if Allah came for them; they are in a better place now.

The *Cyclone* picks up all the military drones and reconnaissance slips as it orbits, passing over Iran. Then back to LA. The *Saber* is reloaded into the *Cyclone*. The *Ship Tender* takes us down to Anna's house in LA and parks in the backyard.

CHAPTER 34

DAY TEN

We are home again in LA; last night we were both in bed within twenty minutes, exhausted and asleep immediately. Then I am up around six in the morning, swimming laps in Anna's house pool, loving it. While I'm swimming, Anna is sleeping, then later, with a phone call waking her up, she ends up talking to her mother and sister, all three on a conference call conversation, as there is much to talk about. They have several reasons for concern. Anna's mother is saying her stepfather is missing, and the world is a mess. Sam Jordan has disappeared; no one has heard from him for two days. His Secret Service team is at a loss. Anna tells them I am leaving the following day as part of my work, called away.

The TV morning news carries the president's press conference live. He tells the story of Iran's attack on the United States and their fate. All people on the entire planet feel frightened about the possibilities of what could have happened. The populations of the world and especially of the United States want to know about the alien saviors. Who are they? How long have they been here? Do the other governments of the world know about them? Where are they from? Do we need to be afraid? Why were they kept a secret?

The president explains and answers questions as much as possible. He says the whole situation with Iran's planned attack was a close call, saved by a bizarre situation. Crazily enough, a visiting alien starship that was here temporarily helped us. In communication with them we asked for their help, and they did supply a critical military operation, vaporizing Iran's nuclear bombs, preventing the death of millions. They are leaving soon. No one knows if they are coming back, why they are here, where they are from, or why they helped us. The president says we are grateful for their help. No one knows anything more. There is much discussion on the TV networks and much speculation about the last ten days of UFO activity. The networks replay previous John Jacobs's interviews.

Anna invites her mother and sister to come visit. Her mother is frantic. Her husband is her whole world, and there have been no phone calls from him, nothing for two days. She called the Secret Service, and Sam had told them he was on vacation. Anna wants some company, as do her mother and sister. They are coming tomorrow. Both will catch morning flights and will be here before lunch. Anna says she will pick them up. They know I will be gone.

The news agencies know nothing about the senator's disappearance, as this has been kept confidential. The Secret Service is afraid he may have been kidnapped, or hopefully he just took some time off without telling his family. He was last seen at his Senate office in Washington, DC, two days earlier.

Nikki and her mother say they will miss me. Anna says I have business to take care of, have to leave the following morning. I am sorry I will miss them and really sorry about the senator. I know more than they know. Sam Jordan is dead, kidnapped by his buddy Luca, tortured, then his son, Anthony, killed him. His body was disposed of at sea, a long way from Washington, DC. I could not save Anna's stepfather, yet I can certainly take care of his killers. Tomorrow morning will be interesting for the Deforleo family, especially for Luca and his son, Anthony.

After the call, Anna is looking for me, saying, "Henry, where are you? What are you doing?"

Seeing me in the pool, she laughs and yells at me, "I am not wasting our last day together. We have things to do! Get out of that pool."

"Yes, Anna, I am ready and have been for some time, waiting for you."

"Why didn't you wake me?"

"You needed your sleep. It was most pleasant just watching you. What do you want to do on my last day on Earth? I have until the end of the day, maybe a little more."

"We'll have a normal day. Pretend you're not leaving, and don't mention it. We will also pretend to be married and thus have a boring, normal day. We save no worlds or countries today. And no one who wants anything from us gets to talk to us. Maybe we will read the paper or maybe a good book. We could go to the library or the zoo and take the bikes. I want the whole day. I will make you breakfast, whatever you want, and then we will take a bike ride. Is there anything you want to do today?"

I reply, "Maybe this evening, only if you are in agreement. I thought we could take John Jacobs and his wife to dinner tonight wherever they want. It would be a thank you. I like them, and they seem like a nice couple. I need to talk to John, too. Dinner would be good, my last decent meal. What do you think?"

Anna responds quickly, "It sounds perfect. Except we need to be home by nine o'clock, as I want the last three hours to be just you and me. I'll call the Jacobs's; actually I will call Judy.

Please have the *Cyclone* provide me with her cell number. She can choose the restaurant, maybe make reservations for us, and we'll provide transportation. We could have dinner anywhere, right? Maybe London? Or New York? Where do you want to go?"

"Anna, I'm thinking New York. I have a surprise for you there, something I need to show you. I think you will like it. Something you might use in the future. We can be there in ten minutes."

She reacts, "Sounds interesting and mysterious. Let's do it. I'm taking a shower. Actually, you should call John Jacobs and find out where he is. He may be here in LA, as he was heading up our surveillance detail. Then we can give him a ride home, pick up his wife, too. He would like a call from you when it comes to us having a social outing. You know having dinner with an alien has ramifications for him." Anna smiles. "He does not know you like I know you!"

"I will call him," I reply.

In the shower, ignoring the hot water spray, Anna finally acknowledges in her mind that this is the last day with me. She can feel it from me; I will be gone, and I am not coming back. She is thinking about why all this has happened. In just ten days, her life has been upended; so much has happened, it's hard to comprehend. She feels the tears coming.

She prays, crying out, "Why, dear Lord, did this happen? It must have happened for a reason. This was not planned by either Henry or myself. Please Lord, help me." She breaks down more, her hands over her face, sobbing, and thinks, *Can this be fate, just the ten days together, a brief romance? Is this my destiny with Henry? I never planned for this or even thought it possible. Then it's only a short fling? Is this Henry's destiny: a lonely life for him, no family, just desolation, dying alone somewhere? Those who know the future know our fate, and please God, may they be kind to us.*

She weeps as she showers, overwhelming sadness overcoming her.

Anna is drying off, recovering, feeling her courage again, and thinking: *Our salvation and our strength is our love for each other. We will need to fight for each other! Henry must fight for me; he must battle for our unborn children. I need to sacrifice, no selfishness, need to compromise, keep us together no matter what, stay strong and keep Henry strong. We will be life partners. Henry knows his happiness is in that direction. He must not fail us. Someone else can serve the Consortium. It will be our destiny. We will make it so!*

She finishes drying off then brushes her hair, refreshed and ready to take on the day. She puts on some respectable shorts yet tight to her bottom and made of soft white cotton. She puts on a light-blue T-shirt covered by a navy silk blouse, wearing a sports bra, then reviewing the results in the mirror. She thinks: *I need to look decent yet I think Henry will be pleased. Time to find him.*

She strolls through her home, sees him out on the deck on the phone, waves at him.

I see Anna, waving back at her, signals her, showing the cell phone to her, and waiting. I project: "Not long."

After making several calls, I finally reach John Jacobs on his cell phone, now waiting for him, as John is saying he is boarding a flight going back home, currently finding his seat, wants me to hold for a bit. Finally, he is listening, and I invite him to dinner tonight, Judy, too. He is nervous about the call and is even more than surprised by the dinner invitation. He does not respond quickly, and I laugh, saying, "John, it's not a big deal, just a social dinner, time to relax. It's my last night here. I'm not sure when I'll be back, and I'm taking Anna out for dinner. We both want you to join us."

After a pause, trying to be persuasive, I entreat, "John, you and Judy are the only couple I know on this planet. And I also have a proposal for you, something you'll be interested in. I can explain it to you before dinner. It's my treat. Let's go to New York. You and Judy will have a ride in a military light starship that I call the *Saber.* It's very fast! We'll pick you up; let's say around five o'clock. I'll have you home at eight thirty. Please check with Judy. The dress is casual."

John stutters, "I—I'll need a babysitter for the kids."

I smile. "Please bring them. I love children. It would be a pleasure for me."

John is shocked, not sure how to answer. "Does the president know we're going to dinner? Meeting with you, even on a social basis, could have political ramifications."

"Yes, the president knows, if it makes you feel better. We had a long conversation, and he agreed with all my requests, including dinner tonight. I guarantee he will not interfere, nor will you face any ramifications in the future. Just check with Judy. If she is interested, then there are no issues. Let's make it easy. We'll eat at my place in New York City, no public restaurant. There's staff there to help us, a superb cook, too. I'll pick you up at five o'clock in the park down the street from your house. With your permission, if we have time, we will take the kids for a short spin, too, up into outer space, just for a few minutes. There is a pool where we're going if they want to swim, although I know it is a school night."

John laughs. "I know Judy would love this, all of it. It's not your normal evening, and she loves Anna Summers. The chance to meet Anna will be a thrill for her and the kids. I will speak to her, and five o'clock is fine. The swimming possibility for the kids probably won't work because of their bedtimes, but thanks for asking. By the way, we know you have a place in New York, just so you know."

"I know you know, and thanks for your honesty. My law firm was the leak; one of the new associates felt compelled to give in to FBI pressure. I have a meeting planned with the law firm to talk about it. Fortunately I know everything the FBI knows. Luckily for the FBI, I am on their side, and they are on mine now."

John hesitates, then says, "The FBI loves you for saving the country. Yet they are terrified of you; they think you use mind control; they think you have your hooks into everyone, maybe even the president. Everyone acts as if you know whatever is said, thus no one says your name or talks about you. They also know what happened in Iran, the total purge of most of the leadership, not a trace of them, and all the key people, the right people. You didn't miss one, as if you had inside information, meaning their own thoughts. You could do that anywhere. Every leader in the world is terrified of you, even if they say they aren't. Everyone knows what you did to the Chinese and the Russians. They all wonder what your real agenda is, what you're going to do next. Of course we are all hoping for the best."

"What do you think, John? You certainly are honest and candid. Please give me the truth."

A long pause; finally John responds.

"I think you have your hooks into everyone, including me. I'm not sure how. I sometimes feel you're listening, maybe even guiding me, or maybe I'm just imagining it. I hope—or think—you mean no harm to us, and I am not real worried about you, not sure why. I want to consider you an ally. You saved my daughter. You certainly saved us from Iran and a terrible destruction, my life was saved as was my family, millions were saved; you will always have our gratitude. Judy and I will always be your friend, as we owe you big time. Yet, I also have acute anxiety and real bad dreams about visitors coming from out there, your comrades. The whole universe is out there, and now we know they know about Earth. Nothing is certain. Many here have real stress, and the fear is real."

"John, for right now, two things are certain: We have a fantastic dinner planned tonight, and I leave Earth in the morning. Let's enjoy the evening. See you at five."

Anna is looking at him with a frown, standing there with her arms folded, looking really hot in her white cotton shorts, showing off everything I love. I know she must have been listening to my conversation with John.

I sheepishly say, "I guess you heard about the New York place in my conversation and are wondering why I never mentioned it."

Anna continues to stare at me, not a pleasant look.

I continue, "Yes, I have a place there, but it's not really a home to me, just a place to go. I never think of it, or I would have told you. I already planned to give you keys to it, one of the things the law firm will go over with you within the next couple of weeks. This way you'll have a chance to meet the staff."

She continues to stare at me; I feel her mind probes.

"Anna, honest, it's not a big deal. I haven't been there a lot myself. I don't even know the neighbors." I say this honestly, as there are no neighbors; I own the whole building. Yet in truth, I spend little time there.

Anna shakes her head, says, "All right. We're eating dinner there tonight. Judy will want to know what to wear. You said casual, which is a nice dress. If you have a staff, I guess you have a cook there, thus nothing for Judy or me to be concerned about regarding dinner. I'll call Judy. Then a bike ride. No time for breakfast—we eat out. You need to wear shorts and a T-shirt, as you will get hot. It will be a long bike ride. I know this great place to go. We can take fruit, too, make it a picnic. It's my surprise. You'll like it."

She talks to Judy, who is delighted, thrilled to meet Anna, and we have a dinner date. Then, we are on the bikes heading out fast, and I am trying to keep up.

I am trying not to worry about Anna, her weaving in and out of traffic ahead of me, although she is good on a bike, well practiced on it, lots of miles under her belt. My skills are working well enough; however, this is not like running. I laugh as I think about the FBI and everyone else on the surveillance team following us. The helicopter above is probably them, too, and then the *Cyclone* up above it. The *Cyclone* is anxious, ready for the trip out, trillions of miles to cover, waiting for me to return to duty, enough of the silly stuff. The Consortium is waiting, I know; Gabriel will want to talk about my trip.

The car next to us and then another in front of it, have guys in them who are taking photos of Anna and me, too. They know who Anna is, yet today is not the day to take photos. I am off limits. Two LA police cars come up behind them, lights blinking, and then another, then two FBI cars. Then two more unmarked military cars are waiting for them at the stoplight. The police are out of their cruisers, halting the cars, pulling the men out, arresting them, handcuffs, the whole thing. Then more police cars arrive, their lights flashing, sirens on.

Anna and I keep going fast, looking at each other. She laughs and yells at me, "First time that ever happened. You must be really important, Captain Johnson! You think they're watching us close? They're not taking any chances with you. Wow! You won't be getting lucky on this picnic, Henry!"

We finally arrive, gliding down a big hill, a surprise ahead. We are at the LA Zoo. We are going to the zoo! Anna has her money out at the entrance gate, ahead of me. She passed all the cars waiting, her bike now resting against her body, paying at the window the nineteen dollars apiece; she is yelling that it's her treat. The ticket guys know her and let her in the line without complaint; they're just glad she is at the zoo. It does not hurt to have her there. Some of the people in the lined-up cars are taking her photo, as they recognize her; others are getting out of their cars, walking up. She smiles at them, her entire face lighting up. She has no disguise; she is gorgeous, and it's not hard to tell who she is. She stands out, one of the celebrities they are all hoping to see. She signs some autographs. Her photo is taken many times as I hang back. She is still wearing the white shorts and the navy-blue shirt, now clinging to her; she looks like a super model from New York. I come up. No one can figure out who I am, sure not a famous actor. Many more are getting out of their cars, heading our way. The police and FBI have caught up, too. Anna waves at them, back on her bike, and off she goes, yelling at me to keep up.

I am thrilled, seeing all these people, the kids, and all the zoo animals. What a sight. The grounds are huge; we bike everywhere, riding on bike lanes, perfect as long as we don't run anyone down. I think this is a wonderful surprise, although our surveillance team must be miserable, yet now I see a lot of LA police bike officers here and there. They are certainly there because of us. I laugh, and Anna turns to the sound, looking at me. We are riding close to each other down a walking path, side by side.

She is smiling, "Henry, I think you are having a good time!"

"Yes, Miss Summers. This is wonderful, perfect. Let's eat the fruit we brought!" I see a table under those trees, over by the lion pavilion.

"How about there?"

We pull over. It's an appealing area, with several trees with a lot of shade and one wood picnic table, no one else close. I sit down at the table and enjoy a good view over the lion yard, close enough to see some of them sleeping or casually looking at us, sensing we are here. All of a sudden they are up, frantic, pacing back and forth, in panic, then growling, roaring, obviously upset, staring at us. Anna looks at them, startled, and then she gets a strange look on her face. She gasps and looks at me.

"Henry, I can hear their thoughts; yes, really, I hear the lions. I think they hear me, too. This is wild! Is it the telepathic thing? They're curious about me; no, they are terrified of you. They know I'm female and you are a male. They all like me, but they are all afraid of you, really afraid of you. If you look at them, they might really panic; they might try to climb over the fences! Henry, please, just reassure them you mean no harm. I think they know you're not like me. Maybe they sense you're an alien."

"Henry, how alien are you?"

"Anna, it's not me. They sense the *Cyclone*. I will soothe them."

They sense my presence, too, although I think it is the *Cyclone*'s presence that's creating the real terror. They feel the *Cyclone* through me. The biggest lion is really intense, an older male, roaring, fierce. I can smell his fear, and his courage is outstanding. I have to admire him, a true predator. We lock eyes, and I hear his thoughts, and I simply respond to him, projecting my thoughts. I tell him who I am and that I have no plans to hurt him or the other lions. He feels my admiration for him. I make him feel better about me, another visitor from a long distance away, not a threat. I want peace between us. I project a strong thought of calmness. He responds in kind. Finally he is lying down again, at peace. I see they are all relaxed again, following his lead.

"Anna, I just needed to respond to them, let them hear my thoughts. I don't scare them anymore. Maybe I did before. I know they sensed the *Cyclone*. Remember, the *Cyclone* is part of me, part of who I am; I cannot do anything about it. I'm sorry if I scared them and you."

Anna heard it all, including the thoughts of the lion, and she sees my sadness, feels my feeling of desolation. She comes to me, her hands to my face as she tenderly kisses my forehead. She whispers, "I understand, Henry. I am so sorry. I know you're trying your best to be a regular guy. I love you, Henry!"

The rest of the time at the zoo is great, although all the animals react strangely to me, forcing me to reassure them mentally. The birds all become agitated, as do the zebras, moving quickly from me, scattering in their areas. I am not able to soothe them quickly enough. The zoo staff notices the behavior of the animals and look at me strangely, although everyone is delighted to see Anna. Taking the spotlight off of me, she handles it all well; it's easy for her. She just knows what to say and makes everyone feel special. She has a good heart, and people feel it.

From then on she becomes an attraction at the zoo, as word spreads fast that she is there. The zoo staff are delighted she's there; she's like another exhibit. The LA police are everywhere, lots of them. The FBI guys are subtler, yet they're there, too. I provide security sometimes, mostly with a hard stare, and just when the crowd is surrounding us, pushing us too hard, always asking for autographs. To my amusement I am asked for my autograph. Thankfully Anna always stays close to me.

We take off for home, Anna riding the bike hard and fast, saying she needs to get home. It's time to get ready for New York City. She says she has a date with a big-time billionaire with a huge New York penthouse and a ride on his private jet for the trip there. She wants to look her best.

⇒⇥ ⇤⇐

We both have showered and are mostly dressed. The TV is on, showing the news; both of us half watch as we dress. Anna has been kind to me, as I have a closet now, just my stuff. I'm pulling out clothing when my cell phone rings. John Jacobs is on the line.

"Captain Johnson, I apologize. I'm having a family problem, still occurring right now. Actually it's more of a crisis. It might mess up our dinner plans. I wanted to warn you. And I thought you might be able to help me."

"John, please let me help you," I respond.

"Yes, please, I really need your help." Jacobs pauses, and then says in a worried tone, "My son and his date are missing. He was due home three hours ago, as was his date. It's a school night, and this was a study date. I do not feel good about this. He's never late. I've called the police, and they can do nothing at this point."

I say, "John, I can find him, and I'll bring both of them to your house. Then we can meet as we planned. I know where he is now." As I am hearing information about his location, provided by the *Cyclone*. "I'll pick him up."

John does not ask how I know, just tells me his son's name, Michael Jacobs, and what he looks like. I know exactly where he is, as the slip in his son's brain is a homing beacon telling the *Cyclone* where he is at this moment. I put slips in Jacobs and his entire family when I told him I would look out for him. These slips signal the *Cyclone* if any of them is in mortal danger, and the slips will also kill the threat. However, it has to be lethal and imminent.

Currently Michael and his date are at a diner on Highway 9, not too far from his high school, where he is a senior.

Anna heard the communication from Jacobs as she followed my telepathic thought process; most of the communication between us now is telepathic. We rarely talk to each other physically. The brain-to-brain thought transfer is so personal and clarifies messages so well, and the emotions are strong between us, making the intimacy feel good. We know each other's feelings without confusion, and they are always sincere. The mind meld has helped us, as our minds are in sync now, and each of us comprehends the love bond between us. We each have evolved in unexpected ways.

She says, "I am ready to go if we need to leave early. Is he in a lot of trouble?"

I look at her. "Anna, you are absolutely beautiful. That black dress is perfect!" I think it's some kind of soft velvet, and it complements her figure. I am wearing a sport coat. "You should know

I dressed up for you. And yes, Michael is in trouble, not sure how much. We need to leave. We need to take the *Saber*."

⟩+ +⟨

The *Saber* is above the diner, hovering, and I alert Anna there is a problem below. Apparently two large biker-gang guys have taken Michael's car keys away from him and are harassing him and his girlfriend, Natalie. Both are sitting in a booth, with the two drunken guys. The bikers also bought their own dinners with the money from Michael's wallet. Both Michael and Natalie are in tears. Both have been roughed up. The restaurant's employees have been more than intimidated; they're really frightened, trying to stay out of it, looking the other way, not wanting to get involved.

Anna says she's going with me as the *Saber* hovers above the field behind the diner. She is saying she might be able to help, try to keep it from turning ugly for the bad guys, no bloodshed. Anna is saying maybe reason could prevail. It's worth a try. We go down on power beams; she learns fast. She warns me to stay back and let her try to resolve this. We walk in and see all the other customers have left or run out, and the employees are hiding back in the kitchen.

The bikers look Anna over as she comes into the diner, and after a few seconds of looking at her, both of them are getting up from the booth, hollering and making a fuss about her good looks. They come toward her, saying they want to buy her dinner and party with her. They calm down quickly as I come up behind Anna. She is looking at the two high school kids sitting there in tears. Her anger is not calm or of a reasoning nature.

She tells the kids to get up as we are leaving. She is clearly angry.

The one big guy tells her to mind her own business. Anna maintains her ground, irate, calling them idiot bullies. She is totally disgusted by them. The first guy grabs at her, and she is fast, avoids his hand, backs up, and she then blasts him mentally, an extreme thought probe, just like a Taser bolt; so strong, it penetrates his mind; Anna is surprised, too, not realizing she could do such a thing. The slips in her head have reacted to her possible peril, attacked him, energized by the *Saber*. The biker jolts backward, like he touched an electrified fence, falling fast backward to the floor, hitting hard, now moaning, holding his head, tears running down his face caused from the intense pain, blood coming out his nose. So much for talking. The second guy is looking at her, then me, fear clearly on his face. Anna is backing away, shocked by her newfound skill, this telepathic bombardment capability. The second guy pulls the guy on the floor up and heads for the door, dragging him.

I walk out behind them, hold out my hand, firmly saying, "You forgot something. You owe the boy his money back."

There is fear in their eyes. They say nothing, then the guy standing pulls out his wallet, giving me all the cash he has on him. They both apologize, saying they were stupid and it will never happen again.

Out in the parking lot, an excited Natalie asks, "Are you Anna Summers? You look just like her. Why are you here? And thank you for saving us!"

Anna tells them Michael's father called us, and we are going to take them to meet him. She says she really is Anna Summers and hugs Natalie, who now is more than pleased.

We are all back on board the *Saber*. Anna and the kids are talking a mile a minute, the kids explaining what happened in riding the power beam to board the starship. We are moving fast, heading for the Jacobs's' home. Anna has already shown them the ship, telling them it's a new private corporate jet. The

Saber lands in a large park down the street from the Jacobs's' house, a really tight fit between the trees, a couple of trees pushed down. Fortunately it's raining, making it hard to see the starship.

The kids accept Anna's explanation of the ship without questioning. When home, they defend what they did, explaining all of it to John and Judy Jacobs, said they did nothing wrong except to be at the diner. They were studying together and ordered two soft drinks, and then the biker guys descended on them.

While we are at the Jacobs's' home, they thank us for helping the kids, and we say it was nothing. I say Anna did it all. Afterward, alone, she pokes me saying I forgot to mention something about one of her new skills. She says we need to talk, not now, yet later for sure.

Everyone loves the starship. We are back on the *Saber* and loaded up: John, Judy, and the rest of the kids as well as Natalie, after she called home for permission. Due to time constraints, the *Saber* takes us directly to New York City. The ship is on self-pilot, operating with perfection, totally camouflaged.

As we come in low over the city, it is late in the day, no rain, and a blue sky. The sun is starting to go down; the city is reflecting the light of the sunset, the light shimmering off of the skyscrapers, sparkling in the contrast of the darkening blue sky, the sun still a golden radiance on the horizon. We land at my building without issue, and no one knows we have come into New York, except my staff. They are lined up at the inside door of the roof garage as the hydraulic arms spread the roof out, each half totally opens, rising up like two angel wings. Then after the *Saber* lands, the extended roof sinks back down; the cover comes back over the *Saber*, a tight fit, yet covering it and hiding it from prying eyes. The staff is all smiles and greets us warmly. I rarely have guests. I had called ahead and the chef, Brett, has prepared several dishes. Everything is ready.

I have a fun time showing my guests the penthouse. With fifty thousand square feet of living space, it's quite a tour, although 30 percent is the living quarters for the staff and their families, which was not on the tour. The staff has use of the fun stuff, too. They can use the theater for movies; there's also a video-game room, an exercise room, a swimming pool, and much more.

Anna is smiling the whole time, acting overly impressed, giving me a hard time, kidding me about which room I use for my mistresses. She laughs about how the New York City nightlife is famous for handsome, single, rich, young playboys. She wants to know if she has use of it, as she might want to entertain guests when she's in New York. I laugh and give her the keys. She looks at me, surprised.

The Jacobs's are all impressed, and I tell John he can use it when he wants, if here in New York visiting. The kids love the movie theater and are delighted with the pool. There's a lot of luxury in one place. I tell them, in the past, I have used it only every ten years, maybe five or six times over the many years. They do not know what to say. The kids ask me how old I am. I laugh; tell them I'm much older than I look. They ask if they can use the video-game room before we have dinner. I show them what to do, giving them half an hour, then dinner. Anna and Judy sit down on a comfy couch outside the video-game room, in an adjoining side living room, one of many, allowing them to talk yet still be able to watch the kids. They are each served a glass of wine.

"Anna, I'm taking John to my library study, three doors down. Please excuse us, will not take long. We are also having a drink. We need to talk for a bit."

She smiles, waves me off, then laughs and exclaims, "Henry, try not to scare the hell out of him. This is a fun night, remember."

I shake my head, amused. "John, don't pay any attention to her."

We walk into the library, my favorite room. It is large, walls covered with books, dark mahogany paneling, leather chairs, side tables with brass lamps, a big dark-cherry desk on one side, a large mahogany conference table on the other end. Drinks are waiting for us—a beer for John, bourbon on the rocks for me. We sit on two leather chairs facing each other. We tip our glasses at each other, make eye contact, smile, and take a drink.

"John, I'm leaving Earth tomorrow, going back home, meeting with the Consortium. I want to finalize Earth's induction into the membership. I think I will be successful. I have some personal issues to resolve also. I have a proposal for you. It has been cleared by your president, a favor he is paying off to me, approved by all who need to be involved. It is top secret and confidential."

I pause. "I want you to go to work for me, become an employee of the Consortium. You will work for me yet keep your current job with the government, still in Section 58. You keep your pension, seniority, health insurance, everything. You will also have additional duties and responsibilities working for me; this is a new job—not that hard, about the same things you are doing anyway. Are you interested?"

John has a look of disbelief on his face, totally surprised. He takes another drink. "Do I have to give you an answer right away? And what exactly would I do?"

"Good questions. Yes, I am leaving, thus no time to wait, need to know tonight. Of course you can talk to Judy. This job is one you will like. You will be representing me while I am gone, responsible for documenting activities here and reporting to me with your evaluations. There is an office on the floor below us in this building. It will be yours. You will also be in charge of the building. You will have massive communications capability here, your own energy supply, access to drones, and total security. The building is a fort; no one else lives here except for my staff plus their families.

The staff will take care your needs, cook for you, clean, whatever you need. It is protected much more than it seems, as I built it, along with my drones, and has the same technology of the *Cyclone*. It has a security shield when needed, activated automatically, as when it is threatened, it deploys. The building also has weapons; defensive and assault. You have access to all data, every system in the world, classified or not. You will also be telepathic, able to read minds to some extent and communicate mentally with me. You will be programmed and enhanced mentally tonight. The building will communicate with you mentally as will the drones."

John looks frightened: his face is pale, blood pressure higher, and he is about ready to be sick.

"John, stop worrying. It's already done. You can hear me mentally right now. It does not hurt, and the enhancement package makes you smarter but changes nothing about you personally. You are the same person, yet may live a lot longer now. You were enhanced this minute; you did not feel it, and you will never be affected in a negative way."

Hearing John's thoughts, I respond telepathically, "First of all, call me Henry, and yes, I did have a lot of nerve. I regret if I offended you. It is necessary to keep you alive, as you have a lot of enemies, some new. Please forgive me. You are going forward with this because it is your free will; you would never turn this down. Your family will be helped, too. The pay is five hundred thousand dollars a year guaranteed for one hundred years, going to your family if you are dead. You should live longer now. Your salary will be increased yearly depending on inflation and performance. I have arranged for my law firm to contact you with the details and paperwork."

I speak out loud again, as John is freaking out with the telepathy. "John, the drones will guide you on the government stuff and reporting to me. The most important task is to guard Anna. I will not be here, might not be back for ten years. Anna will be upset with me, angry, hurt, and not able to think rationally about me. She is in a dangerous place. Knowing me and then not being on the starship makes a possibility of someone kidnapping her a very real threat. They would interrogate her to find out about me and starship technology. And I also have my enemies seeking revenge, try to use her to get to me."

"I asked the president for three favors, which he agreed to. You were one, the approval for working for me, and then protecting Anna is another. He has made you the coordinator of her protection, giving you unlimited resources. You have the Secret Service, NSA, FBI, CIA, and any military you need. You also have this building and the drones. However, the drones capability is limited if too far from this power source; thus, she needs to live here. The last favor is to give you and myself immunity from any legal prosecution. You are above the laws of this world. All the other countries will go along with this, as they have no other choice. They have no choice as they have no jurisdiction over the Consortium. Yet you still are subject to Consortium laws." I smile. "John, what say you?"

John is intently looking at me, his face flushed, a facial expression as if he just saw God. He slowly speaks. "I can't believe this is really happening. It is a shock. I never saw this coming. It is impossible to say no; I could never live with myself. Yes, I will take the job, and thank you! You are right on all of it. I would never turn this down; it is everything I have ever dreamed about. The money is also more than I ever dreamed about. You will not be disappointed. I will not let you down. I already love Anna, and protecting her is an honor and privilege."

I reply, "Excellent; you start tomorrow. Do you have questions?"

John responds quickly. "I have two questions. Will I ever have a chance of visiting your starship? And what are my chances of survival with this job? Please, an honest answer."

Answering, "As of now, since you are on the team, excellent. There are lots of things that will be put in place to protect you, yet you could be killed, although it will be hard to kill you. You have already been given an internal medical repair package that will help you stay alive; it is in your body right now, working fine. The same thing your daughter was given, everyone in your family has it now. While it's impossible to control all threats, it is up to you, and I have great confidence in you. You will have to make the right decisions. My law firm will help you sometimes. You have unlimited funds at your disposal; they will supply you. They will also sign you up as an employee and you technically work for them, receive their benefit package, which is a good one. Most of the time you will not hear from me, yet you can try, using the beacon transmitter on the building. Most of the time I will be too far away to respond. Of course the president has promised to give you resources."

John asks, "Henry, this is a personal question, but I hope I can ask you this: what is your relationship with Anna?"

I look at John. Then I look away. I can't help it—moisture comes to my eyes. I'm feeling the sadness.

"John, it's hard for me to talk to you about this. She is the love of my life; found her after all these years. I am not sure I'm good for her, and she is the last person I would want to hurt. I live a dangerous life, and my enemies are ruthless. They would do awful things to her because of me. My employer has made it clear I am needed, and I will never make a good family man. Retirement is probably not an option. Starships are not great places for children. She is better off without me. She has a wonderful life here if I have not screwed it up for her. She needs to find a better man than me. I am not sure I will be back soon, maybe not for a very long time. She does not deserve having to wait."

John's eyes now have tears as I have been talking. He says, "Henry, I know she loves you. It's obvious. Not to be the one to give you advice, yet it is clear to me. You must try to build a life for her. There is no going back."

"John, just protect her; now you understand why it is critical to me. I will try to bring you more resources. This planet is vulnerable, too. That is another reason I have to go. I want to bring in a fleet, maybe make this my base of operations. It's the only chance I have to make this work. I just don't know what will happen. This is new terrain for me, and I'm not sure what the Consortium will do."

"You start work tomorrow. Be here in the morning. The drones will teach you what you need to know. The staff knows you are coming, as does my law firm. Judy and the kids are welcome to move in here. Try to talk Anna into moving here; it's much safer. The drones can help you here, too, although they are worthless away from the building for any length of time. Otherwise, if Anna will not move, it will be tougher protecting her and you will be in California a lot. You can work whatever hours you want; please travel as needed. File expense reports, any cost is reimbursed. I just need results. Protect Anna."

⊨⟨⊦ ⊣⟩⊨

As they are sitting there watching the kids playing video games, Judy looks at Anna, smiles, then tenderly says, "You are so young. You are beautiful. I have followed your career, and you have incredible talent. You and Henry make a cute couple; you are good for each other."

Anna looks away, feeling sad, and her mind is somewhere else.

"Are you in love with Henry?" Judy asks.

Anna jerks her head up, changing focus, intently looking at Judy, making eye contact. She relaxes, smiles back. "Yes, I am. I'm worried; maybe *frantic* is a better word. He is leaving tomorrow, and I am not sure he is coming back, at least not soon. I miss him already. I have told him I will come with him. He is afraid I will ruin my life if I come with him. He says living on a starship is not pleasant. I am afraid, too. He might be right. I am like a moth drawn to a flame. All of this is overwhelming, as were the last ten days, way beyond description. Yet I feel like I have known him forever. I think we are destined to be together no matter what. I can rise to his needs, be a true partner, if he would just give me a chance."

Judy, alarmed, shakes her head, in a concerned voice, exclaims, "I am so sorry! I agree with you, both of you should be together. It fits. He needs you much more than he knows. The Lord works in mysterious ways."

"Judy, I know more about starships and aliens than I ever thought possible. I am in over my head, sort of like Lois Lane in the *Superman* movies. I have nothing to rely on in my past experiences to predict our future together, yet I absolutely know this is the right path. We have one chance. He must fight for us, or we will be ruined. If he doesn't, I will be heartbroken and furious. It is his one chance for happiness. He needs me. I don't care about his other responsibilities or the Consortium. I know I sound selfish and immature."

Judy sadly says, "Anna, I wish I could help. You sound like you know Henry well, something everyone on Earth would want to know. Either way, you could help Earth go forward in a transition to joining the Consortium. It is frightening to think what might happen to us, the aliens supervising us. They are so advanced; we must seem primitive. John is worried, as is everyone who knows about it. I know Henry has worries, too; he has those sorrowful eyes, like he carries huge fears and concerns. I think he's sad for you, too. I think he loves you. It does seem impossible for you to have a life together. I don't know what to say. I always pray when faced with an unbearable crisis. I will help you in any way I can; just call me, Anna. I will pray for you both."

They both look up as they hear me call them to dinner.

The dinner is terrific, with several kinds of dishes. They all are delicious. The wine is superb. Brett, the chef, is out in the dining room asking about it. I am really pleased with her. The dining room is formal and huge, with classical music playing in the background, and it is a nice evening for all. The kids ask Anna about being a movie star, and she jokes with them, making fun of herself. Everyone laughs. Then it ends, and we are back on the *Saber.*

We drop off John, Judy, and crew and head home to LA, back home by eleven-thirty. I park the *Saber* over the pool. Anna and I are in bed at twelve o'clock, watching one of Anna's films, her last one, the possible Academy Award winner. We eat popcorn and snuggle up together, nothing more. The film is great, and I love it. I cry at the end, causing Anna to cry, too. We laugh at each other and talk about John and Judy and their kids, then fall asleep in each other's arms.

At six o'clock in the morning, I am up and dressed; I am ready to go, with things to do before I leave Earth. Overnight, I know, as I heard the diesel engines, metal clanging, and all the noise outside, the military has arrived. The president is keeping his promise to me, providing protection for Anna. He has sent an entire battalion, now set up around Anna's estate, with streets blocked off, angry neighbors evacuated from their homes, tanks at all intersections, and troops and machine guns everywhere. The FBI, CIA, and NSA, Secret Service, plus the local police, are all here. Helicopters are coming and going, serious-looking military Apaches armed with missiles. They know the *Saber* is here and are keeping their distance. An aircraft carrier will be stationed off the coast when we are gone.

It is dark. Anna is still sleeping, exhausted. I leave a note for her, telling her not to waste her life on me, not to be optimistic about what I will be able to do about Gabriel and the Consortium. With me she always will be a target. She will do better without me. I write that I will see her later today, on the way out, to say good-bye in person; I will see her and her mother and sister at brunch. *I will find you.* I slowly sign it, "With all my love, always, Henry."

The *Saber* growls as it is starting up. Then it is rising slowly, wind rushing everywhere, the burners heating up as it rises in altitude like a helicopter, hovering, gaining speed, then leveling at four thousand feet, slowly rotating, holding at this altitude. I look down at Anna's home, wondering if Anna is up, reading my awful note. I see the army tanks now in position around the perimeter, and then looking out over LA, with the ocean view, missing this life already, feeling a hole in my stomach, the ache for Anna, and loneliness. My feeling of bleakness and desolation is unbearable. I know I will never be the same and, worse, that Anna will feel the same despair.

The *Cyclone*, although many miles away, also feels my emotions: my anguish, hopelessness, and desperation. The *Cyclone* thinks this problem was foreseeable and truly sad. The *Saber* has the destination interception point calculated from the current location. The *Cyclone* is now orbiting ninety miles up, fifteen thousand miles away, moving at thirty thousand miles an hour. It is waiting for me and preparing for the long trip home. My arrival back on board is due in about one hour.

The *Saber* rises quickly, on the move, the burners hot. I signal, and then there's the roar and thunder as it blasts off, heading for New York City. There is no time to waste.

CHAPTER 35

TAKING CARE OF BUSINESS—LAW FIRM MEETING—FAREWELL TO ANNA IN LA AT CAFÉ

I am heading for New York City. The time zone there helps, as I will be there close to 5:00 a.m., still dark.

I know I need to take care of Luca and his son Anthony, two dangerous people, guilty of horrific crimes. I will kill them both for their crimes against the United States, for Sam Jordan's death, and because of the danger they pose to Anna's life. If all goes well, she will never know how Sam Jordan died; Luca tortured him before he killed him. Luca wanted to know who Sam had talked to and how much he talked about Luca. Anthony finally killed Sam, after terrific suffering, death ending his misery. It was gruesome.

I think grimly, *And it will be just as bad for Luca. If Anthony is found, he will also get what he has earned. Both of them will find their ends in a gruesome justice, well deserved.*

The *Saber* is hovering six thousand feet over Luca's estate in New Jersey, not far from New York City. He has elaborate security: cameras, dogs, guards, electric fences, motion detectors, and infrared detectors. Yet nothing will defeat several cell-size killer drones, three deadly slips, as they enter his bedroom. Luca sleeps alone tonight, his mistress gone and his wife long ago dismissed from his bedroom. The slips enter his brain through his nose, taking over his motor functions yet leaving his frontal lobes alone so he will know what's going on.

Luca wakes, tries to talk but can't, nor can he move. The slips move about in his brain, copying memories as needed, the probes causing a great deal of pain. Then he slowly rises from bed, prompted by the drone that has assumed his motor functions. He has no control and tries to fight it, desperation in his eyes. The terror is overwhelming, and he vomits down his chest, not able to bend over, his head looking directly ahead, the vomit running down his chin, and then he pisses in his pants. His eyes are wild as he turns on a light, his hand not his, then with no control over his legs, he slowly walks over to the dresser and opens a drawer. He fights it, the terror in his eyes, yet he pulls out his Glock, his semiautomatic handgun, a large-caliber pistol, kept loaded, looking more like a cannon. He can't gain control of his functions as he is forced to slowly walk out of the room, holding the gun tightly, with jerking movements, trying to fight it, going down the stairs and out the back door. He stops at the pool, looking down, chambers a round, then slowly putting the end of the gun barrel into his mouth, his eyes wide, tears streaming down his face, trying to scream, yet no sound leaves his lips. He waits, looking down the barrel. Then, after a few more agonizing seconds, a loud explosion instantaneously after his finger pulls the trigger. The drones have already vanished, and his brain splatters over the concrete as he falls into the pool. The security cameras pick up the whole thing, making it easy for the coroner to sign the death certificate, cause of death: suicide.

Unfortunately Anthony is gone, not in the United States anyway. Maybe John Jacobs can find him another day.

The *Saber* lights up, burners thrusting, heading for the hook-up with the *Cyclone*, now close, only five hundred miles away. There is one more visit in New York, and the *Cyclone* will work well for that event.

—⟨+⟩—

It is 6:00 a.m. It is time. I need to visit Mr. George Beagle, the oldest law partner at ninety-two years old, yet younger than me. I know him from the first day I hired the firm. He will have his son there, too, Mark Beagle. All the rest are gone, dead or retired. I need to talk to him, go over Anna's new role in my trust; and John Jacobs's new position. I need to meet some of the junior partners, although I have met some of them through the years. One in particular needs a reminder about confidentiality, as he was the FBI leak. I will meet all of them on the roof of their office building; pick them up there for a ride in the *Cyclone*. I smile and think, *It will be exciting for them.*

I have a 7:00 a.m. appointment with the entire firm, all the partners. They are all fearful; I did not tell them the purpose of the meeting. George knows about the leak, as do all the partners. They know who it is. They are not sure what is going to happen to him, not sure about themselves, either. They are all on the roof of the building, eight partners, thinking this is bizarre, wondering about their wills, if their wives will miss them. Why did I ask them to meet me at seven o'clock on the roof? Will I throw them all off the roof or hopefully just the guy who fed the FBI information about me? Nobody talks as they wait for me to arrive. They are watching the sun come up, a wonderful thing normally.

Of course the FBI is claiming they know nothing about me and that they never asked the law firm for information. The partners are on their own. And by the way, they told the firm the president has given me total immunity for whatever I do, including what I might do to the partners.

By now the partners have a good idea who I am, *an alien*. They always suspected it, and since I am from another world it is terrifying to think about what I might do to them. Breaking their confidentiality about me after all these years was silly; I am their best client, one who has paid well and whom they knew to be scary. They know I have been busy in the last ten days; they read the papers, figured it out.

Suddenly the wind kicks up. Even on a twenty-story building, a gusting wind is a concern. Then a thunderous, hot jet engine blasts right over their heads, and they feel the heated air blowing down on them. Trying to hang on, they are all swept up into the air, all screaming out, asking to be forgiven, please, they're so sorry. They are suspended in the air by some force, and then they are thrust into some kind of massive opening, yet landing on their feet, a large hangar door closing behind them. It's hard to see, and it's silent, but they can tell they're in a huge hanger. Their worst fear has come true: it really is an alien starship. It is miles long, as they saw a brief glimpse of it when flying up into the ship, two hundred feet up. Now it is mostly dark. They are in some kind of enormous hangar, like a runway, just a little light coming from the far end. They are all speechless, stunned by the surreal impossibility of all of it.

I come out of nowhere. The light becomes brighter in the hangar, still a reddish dim, yet I am visible. They are all shocked, as I am young, even more than usual. I am not more than thirty, yet they know George has known me for almost sixty years. They all wonder if I am immortal. Now that they know for sure I am an alien, anything is possible.

I laugh. "It's OK. You all look like you have seen a ghost. You don't need to be afraid. It's good to see you. You will be fine, just wanted to give you a starship ride. It is not easy to board a starship; power beams are the safest way. Since you have been my trusted law firm for so many years, I thought you were due for a little excitement. Consider it a bonus. We also need to get to know one another better."

"Please follow me. Hold on, as we will lose gravity soon. Use the handholds. We're going up to the captain's bridge, where you will see us circle the moon and slingshot back at five hundred thousand miles an hour. You are aboard the Consortium starship the *Cyclone*. You will be back in your offices in about two hours—plenty of time for us to talk business."

After we are all strapped down into the big seats on the bridge, plasma screens light up, and the world around us is all visible. The Earth is there in all its majesty, shining in the sun's benevolence. The *Cyclone* is already accelerating through the upper atmosphere, two hundred miles from Earth, moving fast, hitting one hundred thousand miles an hour in the next three minutes. The Earth quickly becomes small as the *Cyclone* heads toward the moon. The attorneys are spellbound, still unnerved, emotions high, astounded by the experience.

I say, "You are welcome to watch the voyage. I will do all the talking for now." Looking at them, I see they all are watching me, a lot of anxiety in their facial expressions.

"First order of business is the FBI leak by Mike Sanderson. Mike, you need to talk. Give me your reasons, why you did what you did. Be clear. Be totally honest. Your partners need to know, too."

Mike Sanderson is terrified of being called out and can hardly talk. Finally, in a quivering, breaking voice, he says, "Mr. Johnson, please, I am so sorry. It was intimidation by the FBI. They told me it was national security, said I could go to jail on conspiracy charges. I told no one, none of my partners, as I did not want them to be in the same fix. It was bad enough for me. Please punish me only; I am the only one guilty. I should have told you.

It was a breach of my legal duty to you. For what it's worth, I have children and a wife. I am so sorry. I beg your forgiveness!"

"Mike, no problem. You are fine. Nothing is going to happen to you. Don't do it again, though! Stay firm no matter who pressures you. You have access to me; use the laser beacon if necessary. You have John Jacobs, too; he is now an employee, as was discussed by Mr. Beagle previously. He represents me, and he has resources you do not have. He can bring you some government help, too. That's it. George and I need to talk. Thanks for your honesty. George, and Mark, too, please come with me."

Mark easily moves along, as he is much younger, grabbing handholds. George also pulls himself along and is having issues because of the lack of gravity; I reach out and pull him along. We are in my cabin quickly.

I begin, "George, Mark, you have seen me with Anna Summers in the newspapers?

Mark smiles. George nods his head, intently looking at me, saying, "I have prepared a will and a power of attorney to be signed by you. Per your instructions she will own half of the fund now, then all of it upon your death."

I say, "You will be contacted at the time of my death. The power of attorney gives her control of the trust in the event of my death. She will be treated as my wife, with every consideration and respect to be given to her. George, you, too, Mark, I want you to know, the president of the United States has guaranteed her safety and will provide protection. John Jacobs will also be in charge of those resources. So you know if anything happens to her, for example, if she is kidnapped, no matter who is involved, the guilty will suffer a thousand deaths; they need to know. Nothing will stop me. Please, I want you to keep tabs on her. Anna will not be high on me, as I am leaving Earth. Mark, you are younger. Please go see her; get the paperwork done. I will eventually be back, although it could be years from now. Can you do this for me?"

Mark responds, "Mr. Johnson, I will do whatever is needed. Do you have to go, to leave Earth?"

"Yes. I am concerned about threats from outside this planet. I have to be proactive, prevent the possibility."

George raises his eyebrows, a frightened look. "Yes, I understand. I'm sorry. Should we be afraid?"

I respond, "You should be fine, not to worry, at least not today." I smile.

The attorneys are delivered back to their rooftop, all excited, all thankful they survived, grateful to be living. They thank me, promise complete loyalty, saying they will serve me in any way needed. There will never be any issues coming from them ever. After I am gone, they call their worried wives to let them know they will be home for dinner, and to tell the kids they love them.

⊨⊣⊢⊨

The *Cyclone* is heading for Los Angeles. It is about ten o'clock in the morning there. The slips act as homing beacons helping in finding Anna, who is picking up her mother and Nikki from the airport and heading into LA. Anna has told them I will probably join them for lunch; I want to say good-bye. Anna has never told her mother about me, about the alien thing. She has no clue, and Anna hopes to leave it that way. She has also not told her mother that her period is five days late. She is shaken; she is never late. Could it happen that fast? Could it be possible? Talk about complications.

They are at the best restaurant in LA on a street off Rodeo Drive, a very fancy outdoor café with many tables, all with uniformed waiters, white gloves, and good manners. Hollywood stars routinely come here. There are large green umbrellas covering the tables on a big patio and a grassy area in front of a patio, twenty yards from the street, with white fencing, there to keep the tourists from bothering the guests. Then there is the sidewalk with lots of people. Some are waiting in line to come in to eat. The street is wide, six lanes across, divided in the middle. There is a park with a lake next to the restaurant. It is a gorgeous day, blue skies and not too hot, just right.

Anna is given a table immediately, as everyone knows who she is, and it helps business to have her there. The meal is not charged, either, as restaurants are always grateful when she is there. She is treated as a prized celebrity. The other patrons are taking photos of Anna, and she signs autographs with a smile. Her mother and sister are more than proud, both beaming.

They settle in at their table, order food, and drink and chat. Nothing has been heard regarding the whereabouts of Sam Jordan. Anna's mother is fearful, tells Anna she knows about his dealing with the Mafia. Anna talks about the security around her house—military tanks, troops, police, FBI—and how the neighbors are all mad at her. TV cameras and reporters are everywhere, asking about Henry, who is he, and is he the reason for the military security guards? She says it is crazy. Even now there are troops out on this street, here, sitting in armed jeeps. Police have surrounded the restaurant. Secret Service guys are within twenty feet of their table, sitting at another table, watching.

Anna tells her mother that I am more than I seem and that she will explain more when they have some time. It could get real complicated. Nikki tells their mother she knows about me, and it's better not to know.

Anna's mother raises her eyebrows. "Is there anything else I should not know?"

Anna responds, "Mom, this is not the right place to talk about it. I promise, you will hear all about it when we get home. There is the possibility Henry will be here to join us; he mentioned it would be about this time, about ten o'clock or so. He has a lot to do before he leaves, and I am not sure he will be here."

Her mother replies, "I like Henry, and if he said he was coming he will be here. I don't understand his leaving. Where is he going? You two are perfect for each other."

Anna looks at her mother, tears starting to come to her eyes. She says, "Mom, let's not talk about it now. You have no idea how complicated it is. Let's just enjoy the day."

They eat, and it is excellent. Nikki and her mom have glasses of wine, then second glasses of wine. Anna does not drink wine today, having coffee, just in case. They laugh about things they did when they were little girls, her mother laughing, too.

Anna keeps looking around, wondering about me. Not to see me to say good-bye would be tough. On the other hand, this could really be awkward, with all these people, the security guys, reporters, and TV cameras following her around. What will I do? The *Cyclone* is massive. These people have no idea. She is thinking, *Please, please, Henry, sneak in the back door. No starships descending from the heavens.*

All of a sudden, an enormous dark shadow starts to darken the restaurant, looking like a storm coming in, and everyone looks up, shocked to see the blue sky blocked up high; something big is up there, and then the place is starting to pulsate; the ground is vibrating like there's a minor earthquake. The whole neighborhood is being shadowed now, the sun blocked from view for several miles. The winds are picking up, even gusting, the umbrellas start rocking, dust blowing up; a blasting, thunderous noise is coming from above, small dust tornadoes spinning here and there. The ground is vibrating more. Her hair and light summer dress is blowing with the wind. She can feel me mentally and the *Cyclone*. She knows we are coming. She can see the bottom of the huge starship descending, maybe three or four miles up from them, no question, right over them, straight up.

Everybody at the restaurant and beyond it, is out in the streets; they are looking up, seeing this massive thing straight up overhead. Shocked and dumbfounded, no one is sure what to do, everyone astounded at the size of this obvious alien starship, coming right down on top of them. Everyone is thinking, *This is way too weird, can't be happening; yet this is Hollywood, right?* Then, all of a sudden, they comprehend this is real; in a second all are running, grabbing their things; flight is critical, everyone going in different directions as fast as they can, screaming for dear life.

Anna shouts to her mother and Nikki, "Damn! Wait here! Henry is here, and the *Cyclone* is coming down on top of us."

So much for sneaking in. Looking up, she says, "Thanks, Henry!"

Anna is abruptly up, her chair falling over, her shoes off, and she is running out to a flat grassy park area, fifty yards to the side of the restaurant. Looking up again, she sees the *Cyclone* much lower, still descending, and it looks twenty times the size of an aircraft carrier. She mentally tells me not to come lower.

The *Cyclone* suddenly stops. It is about four hundred feet up now, really low, easy to see how gigantic it is, and the real thing, an intergalactic starship. Thankfully it has stopped; the noise subsides, and the wind gusts slow down. The ship is slowly hovering, staying at that altitude; the only sound is the buzz of massive static electricity sparking off the hull, like small bolts of lightning. The ship is vast, looking like it is miles long. To see an alien starship this close is terrifying for most people. It is also shaded under the starship, dark, as the ship is blocking the sun. There are police helicopters and army helicopters circling the starship, yet keeping a safe distance, looking like small insects buzzing here and there.

Anna looks around, seeing the restaurant has cleared out; the streets are empty. Everyone still running away. She thinks, *The damn reporters are still here, though, along with the TV cameras, and of course the security people are gathered around, protecting me. You have to admire their courage.*

She waves to the security people, feeling grateful, yelling, "You're heroes to stand here with me. I'm OK though; the starship is friendly. There is no threat. It would be better for you to back away. I have a visitor from the ship; a good friend is coming to see me in about ten seconds."

Anna's mother and sister now run up and stand next to her. Both are scared, yet they are not about to leave her. Nikki says, "We are in this together." Anna tells them it is Henry—he's here—and not to worry. She looks at her mother and says, "Mother, keep an open mind. I should have told you, Henry is not exactly from this planet."

⊷⊶

Anna is amazed again; she is thinking Henry never ceases to surprise her. He did say he would see her before he left although this is a little much, a tad too dramatic. She is looking at the *Cyclone*'s underside, and it is astonishing. It is so long—miles long; the silver metal is perfect, not a blemish, and the starship is so mammoth. The vision of seeing the *Cyclone* this close is just astounding.

All of a sudden, there are bright lights everywhere, many powerful beams shining in the shadow of the starship. Torches of massive lights are streaming down like mighty sun streams, sizzling with heat, and all coming from the *Cyclone*.

All of a sudden, Henry is there, like a wizard, just appearing, now hovering two or three feet off the ground. Anna knows he rode a power beam down. She knows it is Henry because she can feel him, although he does not look like her Henry. He looks like an alien warrior, a knight. He has on an armored suit, with steel shoulder pads and the rest a smooth, silky stainless-steel mesh, like a thin, light cloth mesh, yet metal, threaded with sparkling gold and silver. All of it is covered with thin, flexible metal straps, bigger ones at the joints, expanding and flowing with his movement, acting like muscles, giving more power plus a glide with his momentum, like a lion striding.

His sealed helmet is made of an exotic metal, with silver- and gold-embedded streaks, and across the front of the helmet there is a horizontal red-lighted slit, for the eyes to look out, and a dark cover pulled down over the front, made from a dark-silver glass. The glass hides Henry's eyes, and there is a red infrared light beaming out of the slit, looking like torches. The overall look is scary yet awesome. Henry looks about nine feet tall as he is walking on air, three or four feet off the surface, striding toward her with no gravity. His boots are almost to his knees.

Anna is thinking he looks really great, not that she's much of an expert in military fashion. She thinks Henry would be a super leading man in her next movie. She sees there are more Henrys everywhere, his security troops, looking like Henry but with no gold and silver on their suits or helmets. They are each armed with a gun locked into each right arm, extended over a gloved hand, pointed out. All of them, including Henry, have several fast-spinning, bright-lighted gold basketball-size halos encircling their heads a few feet up, glowing and slowly orbiting around them. It is astonishing to see, hypnotic to look at them.

She is thinking, no doubt about it, *Henry is a magnificent warrior.*"

I hear Anna's thoughts, and now I'm about ten feet from Anna. I stop; hover, then my feet lower. I am on the ground. I just look at her, stand there admiring her, knowing it might be my last chance to see her and to talk to her.

My voice sounds weird through the sealed helmet, amplified, thus a little too loud, saying, "Hello, Anna; I'm sorry I'm late, never enough time."

She says, "You look good in your warrior armor, it suits you, and the hovering is impressive. I am not too high on your voice."

I plead, "Anna, I know you are mad at me. I understand, and it is my fault. Please forgive me for any pain I have caused you." I'm now in telepathic mode, no one needs to know what I am saying to Anna. It looks like we are staring at each other.

Continuing, I say, "I'm sorry as I know I left early. I had a couple of critical jobs to do. I did want to talk to you. I am also sorry, as I cannot get closer to you. The halos are really security shields, and they are activated when we are on the surface of any planet. They can be deadly if you are within four feet of me. I am forced to wear them off ship, as it is one of my rules for all troops on duty, and I have to set an example."

"Yes, I see you are back on the job again," Anna responds out loud.

Looking at Anna's mother and sister, I say aloud to them, my voice sounding eerie coming through the helmet, "I am sorry we did not have more time together. I wish you both good lives, and I am delighted to have known you."

Anna's mother is speechless and looks like she is going to faint.

Nikki laughs and says, "Henry, you would make a great brother-in-law. Come back, and good luck to you!"

I look at Anna, mentally projecting to her. "I do not have much time; it is a long trip, and I need to head out. There is much to do. I want to give you something. It is a locket on a chain, not much to look at yet very valuable. It will protect you or help to guard you. I want you to wear it always." I extend my hand; a light-gold locket appears, and then travels across the space between us as if on some invisible power beam. She reaches out and takes it.

She projects back, "Henry, I'm not sure I want any protection from you. Your note made it clear you were ending our relationship. I am furious with you. You have no right to think for me. I want you to fight for us, not only for my happiness and our children's but for yours, too. Think about it. This may be your only chance at happiness. Choosing a miserable life of loneliness is not my choice but yours. I love you! I cannot stand the idea of you being alone, without me. You are a fool if you choose this."

I speak mentally. "Anna, I do not choose this. I am trapped. I am military, part of something bigger than me. There are severe repercussions for others if I am not there to protect them, maybe terrible hardships for others. Many beings depend on me. I have a duty greater than myself. You love me for who I am; you know who I am, have known from the beginning. I am sorry. For your sake don't count on me. The *Cyclone* ran the probabilities, and I would cause you much hardship if we were a couple. If I left the Consortium, we would be dead within six months due to one of my enemies striking us. For you, living on a starship would be misery, your mind and health broken within two years. Your survival on an alien world would not be good either. You would hate it, and it would be misery for our children. I never should have done this, causing all this pain."

Anna is crying, tears rolling down her face, angry. She yells loudly, "Henry, you be here January 12, at the Academy Awards, at eight o'clock. I will leave a pass for you at the box office window; you will have a seat next to me, as my date. If you are not there, I will know you have chosen a different kind of life, not with me."

In a loud, eerie voice, deeper than before, using words, I say, "Anna, please put the locket on; never take it off. I will do my best. I have to go." Hovering up, gliding away slowly, I intently look at her for a few seconds, then I salute her, saying loudly, "Calabra!"

Anna hesitates, pauses, finally smiles, pauses again, then in a sad, loving voice, loudly cries out, "Yes, Henry, Calabra to you, too!"

I can only stare at her, feel her heartbreak, feel my own sadness, force myself to turn away.

Then I finally look around, slowly turning each way, taking it all in, unbelievable! I can't believe what I am seeing.

I am looking out at an enormous crowd of people standing maybe only sixty feet back, maybe closer, and many, many people behind them, lined up as far away as several football fields or much more, thousands all staring back at me. Cars are everywhere, more people pouring in from surrounding neighborhoods, some running, all crowding one another, all trying to get a good look. Then there are TV cameras and more, all kinds of cameras, plus reporters, police, firemen, priests, soldiers, then old men, plus young men and women, children, all ages, people, all humans, all wide-eyed, everyone videoing with their smartphones; even the police are taking selfies. My troops are holding them back.

I realize no one is afraid; they are smiling, excited, maybe thrilled; yes, they are delighted, just glad to be here, to see this!

I am surprised, can only imagine what they all must be thinking. I then comprehend.

They think this is history in the making, and probably millions will watch this event on TV tonight. This moment in time will be recorded as the first contact with aliens, seeing a real starship, a real alien contact made with Earth people, those that were here today. It is documented by thousands, thus real evidence. They were here to be part of it and to see it.

I laugh out-loud; thinking it probably will make some kind of Twitter record, too. I hover upward about ten feet, rotating slowly, then rising more, looking out at everyone. I laugh again and slowly wave, shouting out to them loudly, "Calabra!"

I look at Anna one last time, pause, then I'm gone.

As it ends up, the entire planet, almost every single person, will eventually see their first alien, me, my troops, and my massive alien starship, as the video is played over and over, across the world. Millions will be astonished by this first real contact with an alien being, this vast starship, the soldiers, and his weird voice. "Of all things," the news anchors will say, "it looks like he is a fan of Anna Summers. She invited him to go to the Academy Awards as her date. Everyone heard it. No one could invent that story. He will be back...maybe."

My troopers and I disappear as quickly as we appeared. Within seconds the ground shakes again. The massive starship almost immediately starts to climb, heading due east; the dark shadow disappears. There are strong winds and dust spiraling everywhere, little tornadoes spinning off the ground, with clouds of dust forming, static electricity like lightning sparking off the hull. The ship is climbing up to fifteen thousand feet, then the thunderous sound of massive rockets starting, with the hot thrusting fire streams surging west, then the roar rushing out for miles in all directions as the starship blasts east, climbing faster and faster. Finally, at ninety thousand feet there is a massive explosion as the burners blast out more, and a huge fiery tail thrusts out for miles as the *Cyclone* surges up into the heavens, disappearing. It is gone that quickly. Within several hours I am a trillion miles away, still gaining speed.

CHAPTER 36

ANNA WITHOUT HENRY

I watch as Henry and the *Cyclone* are leaving, and surprised, as I think I hear the *Cyclone* mentally saying good-bye to me, and I feel a strong wave of emotion, the projection is a feeling of great kindness coming from it, then I feel the *Cyclone*'s great sadness, and then I know for sure the *Cyclone* is saying good-bye to me, actually missing me, feeling a tender affectionate concern for me. Plus, the *Cyclone*'s admiration for me is there, praising me, even proud of me. Finally a feel a farewell salute, wishing me the best. Also, strange enough, I feel encouragement, a nurturing feeling that makes me happy. I know for sure it is the *Cyclone*, and I wish the same for it, also sending my love back. I thank the starship and ask that Henry be protected, knowing how important their relationship is to each other and my love for both of them.

I look around, thousands of people are still here, many of them staring at me. The news people are here, too, trying to cover the story. They want to interview me, calling out questions. The security people stand guard, holding them off. The military has started to ask people to go home, saying the show is over.

I think the best thing to do now is to go home as fast as possible and hide out. The newspapers will go nuts with this. Everyone in the world knows about Henry now, or they think he is the alien in an armored suit and visiting me. How special. Brother! The tabloids will have a lot of fun with this, my new alien boyfriend. Does he have a day job? Does he have a penis? Does he eat food? Why does the government protect me?

I look around to find my mother and Nikki, seeing them both, and they are in a daze, both speechless, which is saying something. Of course, they have not seen the *Cyclone* before. The sheer size of it shakes you up, then close up and personal is humbling. Naturally I am an old-pro starship princess, knowing everything. Time to go home; I grab their hands and walk for the car. The security people follow, although they have new respect for me, I can tell. The crowd that is still here just parts for me, looking at me in awe. Crazy world!

As we travel home I can't help but think how bad this could get. The news people will be awful, and they will be everywhere I go.

I think, *how do I handle being pregnant?* I can only pray I am not with child. Imagine the awful questions. Did the alien get you pregnant? Yes, if I am pregnant it will get really scary. I will be accused of having the evil seed, spawning a devil child. Maybe it is good to have the security and Henry's locket. I'm wearing the locket now. It makes me feel good to have something from Henry. Even if I never see him again, I still have the locket, and I might have much more. The appointment with her doctor tomorrow will settle the question. I will take a pregnancy test. I never miss my period; it is never late. Why was I so careless? Who can I tell? My mother, yes, and my sister. Who else can I trust? I feel the fear in my stomach.

Henry, where are you when I need you?

As I return home with my mother and sister in tow, there are at least ten police and military vehicles escorting us. The neighborhood is a war zone. There are guardhouses and barbwire fences everywhere, checkpoints at every corner. The neighbors have been moved out and paid off. Their houses are now full of troops and security staff. They are from everywhere: FBI, Section 58, CIA, Secret Service, Homeland Security, state police, local police, Interpol; even Scotland Yard is there. There are TV network trucks, camera trucks, satellite feed trucks, foreign country networks trucks, and reporters. The whole world is camped out next to my house. There must be three thousand people around my house. The tanks and missile-launch equipment are over-the-top frightening. My mother is completely freaked out. Nikki is laughing, thinks it is great. My home looks more and more like a fortified prison.

It is decided my mother will move in with me, at least until Sam turns up. He may be hiding out from the FBI. The FBI wants him for questioning; something is up, something not good. Nikki is also staying with me until the end of July, maybe a little later, until the end of her summer break. They laugh together. The hell with it all, I say. Let's go swimming in the pool!

⟞⟝ ⟞⟝

I'm in the doctor's office, which was cleared out before I was allowed to go in. Of course there is no privacy; female Secret Service agents are in the office with me. Everyone knows about the upcoming pregnancy test. How embarrassing. Mother is pleased, crazily enough, when it tests positive. Yes, I am pregnant. Knocked up! It is very early, I am reminded, and it might not make it past the next two months, but I know in my heart I will have this baby. It's destiny.

Nikki is delighted, says I need to let Henry know what has happened. How do I call him? Would it make any difference?

Lord, it is really complicated now. Days pass; I am sick in the mornings. The Secret Service is most protective; they even call the president regularly; I overhear them. The president must have gotten excited about the whole thing, as there is a Secret Service detail inside the house now. The baby and I will have guards twenty-four hours a day, meaning lots of issues for me. There will be no media coverage of the pregnancy; people will go to jail if anything gets out. An aircraft carrier is currently in the harbor, stationed outside of LA, now with an additional purpose, to house prisoners. The fighter jets might come in handy, too. The baby news is top secret, classified, at least until I start to show. No one is sure of the political ramifications. No one wants to face Henry if anything were to happen to me. They say, "Technically, this could be a baby of an alien civilization."

Oh brother—I think—*give me a break!*

Mother comes into my bedroom every evening, even several days after the doctor's visit. She sits down with me, right next to me on my bed, as I am finding it impossible to sleep at night. She strokes my hair, holds my hand. We talk about everything, mostly Henry, and I tell her our story from the beginning. She listens intently, and I feel like her little girl again.

Mother not only listens, she cries and asks questions. Sometimes she laughs; she has fear in her eyes, too. She tells me about when I was born, how proud she was, and that I was a beautiful baby. Her eyes light up, and she tells me her best memories of us together.

Finally, one night, she asks, "Anna, do you love Henry?"

I look at her for a long time, and then I respond with a smile, "Even though we had a very short time together, I do love him. I think of him constantly; he is part of me. I include him in my day, every day, thinking about how he would think about this or that. I say a prayer for him every day. He is the father of our child." Tears come to my eyes. "Mom, I know what you're thinking, and I am frightened, too. Is the baby normal? Will I be able to take care of a child, especially Henry's child? Will the government take my baby? Will some alien civilization take my child? Will the baby look like a human? Will schools accept our child? Will other kids be his or her friends?"

Mother tenderly reaches out to me. "Anna, Anna, this child is your child, and you are wonderful. Your child will be wonderful, too. Don't worry about any of this. I will be here for you, as will your sister. I like Henry, and I think he will do all he can do to be here for you. Do not worry; many people want to protect you. Many people love you, including me."

I fall asleep. For the first time in a long time, I really sleep.

After a couple of days, amazingly enough, coincident with the pregnancy, Henry's law firm wants to visit. They have to talk to me about a financial gift to me from Henry and about his will. A Mr. Beagle and his son, Mark, are coming to visit; they will fly in tomorrow. The Secret Service approved the visit; they know all about the law firm.

Mr. Beagle is quite formal, extremely courteous, says he has known Henry a long time. He is wearing a three-piece suit and must be in his late eighties, of an older generation; he is impressive, seems really smart. His son is the same, also charming. Mother likes them both and keeps smiling at the older Mr. Beagle.

His son is my age or maybe a little older. He is also formal, professional, an attorney who takes clients seriously. Both of them seem smart, with a lot of expertise. They respect Henry, to say the least; they are maybe even in awe of him. People are always unnerved by Henry, so no surprise there.

Mr. Beagle's son, Mark Beagle, says, "Miss Summers, you are significant to our firm as you and Henry are our largest client. My father and I want to make you happy with our services. Please, we want to be of use to you. Henry said any problem you have we are to spend whatever time is needed to help you. Actually, he said to treat you as if you were his wife. I have a copy of his will for you. You are the sole beneficiary. He also has indicated we are to add your name on an account set up for him at National Bank, and all his other banks, which makes you half owner. Some of it can be transferred to your local bank if you wish. You have his power of attorney. You are a primary client for us thus we are ready for your needs twenty-four hours a day and seven days a week. Most of his money is invested, yet there are a massive amount of liquid, or cash, deposits. We handle all of it, and we take our responsibilities seriously; we have done so for years. There is about a hundred million in cash deposits."

"Mr. Beagle, wow, that is a lot," I say. "Now, I really am curious, how much is the estate worth?

He coughs, hesitates, looks around, and then exclaims, "The stock market investments are over three billion dollars!"

Mother almost faints. Nikki gasps, then yells, "Thank you, Henry!"

"Lord, Mr. Beagle, are you sure?" I respond.

"Please call me, Mark. Yes, it grows quickly, and it is definitely over three billion. There are also the real estate and gold investments."

"Mr. Beagle, or Mark, if I can ask, how much is the rest of the estate worth—with the real estate, all of it—the total as of now?"

"Nine billion give or take a few million. You could be one of the richest women in the world."

Anna's mother and Nikki are shocked, yet Nikki recovers fast, laughs, exclaiming to Anna, "You go, girl!"

I looks away, my eyes wide, tearful, then I feel full of anger. I whisper to myself, "Henry, Henry, you are so wealthy, just as you said. I said I never wanted your money. I want you for my soul mate. Don't be stupid! You can't pay me off. Please come back to me."

I hear the older Mr. Beagle talking, and I try to tune back in; he is saying, "Miss Summers, also..." He hesitates. "We have been in touch with the president of the United States and John Jacobs, letting them know we represent Henry in any legal issues and, with your authorization, we would like to represent you also, in the event of any issues."

There is dead silence. I am not looking at them, and then I react. "Yes, I am sorry. Seems logical. That works for me. Do you have any way of contacting Henry?"

"No, not like a phone. We have a laser beacon we turn on at the top of his building. He sometimes responds. We will turn it on for you if you want. Of course you have full joint ownership of the building, and you can turn it on without us.

"Last item, Miss Summers. My daughter is a big fan of yours, and she will be in LA sometime next month. Would it be OK for her to call on you? She is the same age as you. I thought you might need some company. Don't answer now; when she calls, just let her know then. There will be no hard feelings if you are busy."

I smile. "Of course she can call me. She is welcome to stay here, too. Don't worry about the beacon. I am hoping Henry will contact me."

CHAPTER 37

POSSIBLE MOVE TO NEW YORK CITY

I see John Jacobs every day; he is becoming like a brother. He goes out to get groceries, does laundry, everything needing to be done. Other people could do this running, but John feels this is far too personal; he needs to be the one to care for me. It is too difficult to protect me if I go out. Thousands of people gather for the chance to see me. Photographers and camera guys and their news trucks, they are all also aggressive, anything for a photo of me.

He tells me, "The media people are everywhere, camped out, roaming around, searching your background, checking everyone who ever had contact with you. They are frantic for information on you. Much of the reporting is gossip or just not true. If there's no news, they make it up."

I have been in the house for four weeks, with no outside contact and refusing to watch the news, as it's too embarrassing. Everything I ever did is under media scrutiny, from my being born to the first day of school to my natural father—every event and every person I ever talked to. They all act as if they're close to me, yet most of them I never even met. All the photos taken of Henry and me, for example, by private citizens at the zoo or people on the bus in London, are worth huge amounts of money. These people are being paid for these photos.

I do not answer any phone calls. There are too many calls to respond to, so I gave up. The Secret Service answers every one, tracing every one of them. Thousands of calls come in daily.

I ask John if it is OK to call my business agent, Jeanie Cox. He says he will hook up a secure line since foreign countries may be hacking my calls. Finally, a day later, I call Jeanie.

"Jeanie, it's me, Anna, your long-lost friend you never call."

Jeanie, talking fast, excited, responds, "Anna, my God, is it you? I can't believe it!"

She continues, "My god, I've called you every day for a month, ever since *the day*. I can never get through; it's constantly busy. I thought maybe your phone was off the hook, and no way will your Secret Service let anyone visit you. The president of the United States is easier to see than you. You have the entire US Army out there. And there are thousands of people wandering around, trying to get a glimpse of you. I think they think you married Jesus. Saying that, did you marry him? Are you pregnant?"

"Oh brother, where did you get that from?" I reply.

"Anna, someone saw you coming out of a doctor's office, and a reporter bribed the receptionist. You know how it works. Vegas odds are three to one you are pregnant. Same odds he's coming back. Maybe not good odds if you want him back."

"Why do people care?" I retort.

"Anna, are you kidding? You are a legend in your own time. Every single person on this planet knows your name. You are the most famous person ever. Henry coming to Earth is like Jesus coming! You are like the Virgin Mary, except not a virgin. They are naming babies after you and Henry, and video games are named after you. Every country in the world wants to know what you know. By the way, how was Henry in bed? He is hot—good taste, girl. I would not kick him out of my bed.

Does it work like every man's equipment, or did you have to help him?"

Angry, I exclaim, "Jeanie, I am close to hanging up!"

Jeanie, talking faster, sounding anxious, responds, "Lord, please, don't hang up! I'm sorry. I am just giddy that I'm your agent, and everyone in the world wants you. You have any movie you want; all the talk shows across the world want you, willing to pay massive amounts of money. You are a shoo-in for the Academy Award nomination, and probably the award, too. Since there is a possibility Henry is coming, per your invitation on *the day*, the Academy Awards will be the highest rated show on television, thanks to you. By the way, this is brilliant on your part. And, by the way, every foreign country will be there—the top guys, not just ambassadors. They all think Henry will come. You are his woman; some say you are a princess from another galaxy hiding out here. Henry rescued you."

"Anna, even the pope wants to talk to you. Something about the Gabriel thing you talked about on the London bus intrigued him. You were being taped, and on video the two of you looked real close. You looked horny. He is handsome, even if he is an alien. The girls of the world are cheering for you. And if you get tired of him, there are fifty million women who will take your place. Did you ride on his starship, no pun intended?"

"Jeanie, hush. You are on some kind of high! Calm down. I can't talk about any of it. This phone conversation is probably being taped by at least fifty wiretaps. What do you mean by *the day*?"

Jeanie acts surprised, exclaims, "What? You know, *the day;* it's the day Henry came down from his starship, guarded by his soldiers, all of them with halos, looking like God's angels. The day you told him he better come back, and he said he would try his best. The day he gave you the locket, which is now worth millions according to the talk shows, if anyone could get it off of you. It was leaked that you wear it twenty-four hours a day, and it will grant wishes."

"If it granted wishes, don't you think I would be asking for them?" I say, "What do you think?"

"Anna, I think the whole world is nuts. Everyone is curious, though. Another question for you. Remember speaking in an alien language, saying good-bye to Henry? They have it on tape. He said 'Calabra,' and then you said it back. What does it mean?"

A long pause; nothing is said. I am too shocked to respond. Finally I say, "This is absolutely nuts. The world has become a crazy place! It is not a big deal. On *the day* I said 'Calabra' to Henry I was saying good-bye. It means 'May the divine light embrace and guide you'!"

Jeanie lowers her voice, talking slower, "Anna, that is more than crazy; that is godlike! Does Henry heal people? This is a lot better than Jesus! Please tell me!"

I laugh, retort, "I am glad I don't have to talk to all the people you talk to, much less listen to them."

Jeanie replies, speaking much slower, in a low voice, "Honey, I'm serious now. Be careful! Actually, you need to know, the world has become dangerous; something more serious—you don't know this—did not come from me. You remember James Algeir, your old flame who turned into a jerk? He was saying some pretty weird things about you and Henry to some reporter, and then Algeir disappeared. No one has heard from him since. The reporter has also become real quiet. As you know, your stepfather disappeared. There are others in other countries, just gone. They all have some connection to you or Henry. Some think it's the government hiding something, and they are behind it, kidnapping these people."

She continues, almost whispering, "Sweetheart, of course nobody, me included, talks about Iran. I don't have to tell you, as

I figure you know everything there is to know. Maybe that's why they guard you; maybe it is really a prison. On the other hand, don't leave there. I am not kidding; there could be millions of people who would come to see you, anywhere you would go, to go there just for a chance to see you. Just to touch you. Some think you can read minds, something you did at a dinner party. That you're telepathic. Henry supposedly gave you the power. Are you telepathic?"

Silence, no response from me.

Jeanie waits for me to answer, finally smiles, knows her answer, and adds affection in her voice and now feeling her confidence back, quickly saying, "Darling Anna, I don't think this—yet, just so that you know, as a heads-up. Some think you're an alien, too, and maybe immortal. They say you also have the ability to heal yourself. When you were at the doctor's, he noticed you had a blood chemical content different from any human, and you instantly repaired yourself; the needle mark just disappeared right after he gave you the prenatal vitamin shot."

She continues, "The doctor told someone who then told reporters you might be immortal. Of course he is not talking to anybody now."

Anna, be careful, they might dissect you. You are safe because they are afraid of Henry, really afraid. They do not think he is human, and they wonder about the baby. Some say it is the best thing that could happen for Earth; some say it's the worst. As long as they are afraid of Henry, you probably will be fine. By the way, apparently Henry said if anything happened to you, the accountable parties would suffer a thousand deaths. He could do it; who could stop him?"

She continues, talking fast again, "Be careful, girl. Let me know when you're ready to come back to work. Everyone wants you, millions of dollars. Of course, wait until after the baby is born. You have that glow, the one-in-the-oven glow. I will be at the Academy Awards, too, sitting five seats behind you. You will be showing. The ticket cost me thousands! Worth every penny. I love you! If you talk to Henry tell him I love him, too. Got to go; bye, sweetheart!"

John Jacobs is knocking on the door. He does not stop and opens the door. Coming in, he says, "You look tired, Anna. Are you feeling OK?"

I grin. "Yes. John, who needs a father with you around? I was just talking to my business agent. She says my career is taking off as long as I have an army to protect me."

"Anna, that's just the right thing to talk about. Thanks for bringing it up. We need to move you to Henry's New York penthouse; it's much safer. Henry said it is like a fort, and the energy source works for the drones, or the slips. Most of the slips protecting you have gone into hibernation, with no energy source. Henry's slips are the most serious defenses we have to protect you. I think your locket is your primary defense against other aliens, although I am not sure. I am sure you are safer there, also safer from a human threat. It is humans we worry about. Just think about it, as I think we have time, though not a lot. Maybe move next month. I know you don't want to go, but just think about it.

"Anna, something else: Judy and the kids could come out and visit you. The kids are out of school. I know you are lonely. Might be fun for you, change of pace."

"Yes, I would like that; I adore your family. Just give me some dates. They would stay here of course. Also, I know you would tell me, but you have not heard from Henry, have you?"

John sadly responds, "I am sorry, Anna. Nothing."

I shake my head, hear my mother calling for dinner, then say, "John, have dinner with us."

John says, "Sorry, no time. I have a meeting with the Pentagon, a conference call. Thanks! Next time. By the way, are you still practicing with my second gun, the nine millimeter, the Walther? You might need one someday."

I respond, "You will be proud of me. I practice every day. I am actually good with it. I like using it, too, sort of makes me feel good, can't explain it. I want to buy one."

CHAPTER 38

ISSUES

The dinner is wonderful. My mother always comes through for me. Over all the years she has protected me, loved me no matter what. She never said a critical word about Henry, nothing about getting pregnant, as in how stupid it is. Nikki is the same, just fantastic, really my best friend, just fun and good to everyone I know. I feel blessed.

Mother and I clean up the dishes together. We laugh and joke.

"Anna, it's been weeks now since the doctor's appointment. Are you due to see him at the sixty-day point?" asks Anna's mother.

"Yes, Mother, next week, on Wednesday. Are you coming?"

My mother beams, "Yes, you cannot prevent me, looking forward to it. My little girl having a baby, can you believe it? You are two months pregnant, with seven to go, and I will have a grandson. I think it will be a boy. I know Henry is not here, yet could be worse. At least you will never have money problems, and you never need to work again. My grandson will be able to go to good schools. I am so happy for you, and my grandson, too."

She continues, "By the way, I think you are showing just a little, although no one will notice. You are still in good shape. The daily workouts and swimming keep you looking good. You are a beautiful girl, and I am so proud of you. If Henry never makes it back, you will be fine. Nikki and I will always be here for you."

I smile, then walk over to where she is sitting and I hug my mother, telling her I love her and I am very lucky to have her.

She smiles, looking up at me: "Anna, also, is John Jacobs still giving you gun-shooting lessons? I agree with him; you need to be able to defend yourself. You are a target now. There are some wicked people out there. I think Sam was involved with the Mafia. He knew it was dangerous, yet he was pulled in, trapped, even forced to do things. I am not sure all that happened, as he never said; he did not want us to be part of it. I worry it might have cost him his life."

My mother continues, "Anyway, we all need to get out of this house. This will be the first time you have been out of the house since the last doctor's office visit. I suppose security will be tight as usual. I guess John and the rest are planning a military campaign to get you there. No matter, it will be good to get you out of here. Nikki and I are both coming."

I respond, "Yes, Mother, it's a major deal. They are evacuating the streets between here and the doctor's office. It will be partially lined with troops. I am not sure all this is necessary. Why would anybody hurt me?"

Looking at my mother, I laugh at her expression as if I have lost my mind, and then say to her, "Hey, I am getting good with the gun John loaned me. Maybe at some point I can take care of my own security."

My mother laughs, too, saying, "Anna, by the way, I got a call from someone named Anthony saying he knows you and Sam. He had some information for you and said to call him. He had a heavy New York City Italian accent, almost hard to understand him. Do you know him?"

"When did he call?" I ask.

"Yesterday. Why, who is he?" Mother replies.

"He is Luca Deforleo's son," I reply.

"My God! Do you think he has information on Sam? Please call him right away," Mother exclaims.

In a heavy New York accent, he says, "Anna, thanks for calling me back. I am Anthony Deforleo, Luca's son, a friend of your stepfather's. I know ya! I know you're famous, too. I guess we are introduced now—by phone." He laughs. Then there's a long pause. I don't respond, regretting I called him.

He quickly says, "Don't hang up. Just so ya know, we have your stepfather; he decided to take a little vacation—with us. Please tell your mother. To be up front with you, his life depends on us. Ya know about me, right? Ya know who I am, and you know my father? Your papa was our partner, our buddy; he has been for years."

I am now anxious, really alarmed, not sure what to do. Damn! If only Henry were here. I say, "All right, what do you want from me? Do you need money?"

"Anna—'Na'—of course not; ya got me wrong, absolutely not! No worries, I just want a visit. I won't bite you. I am taking my corporate jet to LA today and thought we could hook up. I can tell you all about your father. He suggested I call ya, wanted you to meet me. And, my first time there, maybe you show me around and we have a good time. Ya end up having a little time out of that prison you are in."

No response from me.

Anthony continues, "I think we could be friends, maybe more. I've seen your movies, and I'm sure lookin' forward to spending a little time with you. I guess ya know about me, too. I'm famous, too, just in a different way—like notorious!"

No response from me.

Anthony laughs a wicked laugh, saying, "We are goin' to get along great, Anna. What if I pick you up at five thirty, your place? We could go out to dinner and see where the evenin' goes. I am up for anything. Afterward we could go back to your place. I don't have a hotel reservation—figger I don't need it. I thought I might stay a few days with you, so we can get to know each other—maybe really well." Laughing, he says, "Ya knows what I mean. Your papa needs you to do this, if you know what I mean. I will tell ya all about him. I know your mother is worried, too, needs to know."

I hesitate, saying nothing, a little tremor going through me, and then fear in my stomach. I feel sick.

Anthony says, "Are ya there, Anna? Did you hear me?"

"Yes," I reply. "I hear you. Tonight at five thirty is good. I will make reservations at a good restaurant, and I will meet you there. You need to get a hotel reservation; you will not be staying here. I expect to hear a full report on my stepfather."

Anthony says, "No problem. Don't bring anybody if you want me to talk about your father. Ya can make it a really expensive restaurant. I'm treatin'." He hangs up.

I whisper to myself, "Henry, where are you when I need you?"

I will have to sneak out with Nikki. She will have to go with me. Nikki will tell John she is going to the drugstore; he will agree. I will be hiding in the trunk, letting my sister drive us out. Nikki will have to go to dinner, too, no matter what that idiot Anthony wants. But only Nikki. No way would Anthony talk about Sam with the FBI there. Nikki and Mom need to know if he is still alive; there is not much choice. Could Anthony be so stupid to try something in a public place? Nikki will be there, too. *John Jacobs would not like this plan.*

━╬ ╬━

The dinner goes well for Anthony. He drinks and talks the entire time, mostly bragging about his exploits with women and the world, miserable for me and my sister. Nikki hates him, too. He is not modest about being part of the Mafia or, as he calls it, "The Family" and how important he is. He proudly states how he is a natural-born killer, not afraid to do the wet work himself.

I just listen to him although his accent is so strong he is hard to comprehend, and he is disgusting; he grins then looks at me with a leer, but I politely nod. I keep looking around. He is scary, probably dangerous, and, worse, truly boring. I'm thinking, *Maybe somebody will recognize me, get me out of this. But I put on a wig so I would not be recognized, so no surprise no one knows who I am. Stupid!*

Anthony says, "Sam is at our place hidin' out, a safe house we own, not in this country. He is fine." He then laughs. "The senator has done some bad things, could go to jail. Good thing we are helpin' him."

Anthony is saying that ever since his father died, there have been constant problems. He says he committed suicide, shot himself over the pool. He was getting old anyway, not doing all that well. Anyway, it was good for everyone, as he is in command now. He says, "Don't worry, I will make sure Sam is protected; the FBI will never find him. You and your sister owe me for helping Sam."

Nikki laughs at him, tells him he is full of shit. She says she is going to the bathroom and we are going home after she comes back. I tell her I am ready, too. Anthony makes a cell-phone call and, talking intently, ignores me.

Except Nikki does not come back. Anthony is off his cell phone, grinning at me. I leave the table to search for Nikki and find out she is nowhere in the restaurant. "That damn Anthony has done something," I hiss. I am thinking about the phone call he made while we were telling him we were going. I reach into my pocket for my cell phone.

Anthony comes up behind me, grabbing my phone away. "Don't touch me! I yell. I'm calling the police. Give me the phone or I'll scream."

He responds, "No problem, Anna. Stop hollerin'. Here's your phone. Your sister is in my limo waitin' for ya. I just wanted to have a little time with you without her. Let me pay the bill. Don't fret. We will go get her."

When we are outside the door, in the parking lot, Anthony is brave enough, mostly because of the booze controlling his brain, to manhandle me. He reaches under my skirt, squishing my bottom with his hand. It hurts. I shout at him as I push him off, quickly trying to make my way toward the limo, across the parking lot, to escape him and find Nikki. We need to get out of here.

I think, *She'd better be in here!* I open the door and stare in disbelief, no Nikki. It's impossible to believe I fell for this. Anthony comes up behind me as I start screaming, trying to run, fighting him off. He grabs me, throws me into the limo through the open door, the bodyguard holding me down. Anthony is on top of me before I can do anything. The bodyguard puts tape on my mouth, muffling my screaming, and then goes to the front seat. Anthony has my arms pinned back.

The limo takes off; the driver ignores my muffled cries. Anthony takes the tape off my mouth, tries to kiss me.

I push him off. "What happened to Nikki? Let me go! " I scream, terrified.

The driver and the bodyguard are now sitting up front, and the window now closes behind the front seat.

Anthony is sitting across from me now, saying, "Anna, calm down. If ya behave you will see Nikki again. No one can hear you in here. It's soundproof. Just give in and no problems; ya might like it."

I loathe him and his sarcastic tone, his eyes revealing an ugly, sadistic look. If possible, he looks even more ugly now, with a face and body that looks like a junkyard dog. He is about six feet tall, well built, with huge brute hands. He is the kind of man with no friends; it's doubtful his mother would even want to spend time with him. He needs more than two bodyguards, for when John Jacobs comes for him. The other bodyguard must have Nikki, as he is not here, maybe using her car.

Anthony smiles. He can see Anna is really frightened. This will make it easier. He has been looking forward to this for a long time. Afterward she will tell no one; she will be too ashamed to tell anyone. *She will be a good girl when I'm done with her.* He reminds himself how much he likes this.

I see that idiot looking at me with that look. I am scared more than at any other time in my life. I think, *Stay cool. How can I get out of this? A gun would help. This is a huge error on my part. I am alone with him, other than the bodyguard and the driver. They could not care less.*

The driver is driving them into a bad area of LA, and my mind whirls. *Oh my God, what did they do to Nikki? I am so sorry. How stupid can I be? Henry, if you are listening, I could use some help here right away!* I try to twist the locket and wonder, *How do you activate it? I know there are no drones or slips to help me; I'm too far from a starship or an energy source to energize them.*

I yell at him, "Anthony, where is my sister? You better not have hurt her. You will have more heat than you can imagine. You will not get away with this. It is not too late to take me back. You don't want to face Henry. You have no idea who he is or what he will do to you. You will never escape him."

He just looks at me. "Ya came with me willingly. Those two up front will say you wanted it. And yeah, I know about your so-called boyfriend. Where is he now? Maybe you got a little love 'em and leave 'em. Ya better be a good girl if you want to see your sister alive again. Your stepfather wants us to be a couple. Did ya know that? Think about him. You know what is going to happen to him. Ya can take that look off your face. I know how to give you an attitude adjustment."

He eyes my skirt and legs although I am wearing the longest skirt I own. Then, in a quick second, he tries to take off my skirt, actually tearing it off, then jerking my blouse off, trying to undo my bra; I desperately fight him off, screaming at him. He slaps my face, rips off my bra, then pins me, holding me facedown; my arms are behind me, and my legs are trapped under his legs yet he manages to pull my panties off, slapping my butt hard, then splits my legs, starting to probe me with his free hand.

Though struggling with everything I have, I start thinking plainly. *He is going to rape me, maybe kill me. I realize there is nothing I can do about it. He's too strong for me. He is a total dumbass. How stupid, and I got Nikki into this. I would love to see Henry now; even John Jacobs would be good. Why in God's name did I sneak out? If only I had John's Walther nine-millimeter, or any gun would be good. Damn it!*

My rage fires up. I free my right hand and strike out with my elbow, hitting Anthony in the nose hard, blood spurting every-where. He is enraged, yelling at me, cursing. I pull myself up; he grabs for my throat.

Suddenly police sirens on screeching cruisers are close; then shots are fired. I can feel the tires blow out. The limo comes to an abrupt stop, throwing us forward.

I yell, "Thank God!" Then I shriek, "Please help me! Help! Please help me!"

There are police cars with blinking red lights all around us. The doors are opened, the FBI and the police are ordering

Anthony and his bodyguards to get out, grabbing them, cuffing them, and saying they are arresting them for kidnapping and assault. The driver fights, and then is put on the ground, bleeding from a head wound where a policeman had hit him.

John Jacobs is there, looking mad. "Thank God," I say as I see Nikki is with him. The military cars are here now, and more police cars are coming in, sirens blasting, lights blinking, then blocking the road. There are three military helicopters hovering a couple hundred feet overhead.

I am embarrassed and humiliated to have to look for my clothes in the limo, including my panties, then to put them on, with everyone there, all standing outside the limo. I need some ice to reduce the swelling on my face and neck. Anthony was brutal. I am totally mortified. *No one ever needs to ever know.* I think, *I need to carry a gun. Could I be so lucky as to have a chance to put a bullet in him?*

The other bodyguard is in a huge police van, looking bad, face swollen from being hit several times. I am glad to see him helpless. Anthony is handcuffed and surrounded by police, him yelling, protesting that there is no reason to arrest him. He says he has done nothing. He yells at me that it is not over; he will be seeing me again. They jerk him into the police van and then slam the door. I hope he does not get released, ever.

John Jacobs asks me if I am all right and if I want to go to the hospital. I shake my head, saying I'm fine. He says he will take me home but does not look pleased with me. I ask him about Nikki. He walks over and opens the door to an unmarked police car.

Nikki is there, and I jump in. We are hugging, crying. I bawl, "Nikki, I am so sorry. How could I be so stupid! What happened?"

Nikki tells me she was able to call John on her cell phone in the bathroom. She knew it was going bad when the bodyguard followed her to the bathroom, but she managed to lock the door behind her before he was able to enter. He grabbed her when she came out.

Nikki says, "John has GPS tags on both of us, in our cell phones, so when he found out we went AWOL, he was there fast."

John passes all the security gates and checkpoints and drives up to the front door. Nikki goes in, and John asks me to wait a bit, to please listen to him, just a little talk.

He says our mother is frantic, as they all are. "You scared the hell out of all of us! It could have turned out badly. All this security does not work when you sabotage us, no matter the reason. Please, Anna, never do this again! For sure now you need to think about moving to New York, to Henry's penthouse. Henry's drones weren't helpful today. They must not be operating, no energy left; they need to recharge at Henry's building. It is dangerous and stupid not to have them. Please, seriously think about it. By the way, Nikki's car is being driven over here by Mark, one of my guys. He will leave it in the driveway. Are you sure you are OK?"

I reply, "John, I am fine. I am so sorry about today. I owe you my life and Nikki, too. God only knows what that thug would have done to me. He is a scary guy, and I was reckless. I will talk to my mother and Nikki about New York. I will let you know. We will do it, just not this month. I know you know about my pregnancy. Thank you so much for all your help. I am not doing well without Henry. I am in constant fear. I need him terribly, and I don't know what to do. He doesn't know I am pregnant. I am so lonesome, and I just can't imagine life without him. I feel like a fool." I start to cry.

John says, "Anna, don't blame yourself for the recent events. We know you went to see Anthony Deforleo because he told you he had information about your father. You did it for your mother. By the way, we think your stepfather is dead. We think the Deforleo Mafia family killed him, as he knew too much about them. We may never find his body. Anthony Deforleo may have done it. He is a pimp and a thug. However, he probably will not be held long. The Mafia has good attorneys, and I doubt if you want to testify against him. Stay clear of him as he runs the family now. His father just committed suicide not long ago, shot himself in the head. The FBI will eventually get Anthony, as he is a genuine criminal; and, he will continue to commit crimes. But until they catch him for some awful thing, he is dangerous."

Continuing, he says, "Anna, again, please tell us your issues before you react. Never leave your security team! The entire world is watching you. I know you're young, yet the people of planet Earth are going to be making a massive transition. You could be a big advantage and truly help in making the shift to becoming a member of the 'Civilizations of the Universe,' the Consortium. This is a huge historical passage, this specific time in the evolution of the human species, and you are right in the vortex of it. You may be leading the way. You are already famous, probably more than anyone ever in the history of mankind."

I shake my head, looking directly at John, declaring, "I am afraid I am not up to what people want from me. I may not be able to do this. I know I should not be this way, yet I can't help it. I am in constant fear."

John replies, "Join the club; the entire world is in constant fear. This whole thing with Henry could be really good for Earth, or it could be a complete bust. I choose to hope for the best."

He looks at Anna with a tender expression, "Don't burden yourself too much about Henry. He has a lot of savvy. Don't count him out yet. I think he will be back if he's allowed to come back. He committed to helping us, and I think he keeps his word. I know he loves you; you can see it in his eyes. He is motivated to come back to you. Please have faith, as it will all work out. I probably should be more cynical, yet I have faith in Henry. Also think about your son. After he is born, he will need you to be strong. This is your first child, and everything will change after he is born. You are not alone in this. Your son is a citizen of an alien race. He might help us become part of the family of worlds. It can't hurt. I know you have the prayers of thousands. I know you are a true leader, and you will prevail." John smiles. "For what it's worth, Judy and I will always be here for you. You are family."

I look at John in a kindly way. My eyes are moist. "John, you are such a blessing. Thank you again. Your friendship, and Judy's, too, have been comforting, to say the least. You have no idea how much it has helped me, and you are right, of course. I hope I live up to everyone's expectations, yours included. I will do my best."

At night, the massive oblong starships, alien battleships, silently slide into Earth's orbit; all six ships are orbiting seventeen hundred miles out with a speed of fifty-six thousand miles per hour. They look like oversize stadiums, each almost two hundred miles long and forty-eight miles high and sixty-four miles wide. At night, when viewing them from Earth, looking up, they could be orbiting moons, although no one notices them until daybreak. Yet they are so enormous, at sunrise, anyone eyeing upward can easily see them from Earth's surface as they block the sun as they pass in front of it.

It is early September; most of the world worries about the drought conditions, as no real issues like wars, and it's been a hot, dry month so far, causing concern. Some say crop production will be thirty percent less than normal. Yet no weather guys across the world are announcing weather this morning when everyone turns on their radios. When daybreak arises, no one is talking about the weather. All those concerns disappear. Everyone on Earth has one common thought: who are these aliens, coming from somewhere in the universe, with six massive starships, ominously circling Earth?

The president is talking to John Jacobs, using a secure cell phone connection, knowing he is still on Anna's protection team in California. "John, you know about the massive starships orbiting us. Do you think they're Henry's?"

"No, Mr. President, I think they are the Seatisveres. This is our worst nightmare; we do not have Henry; and we do have some pissed-off aliens. This is the enemy Henry battled. He destroyed one of their ships, and that ship looked just like those above us, just smaller than these things. I saw the satellite video. I understand we have no communication from them. I would expect the worst from them."

"John, should we prepare for war?"

"No, Mr. President. Henry said if they come before he gets back, we should light up his beacon to call for him. You know how, as he left you instructions. They will know about this SOS, and they cannot turn it off; it's beyond their ability without destroying themselves. The beacon is located on Henry's building in New York City. The building has the ability to destroy them if they get too close to it. They will stay away. The beacon will also make them nervous, cause them to hurry, to get out before he gets back. He said to stand down, give them whatever they want. He will get it back from them later. He said we could never recover from their all-out attack. Earth would be mostly destroyed."

John continues, "He said whatever happens, tell them he is coming with several fleets. Tell them he will find them, no matter what it takes, and they will pay the price for their actions. Henry said they will not stay long after you tell them he is coming for them. They may take energy and metals, as fast as they can, as much as they can carry, then leave. They will plug in to the nuclear reactors at the power plants around the world. They will do this for their energy needs. People will die, as they will have no regard for human life, think of us like cattle; anyone getting in their way will be destroyed, then actually recycled, the chemicals used again. They use all kinds of metal and are good at finding and taking it. Sometimes they take beings, hold them as hostages, and then ask for tribute. Henry said, no matter what they say, they always kill the hostages."

"Mr. President, you need to warn the rest of the world."

"John, take Anna and her family to Henry's New York building immediately. If they know about her, they will take her. I doubt we could do much to stop them. Henry's building is her best bet. We should have taken her there a long time ago. We will turn on the beacon and signal Henry. Hopefully he is listening."

John hangs up, afraid, not sure how all this is going to work, and then his mind goes to trying to protect Anna. He can't help but think about Judy and the kids. He needs to head east immediately. Where is Anna, and her family? Time to collect everyone for the trip east, to head out today.

Finally, he is heading for Anna's house, with a massive convoy following behind, including lots of big coach buses, police cars, and many military vehicles. Troops and security people are on board; also the buses are loaded with fuel and food. He had told Anna to be ready, and he has called her again.

I am telling John on his cell phone, "Nikki and my mother are in the city. I have called them, no answer, and I will not leave without them. And no, I am not ready. I have to wait for them. I know the enemy starships are out there. Everybody can see them. How can you not see them? They are massive, like six countries orbiting Earth every thirty minutes. Yes, I know they are Henry's enemies. I know you are angry."

"Anna, this is serious," exclaims John. "You are in real danger; we are all in harm's way. Lives could be lost. We need to get moving. The convoy is coming for you. We need to go right now."

"John, yes, I know. I am packed and ready to go, and as said, just waiting for Mother. I have called her cell several times, Nikki's, too. Nikki is here because of me. They went to the bank for some money. I will not abandon either one."

"Anna, we have a convoy ready to go. There is no time. We will drive nonstop to New York City to Henry's place. You have the best chance there if the aliens come after you. We think a flight would tempt fate, so we are staying out of the air; we think it's safer to drive. We expect the aliens to come after you. Call me when they get there." He hangs up.

My cell phone rings again. I answer, thinking it is John again. I feel my face go pale. It is Anthony; he says he has Mother and Nikki, says to come to the vacant hotel on Maple Street, just down the street. Bring no one or he will kill them. I say, "Yes, I understand, and I will be there. I understand. I know! I will tell no one." There is fear in my voice; I cannot panic.

I hang up. My voice is shaking when I call John Jacobs; I exclaim, "John, Mother's car broke down about eight blocks from here. Her security team will stay there with the car. Triple A is coming for the car. I will go get her and Nikki. They are close, five minutes away. You don't have to go; I will go get them, and then we can head out."

John forcefully says, "No way. I will drive you. No arguments, and I will take one of our guys just in case there are problems. We need to radio the security team; forget the car. We need to hurry. I can't believe it, of all times!"

I start to object, but I say nothing when I hear John's reaction. He says he will be there to pick me up in a minute.

━╡╞ ╡╞━

On the way to get Anna's mother and Nikki, John drives the car fast, and is wondering about Anna, thinking she is not herself.

Anna is looking fearful, distraught, and panicked. He asks, "Anna, what is wrong?"

"John, I am so sorry. I have lied to you. I'm really frightened. This is bad, really bad. Anthony has my mother and Nikki. He's taken out the security guys, killed them. Anthony just called; he says he just wants to talk. He said for me to come immediately, by myself, with no security; otherwise he will kill both of them. I do not want you to face this, John. I don't want to be responsible for your death. Let me try to save them. I have no choice. You do. They're just around the next corner. He's waiting for me. Please stop; let me go on; it's the best chance to keep them alive. He is crazy. He will kill them. He really will kill them!"

"Damn it, Anna! You have made it worse. I can't believe you are just now telling me this. We could overpower him with a lot of troops. He is too cowardly to face death. I am stopping the car. We are going back to the house!"

Before they can completely back up to turn around, three black SUVs come up behind them fast. The first one slams into their car, hitting one corner, spinning it like a toy. John is staggering out the door as soon as it stops, his gun out. He does not realize two more SUVs have come from the front. Two gunmen with black ski masks are shooting out the windows with assault rifles, then hitting John with several rounds, exploding into his chest, leaving ugly, bloody wounds. He never had a chance to get his gun up. He falls, bleeding from his mouth, gasping for air. His fellow officer, attempting to save John, shares the same fate, shot several times and hitting the ground, thrown back hard.

I scream. Fearless, I am out of the car, rushing to John's body. I am tackled by one of the gunmen, and then roughly forced down to my knees. Anthony gets out of the SUV, walks over to me, and grabs my hair, forcing me to look at him. I can't help it, I spit in his face. He wipes it off and bellows at me, "So, ya want to see your mother and sister?"

Another thug pulls Anna's mother and sister out of the second SUV, dragging them over to Anthony. Nikki fights, tries to break free. Anthony raises his gun at her, then, hearing a shriek from their mother, points the gun at her as she jumps in front of Nikki, trying to protect her. He shoots her in the face twice. Their mother falls backward silently into Nikki's arms, blood everywhere. Nikki catches her, letting her mother down slowly, moaning, and holding her.

I gasp. I can't talk, and I feel the horror. I see my mother lying there in Nikki's arms, without moving, her open eyes staring up, blood covering her. Nikki is screaming at Anthony, a wild look in her eyes. Anthony calmly walks toward her. At ten feet away, he raises his gun and shoots her in the chest twice. She goes down like a rock, bleeding out everywhere.

I feel pure rage. I can see John's nine-millimeter gun on the ground next to me. The gunman holding me sees it, too, but not soon enough. I slam my fist into the gunman's nose, knocking him backward off of me. I lunge over, grab the gun, and come up firing. The first shot puts a hole in the gunman's forehead as he is trying to grab me again. I turn, aim, and fire at Anthony, who has turned toward me, the rounds hitting him in his chest; his vest protects him. I fire another round in one arm and a third in the same arm. Anthony, shrieking in pain, falls backward.

I see the gunman next to Anthony aiming at me. I fire at him before he is able to take his shot. My round enters his neck; he falls forward, splattering blood all over the pavement. I carefully aim again, catching another gunman ten yards behind Anthony. The round enters his forehead above the right eye. I know they have vests on and that the head shots are necessary. I shoot one more gunman in the leg, up high, blood spurting from an artery. I know I am out of ammunition as I end up trying to fire an empty gun. Then I feel the impact as a bullet slams into my shoulder, entering high and knocking me backward; I land flat on my back. The round has exited out the back of my shoulder, the hole gushing blood. The shock of the pain with the impact is incredible, and then all is dark and quiet.

⊷ ⊶

I wake up; looking up to a ceiling of an airplane seat, see a dim reading light. I can't move my arms, although I feel little pain. I hear the whine of jet engines and I know I'm in an airplane, maybe a small corporate jet. I am strapped down onto a seat that is laid out like a recliner, just about level, almost horizontal, like a bed. There is a plasma bag above me, feeding me blood, attached with a long tube stuck into my arm. I look around and see several men sleeping in seats spread out, here and there, in a long cabin, of a big plane. I can see the pilot's cabin lit up with red lights. I notice one passenger is also laid out like me, hooked to a blood plasma bag up above him. He is moaning in pain. I laugh, knowing who it is. I can see him; it's Anthony. Too bad he is still alive.

Then I remember: my poor mother, then Nikki, John Jacobs, and his friend. All are dead. I cry silently. The anguish of it all, the pain and grief hit me, and it is unbearable. Is my baby still alive? Why am I alive? Where am I? It must be Anthony's corporate jet. He has kidnapped me. If I could get out of these straps, I would kill him, finish the job.

I'm thinking I have surprisingly little pain. I feel strong, and my shoulder is fine. I know I was shot there. It was not an illusion. It must be Henry's little medical repair slips. They are working. I do heal, and I feel well. I know my baby is fine, too, as I feel the little guy. They have saved our baby and my life and more. I still have a chance to get Anthony for all he has done. Thank you for that, Henry!

If I could just do it over, of course, I should have told John immediately. I was so stupid. I lost the most important people in my life. My poor mother and sister are gone because of me. John died a horrible death. Then there is John's family. His wife, how could I face Judy? And John's friend died defending me. My stepfather is gone. My whole family has been destroyed because of my actions. All because of me. I caused all this grief. Even Henry is gone.

I am sobbing, can't control it. That damned Anthony. May he die a horrible death!

The cabin lights come on, startling me. Speaking of the devil. I am looking up into Anthony's ugly face, now puffy, and his arm dressed and bandaged. His eyes are wild from the pain and the medication. He snarls at me, then in his awful New York accent, part Italian and part mongrel, "Good mornin', Anna. You woke me up with your cryin'. Maybe ya're learnin'."

I respond with acid in my voice, "Good morning, Anthony. I am delighted to see you are in a lot of pain. Dear me, what happened to your arm? You would be dead if you had not been wearing a vest. You are going to wish you were dead before this day is done."

Anthony, grimacing, responds, "Anna, same for you. Since you are feelin' better, you will be able to service my needs. Then ya get to see some aliens. I sold you to them. Since ya like aliens, I am doin' you a favor. They are comin for ya. We have just enough time for some fun."

"You fool! Do you think they will let you live? How did you contact them? They will track you now."

"Anna, you will never learn to be a good girl with that kind of attitude. I called them on this plane's communications equipment usin' all channels. They actually responded! They had a translator who spoke American. I told them ya are Henry's girlfriend, and they said they would pay me whatever I want. I am gettin' as much gold as this plane will carry. We meet them in Rio, Brazil, at the airport. We will be there in two hours. They must want you bad. I did not tell them about ya bein' pregnant, and since you are not showin' much, maybe you will be able to hide it. See, Anna, I am not that bad a guy."

Two of Anthony's guys get up, coming at his waving for them. They grab me, holding me down, releasing the straps enough to turn me over. I fight, yet they easily overpower me, and they tighten the straps again. I am now facedown on the seat, pillows under my belly, causing my bottom to be up in the air.

I feel the dread of what he is going to do, knowing he will show no mercy unless I give him what he wants. I feel him pulling down my jeans, then pulling my panties down slowly, with his good arm he spanks my bottom hard, trying to humiliate me. I fight, scream at him to stop, that I will kill him slowly, that—

Baaaammmmmmm!

The explosion is loud and massive. I grab the seat for dear life as the plane jolts upward out of control!

The plane has crashed into something, causing it to violently surge up, maybe a hundred-foot bounce up, then drops down fast, sending Anthony and his men flying into the air with the loose baggage. Another explosion!

Boom…bisaaaaaa…ah!

The continuing explosions are ear splitting, painful, disorienting everyone, then causing overwhelming horror as the plane partially tears apart, still lunging up and down. The wings are coming off from the pressure of some kind of force field slowing the plane down. The forward momentum is ceasing; instead the plane is rising, slowly gaining altitude, going straight up, pulled up by some gigantic force. Then there are more unidentified loud noises, wild snapping sounds, wind blasting through the plane, the air pressure lost to the outside atmosphere, making it hard to breathe.

Another big bump, and the plane has rolled onto its side, the pilot's cockpit now slanting down. Anthony is trying to move up the aisle, howling in pain, frantically holding on to a seat. The rest of the passengers are hurled up into the upper cabin space as the plane is turned over, everyone feeling it rising in midair. The pilots are screaming. The passengers are screaming. I am screaming. I am desperately hoping it might be the *Cyclone: Maybe, could it be Henry? Maybe the locket called him.* It is still around my neck. *Could I be so lucky? Although I would not want him to see me like this; my bottom is still bare; it's embarrassing, to say the least. Henry, is it you?*

The seats are overhead now. The plane is upside down, still rising up higher in attitude. It is entering into some kind of hangar, pulled by some force, drawn into a hangar of some sort. It has to be a starship. Just who's starship? It is too dark to see much of it, just some light from the hangar shining through the window portholes of the plane. The pungent odor is awful—must be coming in through the broken holes in the hull. It is like something died, a revolting odor. The plane is finally resting in the hangar now, the jolt of landing obvious.

I realize this is not Henry saving me. These are the aliens that attacked Henry. I am sure now as I can see them outside the jet's portholes, looking into the cabin. These guys are the real thing, really bad-looking beings, just really ugly. Henry was right—I am not cut out for this kind of thing. I am terrified. My heart is racing, and I want to run but run where?

The plane starts to shudder, vibrating terribly. A laser saw is cutting down the middle, starting at the tail, moving fast. Everyone conscious is moaning or saying prayers. I can hear the pilots trying to use the radio, yelling, "Mayday," asking for help. They are more than panicked, truly freaked out. I hear Anthony actually weeping. I know he is hiding in the restroom and has probably pissed in his pants. I hope I live long enough to see him get it. I have given up on the locket saving me and then remember I am still strapped to the seat with my bottom up in the air.

The aircraft simply falls apart as it is forced open, each half separated, and you can see the ceiling of the hangar about forty feet up. Then three god-awfull ugly real-life aliens climb in, ducking their heads, staring at everyone, using torch beams to shine down upon them. There is a little light in the plane. They are speaking in high, shrieking voices, grating like cat screams, not even close to English. No one understands what they are saying.

Four large drones, about the size of huge dogs, are now hovering around Anthony's men. The drones attack randomly, spitting an acid-like liquid on each man and seeming to be energized by the shrieks of their victims' extreme pain. Within minutes the men are turned into a jellylike substance; then each is sucked up into the drones' large mouths; they look like large fish mouths, measuring about three feet wide and lined with sharp metal teeth. The drones chew with gusto. It is an efficient process, leaving no waste, although blood is everywhere.

It all sickens me as I watch everyone trying to get away from their imminent fate. I laugh as I think of that dumbass Anthony, who is thinking the restroom will protect him. The odor and the sizzling of the acid on human flesh is unbelievable, truly horrific; the pain must be intense. This is unreal; it is some kind of gruesome nightmare.

I can hardly wait for my turn! I think, *Damn, Henry, where are you?*

All are gone, except for Anthony, still in the toilet hiding. They are all dissolved, all eaten, yet the aliens and the drones continue to ignore me. One of the bigger aliens now comes down into the craft. The other aliens treat him with respect, maybe afraid of him. He has to lean down, as he is so huge, maybe nine feet tall, with long side limbs that are like big arms with long tentacles for hands, if you could call them hands. He looks like a big muscled rat with two long legs, not four legs, and no fur on him, as the skin is comparable to skin on a big dark-yellow hog. The clothing is some kind of filmy, gel-like covering with weird colors. On top of huge shoulders he has a massive head with a huge mouth, long jaws with a lot of wicked-looking teeth, no ears, no hair anywhere, and he smells bad. Surprising, his nose is like a human's nose yet flat against his face, with really big eyes above his nose that could actually be called handsome.

He walks right by me, and then he comes back. He's petrifying, and I almost pass out. My bottom is up in his face, embarrassing as hell. He squeaks something, and amazingly enough, totally unbelievable, I can understand him. I am connecting, as he is using telepathy. I have to smile; Henry's slips are now working. I guess they must be energized by this starship. I can hear the alien's thoughts resonating in my mind. This is so weird.

Astonishing enough, he is saying, "Calabra!"

I can't believe it! Who would think? Absolutely crazy. I respond in kind: "Calabra!"

I hear him mentally when he asks, "Are you OK? I am going to remove your straps, thereby releasing you." He unties me, saying, "Do not try to run from me; never try to escape; always stay close to me, especially when we leave here, as it can be hazardous here on our starship."

I thank him and tell him I am fine. I try not to stare at him. My fear level is off the charts.

He nods his head. He asks, "What do you want to do about Anthony? He's hiding in this little room here. I know you know him, as he told us about you. We have some of his memories concerning you. We know he killed your stepfather. One of our drones, like Henry's, has downloaded many of his memories from his brain. The recent memories of your mother and sister are there, too. We do not need him alive, and his proteins and body chemicals will be recycled. Do you want to save him?"

I can't believe it. Who would think he would ask me about saving Anthony, after telling me he knows Anthony killed my father? Did not see that coming. This is all so surreal. I stare at him, repulsed by his smell, thinking, *Lord, he will take some getting used to!*

He continues to look at me, expecting a reply. I am remembering my mother, Nikki and John.

I quietly respond, projecting my thoughts like I used to do with Henry. I respond, "No, I certainly do not want to save him. He is a hideous man and deserves a bad death."

The alien turns from her, strides down to the plane's restroom, and tears open the door as if it were paper. He pulls out a shrieking Anthony. Then, grabbing him in a better grip by his neck and thigh, he lifts Anthony's whole body and hurls him down the plane's center aisle.

Crumpled up at the plane's firewall, several limbs fractured, bleeding from his head, horrified, Anthony screams, "Anna, for God's sake, please save me. I am sorry…I was stupid…Please help me!"

I laugh at him, looking him straight in the eye. One of the huge dog drones then attacks him, and he is screeching, horror in his eyes. The drone eats him alive, using just a little acid, burning him where the jaws hit, eating the smoking tissue. He is crunched up slowly and swallowed finally. He is screaming for a long time. It is absolutely dreadful!

I have to look away. I feel remorse, as even Anthony did not deserve that. The laughing at him was not necessary. These last two days have been the worst of my life. I am totally freaked out!

I turn back, terrified again, trying to remain calm, making eye contact with the alien, inquiring, "What happens to me?"

The alien intently examines me, and then finally speaks. "Anna, my name is XTOX. I am admiral of this ship and head of our civilization. I am trying to use words or thoughts that make sense to you, yet they might not fit every meaning. Please bear with me. You know why we are here. We do not hold you responsible; however, Henry is our enemy. Of course I know he represents the Consortium, and you carry his son. We will be careful with you for a lot of reasons. I will warn you, however, to always follow my commands. You need to do what I tell you. You are my prisoner. Communicate with no one other than me. You will be treated well, and you have nothing to fear as long as you do not fight us. If you create a problem, you will be punished."

He continues, "Please follow me. I will lead you."

I step down out of the plane, and we enter into some kind of holding hangar. It is huge and has a terrible smell, like rotten fish or worse. I gag, then I look down, barely comprehending what I see: as I'm stepping on something and they are spread everywhere: small white broken bone splinters and scattered small fragments of clothing and lots of dried blood. I have seen these kind of bones before. *My God, they're human!* I also see something else, truly nauseating. I am revolted; I can't believe what I am seeing. Now comprehending what this is, I feel disgust and feel the bile in my throat as I start to vomit. I have realized there are also some really little white bones mixed in; they're fragile, small tiny human bones--- the bones of children!

XTOX reacts strongly as he sees what I am looking at, feels my revulsion. "Stand up straight, and do not move. You will not be allowed to see any more of this. Look at me. I am going to blind you, burning your eyes with lasers. Stare straight ahead. It will hurt. Don't move, or it will be worse for you. You are not allowed to see the inside of our ship."

He grabs my arms tightly. My head is grabbed from behind, compressed in a vise grip, painful, not able to move, staring at a small flying drone, then a bright scorching light. I feel a burning pain in both eyes, like a hot torch, then a really bad migraine hits across my forehead. Just like that I am blind, can't see anything. Nothing! I have been screaming the entire time.

Finally I stop screaming. The pain is awful. I put my fingers to my face and feel the hot, burned flesh. No eyelids left. They have been seared off. I can feel the hot scar tissue. I can smell my burned flesh, and I am horrified as I feel no eyeballs, just burned, empty sockets.

I wonder what else could happen. It hurts like hell. I moan; it really hurts badly, and then I think, my acting days are certainly over; blind is not good! My chances of living long are not seeming too good either, much less of going to the Academy Awards. Of course, much worse, I could end up living here the rest of my life.

Lord, my eyes, my face! The pain! What a great finale to a great day. What a nightmare.

I am now totally traumatized. No feelings are left, and all of my emotions have been used up. I don't care about anything. I am now following the alien at his command; I can see him with my mind, like I'm in a fog, walking with him as he is leading me. I am blind as a bat. I feel myself being lifted into some kind of bedlike chamber, like a coffin. I am saying prayers for my baby, for my mother, and for my sister. I am saying prayers for Henry and for myself and I am thinking about John Jacobs and his wife. My mind swirls in horror and disbelief as I welcome the blackness and quiet serenity; I am grateful for it. I feel my self losing consciousness.

The president thinks, *It's a new day all right. I thought the Consortium took care of these things. I am dealing with several aliens; really they are nothing but criminals. They are all sitting in my office staring at me. They are communicating with me using telepathy. They say they are transmitting through the cell-size drones I have in my brain that Captain Johnson left. Somehow Henry forgot to tell me about them. I think these*

big guys are as ugly as you could imagine, and they smell like shit, liter-
ally. I am helping them with everything they want from this planet. They
have already killed thousands, including women and children, mostly the
hostages they were supposed to release. Those who put up any resistance
were also slaughtered. Their bodies were turned into soup, then sucked up
into big dog drones, recycled into their starships. These assholes have been
here for ten long days. Now they want to meet and talk.

They love aluminum. They stopped at every aluminum smelt-
er in the world and helped themselves. Of course every bit of
uranium was taken from the power plants, and nuclear bombs
were confiscated from every country. Everyone was warned by
their governments to stay home, stay off the streets, and stay hidden. There was nothing else they could do. Every military organization was shut down, all their equipment no longer working,
jammed from some energy-sucking device.

God, please help us, and send Henry.

All of a sudden these alien guys that were sitting here relaxed,
like they own the place, they jump up. They are anxious, maybe
fearful. Something is happening. They are chattering to one another too fast to follow. Maybe it was my prayer for Henry. That
was fast.

Maybe Henry is actually coming, finally!

They announce they are leaving Earth right now and are saying good-bye. Even more weird, bizarre, they thank me for our
hospitality, apologize for the grief they have caused, reassuring
me, as don't worry, they say, they will not be back, ever. They say
it could have been much worse.

More important, they want me to pass on a message to Captain
Henry Johnson and the Consortium, who will be here soon.
They say they have Anna, and they just found out Henry knows
it. They know that I know who she is, and they tell me they need
to head out because of her. They say Henry will be here soon,
well prepared, with several Consortium fleets. They know about

the beacon, too, know we turned it on to signal Henry. He will be asking about Anna when he gets here with his Consortium fleets. The aliens instruct me to tell Henry she will be treated well, not to worry. They will be willing to trade her and his unborn son, leaving a drone behind to negotiate the terms. They are all going in different directions, and he will not find Anna without their help. He needs to listen carefully to the drone they are leaving with me. Anna's life and his son's life depend on it.

Poor Anna, the aliens have her. I feel so sorry.

They practically run out the door. Within two hours all the ships just disappear, no more six moons orbiting Earth. The world will be partying tonight. We have become one race, the human race. It is amazing how close and kind to one another the countries have become since the aliens arrived. The human race might make it after all. It's a shame it took something like this to happen. Now we need to clean up the mess that's left.

CHAPTER 39

THE CONCLUSION

Three days later Henry enters into Earth's solar system hard and fast. Two fleets are following him. There is one *Titan*, a city starship, several days behind him. It displaces a six-teen hundred square miles, massive even for the Consortium. It carries many thousands of troops. Then there are several hundred *Eagles*. They are like the *Cyclone* yet bigger, newer. Each carries two *Tigers* in its storage hangars. The *Tigers* are like his *Saber.*

Except for the *Titan*, the rest are coming in with Henry. They are in formation, threading in and out for several thousand miles, as a lot of starships. They are all trying to slow down to orbit Earth, spaced evenly around the planet. The orbit will be two thousand miles out; none will land for now. The *Titan* will orbit five thousand miles out due to its massive size. They will use the *Titan* as a base, spreading out to find the Seatisveres' starships, soon to be destroyed or taken captive. Of course all now know about Anna, that one of the ships has her. They know she is carrying Henry's son.

The *Cyclone* comes in hovering over Washington, DC. Henry called ahead. The president told Henry all the events that occurred while he was gone. Henry knew most of it already. The president is delighted Henry is here, finally, his actual presence here at the White House. Henry is in the hallway coming from the front lobby, to meet the Secret Service who are all smiles as they lead him toward the Oval Office to meet the president and his staff. There are also a select group of reporters here, too, those that can be trusted.

They are all standing and sitting in the president's office. Henry sees a lot of people, as many as can squeeze into the room. They are awestruck by Henry, trying to see him, the women smiling at him, the men offering to shake hands.

He is here officially as Captain Henry Johnson, looking quite regal, as he has come formally dressed in his Consortium uniform, built not of any cloth anyone on Earth has ever seen or touched. It is thin yet strong, with a lot of dull-colored threads mixed with light gold and silver threads with tiny sparkling dark pin-lights changing colors constantly, internalized in the material. The material can change colors to match a background like a chameleon in camouflage mode. The uniform also perfectly conforms to his muscled body yet always allows space for free movement.

The look is astounding, pure magic. The external workings are astonishing. There are thin dull-silver and brass-like metallic straps matching up with all of his larger muscles, traveling together and working in unison with the muscles. Then his shoulders are draped with some kind of short, lightweight, dark, flowing cape, extending down his arms, with some kind of darker markings. They are probably some alien language. He has a dark-brown belt that might be some kind of leather, holding some small leather cases, and one leather strap crossing his chest with different emblems attached, like small flags. A holstered weapon of some kind is attached to the shoulder harness under his arm. He has on some kind of protective boots that are almost knee high, looking like leather, tight to his legs, yet looking soft and comfortable. It is hard to identify the color, yet close to dark-gray-brown leather. His tight gloves are dark leather. There is a halo circling him about three feet above and in orbit around his head. There are also small firefly drones everywhere, moving here and there.

The president shakes his hand, smiling, welcoming him back. He is thinking, *Wow! Yes, Henry is impressive, and it's not easy trying to figure him out: he's mysterious, sensitive, yet strong and looks great in his amazing uniform. Henry really is the universal hero: a good guy in a fantastic uniform, movie-star looks, and totally charming, smart, and empathetic, too. No wonder Anna fell for him. Everyone here loves him, too; yet they are all shy and nervous. I guess trying to impress him.*

No question, he is also intimidating, and everyone is mesmerized, they can't take their eyes off of him. Of course this is history in the making, something to tell their grandkids. I wish my wife and kids were here.

Henry smiles at everyone. "Mr. President, I appreciate your meeting with me along with your staff. I know a lot has happened in the last couple of months, and now September is almost over. I apologize for not being here earlier. Believe me, I tried. I have been briefed on the events and the tragedy of the alien attack. I cannot express how sorry I am, and I speak for the Consortium also. We will avenge your loss; those responsible will be found and punished."

He continues, "Good news, however, as Earth has been accepted into the Consortium of Civilizations. Congratulations! We will set up communications; we will notify the rest of the world. We will keep you up to date on all we do. The transition plan has already started. There will be daily broadcasts to teach everyone about the new way. The changes will be alarming, yet they are common-sense concepts, nothing harmful or threatening. Local government continues; nations stay the same; leadership will remain the same or get better. Elections will take place where needed. Freedom and free will are still the goals as is responsibility for one's actions. Of course criminals will be rehabilitated, as you will have access to new behavioral technology. You will end up with no prisons or prisoners, or very few.

"Our *Titan* city starship will be here in several days. It will orbit five thousand miles out. All critical people on Earth will be trained either here or on board the *Titan*. It is a thousand miles in diameter. It has classrooms as needed for the technology that will be given to you, and you will also be given the training to use it. You will be given several small starships for exploring your own solar system, a gift from the Consortium.

Each country will utilize the United Nations as a platform to politically deal with the Consortium. We will have one appointed representative, and Earth will have three, thus composing a four-man board of directors to act as oversight of the governments of Earth. The United Nations will elect the three representatives for representing Earth on the board.

"I also have two military fleets here. They are orbiting Earth right now. We will make sure your alien friends who visited you a few days ago are punished. There is no question they all will be caught. We will also scan the planet, do a census of populations and make an evaluation of the planet's health. You have nothing to fear again. The *Titan* will be here a long time, and it is a virtual fortress, capable of defending this entire solar system and much of this galaxy."

Henry coughs, pauses, and, with serious sad eyes, slowly says in a lower voice, "Of course we will find Anna and return her too. I am heading out to find her. I assure you she will be back here within a short time. I know she is enthusiastic about being here for the Academy Awards." Everyone laughs, although nervously.

Finally finishing, Henry says, "I am leaving immediately. By the way, the transition starts tomorrow without me. You will have lots of good guidance, and it will be easy. It will be fun, really; enjoy it."

⚔️

I found the Seatisveres' main ship within seven days, after pushing the *Cyclone* hard and covering trillions of miles, partnered with ten *Eagles*. I know Anna is there, her locket slips signaling me by using the communications systems of the Seatisveres' ship. She did not know they were there to prevent her from giving them away. Her not knowing protected the hundreds of slips she carried in the locket, as stored there in hibernation, only activated with internal energy resources, triggered upon arrival on the Seatisveres' starship. Meaning they opened the locket by themselves, then immediately spread throughout the huge starship. They have infiltrated all their processing centers and most of the minds of the commanding officers on the Seatisveres' starship; meaning it will be mine to control and the defense grids will be shut down when I approach.

I also realize the starship crew is not quite yet in my control and they know nothing about my slips being there, waiting for me, there on board with them. The Seatisveres' admiral and crew will never know I am there until I board, then it will be too late to do much to stop me. If the admiral does anything to Anna or my unborn son, he will die a thousand deaths, not bluffing this time.

Tomorrow I will see Anna again; my heart is pounding, and the anxiety is tough. We are only one day apart. I am still afraid, though, as too many things could go wrong. I pray our destinies will fall in together; I have certainly moved heaven and hell to get here. I laugh as I hear the *Cyclone*. Of course, I know the *Cyclone* did all the work.

They are in a strange galaxy, too, called the Antennae Galaxies, using Earth terms. I have not been here before, although the *Cyclone* is familiar with it. I am getting a download from the *Cyclone*, receiving all the data on the area available in these galaxies. There are not many beings here; it has been going through some violent changes, as they are merging galaxies. Unfortunately I am trillions of miles from Earth.

XTOX is trying to awaken Anna. She has been in hibernation for nineteen days, fed intravenously. She is not waking up, and he is anxious, knows his severe peril if anything happens to her. The massive starship has an onboard hospital, yet they know little about humans. Each room has a chamber and Anna has been in one, in a forced coma. They scan her daily as she heals. A few molecule drones left in her body do the repair needed. The slips in her brain work; she is fine, as is her baby. Her eyes even heal, repaired by Henry's medical drones, back to full vision again. She has been bathed, moved about, yet she is still is not awakening. The sleep should have done her well, been good for her, as she was highly traumatized.

He pulls her up to a sitting position, legs over the side of the movable floating bed, next to the room chamber. Two medical nurse drones help him. Her vitals are good. Why is she not responding? She is trying to open her eyes. He has to hold her head up, and she looks sick. He asks her to focus.

Then, just as he is starting to unnerve, she is awake fully, eyes open, coughing, then jerking forward, vomiting some fluids on the floor, finally trying to talk. He holds her, mentally reassures her, and tells her to use thoughts not words. She is trying to pull herself together, still dazed, weak.

He holds her up so Anna is sitting, her legs still hanging over the bed, although she is having a hard time. She is looking wild-eyed at him.

She asks, mentally projecting uncontrolled fear with her thoughts, *Please tell me. Is my baby fine? Healthy? I am so weak! How long have I been under? I'm not blind? I can see you! What did you do to me? My head is throbbing! This is awful!*

She gasps as she remembers her burned eye sockets. Her hands fly to her face, feeling for her eyes. Her eyelids are also back on her face, and she feels no scars. *What a relief; thank you, Lord.*

"Anna, remember to project your thoughts so that I will understand. And yes, your child is fine. And you are alive, healthy or close to it. Your vitals are good, and your child is well. It could be much worse. Your eyesight is restored. Your medical drones, or Henry's slips, repaired everything during your sleep. You just need to move, push yourself. Your strength will come back," responds XTOX. "You have been in hibernation for nineteen Earth days, longer in flight days. You are trillions of miles from Earth. We have just entered into the Antennae Galaxies, where we spend a lot of time. It is off the beaten path, as you would say. Henry does not know where you are, so don't get hopeful. Your best bet is he trades us something we want badly, pay our price for you and his unborn son. He will do much to get his son back. You need to make yourself comfortable here. It could be a long time on board."

Anna shakes her head. "I feel dreadful. My mouth is sticky; the taste is terrible. I need a mirror. You said he knows about our son?" she asks, now fully awake.

XTOX replies, "Yes, he does; we left word for him on Earth after we took you. Here, drink this fluid. The drone will pour the drink into your mouth. It will clean and refresh you."

Continuing, he says: "By the way, Anthony would have killed you except for us. It was a lucky break for you that we came for you. He has done the same with other young human women. We pulled some of his memories when he was in the toilet in the plane. Henry is not the only one with brain memory slips. We saved you from him."

XTOX projects his thoughts strongly, with passion, exclaiming, "Only Henry would do this to you, not protect you, leaving you vulnerable. Now we have you and your son. Henry is not worth your loyalty. He is more ruthless than we are, more than cruel. You doubt me; Henry really has done many terrible things in the past. As punishment, he sometimes kills his victim, restores him, and kills him again in a different way, always painful, doing this a thousand times. Everyone in the universe knows about it, and it does frighten those who never frighten. Actually I am not too keen on it either. Since he is the top military guy for the Consortium, no one interferes. It is a bad death many times.

You probably know very little about Henry. Why do you think the Consortium has him, made him what he is, utilizing his expertise, his killing instincts, his best talents? He is no better than us. Henry has done some dreadful deeds for the Consortium. He is basically a predator's predator. He is trained to hunt down his victims, other predators, with no mercy. It makes you wonder about your unborn son. He will probably become the ultimate predator. Think about it, Anna, the Consortium could use Henry to get to your son, make him the next Henry or worse. We can take care of you and your son, protect you. You could even visit Earth every so often, as we have business there, too. You just need to trust us."

Anna stares intently at him, projecting her thoughts: "XTOX, you forget, our son belongs to Henry, too. He will love his son. I know Henry. He will come for his son and me. You have no chance. I trust and love Henry. Your poisoning words are just so much rhetoric. Give up while you can. If you give up now, return me to Earth. I will tell Henry to have mercy on you, no thousand-death thing."

XTOX shakes his head. "Anna, you are foolish. The Consortium will take your son."

She responds, "Why would I believe you?"

XTOX looks at her intently, then responds, "Yes, yes, you are right. So be it. Henry also should be happy with us, grateful we saved you, as I have saved you and his son. You might put in a good word for me, just in case it all goes wrong. I am just saying there is much you do not know about Henry. You might be surprised about Gabriel, too, and the Consortium. We will talk more later, when you are stronger. Please, Anna, maybe listen with an open mind. We just want to make a living. We want an exclusive license to broker our goods, which are exotic metals. We are sort of like one of your pawnshops on Earth. We loan out money to civilizations with no credit. They give us metals we desire for collateral. If they don't pay us back, we sell the metal for a tidy profit.

"Of course Earth donated quite a bit of aluminum to keep from being destroyed by us, as we lost a valuable starship there. Someone needed to pay. We also helped Earth get approved into the Consortium, us being the villains attacking Earth. This happening to Earth, an event we caused, means an automatic acceptance into the Consortium. We did your Earth a favor, as the Consortium approval is worth trillions for Earth just in tourism money alone. Tourists love new primitive worlds, tribe-like beings, especially those who still have sex."

XTOX looks intently at Anna, projecting his thoughts to her. "Anyway, you are tired; you need your dinner. Here, drink more fluid. You have your baby to think of. You need some exercise, too. The hibernation weakened you."

"XTOX, where is my locket?"

He replies, "Sorry Anna, we took it—too dangerous to leave with you. We locked it away where the beacon will not signal Henry. Once he agrees to our terms, we will send you to him, and for now you will be our..." XTOX stops, has a strange, freak look in his eyes. She sees he can't move. A dazed look comes over him, and he tries to move; his eyes become frantic.

Anna notices XTOX is looking really sick suddenly, turning different colors, and then he starts to pass out, dropping gradually toward the floor. Anna reaches out with her arms, just barely catches him, then tries to hold on to him using her legs wrapped around him. This close, she thinks, he smells worse, terrible! He is so large, lucky there is only a little gravity on the ship, as she keeps him from hitting the floor.

Thankfully he suddenly awakens, startled, in shock and speechless. He pulls himself up and regains his composure. He shakes his head. He finally mentally exclaims to her, "Yes, yes, it was too simple!" Shaking his large head in rage, he cries, "We are finished. Damn! Damn!"

There is a wild look in his large, protruding eyes, projecting more anger and words she cannot understand, maybe swear words. He rages, "Your Henry set us up. Your locket is not a locket but, as you would say, a Trojan horse. How clever of Henry! It opened when you boarded and signaled Henry immediately using our communications systems, corrupted by his drones; your locket released thousands of drones and slips. They probably spread throughout the ship immediately. The mental drones, the slips, entered our brains, and then entered our system's intelligence centers and the navigation; everything on board worth anything was corrupted. He has influenced me from the beginning, even at our first meeting with you. I realize it now. I can feel him now in my brain; he has a slip in my brain, and I know he is on board, coming for me. I fainted because of his scanning the ship looking for me. Henry created a mental wave, and the first impact knocked me out. He is here with many troops. They have all boarded us. We are done for."

XTOX's speech is high-pitched, not understandable; he pauses, the telepathy now continuing, sorrowful, passionate, pleading: "Anna, please save me and this ship. I have done you no harm. He has many starships around us and he intends to destroy us. Please save us! There are 223,000 of us on board, females and children, too. Henry is coming. I beg you, don't let him destroy us."

Anna tries to stand up; she is so weak, yet the possibility that Henry is here thrills her more than her current condition. Could it be possible? She can hardly breathe as she hears all kinds of commotion down the tunnels of the massive starship. She does not have the power to stand up. She tries again.

Then she almost faints as she actually sees Henry at the end of the tunnel, striding toward her with a huge smile. His helmet is off, and he is yelling "Anna!" fifty feet away; he starts to run toward her. There is noise all around them. More troops are pouring down the tunnel toward them, and XTOX steps forward in front of her, almost protective, walking out to meet them. She can hardly move, still sitting there, holding on to the bed. She is weaker than she thought possible, trying not to faint.

XTOX steps forward, bowing, saying, "Henry, you have taken the ship. We surrender under Consortium protocols, thus we are entitled to due process. We make the declaration, as we want to repent, and we ask for forgiveness. We understand the ramifications and accept them. We will also compensate our victims."

Henry laughs. "XTOX, people died on Earth. The Consortium will have a trial, and you have a chance. You can give them your side of the story. Your starship will be escorted back to KA*AM. We have all the others; the rest of your group is captured. They will go to KA*AM as well."

XTOX bows down, then stares at Henry's eyes. "As it will be, as it should be, per my fate. My providence awaits me. Yet we have performed a service for you, taking your Anna away from certain death, as she had been kidnapped by a rogue human. We have saved Anna and your child also, and as you can see she is here, behind me, protected by me in preparation for your arrival. Granted it was not an exact plan, yet Anna, I think, will testify to our prudence in watching over her."

XTOX turns, staring at Anna, pleading silently for her response.

Anna looks at Henry, projects agreement, saying, "He saved me from Anthony, kept me safe here."

Henry turns to XTOX, saying, "I appreciate you taking care of Anna, and I will put in a good word for you at your trial. If you are responsible for killing beings on Earth, you know the law."

XTOX looks at Anna, and in a lower, softer mental tone, almost affectionate, still telepathic, continues. "Anna, it has been a pleasure meeting you. I am sorry it was so brutal; I have no ill feelings toward you. Our link in this life was destiny. We both face limitations to our choices, our free will defined for us, our inevitable fate to come for us, and yet we step forward in the dark. Yes, it is a constant challenge of survival, one of the decrees of this life."

XTOX bows slowly, eyes closed, as he whispers, "Calabra, Anna." He then turns proudly, standing tall, looking at Henry, who nods, directing him to his side.

Four soldiers approach him, salute Henry, and then escort XTOX down the tunnel.

Anna breathes deeply, stands, tries to run to Henry or more like staggers to him, can't do it, stops, crying, "Henry! Thank God you are here. It is about time. Where have you been? Help me."

Henry strides forward; he grabs her in a clutching embrace as she almost falls, Anna holding on for dear life. Henry picks her up easily, holding her in his arms. Both are crying. She is kissing his face, and then they kiss deeply.

Anna says tenderly, close to his ear, "I have missed you terribly! Henry, you need to know we have a son. I am pregnant."

He laughs. "I know, and I am delighted, happier than I have ever been. Our son! I have missed you, too, more than I thought possible. I am so sorry about not being here sooner. I should have been here."

Tearful, with sad eyes, Anna says, "Henry, you need to know, it is awful and all my doing. I caused it all. My mother and Nikki were killed by Anthony, as was John Jacobs and his friend. It was terrible. I saw it all. It was all my fault."

Henry exclaims, "Yes, Anna, I know all about it, and you also killed five of the bad guys. I have good news, though; you are wrong, as John, Nikki, and John's friend did not die. The medical slips saved them. I'm sorry; your mother did not make it. She had too much brain damage to save. I am so sorry. I deeply regret not being there for them and you. I failed you. It's not your fault. Never think that you caused it."

"Nikki is alive?" cries Anna. "John is alive? Medical repair slips? How is that possible? They are alive?"

Henry responds, "Yes, yes, alive and healthy and worried about you. The repair slips were in each of them, as I installed them a long time ago. The slips in your mother's body moved to John's associate when they could not save her. She had too much head trauma to save her memories; thus it was impossible to save her identity. She would not have been your mother if saved. Anna, I know you loved her dearly; I am sorry. Nikki made the funeral arrangements. Many, many people came."

He continues, "Nikki is now on the *Cyclone*; she wanted to be part of your retrieval. Both of you will switch to one of the *Eagles*.

They will go back to Earth with you. I am taking the *Cyclone* to meet with Gabriel. He is meeting me halfway. Nikki is waiting for you. You need to leave for Earth right away."

Anna asks, "Henry, how did you do all this without the Consortium's consent?"

Henry laughs. "You know the irrational old cliché: it is better to ask for forgiveness than to ask for permission." He then says more seriously, "I need to work out the details."

Henry stares intently at Anna, leaning down, unwrapping his arms around her, and letting her stand. She is almost too weak to stand yet she pulls herself up.

Henry awkwardly drops to one knee, brings out a little black jewelry box, looking up at her, opening the box, nervously saying, "Please forgive me, Anna. I am sorry for all this. It was not my intent. I love you. I need you, and you were right. I hope... please, Anna...will you marry me?"

Anna laughs and looks at him with amazement.

She responds, "Henry, when did you have time to buy that? She drops down, takes the ring, kisses Henry's cheek, nuzzling him, and she responds in a whisper, "Yes, of course Henry. I will marry you. I love you with all my heart. I need you, too. How will we do this? Where do we get married? Where do we live?"

Now looking at her, their eyes locked, he smiles and says, "I am working on it. You might have to go to work for the Consortium."

Anna looks at the ring, exclaims, "It is gorgeous!"—she slips it on, beaming a huge smile—"I'll do anything, as long as I am with you."

She beams more, laughs, and then asks, "How bad can it be?

She changes her tone, more serious, exclaims, "One more thing Henry, are you going to be at the Academy Awards?"

"I am not sure. I will try my best."

"Just be there! It's important to me, Henry. I need you to be there."

Henry nods his head. "Anna, I am forgetting where we are... we still have some issues here. We have to get going right away. You need to leave this ship for a lot of reasons. For one, it is dangerous to be here; things are still moving fast. I am taking you to a starship like the *Cyclone*. Nikki is there. I will be making my trip on the *Cyclone*. You will be taken care of personally from now on, with a constant guard, as if you were me. You are heading back to Earth. Everyone is looking forward to seeing you. John and Judy have been frantic since you were abducted. John blamed himself and is overjoyed about your return. He and Judy and the kids are moving in with you. I will be there as soon as I can make it happen."

———

It is January 12, and no word from Henry. It has been weeks. I am obviously showing; six months is a lot in the pregnancy world, as in little kicks in the stomach. I have been singing to our son, and I'm surprisingly good at it, too. I know our son loves it when I sing to him. It was tough to find a dress for the Academy Awards tonight, something to go with the pregnancy. The morning sickness surprisingly continues, and it is lousy.

I am appreciative of the abundance of security, all Consortium troops and starships and thousands of drones, all sizes, everywhere. John and Judy Jacobs are staying with me at the house; it's wonderful to have their presence near me and very reassuring. John has been a big help. He gave me a gun and I passed the concealed-gun license exam. It makes me feel better to have it. I'm good with it, too. John says I'm a natural marksman. Thank God John and Judy are both going to the awards tonight.

John told me, at Henry's request, and with the FBI's help, he cleaned up the Deforleo family. Most of them were caught. A huge sex-slavery organization was discovered, hundreds of girls held in bondage released. Some stayed in the United States; some went back to their families overseas. The Deforleo organization was legally prosecuted rather than using Henry's way. John said Henry was really upset about Anthony, said if Anthony was still alive to hold him for Henry's return. Luckily for Anthony they never met; he would not like the "thousand deaths" thing.

The guests tonight include every leader of almost every country in the world. They are having the Academy Awards in a massive coliseum. About every celebrity in the world will be there. I know it is not me they are coming to see. All will be waiting to see if Henry comes.

And then there's me, thinks Anna: hardly feeling beautiful, knocked up, with no husband, standing literally in front of the world. Awkward, to say the least.

At least the tabloids are a little more subdued, as they are afraid of Henry, what he might think of them, and mostly what he might do to them. The ratings for tonight's ceremony are expected to be off the charts. It's believed several billion people will see the Academy Awards, as most of the world will be watching. I have already been told I will be getting an award. They are even televising me leaving my home. I feel bad about all the attention. What about the other winners? I wish my mother was here. Thank God for Nikki! Henry better damn well be on his way. They are all coming to see him, expecting him to be here.

I start to cry, which I do all the time now. What if he does not come? At least I have an engagement ring. Nikki says to wear a wedding band if it makes me feel better. My real fear is when I am up there standing in front of billions of people. *What do I say up there at the lectern? I do have to thank everyone. What if he never comes?*

I am trillions of miles from Earth, on the other side of the galaxy. The *Cyclone* is still gaining speed, trying to make Anna's Academy Awards night. It is not possible to make it, yet the *Cyclone* is pushing over all previous records, moving faster than ever, maybe too fast. I'm unsure why the *Cyclone* is pushing the limits with this much danger, maybe actually feeling the urgency, maybe doing this as much for Anna as for me. It's surprising that the feeling of losing Anna has been so deep for me, unbearable, and now both of us feel it. We have changed; our lives are not the same now. Both of us realize it, and there's no going back, Anna is part of our future.

Almost humorously, the *Cyclone* is not complaining that we are using tremendous amounts of energy and definitely taking risks with our survival. The *Cyclone* is usually the first to point out my recklessness; but now it is acting like me, pushing the limits. The universe is harsh, taking lives just like time does. The *Cyclone* knows it all could end in a millisecond as pursuing these speeds is dangerous, yet our propulsion is expanding, cutting through the fabric of space and time. We are violently using gravity as an extreme tool. Trillions of tons of gravity are forcing colossal weight out of equilibrium. This ripples a hole into space and time, leveraging great forces—a violent and dangerous process used for centuries. The result: we are covering quadrillions of miles within minutes.

I am thinking, *I have been on so many lonely voyages, riding the thirty-four billion tons of starship plunging through the cold black emptiness, and after all these years, there's not much to show for it. I think this trip is going to be our fate, a destiny for both of us, the* Cyclone *and me. We are both good soldiers.*

I laugh. *We both appreciate Anna!* I smile. "*Yes, Anna, Calabra! May the divine light embrace us. I love you, whatever happens!*

⟫⊹ ⊹⟪

Anna is walking the red carpet. John, Judy, and Nikki are helping her, making sure she doesn't fall in her dress. It looks more like a wedding dress, silvery champagne in color, with soft, flowing multiple thin layers of chiffon and lace falling loosely from her empire waist. Anna now doubts her choice in dresses, wishes her mother were there to reassure her. Suddenly knowing how proud her mother would be right now greatly renews her spirit, giving her the confidence to walk tall and beautifully as she ascends the stairway into the coliseum.

My God! She thinks. *No need to worry about an alien attack or any attack. There is security everywhere.*

She knows one of the Consortium *Eagle*s is hovering overhead and has laid out a security blanket—a shield, like a big electric fishnet around the entire building. The Secret Service is there because of the president. There are Consortium soldiers outside, lots of them on guard. The protesters keep their distance from them, terrified of them. Many people, thousands, are camped out in all directions, all wanting to have a glimpse of Anna. She is still shocked by this cult status; it's hard to adjust to it.

There are little drones, too, lots of them, everywhere, like little pins of light darting around, inspecting everything. They are a constant part of Anna's life, ever diligent. For the first time, there are also halos over Anna's head about four feet up, orbiting slowly, three of them, projecting a security field around her. She knows it is her imagination, yet she thinks she can feel the force around her. These new things make everyone nervous, some fearful, and they are certainly not calming to Anna. Thank God they only activate when there is a threat.

She thinks, *Still, I am here! Can you believe it, the Academy Awards? I am excited. How could I not be? I have a smile larger than my face. Every camera in the world is here. If Henry could see me, he would be proud of me. He hides it, yet I know his emotions run deep, and I know he will love being a wonderful father.*

It is hard not to worry. She is anxious about Henry, as no word is not good. She needs to make herself think of other things, need to act confident. A happy thought is always her son. It is easy to focus on him, as he is really active now, kicking up a storm.

Everybody, even the President called her the previous night. The Chinese premier also called, a very sweet man. Many directors, producers, fellow actors, and fans sent notes wishing her well.

She thinks, *I am grateful. My life is not going to be easy. No matter, I am appreciative.*

As Anna walks down the aisle, she stops and says hello to the President and his wife. He tells her she looks gorgeous; she thanks him with a big smile.

Jeanie, Anna's faithful business agent, is here, too. She ignores the halos, walks over to Anna, and hugs her, kissing her, saying she loves her. Anna tells her she'd better! Anna continues down the aisle, marveling at the number of people. She knows they are here for her; yet, more likely really here, because of Henry, all wanting to know about the aliens, fascinated by her relationship with them. Some of it is scary, as there are also hundreds of protesters with signs outside. They are being motivated by the fear of the unknown and the massive changes taking place.

She thinks, *I understand, as I feel the same fear.*

She pauses, looks around. There is music, spotlights beaming, beautiful charming people everywhere. It is the definition of glamour. If only Henry could be here to see it; he would love it. They find their seats. Nikki, John, and Judy sit first as they have seats next to her and Henry. She sits down next to his empty seat, close to the aisle.

Finally the lights dim, and it starts.

The host, a national comedian Anna likes, Mason Reilly, waves at her from the stage. She waves back. He jokes that he had to get permission from 120 levels of security just so he would not be shot when he waves at Anna. He says Henry found out Anna had one cooking in the oven, and then found out her father was coming tonight with a shotgun, so maybe he changed his mind, he is not coming. It might all become front-page news on the *Universe Daily Herald.*

Everyone laughs.

He laughs, too, and says, "Let me ask the audience: how many people think Henry is coming tonight?"

Everyone is laughing and raising their hands.

He says, "Does everyone know who Henry is?"

Everyone yells, "Yes!"

The night goes on. Anna knows they have her scheduled at the end of the awards in case Henry is late. The seat next to her remains empty. She is now beginning to realize it was unfair to push his being here for this; he could be trillions of miles from here. She created all this anticipation and the disappointment if he does not come. She also feels remorse for being selfish, maybe putting him at risk.

Then, just like that, Anna hears her name. She is called up for the award for best actress. Anna is truly delighted, a huge smile across her face. It is a big moment, especially as young as she is. She can't help it; she is thrilled. The applause is wonderful. Everyone is standing and cheering. The movie's soundtrack is playing. She slowly walks up, beaming, saying hi to everyone along the way.

Standing at the lectern, smiling, Anna starts out thanking everyone by name who worked on the film.

"Thank you!" she continues. "Of course I want to thank my mother, who recently passed away, always behind me in every endeavor. I thank my sister, Nikki, too, and also a thanks to John and Judy, two dear friends."

"Please know I am grateful, and to everyone here, I am truly honored to be given this award. I have literally traveled trillions of miles to be here and am so delighted to actually be here, *on Earth.*"

Everyone laughs and applauds.

"I thank all the countries that have sent really important representatives to be here at this event, another kindness, one of many I have been blessed with, coming from so many wonderful people. I thank the President and the first lady for being here. I thank the Chinese premier and his first lady for being here."

"The nominations are all about incredibly talented people, and I am truly privileged to stand here among the best. I love my work and love the people in my profession, my extended family. I know you all know I have had a busy year. Many of you have called, and I apologize for not talking to you. Life leads you in unexpected ways, and as you know, some really wild things have happened."

The applause is overwhelming. Anna pauses. Everyone is looking around. One camera is on the door just in case.

Anna finally says, "I know you are all curious about me and Henry, my fiancé. I have been private about it, as it is hard to explain. He would be far better at telling you about his world than me. You will love him as I do. My hope is you hear it directly from him. I can't stall any longer. I know many of you were hoping to see Henry. I guess he is not coming. Thank you all for being here. Thank you for this!"

Starting to leave the lectern, Anna suddenly stops and smiles. She feels it. She notices the floor is shaking just a little, can feel the vibration growing. She knows it is not an earthquake; the *Cyclone* is here, above them all. The building is pulsating. The huge starship must be descending. They can all hear rolling thunder above, and everyone is looking upward. They all know what is happening as this alien ship comes down on top of them. The excitement is astonishing; all are in awe.

Anna feels the presence. Henry! She feels him, warmed by the welcoming emotions of both Henry and the *Cyclone*. In this huge coliseum, the tremors are now easy to feel, and everyone knows he is here. It is more intense. All know there is something above them in the heavens that is massive. They all know it is a starship, and everyone is standing, looking at the main doors, excited, expecting to see a being from another alien civilization yet also a human, part of them.

Bammn! They all jump, startled. The locked closed door in the back bursts open with a loud explosion, and Henry is literally running down the aisle, many drones following him, swirling around him like fireflies. Henry is dodging the TV cameras, putting on his tux coat, yelling, "I'm here, Anna! I am here! What do I do? Congratulations! You are incredible! I made it!"

The coliseum is huge, and Henry is moving fast. The cameras try to follow him; the entire world is looking at him. Anna is waving at him, beaming, overjoyed, watching him run, and she thinks, *He runs so easily, without effort, strong, graceful. What a great athlete.*

He slows down, stops at the President's row, says hi, smiles, and shakes his hand. Everyone is applauding and laughing. Henry waves at everyone.

Anna says into the microphone, "It's about time, Captain Johnson! Come up here and say hello to everyone. I would like to introduce you to the world."

He comes down the aisle and goes up the steps fast, two at a time. He strides up to the lectern and hugs Anna, kisses her, telling her he loves her. She loves his kiss, feels his joy, and knows he feels hers. She steps back to the lectern; Henry is behind her. She is wiping tears from her eyes.

TV cameras are everywhere as news networks from around the world are here, thousands of camera flashes; drones are everywhere, too, warning cameramen when they start to get too close. Smiling, Anna looks out at the audience and the citizens of the world, realizing just now how massive this audience is, as a good chance everyone in the world is watching her, either now or on the news tomorrow. Never before in history have so many people watched and listened to someone speak. Who would think it would be her? She is amazed and honored.

Anna laughs as she thinks everybody in the world is smiling, too. Henry is so handsome, her Starman, and she can't help but be proud. She exclaims, "Let me introduce you to my fiancé, Henry Johnson, someone I think you are going to like and who will be of great interest to you. You all want to hear his story and he can explain it far better than I can. He is from the planet KA*AM, trillions of miles from here. He is friendly, I can assure you," she says with a coy smile. Everyone laughs. "He looks like a human because he is from Earth originally. He has been employed by a Consortium of Civilizations spread across the universe. He is awesome, and you will love him."

Looking at Henry, laughing, Anna says, "Henry, no telepathy. Please talk to these people." He kisses her again, tears now rolling down her face.

Anna then feels it. She feels Henry's emotions and thoughts. It is happening. Now everyone in the place feels Henry's emotions and his thoughts, and there are astonished looks on their faces. All are now applauding; all are standing up; now everyone is tearing up, too. They feel him. Henry is projecting his powerful emotions, his longing for Anna, his love for Earth, and his love for them, all being intimately felt by every person here in their hearts and in their minds. None of them has ever experienced telepathy, much less a mind meld, or even thought such a thing possible. This telepathy stuff is great. Henry is going to do really well in Hollywood!

Henry asks them all to sit down and relax completely, and they will see what he sees. He will show them the universe and his home planet. Everyone is delighted, wanting this, and then they slowly enter into a mind meld, mesmerized by his thoughts. He tells them about himself using both telepathy and soothing out-loud words. Then he talks about KA*AM. They see this wonderful planet in their minds, just like they were there. Henry has gone deeply telepathic; it is very powerful as they can see what he sees and feel what he feels. Two older women faint, and then are quickly revived by ushers with wet towels. Everyone in the audience is in tears and laughing by the time he finishes. They love him! Anna knows they really love him. She knows, as she feels it, too.

Yet Anna's mind is in other places. She knows nothing from Henry about what happened with Gabriel. She wonders what the next chapter in their lives is. Henry looks tired, worn out. What happened to him? Did they agree to his retirement? What is going to happen going forward for them, for the Earth, for their children? What will happen when their son is born? Will he be a citizen of KA*AM?

Anna remembers every television in the world is showing this. It is later reported that five billion households have viewed this event. Many changes will be taking place in the future. What will be Anna's role? And Henry's?

Cameras from around the world follow them, trying to crowd in, fighting for space, although are never allowed too close; as Anna and Henry walk backstage they continue to trail them. He asks her mentally about the baby. She smiles, and he knows all is well.

She looks at him and asks him out loud, "Henry, did you make a deal with Gabriel?"

He turns his head, looks at Anna, and smiles. She hears his thoughts. "Yes, Anna, all is well, or at least sort of. I will tell you all about it, and you will meet Gabriel tomorrow. He is coming here. We will be fine. Earth will be fine. Earth has been officially accepted into the Consortium. He wants to meet you and has come a long way. He wants to come to our wedding. There are ten fleets out there and two more *Titans*. We are here together now, Earth has been adopted, and we all have a new beginning."

The End

Made in the USA
Columbia, SC
28 October 2020